£.2.79

DEATH MARCH

BLACK MAGIC OUTLAW BOOK SIX

Domino Finn

Published by Blood & Treasure, Los Angeles
First Edition

Cover Typography by James T. Egan of Bookfly Design LLC.

Print ISBN: 978-1-946-00806-0

DominoFinn.com

Death
MARCH

BLACK MAGIC OUTLAW
BOOK SIX

Chapter 1

The bottle of Corona slammed the bar with enough force to bubble over. The gruff man tending brews paid it no mind. He was, after all, the one being so forceful in the first place. I dropped a fiver and grunted, feeling a more appropriate gesture of thanks would be wasted.

The establishment, if it could be called that, was more like a storeroom than a bar. The exterior was a nondescript reinforced door in a grungy but gentrifying Downtown-adjacent neighborhood. The interior was stripped down to the concrete and somehow even more grimy.

I didn't know what I'd expected, but it wasn't this. I took a pull from the bottle, bit back the warm beer, and rolled the metal bracelet over my fingers. How the hell had I ended up here?

A heavy shoulder brushed me as a man stumbled against the padded counter. "Whoa there!" he croaked. "Sometimes you catch the bar; sometimes the bar catches you."

I straightened and cast him and his impromptu poetry a sidelong glance. In his thirties, sharp orange hair, freckled face. "No worries," I said evenly.

Another man settled over my opposite shoulder. Jamaican maybe. The weathered bartender turned his back and pretended to disappear.

"Of course," observed the first knucklehead, "sometimes it's your lucky day and you catch something else entirely."

That was when I noticed they both wore bones around their neck. Not finger digits or anything so orc-like—these beads were most likely harvested from chicken skeletons.

I frowned. These guys had nothing to do with my purpose here.

"Careful," I warned, taking a big step backward to look them both in the eye. "I'm not here to start a fight with santero hucksters. And, trust me, you're not here to start a fight with me."

Their eyes narrowed. The Jamaican's gaze dropped to the silver dog whistle hanging from my neck. The skull-and-pentacle belt buckle.

His face went to full alert. "You're..."

"Bingo," I said with a wink. I leaned back into the bar and took a swig of warm beer.

"Don't you turn your back on me," said the white dude, placing a firm hand on my shoulder.

His boy retreated to his side and pulled him off. "Don't you know who that is?" he whispered, doing a poor job of concealing his voice.

His friend scoffed. "Just another asshole who got lost in the wrong watering hole."

"No, you idiot. That's—" He lowered his voice even

more. "The One Who Walks With Opiyel."

My eyebrows reached for my hair. I hadn't heard that one before. Funny how much a legend can grow in a year. I kept my casual attention focused on the bottle in my hands, hoping the santeros would go away of their own accord.

The ornery one stared at me for a good minute, focusing and refocusing and nearly losing his balance once. Which meant his initial stumble wasn't part of the act.

"You sure?" he concluded. "Looks like a dumbass jock to me."

I ground my teeth. Legends, I could deal with. The jock label? Not so much. The physique wasn't me as much as it was an upgrade—part of the all-new Cisco Suarez—but growing up I was a skinny kid. Not a wimp, mind you, 'cause I always fought back. I just wouldn't *win* that often. I'd preferred my battles in the realms of Dungeons & Dragons, comics, and fantasy novels. Basically anything that had cool dragons in it.

That was before I'd encountered *real* dragons, of course. Now I'm not so hot on them.

I frowned and rapped the metal bracelet against the bar.

"I'm serious," urged the Jamaican. "It's him."

"Well, all the more reason to whoop him then."

I sighed sharply and turned. They started, but they didn't need to. I wasn't making a move. "Look," I said, clearing the air. "Things happened last year. Things beyond my control."

The tough guy sneered. "That's not the way I hear it."

"Well, it's the way it was. And I'm sick of explaining

myself to you guys."

The friend didn't want any part of this conversation, but the troublemaker cleared his throat and gained confidence. "I lost my job, you know. Some of us lost a whole lot more."

I winced and took a calming breath. He wasn't entirely out of line. "That... that wasn't me. Listen, how about I buy you a round of drinks and we shake it out? I know what they say about me, but I don't have a problem with other necromancers. I'm one of you guys."

He spat at my feet and made a fist. I twitched my hand. The dog-collar fetish on my wrist thrummed and a sliver of shadow rose from the floor and wrapped up his arm tight. He could no longer lift his hand, much less throw a punch.

My face darkened as the very shadow crept over it. "Not. Smart."

His friend threw a hand up and tugged him away. "It's okay. He's chill."

I let him go even though his expression was anything but. They retreated several steps before getting in a hushed argument. The Jamaican eventually gave up and stormed out of the makeshift bar. Smart guy. The white dude wasn't left alone, however. He glared at me before rejoining his buddies at the pool table. More santeros, by the looks of it.

I settled back on the bar and scowled at the Corona. My reputation within the Miami Santería and voodoo communities was something else, more infamy than celebrity. In a city full of brujos and bokors, that was dangerous business. Lucky for me—or maybe for them—most knew better than to pick a fight.

A girl on the corner barstool chuckled. I couldn't decide if she was a cokehead or a prescription pusher, but I was in the ballpark. A waif of a thing, without the nice clothes or makeup that would've stood out in this dive. When my eyes landed on hers, she took a long drag of her menthol and arched an eyebrow.

So much for flying under the radar. A casual glance at the surrounding patrons showed either an avid interest in my well-being or a strong desire to feign otherwise. The cat was out of the bag.

I slid a few seats closer to the waif.

"You're not gonna ask if that seat's taken?" she drawled. Her voice was a surprising falsetto. Sweet, almost innocent, and decidedly country. It didn't match the packaging, except for maybe the twin pigtails pinning back her light hair.

"I've been here long enough to know better." She exhaled smoke in my face and I pretended not to notice. She had large hoop earrings, a nose stud, and black fingernails, but no apparent instruments of spellcraft. "Besides, I get the feeling you're dying for good company."

She showed her teeth. "No such thing 'round here." They were a nice set of teeth for a rundown girl, and she made sure to accentuate them as she played with her tongue piercing.

I twirled the loose bracelet on the bar. The metal droned like a spinning coin, faster and faster until I snatched it and did it again. The bartender eyed me gruffly. That was his thing, I guess.

"So what's your fancy?" asked the girl. "No spell tokens

here. You don't look the pill-poppin' sort." She appraised me with her lips pursed. "And if it's anything else you're looking for, you won't find it here."

It was an interesting stance to take in front of the only employee in sight. She was essentially claiming ownership of the operation here. The bartender was staring, chewing on a toothpick, too old and apathetic to say anything one way or the other. He simply hovered close and wiped bar glasses with a dusty towel.

"Funny you should say that," I started, "because I *am* looking for something. Someone, really." I pulled a school photo from the back pocket of my jeans and placed it on the bar. "Ever seen this girl?"

She scoffed. "Mister, ain't she a little young for you?"

I rapped the bracelet on the bar. I'd found it in the grass where the kid had disappeared. It was a cheap piece of aluminum with multi-colored beads. Not extraordinary by any measure except for the blood staining the surface. The girl's eyes flared, sending a chill down my back. Something was off about this place.

I continued matter-of-factly. "Her name is Gendra. A lot of people are looking for this girl. Her parents. The police."

Her eyes shimmered as she extinguished her cigarette. "Even little ol' you."

I leaned in. "Not a lot gets by *me*."

I left out my personal interest in the kidnapping. It wasn't that I knew the girl, but she'd been taken from my daughter's middle school. Second one this month, which was a little close to home.

"No offense to Miami's finest," I said, "but I know a trick or two they don't. A discarded bracelet on the side of the road doesn't mean much, but this one has a bit of blood." I held the bracelet to her face. She tensed and sniffed the air like a predator. "Someone like me can learn a lot from a bit of blood."

She regained her composure and playfully twirled a pigtail. "I don't know what you're talking about, mister."

"Then there's the matter of the windowless black van that cruises the school. The same van parked in the back alley right now."

Her eyes shifted to the bartender. I'd definitely hit a nerve. The part about the van had mostly been a bluff, but they didn't know what my magic could do or how much I knew.

The old man set a glass down, draped the towel over his shoulder, and retreated into the back room. I let him go.

"Look, mister... You know this girl? She under your protection or something?"

I grinned wryly. "They're *all* under my protection."

Chairs abruptly scraped the concrete. Two wannabe bouncers stood, puffing out their chests and cracking their knuckles. One was stupid looking and the other looked stupid. I noticed the hothead and his buddies weren't at the pool table anymore. Most in the dive bar had evacuated.

"This guy bothering you, Tutti?" asked the stupid-looking one.

I groaned. "The bartender's not getting the manager, is he?"

They chuckled. "Let's be reasonable, wizard. You can't storm in here and make demands. I don't care who you are." The other one clenched and unclenched a fist in anticipation. Curiously, they both had black nail polish too.

"What, did I miss the flyer for goth night?"

My eyes darted to Tutti's fingers, currently elongated into black claws and scraping a groove in the hardwood. She flashed a predatory smile. Two long canines grew into place, and her lashes fluttered seductively. "My, my. Now there's the face of a man who's never heard of the Obsidian March."

Chapter 2

Unexpected was an understatement. I'd known new players were making moves in Miami in the wake of the destruction of the largest drug cartel in the history of the Caribbean, but vampires?

Obviously I hadn't thought this little meet and greet through.

"The Obsidian March," I repeated. "Please tell me that's your online guild name."

"Cut the shit," snapped Tutti, jumping to the bar top. Her movements were erratic but fluid, toeing the line between capable and out of control.

"Want me to take him?" asked the bigger of the guys.

"No."

"He knows too much."

"He'll keep it to himself," she asserted, turning to me. "You know how this goes, wizard. We do our thing, you do yours. No need for the masses to sniff either of us out."

I scowled at how she lumped us together. I was nothing like them. "I want the girl."

She snickered. "You think we're going to wind down our operations because you walk in here and say so? The Obsidian March has roots in this city that go farther back than your recent rise."

"Then maybe it's time to rip those roots from the ground."

The men transformed right before me. Their eyes milked over, their skin went black. And I'm not talking African-descent black but a polished obsidian, like their namesake. It hardened into a flexible carapace. Their noses and ears melded with their heads. Their faces grew flat. And, you guessed it, their fingers doubled into sharpened knives.

They hissed and swiped at me. In a blink, I dissolved into the shadows. My body became ethereal, slipping past their claws and bulky bodies until I solidified behind and shoved them into the bar.

"Cut it out!" ordered Tutti, standing over us with outstretched arms. The men turned on me and froze.

I took slow steps back to give us some space. Good practice around vampires.

Trashy clogs rapped the bar. "This isn't an ambush, wizard. We're not fighting you."

I cocked my head to the side. "Could've fooled me."

She glared coldly and hopped to the floor. Again, a sudden movement with alien grace. I backed away as shadow billowed over my fist.

Tutti scoffed at the show of power. "But this *is* a declaration of intentions. The March halts for no man, woman, or child. If you have services or property to negotiate, come back when you're feeling more congenial. But never dictate terms, wizard."

A siren broke the city noise.

The vampire smiled. "Speaking of Miami's finest..."

Tutti pointed at the door to the back alley. The three surged forward, leaving me a choice: stand my ground or go. I maneuvered to the door.

I hadn't banked on tussling with vampires today, but it wouldn't be the first time I'd seen something of their sort. The real problem was the police. And...

"The girl," I said.

Tutti twirled a pigtail and pouted. "I'm afraid that one didn't work out. She's beyond even you now."

I went red at the thought. "You sick fucks!" My shotgun materialized from the ether. The bodyguards reacted quickly. They batted my aim to the side. I spun with the blow as the other grabbed at my old position. It was a simple matter to send a locomotive of shadow into him. It bowled him over two tables and the bar.

The police siren grew louder. The second bouncer lunged. I hopped back to avoid the attack while working a rope of shadow around his waist. I closed my fist and pulled, pinning him to the far wall, unharmed but out of the action. That left Tutti and me unmolested.

By now the girl had a serrated blade gripped between two fingers, readying a throw. I was faster. I lifted the shotgun and fired, sending a custom blend of buckshot and spark powder into her gut. A roar of fire exploded and sent her spinning through the air.

Tires skidded in the curbside gravel. I opened the back door and scanned the bar, angry I couldn't finish what I'd started. The bloodlust distracted me. A rubber alternator belt wrapped around my neck and yanked me outside.

The sudden transition to sunlight blinded me. Yes, seedy bars operate daytimes. Hell, it wasn't even noon yet. This unfortunately meant my shadow spellcraft was limited. Before my eyes could fully adjust, a fist slammed into my cheek.

I kicked out and caught a groin with a red alligator boot. The dude doubled over with a high-pitched squeal. It was the hothead santero with his pool buddies, minus the Jamaican who'd had the sense to leave. That meant I was only surrounded by five guys now.

The santero coughed and climbed to his feet. "You're gonna pay for that, brujo."

I checked the back door, which had shut itself. With the Miami sun beating down, it was doubtful the vamps would join this particular party. I also noticed the black van was gone.

"You guys are either very stupid or very drunk," I muttered.

"Could be both," said the guy squeezing the alternator belt around my neck. His friends glared at him. I shook my head.

"Cisco, is it?" asked the santero, deepening his voice to mask his bruised... ego. "This is from Johnny Red." He punched me in the gut.

I cackled. "What kind of stupid name is Johnny Red and why would he call himself that?"

A couple of them chuckled. The hothead's face flushed. "It's me," he snapped. "I'm Johnny Red."

"Tell him he punches like a girl."

He smoldered. "You..."

He telegraphed a haymaker. I waited as it came and threw up an arm block. He struck the armor tattoo along the outside of my left forearm. Blue light flared and several bones in his hand crunched. He reeled and screamed, "Kill this asshole!"

A fist came from the side. I lurched forward, pulling the dummy choking me into the blow. He dropped the belt and stumbled away cupping a bleeding nose. I didn't bother looking for shadow. I punched the surprised guy who'd just hit his friend and then kicked the knee out from another. The last one danced in place for precious seconds as his brain processed the situation, but it wasn't long before he bolted.

A white-and-green police car turned into the alley with a quick chirp of its siren. The runner scrambled and turned, jumping over a chain-link fence.

"This isn't over," swore Johnny Red, hunched over his broken hand.

I sighed and cracked him in the face with my boot, sending him to La La Land. Then I turned to escape around the block.

Another police car veered ahead of me. They had us on both sides. I contemplated the door to the dive bar before it slammed open. An officer on foot rushed me.

I threw up my hands and dropped to my knees, unwilling to escalate this any further. Overexcited police officers in brown uniforms converged on us, barked commands, and slammed me face-first to the asphalt.

I ground my teeth as the handcuffs clinked into place. We were all going in. Not a good day to be a necromancer.

Chapter 3

"Francisco Desi Suarez," read the detective sitting across from me. He snapped my shiny new driver's license on the table and considered it with an arched eyebrow. "Why in the hell would you get a photo ID with a black eye?"

I sighed loudly. It was a long story.

The detective shrugged. He was an older guy with tightly curled black hair that was going gray. The kind of guy who'd seen a lot and had the questions to match. The kind of guy who lamented where society had taken a wrong turn.

His partner was a quiet Cuban guy with greased-back hair and thick eyebrows. He'd done nothing so far but lean against the corner with his arms crossed.

I twiddled my thumbs and frowned at the loose handcuffs chaining me to the table. Apparently Metro-Dade PD viewed beating down four chuckleheads as violent. I didn't like cold iron because it made escape into the shadows impossible.

"Well, it's nice to meet you, Francisco. I'm Detective

Darrow and this is Detective Peña."

"Call me Cisco."

Thus far I'd played things cool. I had to. Going full Baker Act and outlining the vampire menace would've gotten me nowhere. I'd briefly considered tipping the police off in a more reasonable fashion—telling them about the black van without getting into the supernatural nitty-gritty —but that was a no go as well. The van was long gone and so was the girl. The police would be in wildly over their heads.

I had to look at the situation in the cold light of day. I was in custody for a simple bar fight. No assault charges. No attempted murder because apparently Tutti had disappeared. No firearms violations because they didn't have one. At most, I was looking at public intoxication and a slap on the wrist. It pained me to admit it, but the best course of action was revealing nothing at all.

Detective Darrow stroked his mustache and nodded. "Okay, Cisco. That's a good start. We just want to sort things out here."

A plastic bag on the table held my possessions. The silver dog whistle on black twine. A fold of small bills. The dog-collar bracelet. A cell phone. Car keys. My bronze voodoo knife, which luckily was more ceremonial than anything. Darrow had also set my belt pouch to the side, but for now he considered the ordinary items.

"Do we need to ask you where you got the cash?"

"It's not that much," I said.

He nodded. "And the *Knight Rider* key chain? That thing

must be an antique."

"I have a thing for Firebirds."

He leaned forward with a chuckle. "Who doesn't?" He considered the collar and whistle. "You a dog trainer or something like that?"

"Something like that."

He nodded silently. He was just getting started. Trying to build a rapport. I knew how it was. That didn't make me any less nervous when his eyes strayed to the belt pouch. He huffed once and unzipped it quickly, as if taking off a Band-Aid. The detective inventoried the contents one by one, announcing them as he did.

"Two packs of matches, used. Two plastic 7-11 lighters. Five mini road flares." He paused, waiting for a response.

I shrugged casually. "Hope for the best, prepare for the worst."

His eyebrows showed his skepticism, but he continued. "Two-dozen pack, colorful birthday candles. One uninflated metallic birthday balloon. The mirror half of a woman's plastic makeup kit." He watched me carefully as he spoke. "Three sticks of Crayola sidewalk chalk, various colors."

I swallowed. "I don't like how the normal stuff gets dust all over your fingers."

The detective paused for a beat and frowned. "Some kind of gel in a bright-red ketchup squeeze bottle." He flicked off the cap and recoiled at the smell.

"This..." I stalled, scratching the back of my head. "It's, uh, kinda embarrassing."

He waited without blinking.

"Jock itch." I pointed to my groin. "Like a motherfucker."

"Oh!" He tossed the bottle away from his face. Detective Peña laughed.

The stuff *was* pungent, I'd give them that. I just couldn't tell him it was a homemade zombie toxin to numb wounds and prevent infection. Awkward personal problems were more effective at deflecting attention.

Darrow turned to his young partner, still stifling a chuckle. "Well, you finish the inventory, goddammit."

Peña's face fell flat and he approached the table. "Let's see. You got some plastic Easter egg containers filled with powder. What is that? Lye?"

"It's for neutralizing the smell of cat urine."

He rolled his eyes. "You got a little plastic container—"

"That's a film container," commented Darrow.

"Whatever. A black film container filled with dust and... What are those? Snake teeth? And a pill container with powder capsules." I opened my mouth to speak but Peña threw a hand up. "Let me guess. You get bad headaches."

I smirked. "Guess you're a detective for a reason, Detective."

He snorted. "It is, you have to admit, an odd assortment."

"Yet not incriminating in the least."

"Don't forget the last one," reminded the senior detective.

"Oh, yeah," said Peña, shaking the small pouch to produce the sound of rattling objects. "A variety of shotgun shells." He turned the bag over and let the plastic cartridges tumble to the table.

"According to Florida records," noted Detective Darrow, "you don't have a firearm registered in your name."

I crossed my arms over my chest. "I also don't have a firearm. What can I say? You got me. It's weird to have those."

My shotgun was the one possession I owned that could be stuffed into a shadow box, an incorporeal vault of spellcraft that others couldn't access. It meant I didn't need to worry about carry laws.

Peña dropped the bag onto the table in frustration. "You're that Cisco Suarez guy who was dead, right?"

The mood in the interrogation room turned.

If we were being technical about it, I'd died three times. But I wasn't about to fess up to the popo. As far as they knew, Cisco Suarez disappeared eleven years ago. A victim of an occult ritual turned bloodbath. Presumed dead.

After living on the streets like an outlaw, my best friend Evan and his wife Emily had helped me go legit. Got my death certificate rescinded. Filed for a new ID and set me up with some clean money. There'd been a bit of a media frenzy over my mysterious reappearance, but I wasn't special enough to stay in the news.

Cisco Suarez wasn't off the grid anymore. It was a small price to pay for getting my life back.

"That's me," was all I said.

The young detective leaned on the table in an aggressive display. "What's your deal, Suarez?"

I met his eyes but didn't talk. Before Peña could lose his temper, Darrow waved him away.

"Surprisingly," tempered the more experienced detective, "a guy like you doesn't have a criminal record, unlike the other jokers we picked up from the dive bar. Is it true what we've heard? That you've recently become a police consultant?"

It was like I didn't have secrets. My friend Evan was a lieutenant for the City of Miami Police. This "connection" of mine had ironically brought me more trouble than it kept me out of. Even now, the department interviewing me was Metro. County police were entirely different than City, meaning I couldn't ask Evan for a favor and have this dropped.

So I had to suck it up and play their game.

Darrow leaned back and stroked his mustache. "What is it you consult on, specifically?"

I leaned on my cover story. "I spent a lot of time in South America and the Caribbean after my kidnapping. Saw a lot of crazy things."

"Such as?"

I shook my head. "I dunno. I might write a book someday. You could say that, after what happened to me, I'm fascinated by voodoo culture."

"An occult expert, then. If there's a crime scene with decapitated chickens and saint figurines, they consult with you."

I smiled. "It's pretty boring stuff, actually."

"I'm sure it is." The detective sighed and rubbed his

eyes, taking a moment to collect himself. "I'll be straight with you, Cisco. You seem like a decent guy. I don't have a problem with you. Neither does my partner, despite his gruff attitude." Peña hissed. Detective Darrow leaned forward. "But I need to know what you were doing in that alley today, son."

Damn him, this was the part that gave me the most trouble. Sincerity. Give me verbal sparring and posturing all day, but this cop looked like he wanted to make a difference.

I assured myself that the best help I could offer was keeping them ignorant of the nest of vampires I'd stumbled into. Even if it meant getting charged with a misdemeanor.

Before I could muster the appropriate tact for a friendly "no comment," the interrogation door opened.

A rail-thin black woman with hair bigger than Oprah strutted in. She was tall even without the heels, and her stern expression took less guff than her no-nonsense pants suit. She placed a business satchel on the table and seemed to move and speak a mile a minute.

"Thank you for your prompt alert, detectives. I'll share word with the DA that you've been more than helpful." She pointed to the mirror. "I caught the end of that and can take over from here."

The detectives watched her evenly.

"You *were* done with your line of questioning, weren't you?"

Darrow let out a neutral sigh and nodded. "He's all yours." He stood and shook his head quietly at his partner.

The woman smiled. "Would you please re-collect his

possessions before you step out?"

"Peña will take care of it."

The veteran detective exited while the junior partner scooped my possessions back into the belt pouch. As we waited in silence, I studied the newcomer. I'd seen enough cop shows to assume she was a lawyer, but then her jacket fell open and I spotted the badge on her belt. She was a fed.

Chapter 4

I don't know if Peña was supposed to take my stuff or not, but after organizing it he left it on the table and walked out. Part of me thought he did it to annoy the fed who sent them packing.

"Cisco Suarez," said the woman idly as she dug into her satchel. "Your story is an interesting one."

"Stranger than fiction," I quipped.

"I doubt it. But then, I've read some strange books." She slipped a laptop from her bag and powered it up while she stood. The woman chewed her lip and rapped the keys for a few minutes, forgetting I was there.

I tapped my fingers on the table. "And you are...?"

"Of course. I'm Special Agent Rita Bell." She held out a firm hand and I shook it without standing. I was cuffed but had plenty of leeway with the chain.

"The FBI? It was one fight with drunken asshats."

Rita Bell leaned on one hip. "Mr. Suarez, you're not here because of a back-alley dustup outside a Wynwood dive bar. The local police have already released the other men. They, uh, attributed their wounds to accidental mishaps. One man claimed to have broken his hand punching a wall."

I chuckled. A wall would've been softer. "So I'm free to go then?" I asked hopefully.

She smacked her lips, neither confirming nor denying. The special agent sat down and said, "I'd like to show you a few things first." She spun the laptop around as a video played onscreen. It was grainy security footage from outside an airport warehouse. A large ogre was throwing around a man with a white tank top and red cowboy boots. I blinked evenly.

"This video feed was recorded several months ago." I held my tongue as she recited the date. An observant person might notice it was the day before the issue date of my driver's license. The man in the video pulled a shotgun. It fired wide as the ogre clocked him in the face. I winced. It's not easy to give me a black eye like that.

The more I watched, the less worried I was. Because the ogre, as monstrous as it was, didn't look like much more than a 'roided-out lunatic, and the debonair gentleman kicking his ass had a blanket of shadow rippling over his identifying features.

Lucky coincidence. I definitely didn't remember that part.

"Shall I let you draw your own conclusions?" asked Agent Bell.

"I get it. The red boots. But you have to understand, this was after my story had gone public. I was all over the media. Cosplayers were rocking the Cisco Suarez look citywide.

This is probably some prank."

She frowned. "Don't you find that people who refer to themselves in the third person are narcissistic at best, sociopathic at worst?"

"You're the one with the criminology degree." I flitted my gaze to the security footage just in time to see the brawl disappear into a storeroom, where it had ended. Despite being caught on video, I'd somehow escaped incrimination. "Besides," I said, "it's hard to tell what's going on here. Looks like the video's corrupted."

"Yes, well, let's work with what we have, shall we? I want you to tell me what you see here."

I cleared my throat and glanced at the two-way mirror. I wasn't getting any help from there. "Look, Agent Bell, if you want my expert consultation, tell the FBI to stop being a bunch of cheapskates and pay me my normal rate. You don't get free services by dragging me into custody in handcuffs and pretending I'm a suspect."

It took her a minute, but she eventually smiled at my deflection. Like, a full-on grin of admiration. I like to think she admired my stones, but she could've been screwing with me.

"You are, of course, referring to your work as a police consultant. Is that right?"

I nodded carefully.

"So your expertise is not some sort of elaborate cover?"

I furrowed my brow. "No. I'm really an expert."

"Mind if I test you to see for myself?"

"Try me."

She folded the laptop closed and pulled a manila folder from her satchel. She rifled through some photocopies before laying one before me. It was a letter with eccentric handwriting and symbols.

TO WHOM IT MAY CONCERN AT THE HERALD,

THIS IS MY MANIFESTO.

I WAS ONCE LIKE YOU ARE. A MAN WITH SANITIZED IDEAS. A MAN, IF NOT IN CONTROL OF THE WORLD, THEN AT LEAST IN COMPREEHENSION OF IT. BUT THAT WAS BEFORE MY EYES WERE OPENED TO THE OTHER KIND.

I HAVE BEEN CHOSEN FOR THIS HOLY MISSION BY A CHOIR OF ANGELS. THEY TELL ABOUT THOSE WHO WOULD CONFOUND AND MARVEL US INTO SUBMISION. THEY LEAVE ME FULLY AWARE OF THE COMING FLOOD. SO, LIKE A PROPHET, I MUST GUIDE HUMANITY TO HIGH GROUND.

DOING SO WILL COME WITH A BODY COUNT.

YOU WILL DISCOVER THE FIRST CASUALTY OF WAR ON TUESDAY WHEN HIS MAID FINDS HIM IN PERMENENT REPOSE IN THE BATHTUB. THE DEFT HANDS HE USED TO ENSORCEL OUR MINDS WILL

NEVER BE FOUND, BUT I HAVE INCLOSED A
FINGERNAIL TO PROVE MY WORDS AND MY
CONVICTION. IT WAS TAKEN WHILE HE WAS STILL
ALIVE.

DO NOT ATTEMPT TO ACERTAIN MY IDENTITY. I
AM TOO SMART FOR YOU AND MY HOLY MISSION
WOULD NEVER LEAD ME INTO YOUR HANDS. I HAVE
BEEN CHOSEN. I WILL NEVER DIE. I USE MY GRACE
ONLY TO REACH OUT, AS THEY DID TO ME, IN AN
EFFORT TO PROMOTE SHEEP TO SHEPERDS. ARE
YOU A SHEEP?

IF YOU DO NOT PRINT THIS LETTER AND CIPHER
IN FULL IN TOMORROW'S EDITION THEN I WILL
HAVE TO CULL A FEW MORE FROM THE HERD. IT IS
FOR THEIR OWN GOOD. THIS IS MY MANIFESTO.

Agent Bell watched silently as I studied the note for a minute. "What is this?"

"As an expert on the occult, Mr. Suarez, I was hoping you could tell me."

"Cisco."

"Very well."

I frowned. "My expert opinion is: Find this nutcase and Baker Act him."

She cleared her throat. "The Baker Act. The Florida law allowing unwilling institutionalization of the mentally ill.

That's what you think this is?"

My brow furrowed. "You don't?"

The special agent stared at me, spurring me to extrapolate. Or trying to, anyway. I was still trying to figure out what I was doing here.

The bar fight, the security video, and this letter: they weren't linked. Each had nothing to do with the other.

"Can you identify the occult markers in the letter?" she asked.

I flapped the paper in my hand. Normally I'd use my shadow sight to inspect the Intrinsics, but this was a photocopy, removed from physical contact with the original.

"Well, there are the obvious ones," I started. "The Other Kind is a reference to whatever he fears."

"His persecutors. Who are they?"

"It just says they marvel us into submission. It's not a lot to go on."

She nodded. "Any other markers?"

"You see the usual second-coming-of-Jesus stuff. A new prophet, chosen by angels for a holy mission to storm the coming flood. Sorry to disappoint you, but it's more pseudo-Christian cult stuff than my area of expertise."

I was hoping to disappoint her to death, but Special Agent Rita Bell kept at it. "It's interesting that you skipped the part about him not being able to die."

"Interesting?" I arched an eyebrow. "Isn't that par for the course with these nutjobs? They think they're above our banal existences."

"Banal is a good word." She pressed on. "What do you

think of the cipher?"

I examined the note. Two short lines of letters in no apparent order. The first line was "wivo ivo wero ev" followed by a strange spiral symbol. The second line was similar and ended with the same symbol, like a period. "This is a code, right? You replace A with B, B with C—that sort of thing. What's it say?"

"It's gibberish," she said. "Meant to frustrate us and spin our wheels. Inspired by other killers of the past."

"Killers?"

"Manifesto is a killer, Cisco. The body of the Marvelous Mordane was found exactly as this letter states."

"The famous illusionist? The guy who does card tricks? Wasn't that over a month ago? Wait." I sat up. "Why haven't I heard of this?"

Agent Bell pursed thin lips. "Of the Manifesto Killer? You don't think the *Herald* and the *New Times* are stupid enough to play this killer's games. This is an FBI matter. We don't need a public spectacle."

"But his threat."

She pulled another letter from the folder and placed it before me. "This came two weeks later."

TO THE SHEEP AT THE HERALD,

THIS IS MY MANIFESTO. IT IS MEANT AS A
WARNING. IT IS MEANT AS A SALVAYTION
FROM THIS WICKED WORLD. I WAS REBORNE IN

> BLOOD. DID YOU NOT THINK I WAS PREPARED TO
> SHED SOME FROM THE INNOCENT?
>
> BUT THERE ARE NO INNOCENTS WHEN IT
> COMES TO COMPLICITY IN DECEIT. THE WOOL
> OVER YOUR HEADS WILL SMOTHER YOU.
>
> TWO MEMBERS OF UPSTANDING MIAMI SOCIETY
> WERE KILLED THIS WEEK. SHOT POINT BLANK IN
> THE BACK OF THE HEAD WITH A 20-GAUGE. THEY
> ARE SHEEP NO MORE. YOU WILL COMPLY. THIS IS
> MY MANIFESTO.

I blinked at the letter. "Did he do it?"

"Unknown," she answered without emotion. "Of the homicides in the Greater Miami area the previous week, there are three potential matches given the limited information. Two of them appear gang related. None are solved."

"So it's him. At least two of them."

"Unknown," she repeated. "The limited facts were publicly reported. It's not uncommon for killers to take credit for deaths they're not responsible for as a means of self-aggrandizement. You're familiar with aggrandizement, aren't you, Mr. Suarez?"

"It's Cisco. What do you mean?"

"Just that a decade ago you were a poor college dropout who, based on statements by your professors, thought he was smarter than everybody else. Then violently murdered, apparently. Except you return unharmed with questionable financing and find yourself a new media sensation." The agent pulled a few more photocopies from her folder. Press clippings from the local papers. "Dead Man Lives." "The Voodoo Life."

"What is this?" I asked sharply. "What am I doing in that folder?"

"My job is looking for links, Cisco. Do you believe the Marvelous Mordane was complicit in your ritual kidnapping ten years ago?"

"Eleven. And why would he have anything to do—"

"He was in the area at the time, in between shows."

"He lived twenty minutes away in Fort Lauderdale. Of course he was in town."

She leaned forward. "Was he? Was he there? Did you hate him for it?" She narrowed her eyes. "Did you kill him for it?"

Chapter 5

"Wait." The interrogation room was suddenly claustrophobic. I took a slow breath. "Wait. This is crazy. You don't think I'm the Manifesto Killer?"

She rattled off the list matter-of-factly. "A disenfranchised male who believes he's smarter than others. History of trauma, in this case a forcible introduction into the occult. Then salvation—no—infamy. You're a media sensation. Everybody in the city knows you. And you like it."

"It's a pain in the ass," I asserted. "I did the interviews because I needed to. To make sure my name was clear."

"And now you're a police consultant. Do you fancy yourself an occult sheriff of some sort, taking out the metaphysical trash?"

I shook my head at how off base she was. "This isn't me," I said, tapping the Manifesto letters.

"Would you be willing to submit a handwriting sample?"

"This is ridiculous!" I pushed away. The chain of the handcuffs dragged against the table. I wasn't under arrest.

Could I just ask to leave? Would that make things better or worse? Should I call Evan?

"Look at the facts, Cisco. People on the street call you the dead man, and Manifesto claims to be above death. He says he was born in blood. Was that bloody incident on Star Island the moment you were reborn? The moment you became aware of the Other Kind?"

"Lady—"

"Then there's this." Agent Bell reopened and pressed play. "The man in the video used a shotgun."

"That wasn't me."

"It was."

"Prove it," I growled.

Her thin lips stretched into a smile. "Cisco, Manifesto claimed two victims using a twenty-gauge. Same as the shells in your fanny pack."

"Belt pouch."

"Sorry?"

I crossed my arms. "It's not a fanny pack. It's a belt pouch. They're different."

She blinked dumbly.

"And anyone can walk into Walmart and pick up the same ammunition."

Her voice went stern. "Where is your shotgun, Cisco?"

I ground my teeth.

"Where... is... it?"

The hair on the back of my neck pricked up. Much like before, the door slammed open. This time it was Simon Feigelstock.

I jammed my hand in the freezer bag, leapt from the chair, and recoiled against the wall. The handcuffs snapped taut against the table. The dog-collar fetish was at the ready against the powerful lightning animist slash enforcer.

Simon Feigelstock set down his briefcase, straightened his tie, and brushed the jacket of his pinstripe suit. A large grin splayed across his face.

Agent Bell had stood at the sudden movement. Taller than either of us, she stuck out more because she didn't know spellcraft. Her hand instinctually reached for the firearm at her waist, but she wasn't wearing it during the interrogation so she paused. We all did.

"Mr. Cisco Suarez," said Simon carefully.

I nodded. "Pinstripes."

His eyes dropped to the dog collar in my hand. I turned to Rita Bell.

"Oh, yeah. I was... uh... reaching for my cell phone. I grabbed this by mistake." I scratched the back of my head. I didn't put down the fetish. I glanced at the two-way mirror, wondering if this was some kind of setup.

Simon cleared his throat. "Special Agent Bell, they tell me?" His outstretched hand was not met by Rita's. He shrugged and straightened his jacket. "Yes, well, I'm Simon Feigelstock, Mr. Suarez's attorney."

My face deflated. "Of course you are."

Agent Bell glared at the window.

"Oh," chuckled Simon, "they're not there anymore. Attorney-client conversations are privileged."

She crossed her arms. "If your client isn't guilty then he

doesn't need an attorney."

"The hell he doesn't. What is he charged with?"

"He's not."

"Why is the FBI questioning him? Is this voluntary?"

She worked her jaw. "He was already in custody for a separate matter. Why don't you sit down Mr. Fey... F... Mr. —"

"It's Feigelstock."

I snickered.

"And we're not going to sit down. If my client is not under arrest, we're going to leave." He handed her his card. "If the FBI would like to follow up with my client, make sure to contact me first. He has nothing to hide. We're perfectly willing to cooperate given he doesn't become a victim of gestapo tactics and intimidation."

She scoffed but held her tongue.

"Gather your things, Cisco. We're outta here."

I watched in quiet bemusement. Simon wasn't a friend. He was the exact opposite.

Even worse, he was one of the most dangerous animists I'd ever met. His patron was Ishkur the Thunderer, about as ancient as they came. And, boy, did he know how to crack a lightning bolt.

So did I go with the king of static cling, or did I stay with the overzealous FBI agent?

It was an easy decision. I preferred a beatdown to jail time any day. The enemy I knew, then.

I collected my possessions, wrapping the collar around my arm and draping the silver whistle around my neck. I stuffed my pockets and grabbed the belt pouch, wanting to get out of there as soon as possible.

"For what it's worth, Agent Bell," I said, "you're on the wrong scent. I didn't kill those people."

"We're not finished with this conversation," she warned. "And everything we talked about is private. I can charge you with interfering with an active investigation if the details get out. The world doesn't know about Manifesto."

I showed my contempt. She had smarts but lacked instinct. It was a dangerous combination. There was also something else, like maybe she knew more than she was letting on. Maybe she actually believed in magic.

A knock on the door spurred Simon to open it. An officer in a brown uniform stepped in. "I'm here to escort you two out of the station." His eyes snapped to the FBI agent.

She nodded. "It's okay. You can take him." As he unlocked my cuffs, she toyed with the card in her hand. "Kramer Schiff. I'm surprised you can afford a Big Pharma lawyer, Cisco."

Simon smiled sarcastically as I rubbed my wrists. He pushed me out ahead of him. "We handle a variety of clients, Ms. Bell, and this one's pro bono."

"How charitable of you." She walked right up to him and looked down, head and hair towering above. "And it's *Special Agent* Bell, from now on."

His grin doubled in size. "Of course, Special Agent."

Chapter 6

We were silent the whole way through the police station. I put the belt pouch back on and we made it into the light of day. Simon walked at my side.

"So you're a Big Pharma lawyer?" I asked. "Big surprise. You're a scumbag."

He flashed a dry smile. "Like I haven't heard that before. You need to try harder, Cisco."

A gust of wind blew his comb-over askew. I almost said something but didn't want to be accused of being unoriginal again.

Simon waved to a black Lincoln Town Car that pulled to the curb. "Don't worry," he said as he opened the back door. "This is just a company car. From the law firm."

I dug my heels into the sidewalk. "You're kidding, right?"

He looked around, missing something. "What?"

"The last time I saw you I was on the wrong side of being tortured."

His face soured. "Oh, grow up. We didn't break

anything. Besides, I just bailed you out. Metaphorically, anyway."

"If you think I'm getting in that car with you then you're a crazy person."

"Stop being a drama queen. I need to show you something." He leaned close and waited as an officer walked by. "It's about Manifesto."

"You know about him?" I shook my head. "Why am I not surprised? It could be you for all I—"

"Keep it down!" We both hushed as a pair of uniforms eyed us on the way into the police station. One of them glared at the double-parked Town Car. "First rule of Fight Club, Cisco. We don't talk about this in the street. In front of a police department for chrissakes. As your lawyer I need to stress—"

"You're not my lawyer." I crossed my arms. "Did Winthrop send you? 'Cause I don't trust that old hippie."

"No. He's out of state, and I don't blame you."

"The Gray Lady, then. If Margo wants to talk, I'll need assurances."

"You already have them through me."

"I don't trust you. I'll need it from her. Personally."

Simon Feigelstock took a breather. He didn't like terms dictated to him, but that was tough because I didn't trust his club of wizards one bit. Far from some sort of ancient wizard protectorate, they were a business group that operated more like a cartel. Big Pharma was probably only the start of it.

"Margo's not in town either," he said. "Society

leadership is far away from Miami. From Manifesto."

I narrowed my eyes. "Why is that?"

"Let me show you." He swept his hands to the open car door.

I ground my teeth stubbornly.

Simon took a breath and arched an eyebrow. "Darcy's over there."

I grumbled. "The kid?"

"Yes. I know you trust her."

"The problem is she trusts you. She's too young to know better."

"So come along. See how she's doing."

Simon stood with a proud lean, no doubt a product of grandstanding before countless juries. He knew how to read people. He knew I was hooked.

Mainly, I didn't like the thought of Darcy being around these assholes. And they had just saved me a hassle from the feds. But even more than that, I had a vested interest in knowing about the Manifesto Killer. It's not that I was determined to clear my name, necessarily, but it didn't hurt to know more about the guy.

And the worst part was Simon knew it. His smirk was downright sickening.

"Fine," I said, giving him the satisfaction he wanted, "but under three conditions. You need to promise me that you or your cartel won't hurt me while we do this."

"Already promised, but I give you my word again if you need it."

"Also, you give me a ride back to my car when we're

done."

He scoffed. "Of course. What's your last term?"

I cleared my throat. "I get to punch you in the face."

His expression went blank. "You..."

"Get to punch you in the face. Once. As hard as I can."

He eyed several officers loitering nearby and turned to me, incredulous. "We're in front of a police station."

"Don't care. You deserve it and you know it. It's the only way I'm getting into that car."

He hissed but I saw the resignation on his face. I knew I'd hooked him too. He shuffled his feet for a moment and nodded. "Okay. One punch."

"In the face."

He nodded again. "Go for it."

It was bright out. My boot slid into the shadow of a "No Parking" sign as I drew some power to my fist. Simon stood tall and clenched his jaw. A small glimmer of electricity sparkled across his cheek.

"Wait a minute," I said. "You're running your defenses."

"Fair's fair." He pointed sharply at the veiled glove of shadow over my fist. I frowned and noticed the nearby officers had taken an interest in us. They weren't approaching, but the attention was avid enough they might as well have been sharing a bucket of popcorn and Raisinets.

"Okay," I muttered under my breath. "No spellcraft. Either of us."

Simon grimaced at the thought of leaving his defenses down, but it was better all around. He quenched out his electricity and I dispersed the shadow. I squared my body with his and decked him.

Simon tumbled to the cement. The officers straightened, ready to intervene. I shrugged. They erupted into laughter once they saw the fight wasn't continuing.

"Hey, legal counsel," one of them guffawed, "you wanna file a report?"

"No," snapped Simon, clenching his jaw. His lip was busted open. "No. We're two consenting adults. That was perfectly voluntary."

They couldn't stop laughing. One reached for the club on his belt. "I could hand him my ASP if you want."

I chuckled. Simon climbed to his feet and brushed his suit off, glaring at anyone and everything that dared meet his eyes. "Okay, hotshot," he growled. "Get in the car." He turned to the police. "Show's over."

I made sure the back seat was empty and climbed in, grinning like a stupid kid. One punch and my whole day was a lot better already.

Chapter 7

The Lincoln navigated the downtown streets with cool comfort. It was a much smoother ride than I was used to. A professional driver sat in the front behind a closed privacy window, which left Simon and me time to chat.

He rubbed his jaw. "You've got a hell of a right hook."

"I've had lots of practice lately." I kept my gaze outside the window. "Some of that due to you."

"Don't blame your troubles on me. Your checkered past has zero to do with the Society and everything to do with your greedy little fingers. The problem with artifacts is that everybody wants them."

I didn't satisfy him with a reply.

"You know, I really was on your side with the whole thing."

I turned my glare on him.

"Once I knew what you were about," he hedged. "My first impression was that you were a power-hungry prick, but I realized your intentions were more honorable."

"So you had me hog-tied and kidnapped."

He continued snaking his way through an explanation. "Look, guys like us, that's how we communicate. We're muscle. And, technically, I was right about you losing the Horn to Connor. I warned you that you couldn't adequately protect it and I was right."

I swallowed and turned back to the window. The Town Car headed out of Downtown, leaving me wondering where we were going. Was all this really just to make sure an acquaintance was okay?

"You've been difficult to track down," noted Simon. I guess he'd taken the apology as far as he could.

"I went dark for a while."

"I don't blame you. The streets were pretty hostile to you after what you pulled."

"They still are, but at some point a man's gotta dig his heels in and stand his ground."

"Preaching to the choir, my man."

I huffed and considered him. The sharply dressed animist wasn't exactly subtle. Large cuff links and big words. He was just an enforcer of sorts himself, with no real power in the secret society. I'd been hoping his little wizard cartel had forgotten about me as I attempted to turn a new leaf. No such luck, apparently.

"Why are you helping me?" I asked plainly. "You could have left me to fend for myself with the police."

Simon smiled. "This city owes you a debt, Cisco. Even if they don't know it. The Society rewards heroes like yourself."

I rolled my eyes. "Yeah, right. I'm thinking the Society

wants to remain hidden, as always. If the popo digs into me, they'll dig into the Connor Hatch connection. It's only a small leap from there to find you."

He winced in halfhearted concession. "I'm not denying we share similar concerns. At least we're not trying to kill you to keep you quiet, right?"

I tightened my fist.

"A joke! It was a joke!" He shook his head. "Sheesh, brother, you really need to lighten up." He scratched his head nervously. "Funny you should mention Connor..."

"He's gone for good," I said. "That's all you need to know."

Simon's face went flat. "You're acting like you killed him or something." When I didn't say anything, he extrapolated. "Listen, Cisco, I know you're a tough guy, but I don't believe for a second you killed a jinn. Our organization is well informed." He leaned toward me. "You wanna know a secret? We just so happen to have word—straight from the Aether," he added in a reverent whisper, "that confirms Connor was exiled from our realm."

I kept a straight face for exactly three and a half seconds before I burst into laughter. Simon here was trying to impress me with how connected he was, when the truth was I had gone to the Aether myself and saw to the jinn's exile. Simon's hushed words revealed he knew very little of the actual truth, which involved me trapping the jinn in the Horn of Subjugation and burying that artifact so deep even he didn't know where he was. Exiled was right, but by my own hands.

Simon's face flushed slightly as my mirth died down. Far as I saw it, there was no reason for him to know the whole truth.

"You know," he continued, idly picking at the door handle, "Connor was known for his stockpile of magical antiquities. After his final days, when it was clear he wasn't returning, a few of us visited his island compound."

I held onto my smile.

"It was raided. The collection was cleaned out. You wouldn't happen to—"

"No," I said firmly.

He searched my face but I wasn't giving anything up. "Quite a bit of his cash reserves went missing as well."

I canted my head. "Find a penny, pick it up. All day long you'll have good luck."

"And here I was hoping to catch you in a lie." Simon straightened his baby-blue tie. "And thus comes our offer to you. You're a capable animist who gets things done, one way or another. I see some of my younger self in you."

I held up a hand. "I'm gonna stop you right there, Pinstripes. I already told you, I'm not interested in joining the union."

He frowned but wasn't put off. "That's your decision, of course, but it doesn't mean we can't reach a mutually beneficial arrangement. I'm not only proposing a truce, but a deal. A contract of sorts, service for service."

"I don't want anything to do with the Society."

"That's why you're perfect! You're a free agent, without known associations to us. The ideal investigator."

So they wanted me to look into something. In return for... "And what could I possibly need from you?"

His face went flat. "Come on, Cisco, let's be serious for a minute. You have a new condo in an expensive neighborhood. You have a million plus under your mattress. You're trying to hide your ill-gotten gains by having your friends sign the papers to help you out. It's a stop-gap measure to get you started at best. Only a matter of time before the illegitimate money is apparent. As your lawyer I recommend—"

"You're not my lawyer."

"Fine. Then, as your debonair rival, I feel the need to point out the painfully obvious benefits of the Society's influence. We can get you set up with a legitimate financial history, clean all your money and bring it into the banks, and otherwise perpetuate the illusion that you didn't plunder the wealth of a deposed Caribbean drug kingpin."

I bit down my snarky reply halfway through his speech.

He smirked. "Not bad for an ex-zombie hit man, huh?"

I hated to admit it, but he was onto something.

"Besides," he added, the final blow of the hammer mid flight, "with the feds looking into you, how long do you think your little house of cards will hold up?"

I grunted. Game, set, and match.

The car pulled into the roundabout driveway of a large colonial-styled house in Coconut Grove. The columned doorway was elegant but old, and my impression was the place could use a remodel. Something odd struck me about the house. Despite the early afternoon hour, a solemn shadow fell over Simon's face as he gazed on it.

"What do you want from me, Simon?"

He opened the door of the car. "It's pure providence that Agent Bell brought you up to speed, actually." He climbed out and turned to me. "Someone in Miami's killing wizards, Cisco, and we want you to find him."

Chapter 8

Manifesto. Apparently this killer wasn't gonna get out of my life until I did something about it. The fact that I didn't object and followed him out of the car was enough tacit approval for Simon. This was, after all, a deal that greatly benefited me: Dealing with the Society on equal terms. Ridding the world of a killer, with the added bonus of clearing my name with overeager FBI agents. And, of course, there was the money. I had it, but I couldn't openly spend it. Believe it or not, as much fun as it was the first ten times, making living-room forts out of blocks of cash did eventually get old.

So it was safe to say I was on board. A win all around. After my failure to save little Gendra from the vamps this morning, this was the next best thing.

Except I still wasn't sure how the distinguished colonial manor house figured in. Did the Society know where Manifesto lived? That hypothesis was quickly dashed when Simon opened the door and the pungent stench greeted my nose.

"I get it. I'm discreet, I'm a necromancer, and you've got a dead body." Hey, I'm not the sharpest tool in the shed, but I'm no dummy.

"You catch on fast, dead man," snickered Simon.

He led me down a long hall painted red. Black-and-white portraits adorned the walls, giving the impression that a distinguished family had history here. Considering the Society's interest and the Manifesto Killer's MO, whoever was murdered must've been an animist.

I frowned. "Am I gonna have free rein to inspect the evidence without the cops getting in the way?"

"There are no cops. This matter is being handled internally by the Society's best and brightest."

I stopped. "You mean you're not gonna tell them about a dead body?"

"*Two* dead bodies," he corrected. He glanced back and paused in annoyance when he noticed I wasn't moving anymore. He sighed. "The Society is not an official organization. These executions draw needless attention to us. If the authorities find the links between the victims, it'll illuminate us, and we're not interested in the spotlight. Now if you please."

He motioned toward an adjoining room. I cleared my throat and entered. It was a small parlor, midnight-blue, with the red velour curtains on the far wall flung open to bathe an otherwise frigid scene with warm sunlight. A middle-aged woman with dyed-black hair lay dead on the remains of a broken chair. A round table was overturned beside her, as if she had pushed it away when she'd fallen.

Standing over the dead woman was a Chinese man wearing a dapper gray suit. His hair was spiked up and he had an air of confidence that was unearned by someone in his twenties.

"This guy?" I snapped. "This is the Society's best and brightest?"

Shen Santos scoffed at my entrance. "Look what the Shadow Dog dragged in. You're lucky we don't take you out right here and now."

I guffawed. He was a powerful illusionist, but it would be a cold day in hell before he got the better of me.

"There's a dead woman on the floor," said Darcy in the corner, sulking. "Her son's in the kitchen, too. So how about we put the macho posturing aside for a few minutes?"

"I'm Cuban," I said. "I can't help it." Rather than lighten the mood, my joke stuck out like a guy at a funeral on a cell phone. I shook my head, immediately reticent.

Darcy was a teenage witch with a bob of red hair, skinny jeans, and enough gummy bracelets to satisfy a classroom. She was also the most powerful telekinetic I'd ever met. She pouted a lot and hated life, which I gathered was due to her being used by the Society for whatever obligations initiates incurred. Personally, I'd kinda hoped she would've ditched this game of shadows by now, but she was her own person.

"Hey, kid," I said.

She nodded once in return.

I sighed and turned to the body. "Fine. What do you have so far?"

"You're the expert," Shen hissed. "You tell me."

"This is what I'm talking about. The Society is this big

bad collection of talent, someone's picking off wizards, and you get Hugo Boss to investigate?" Before Shen said anything, I added, "Not that you don't look fly in a fitted suit, bro. I just mean there's gotta be someone better." He glared at me but didn't object.

Simon walked to the woman on the floor and pointed. "*She* was the better. Marie Devereaux. The Manifesto Killer murdered two random animists and two civilians and Marie was investigating for us. She was good at what she did. She expected results."

"But she was killed first."

He nodded. "A lot of our people are avoiding the state because of this creep, and you know our handle on South Florida is best described as tenuous. It's a different beast down here. Shen and Darcy are locals so I'm using them. Shen's young, but he's got an analytical mind and is willing to help. Besides, you're here too. And Margo's looking into another mercenary, but I don't have details yet. Let's just work with what we have."

I mulled it over for a minute before approaching the body with a light step to avoid scuffing blood with my alligator boots. This was a seance room, adorned with all the bells and whistles. Chakra stones, bones, beeswax candles, hanging instruments used for calming auras. I'd never heard of Marie Devereaux but there was no doubt she was a fortune teller. If she'd had insights into distant times and places, that would explain why the Society had leaned on her to find the killer. Ironic she didn't foresee Manifesto knocking on her door.

I moved to the swiveling door in Darcy's corner and peeked into the kitchen. The white tile was slopped with blood where the boy had attempted to crawl to safety. He was Darcy's age. It looked like he'd been done in with a kitchen knife.

"Damn shame," said Simon. "The kid was usually in high school when this happened, but he'd taken the day off for some reason. As bad as bad luck could be."

A queasy feeling welled in my gut. It wasn't unlike nausea, except this was fueled by rage. Injustice was one thing. I'd experienced a few lifetime's worth and knew it was a fact of the world. What I really couldn't stand was seeing the downtrodden, the underdogs—the truly weak—abused by those in power. Hurting kids crossed the line.

And Manifesto was definitely in power. Executing animists, taunting police, and then slipping away free and clear.

My face soured. I had a lot of doubts about the partnership. If someone was taking out Society mages, maybe I should stay out of it. Maybe they had a leak from within and I should let them collapse. I even wondered if the Society had been responsible for turning the feds on me in the first place. And if not, getting mixed up in this investigation might do more to incriminate me than anything else.

Christ. I was a suspect in these killings and I was standing smack in the middle of a murder scene.

I growled. I didn't know if Marie Devereaux deserved what had happened to her, but that kid sure as hell didn't. In a city of corrupt politicians, dangerous practitioners, and shady business organizations like the Society, I considered myself Miami's last bastion of defense.

"Fine," I muttered. "I'll do it. We have a deal."

Darcy's eyes squeezed into a smile for the briefest of moments. Simon was more magnanimous with his pleasure. Shen scowled, of course.

"But you need to let me bring my own people into it," I quickly amended.

Simon's smile faded. "It's imperative no one knows about this. I told you that."

"I have a friend in the department. His resources are crucial—"

"The police?!?" His hands pulled at his thinning hair. "Have you listened to a word I said?"

I stepped up to him. Lightly, without aggression, but with a confident swagger that demanded full attention. He narrowed his eyes. "You brought me here," I stressed. "You asked for my help. My way, my people. That's non-negotiable."

The lightning animist swallowed back a glower. Despite all the pressure on me to do this, the Society was desperate. Anything scaring them out of Florida had to be dealt with. I had Simon by the short and curlies and he knew it.

He nodded. "Your way."

"Great." I clapped him on the shoulder and turned to the gruesome scene. "Then first thing's first. Let's get rid of all this light." I stepped around the body and yanked the heavy curtains closed. A wash of shadow surged over us.

Chapter 9

I commanded the darkness to leak into my eyes. The room snapped into sharp focus. I waited a moment to take it all in. Get a feel for the place.

Magic splattered the walls like modern art. The Intrinsics, the building blocks of all life and spellcraft, had funneled through this room more times than I could count. Like oceans that wear down mountains, the friction of magic had changed this space.

The Intrinsics didn't always leave strong signatures, but this was a seance room. An anchor in time and place where repeated rituals occurred. With that much juice, it was hard not to have some linger.

That said, the spellcraft was unfamiliar to me. A lot of formless gray smoke, with white webbing shooting this way and that into infinity. Threads of destiny, perhaps. It was clear Marie Devereaux was no charlatan.

My eyes rested on her body. Prematurely aged, I now observed. She was thinner than was healthy. Her skin sagged. What struck me most was the lack of traces of spellcraft on her body.

"She wasn't killed with magic," I said.

Simon nodded. "Manifesto hates spellcraft. He hates animists."

"He's gotta be ballsy to take them on without magic."

Shen scoffed. "Not really. The old lady didn't have much fight in her. None of his targets do."

I showed my skepticism. Shen was overly brash. Power didn't always come from raw strength. You'd think an illusionist like Shen would understand that. But that was because he lacked the wisdom to see it. The experience, too. Marie Devereaux? I doubted she was as shortsighted.

Yet she had been caught unawares this time. I knelt and turned her head to face me.

"The eyes are missing. Have we found them anywhere?"

"No," answered Shen. "That's gross."

"Well, you *did* invite a necromancer to the party. Without her eyes I won't be able to see the final moments of her death."

"You think that's why he took them?" he asked.

I considered the question and shook my head. "No. It wouldn't have worked anyway unless the body was fresh. Does the kid have his eyes?"

Darcy nodded solemnly.

"That's not it then. Manifesto likes to keep mementos. The first magician he killed—the Marvelous Mordane—was a performer. A card mechanic. The killer cut off his hands. He neutralized his power. It's symbolic." I turned to them. "You said a second animist was killed?"

"A piper," said Shen. "Another easy target. Nothing was missing, but the body was burnt up pretty bad."

I didn't hide my surprise. "Really?"

Simon cut in. "Marie believed Manifesto had made a mistake. He murdered the piper but left the gas stove on. Whatever'd been cooking spilled over at some point and started a fire. The whole house burned down. It didn't leave us a lot to go with."

I pressed my lips together and thought about what made a piper special. In the meantime, Simon had pulled out his phone and opened a gallery of morbid photographs. He handed it to me. Charred body. Not burned to completion but the head had gotten the worst of it. I'd seen a similar thing before. Clean skeletal teeth smiled back, as if posing.

"The lips," I concluded. "The piper's lips were removed, but the fire ruined the display." I handed the phone back. "So we know Manifesto isn't perfect."

Simon nodded in agreement. "Marie believed Manifesto never penned a letter because of the mistake. It was lucky for us, considering. With the apparently different MO, the police didn't link it to our boy."

"Don't underestimate Agent Bell. She has a good head on her shoulders, if overly suspicious." My attention returned to the body. Bruising around the neck signified choking. I plucked at Marie's skin. "She's been dead almost a day. Long gone. I'm not gonna be able to get a lot from her."

"This is a waste of time," complained Shen. He stomped to Simon. "What does this guy bring to the table? He's not gonna help us even if he knows."

Simon clenched his jaw. "He'll help."

"The guy has an ax to grind with us. Hell, if the feds think it's him, maybe it is."

I eyed him sharply but it was Darcy who spoke. "Cut the crap, Shen. It doesn't make him a murderer just 'cause he kicked your ass once or twice." I smiled.

He whirled on her, unamused. "So help me, Darcy, if you don't keep your mouth shut..."

I stood, but Darcy didn't move. She remained casually leaning in the corner like she was bored and waiting for an Uber.

"You'll what?" she asked.

Shen's eyes narrowed.

"Kids?" said Simon, annoyed. "You have two choices. Behave or go wait in the car."

I watched Shen with a smirk. He pressed his lips together and unfortunately decided to hold his ground.

Darcy stomped to the hall. "Catch you later, Cisco. I'm outta here."

Damn. And I'd been hoping to chat with her in private. It would need to wait.

"Now," continued Simon, "you think we can get back to business?"

"Yes," agreed Shen. "Tell us something we don't know, shadow charmer."

I took a breath. I really wanted to show the guy up but they were putting me in an impossible situation. I looked around the room. Noted the wooden stand and silk wrap.

"Well, Marie was a fortune teller, right? So where's her—"

"Crystal ball?" cut in Shen. "Already found it. It's in the kitchen. Manifesto used it to beat the dying boy's head in."

I grimaced. As if stabbing him wasn't enough. The killer had to finish him off as the boy was crawling away. I was about to stand up when I noticed Marie's eyelids. One of them was almost devoid of eyelashes, while the other had a healthy portion with heavy mascara. It was easy to miss with the gaping sockets below.

"The killer pulled her lashes," I reported. "I imagine eyes are difficult to send through the mail. I bet Manifesto's next letter will have hair for DNA evidence." I turned to Simon. "Do we have a note yet?"

"We have a source inside the paper. No note yet but it's expected to arrive tomorrow, which gives us a day lead time. The police might have the hair, but they don't have Marie's DNA on file. If we clean the house real good, they'll never be able to find any to make a positive match."

I raised my eyebrows. "You're talking garbage, toothbrushes, makeup, dirty silverware, combs—everything."

Simon nodded. "We'll get it done."

"Why not burn the house?"

"Too much attention. Plus that would match the MO of the piper and encourage them to link the crimes. I'd rather get egg on the killer's face. Have him send the letter and the police come out only to find nothing suspicious. We're already forging a flight history to make it look like the Devereaux family is out of town."

"You're trying to undermine the Manifesto Killer's credibility. Get under his skin."

"It's what I'm good at," he admitted with a shrug. "And the less serious the police take these letters, the easier it is for us to stay hidden."

"That will only stall them so long, you know. They'll eventually consider her dead."

Shen stepped forward. "That's why we have to find him first. Before he kills again."

"Exactly," said Simon. "The longer this goes on, the more impossible it will be to hide, the more facts and links will exist. And when the public gets wind of this, every internet investigator will be on the case. Nobody wants that."

I could imagine. When I was younger, the internet was just getting its legs under itself. Chat rooms, message boards —it was text-based. But these days we had streaming video cameras in our pockets and tracking data up to our noses. For an organization like the Society, people who thrived in keeping their power a secret, it must've been harrowing.

It was only a matter of time before more and more proof of spellcraft got out. Agent Bell had caught me fighting an ogre. It was only through dumb luck that the shadow had obscured my identity.

At the same time, I was believing less and less of what I saw in pictures and videos. Photoshop had changed the game. Computer graphics were so sophisticated and ubiquitous that I'd just watched a perfectly realistic video of an all-giraffe high-diving team.

Technology giveth, technology taketh away.

"Okay," I announced, getting my bearings. "The killer enters peacefully through the front. No signs of forced entry and Marie was doing her thing. She's likely in the middle of a reading when Manifesto reveals who he is. He overpowers her and the son comes at her cry of alarm."

I stomped into the kitchen and skirted the trail of blood. "Manifesto chases him. The boy's about eighteen, not huge but not a wimp. If he's running after seeing someone attack his mother, there's a good chance our killer is a big guy. Or intimidating in some way."

Shen snorted. "Could just be he had a weapon."

"It's possible, but..." I pointed to the knife rack I passed on the counter. A knife was missing. A long bread knife with a handle that matched the others was bloodied on the floor a few steps down. "How was the piper killed?"

"Stabbed, we think."

"Interesting. So Manifesto's not necessarily strong. He took out an older woman with his hands but used a knife on the others. But still something made the boy run instead of helping his mother." I pondered that a moment before returning to the scene at hand.

"Manifesto grabs a weapon here and goes to work. The boy turns to defend himself. Defensive wounds on his hands and forearms, but also wounds on his back, which means he turns to run again. Then Manifesto drops the knife and..." I frowned and stepped back, processing the pattern of blood on the floor. "I think he goes back to work on Marie. Extracts his mementos. Some time later, he hears the boy coughing or something, picks up the crystal ball, and comes back in to finish the job."

Our eyes landed on the final murder weapon. It was a clear orb, similar to the one Emily used but older, as it had an almost golden imperfection throughout. The spellcraft anchor sat on the kitchen counter, shiny and wet.

I chewed my lip. "Where's the blood?"

Shen cleared his throat with a prideful smirk. "The killer washed it off. I found it in a bucket in the sink."

He said it like it had been an inspired move. I checked the sink and saw why. The bucket of water was mostly empty now, no doubt a result of Shen's bungling. The murky color of blood clouded the leftover water. It could've been easy to miss. Except...

I leaned my nose into the sink and sniffed. My eyes scanned the counter tops and spotted the scattered white grains.

"No," I said. "Why would Manifesto wash the blood off this but not the knife on the floor? Either he was wearing gloves or he doesn't care if the police have his prints."

"Do they?" asked Simon.

"They didn't tell me what physical evidence they had besides the notes."

His face slackened.

Shen brightened up. "Gloves would be suspicious. If the killer doesn't have a record, maybe the police don't have his prints on file so he doesn't care if they get them."

I nodded. It was the first smart thing he'd said all day. But it was hard to be sure either way without getting a true forensics team involved. That was the downside of vigilante justice. With the Society handling this investigation, they were essentially blocking the police from doing theirs. And while we could see lots of things they couldn't, they had science on their side.

"You're wrong about the crystal ball," I told Shen. "Manifesto wasn't washing off the blood. That's salt water in the bucket." I opened a few cabinets till I found the large can of iodized salt with the spout still open. Salt water really screwed with the Intrinsics. Not that it interfered with their existence so much as it blocked the flow of energy through spirit. "The killer was erasing his magical tracks. Marie Devereaux must've seen something in the crystal before she died."

I hurriedly flipped on the faucet and washed fresh water over the orb. I gave it a good wipe and dried it off before finding a box of jumbo plastic freezer bags and dropping it in one.

"What are you doing?" asked Shen. His voice was territorial. He still didn't accept that this was my investigation.

"I'm collecting evidence I might need," I said. I used another bag to grab the bloody bread knife without touching it.

"I was gonna do that."

"No. I want you to oversee cleaning down the house. We need to get a rush on that. Make sure they don't clean anything we might want."

"But that's bitch work."

I glared at him evenly. He blinked and appealed to Simon.

"Let's just do what the man says, Shen."

The illusionist scowled and stormed out.

"He's a handful," I said in a mocking tone like a concerned parent.

"You have no idea."

I ran my eyes over the kitchen and the boy, making sure I wasn't missing anything. "There's one more thing. Manifesto's first note included a cipher. The FBI says it's gibberish but I don't buy that. Have you guys cracked it yet?"

Simon hooked his hands on his hips and shook his head. "It's not a normal cipher, and we only received a photocopy of the letter so we couldn't inspect it for enchantments."

I grunted. "Same."

"I notified my source in the paper to let us have a look at the original if there's another. Depending how many people see it, they may need to turn it over to the police, but they could stall them a bit. I have a picture." He pulled out his phone again.

"Send me what you have." I begrudgingly gave him my number and he transferred the evidence to me.

On my last pass of the boy's body, I noticed more blood than usual welling around the mouth. It was likely from lung perforations, but I opened it for a peek. My face darkened.

"The boy was an animist too?"

"What?" asked Simon, half distracted.

"The boy. His tongue was cut out."

Simon's face twitched. "That doesn't make sense. The boy spoke in tongues, if you pardon the phrase, but he didn't do any public shows. Marie was keeping his talents secret until he got older."

"But you knew," I pointed out.

"Sure, a few of us knew, but our organization thrives on secrecy."

"Shen?"

He shook his head. "Clueless."

I washed my hands in the sink. When I was done, I spun around and rested against the counter. "The Society has a leak."

Simon chortled. "No way in hell."

"Somehow the killer knew the boy was a target as well. It wasn't bad luck that he was here. It was the perfect opportunity to take them both out."

He frowned somberly.

"What if this is intentional? A little house cleaning by Margo or GR Winthrop? He tried the same thing with me before."

"It's impossible," he asserted. "Look, going rogue to take out Connor makes sense. That guy was an animal we were forced into a working relationship with. Margo was too conservative to take action, but if Winthrop took a shot I'd believe it. But outing Society members like this, sending notes announcing spellcraft to the newspapers—that goes against everything Winthrop and the Society want. We stand to lose more than anyone if the feds make these connections." He grumbled. "This just goes to show why having an outside actor like yourself is necessary. If Manifesto somehow knows our people..."

He trailed off. It was a good point but he was too eager to dismiss the possibility of an inside job. I, however, couldn't take that chance. If I couldn't trust the Society before, this was a whole different ball game.

Shen returned to the room, slipping his phone into his pocket. "The cleaners are on the way. Anything else we need to discuss?"

Simon opened his mouth but I beat him to the punch. "No," I said in a rush. "We're finished here." I glared at Simon forcefully enough that he got the message. We made our way back outside.

Chapter 10

Simon made his way to the Lincoln. Darcy waited on an idling motorcycle closer to the street, holding her helmet and looking at me. I broke away and met up with her.

"Still hanging around these assholes, huh?"

"They pay the bills," she said matter-of-factly.

"Pay for this, you mean." I pointed to the sleek sports bike. It was bright red, and so was the helmet she held to her stomach. "These things are suicide machines, you know."

She glared at me. Normally I'd chalk it up to rebellious teenage apathy, but considering she could literally float she was fairly safe from getting thrown.

"I know what you're thinking," she said. "That this is all a trap of some sort."

I snickered. "Actually I'm leaning toward an inside job."

"Close enough." She scoffed, but in a playful way. I figured the two of us were something like friends. Or... close enough. "I want you to know Marie was a nice lady. She wasn't a grifter. She was wise and kind. Nick was pretty cool too." She saw my puzzled face and added, "Her son."

"Oh." I took a breath and scuffed the concrete with my boot, unsure what to say.

"Ha," she laughed. "You're worried about me and I'm worried about you."

I smiled. "If there's one thing I proved, I can take care of myself." I looked back. Simon was waiting in the car and Shen had stayed in the house. "And some of these Society guys might seem okay, but it's the organization as a whole that I don't trust. I'm as capitalist as the next guy, but they care about money, not people."

"And I'm not some naive brat who doesn't know that."

"Fair enough," I conceded.

We were both silent a moment, emphasizing how little we actually knew each other. She slipped on her helmet. "Good luck, Cisco."

I nodded. "Take care of yourself."

She twisted the throttle and peeled down the street. I wasn't sure why I gave a damn. Trying to save everybody was a surefire way to guarantee disappointment. I marched back to the car and told Simon where to drop me off.

As amazing as it was, he was unusually quiet too. I decided to enjoy it for once and thumbed through my phone, making sure I had any photo evidence that might come in handy. Everything appeared to be in order.

Then I backtracked over my already long day. The murder, the Society, the feds, the cops. I swore I was forgetting something. As my thoughts drifted to the Wynwood dive bar, I decided to take advantage of the

Society's knowledge.

"Simon, you ever heard of the Obsidian March?"

He arched an eyebrow. "Uh, yeah. They're only the largest vampire clan in the Western Hemisphere. And a major pain in the ass at times, but that's par for the course with Nether creatures."

So they weren't subhumans; they were fiends from the underworld. Which suddenly lent sense to the name Obsidian March. The silvan circles were well known in the Nether. Less discussed were the various marches in the super depths. "What kind of vampires are we talking about?"

"The OGs of vamps. They're upirs, classic old-world variety—think Count Dracula. Only they're not like the movies. Humans can't turn into vampires. Those legends started because they can expertly hide among us for years. By the time one gets exposed... well, let's just say people would rather think their friends and lovers were turned than believe they'd been vampires all along. That and they collect familiars like Pokémon."

"The familiars can't become vamps?"

"More like mindless thralls. Put it this way: many so-called meth and heroin users aren't addicted to meth or heroin at all."

My eyes widened. It seemed familiars shed a whole new light on the Florida Man mythos.

"Also," he continued, "with the possible exception of powerful sorcerers, vampires can't shape-shift into animals or fog or any of that. They do have a natural monstrous form, though."

Interesting. I wondered how much I knew about them at all. "What kind of magic do they run?"

Simon shrugged. "Common stuff for the craphole they come from. Human guises, super strength, fangs and claws. In the Nether their true form has shiny skin resembling a black carapace. It's pliable armor."

"I've seen it."

He nodded. "Then you know how nasty they can be. Fortunately, it taxes them to hold their monstrous forms in the Earthly Steppe. They keep it to a minimum if they can help it. If not, sunlight forces them back to human."

"It doesn't kill them."

"If only." Simon paused and furrowed his brow. "Why the sudden interest in the Obsidian March anyway?"

"Just had a little run-in with them. It's why the cops picked me up in the first place."

His palm slapped his forehead. "Hey, Cisco, I need you to focus here. Eyes on the prize. The name of the game today is the Manifesto Killer." He hissed. "It would be just like you to start a crusade against a powerful supernatural faction in the middle of my investigation."

"Technically it was your investigation that interrupted my crusade."

He sighed. "What, are the vampires a pressing concern? Is there something that needs to be dealt with immediately? After the Manifesto business is done, I can have someone arbitrate if it'll ease your mind."

I frowned and shook my head. "No. The little girl's

already dead."

He snorted. "Animals. You want your mind blown? The Obsidian March is responsible for over half of all human trafficking in South Florida. Which is, if you're not aware, a metric fuck ton. On the plus side, they don't get involved in human politics. Even though we can't afford an open war with them, they know people like us would retaliate if they tried to take control. So they're content to operate in the background, defending their territory mostly against other netherlings, as long as their supply keeps coming."

My face twisted in disgust. "That's sick."

"Preaching to the choir, my man."

"Why don't you guys do something about it?"

His gaze fell for a moment. His attitude sobered. "I could say because they outnumber us, but the real reason is because it's not profitable to do so." He saw my incredulous look and shrugged. "Hey, you want honest? I'm being honest. I don't call the shots. I'm not one of the fat cats— and don't tell Margo or Winthrop I ever called them that. It's life, Cisco. I survive, they survive, and shit happens."

Part of me wanted to smother on the guilt trip. An enforcer like him didn't lay down the law, but he had enough agency to make a stink about it. Try to effect change. At the very least, he didn't have to be so Zen about it.

But we were almost at my drop-off spot and I needed to think practically.

"If sunlight doesn't kill them..." I prodded.

"Right. Don't waste your time with garlic or silver or

wood. What gets them good is a heartstrike. Upirs store all the blood in their bodies there. They're like blood camels, except with hearts instead of humps. It's their magical core. You pierce that and they'll go down real quick."

I grunted. That was pretty damn helpful, actually.

I suddenly noticed we were two blocks from the dive bar. "This is it," I said. "Stop here."

The car pulled over. Simon held out his hand and I shook it. "You have my number now, Cisco. Call me if you uncover anything."

I nodded and he took off.

I stood on the sidewalk and took a deep breath. Freedom. It wasn't too late in the day yet either. Once again I got the uncanny feeling I was forgetting something important. As I strolled to my car, my train of thought was interrupted by a cry for help.

I spun around. A woman, I thought. She called out again. "Somebody, help!" It came from the alley. I turned my boot on the concrete and raced toward the sound. I rounded the corner and skidded to a stop when I saw them.

The alley between buildings was in heavy shade. And no one here needed any help. That had just been a lure to draw me here. I ground my teeth and faced them.

Chapter 11

"Funny," I announced with a cocky tinge, "I was just talking about you guys."

Tutti strutted triumphantly from the wall where she'd been feigning helplessness. The two bouncers from this morning were with her and fanned out to surround me. It was a stupid trap. I could've backed away and made it to sunlight within seconds. But I reminded myself that it wasn't fatal to them. Probably only slightly more inconvenient than it was for me.

Tutti coyly shuffled her hands behind her back. "You left so early, mister. We never had a chance to kiss goodbye."

She looked a lot different than she had earlier. Still a bit too thin to be healthy, and the same dirty-blonde pigtails, but she now had a fresh coat of makeup. A cut-off white button-up and a plaid miniskirt showed off long legs. She would actually be attractive if she wasn't trying to murder me.

"You're not the brightest set of vampires, are you?" I asked.

Contempt marred her smile and she pulled a pistol from behind her back. "Bright enough to get the drop on you."

I smiled at first, taking in the two thugs as their human forms brandished long black claws. It was too amusing to stifle my laugh.

"What is it?" she snapped.

I shook my head. "You lured me into a dark alley, and you know I'm a shadow charmer. That's what I would call a miscalculation."

"You try something and you're a dead man."

My eyes flashed. "Been there, done that."

"Either way, mister, you're coming with us."

"I'm not going anywhere."

She sneered and pointed the gun at my knee like she was gonna shoot.

I jerked my wrist. A talon of shadow swiped up from the ground and knocked the pistol loose. One of the thugs lunged and I didn't waste time. I warped the darkness into a lance and pierced him straight in the heart. He whimpered and collapsed forward. I tried the same move on the other but he rolled to the side. They were quick when they wanted to be.

Tutti ran to the wall. My shadow pursued as she hopped up the brick, took a few vertical steps, then launched out and over my head. I barely had time to throw up my forearm. The tattoo running its length flashed brilliantly as her claws raked against it. My boot shot into her stomach and sent her to the floor.

I got a bead on the other thug and was readying a

shadow spear when the first one hopped to his feet. What the hell? My blow should've skewered him. What was supposedly fatal had only resulted in a stun.

Had Simon been jerking me around?

I waved my arm over the asphalt. The entire floor gummed up with shadow. The quick-on-their-feet vamps wouldn't be quite so quick anymore. I stepped backward to create some distance, but one of the thugs leapt over my spellcraft and rocketed at my head.

I dove into the shadow myself this time. Not just the thickened goop on the ground. My body *became* shadow. I was pretty sure their claws couldn't strike me in this state but I didn't take chances. I easily drifted away from the blow. The big guy's knee smashed into the asphalt and left a fissure behind. I materialized and cracked him in the jaw. He slumped down face first.

I backed further out the alley and stole Tutti's trick. Left hand up asking for a ceasefire while my right hand was obscured behind my back. The shadow drooped down from it. I layered it on thick, over and over until it glowed amethyst.

"You keep this up," I warned, "and I'm gonna show you what happens when I get angry."

Tutti cackled. She looked hungry. Turned on, even. "You put on a good show, mister." She licked her now-protruding fangs seductively, enjoying every minute of this cat-and-mouse. "But no one gets away from the Obsidian March."

She dove forward. I swung my arm out from behind me,

spellcraft thrumming in the form of a longsword, ready to chop her in half. Her eyes widened and she attempted to roll away. I kept the blow coming and corrected as I could, but her reflexes were better than mine. I missed her heart, missed her torso completely, but her spin maneuver had cost her. Tutti's right arm was severed at the shoulder.

I'd expected blood, but the limb just bounced awkwardly and came to a stop. Tutti screeched in agony and tumbled away, her wound a gaping black hole. Her arm crumbled to ash.

"You asshole!" she screamed.

I didn't have time for an I-told-you-so. I threw my left hand out and the palm tattoo flared as the first thug recovered her pistol and took potshots at me. The small-caliber weapon split the lazy afternoon quiet and echoed off the buildings with explosive power. My energy shield deflected the bullets with little effort. Viking magic.

The vamp on the ground got up and dragged a wounded Tutti deeper into the alley. The one with the gun covered their exit. I wasn't intent on chasing them or sticking around for round two of the county police so I backed onto the street and disappeared around the corner.

And just like that, the fight was over. Heads turned and people pointed, but nobody seemed to agree on where to look. Without missing a beat, I twisted into a casual stroll down the sidewalk. I glanced around in confusion to really sell it.

As I walked down the curb, I pulled the car keys from my pocket. A year ago I would've been climbing inside a haunted pickup truck with a pentagram painted on the hood, but I was a new man now. Legit, on the books, and with a lot of cash to spare.

Somehow, the vampires must've known about my new car. After this morning's incident they had staked it out and set their trap. Lucky for me, Evan had swung me a special deal. Since I was a sometimes police consultant, he'd granted me a privilege usually reserved for officers. My license and registration were as real as they came, but if anyone ran them, the address would come back registered to the police station. Let's see the Obsidian March do something about that.

I took a last look around to make sure no one was coming for me. They were long gone. I shook my head and wondered what Simon would say about my vampire crusade. I'd started a street war without even knowing it.

I clicked the alarm of my 1977 Pontiac Firebird Trans Am and sat inside. I loved this car. Restored silver body with an oversize black phoenix decal on the hood. Hood scoop, T-top, the works. I reveled in the all-silver interior and twisted the key in the ignition. The powerful V-8 responded immediately. I smiled and burned down the street, the aftermarket 4-speed answering at my slightest prompt.

I wasn't followed.

The Firebird wasn't luxurious like Simon's Town Car, and it *definitely* wasn't a quiet and smooth ride, but I preferred the immediacy of the action, the throttle of the horses, and the relationship with the road. This was a man's machine, at least if popular media in the seventies and eighties were to be believed. Sitting behind that tenth-anniversary steering wheel, I had little doubt they were on the money.

It was still too early for rush hour so I made good time getting back to Brickell. The business strip on the Avenue was one of the areas that had evolved the most in my time away from the city. High-rise condos of glass tore through the expansive Miami sky. The street level was lined with swanky restaurants and shops.

For me, the best thing about the area was a little more practical. My daughter, Fran, lived in a local neighborhood. Evan and Emily were her parents, but I was her biological dad. The three of us had long ago settled on the idea, but Fran didn't know the truth. I wasn't sure if she would any time soon.

I pulled into the underground parking lot of the swankiest condo on the strip, parked in my personal space, strolled through the posh lobby, and hit the elevator button to my new home.

Penthouse, of course.

Chapter 12

I stepped out into my private hall. Private not because I own it, but because my penthouse takes up the entire fifty-sixth floor. I found Kasper there working on the door.

Seeing a guy like him in a place like this was comical, to say the least. He was an old Norwegian biker with a long white beard and tattoos over his entire body, several of the naughty variety. A healthy beer belly marred an otherwise scrawny frame. He wore his usual red-lensed glasses and had a stogie hanging from his mouth.

"Just give me a second there, broham," he said without turning to me.

I paused. I'd caught him in the middle of tracing the door frame with a series of scrawling lines. He had an assortment of paint brushes, pens, and buckets of inks and paints to go with them. A few empty bottles of beer sat beside them.

Besides being an accomplished medic from the Vietnam War as well as a sought-after tattoo artist and business owner, Kasper was a scribe. For the last few months he'd been tirelessly fortifying my new digs with defensive wards. It was taking a long time, and it was expensive, but it was worth it. The longer and more layered his spellcraft, the greater the supernatural threats it would keep out. Just in time for my vampire crusade.

Normally, a necromancer like me preferred to keep zombies around for security, either small animals for eyes or large bodies for muscle. My new condo was all-white though, and zombies don't wipe their shoes before walking on the carpet. Command them to die for you and they're gung ho, but try to instill them with manners and suddenly it's an uphill battle.

There was another complication. Since I was a new resident, the head of the home owner's association was being especially nosy, and that was putting it nicely. I had to tread lightly for a while.

As Kasper finished his sweep, he blew lightly over his work. The ink sparkled and faded until it was invisible.

"There," he said, dropping the brush in water and spinning around. "It needs more love but you can go inside if you want."

"I'm surprised you're working so late." I pounded my fist into his. "You don't need to do that."

"Not a big deal. The peace and quiet is good for me. Besides, I felt bad about leaving the little lady inside alone."

My brow furrowed. "Fran?" Kasper knew her as my friend's kid who I watched sometimes, but that was all.

"That's the one. She said you were giving her lessons in spellcraft."

I glared. "She wasn't supposed to mention that."

"News to me," he said, chuckling. "That's okay. You know I can keep your secrets, Cisco."

"Thanks. Her parents would kill me if they found out. You want another beer? Something to eat?"

He pulled on his cigar. "Actually, I think I'm gonna work through this. With the overtime I was able to swing today, I'm practically finished."

"For good?"

"I'll be out of your hair before you know it."

I shook my head wistfully. "I almost wouldn't know what to do without you around."

He opened the door for me. Nothing exploded. "You can swing by the tattoo parlor, you know. Place is usually empty these days."

"Will do." I moved inside.

"Oh, and Cisco," he called, door half closed. "Don't come out without knocking first, or it's your ass."

I laughed as he shut the door. Taken under advisement. The glyphs on his body would likely protect him, but I might not be as lucky.

I marched to the living room. My beautiful eleven-year-old daughter sat on the couch using a tablet. My eyes ran to the TV.

"You've got a seventy-two-inch screen twenty feet away and you're staring at that little thing?"

"Your TV doesn't have Word Wars."

I craned my neck around to see the game she was playing. She was so busy jumbling letters into words she barely noticed me.

"Hello to you too," I joked.

"Hi, Cisco. Sorry for stopping by unannounced. I know our training day is tomorrow, but some creep was bugging Nicole at the park so she wanted to head home."

I smiled. Fran was pretty, sweet, and a pretty sweet soccer player to boot. I'd sometimes pick her up early to watch her play. I ruffled her wavy brown hair. "About that, Fran. You really shouldn't be mentioning your magical talents to strangers."

"Kasper's not a stranger. He's cool. I like his tattoos."

"I'm sure you—"

"You think my mom will let me get one?"

My face went dead. "You're way too young to get a tattoo, Fran."

"Be chill, Cisco. It's not like you're my dad."

I winced.

"Besides, you have some tattoos. They're not as cool as Kasper's though."

I rolled my eyes. My limited tattoos were for cold practicality. "Yes, dear. I don't have as many naked ladies with spiked tails." I tried to sound as sarcastic as possible but I don't think she picked up on it.

"You have a lot of nice stuff here. I took a look around since you were gone. You've been spending money. My dad says you splurge on a lot of expensive clutter because the IRS doesn't track that stuff."

"What?" I crossed my arms. "I don't have expensive clutter."

"You have a leather chair in your closet."

"It's a big closet."

"You have a pool on your balcony."

I blinked. "It's a small pool. Besides, that came with the condo."

"Cisco, your bed has its own chandelier."

I huffed in exasperation. "I like to read, Fran. You should try it sometime with something that's not backlit. That's not a crime."

"Maybe not, but my dad says all your money is."

"Well... I..." I scrambled. My mind darted to my new deal with the Society. "You let your *dad* know I'm working on that."

I shook my head, went to the kitchen, and opened the fridge. What the hell was Evan doing telling Fran about my dirty laundry anyway? Fran was a smart kid and she wasn't blind, so seeing this place it was no wonder she had questions. It was hard to be mad at Evan and Emily too. After all, they were the ones who'd cosigned for me even though it was a stretch for their budget. Like true friends, they did what they could to re-integrate me into society.

Still, I wasn't gonna apologize for living the high life. I'd spent a year hiding out in the Everglades in a shed that legally couldn't be classified as shelter. I deserved some comfort, dammit. And if it was at an ex-drug kingpin's expense, who was gonna complain?

I grabbed a Coke and noticed the beer shelf in the fridge was awfully barren. I pulled a couple of six packs from the nearby cabinet and shoved them in. Then I popped my drink and downed it, savoring the glorious follow-up burp.

"That's gross, Cisco."

"My house," I said unapologetically.

I strutted to the couch, sat down on an adjoining love seat beside my daughter, and fully reclined with my feet up. Not finished, I flicked a switch and felt the automated massage roll under my neck, back, and legs. How's that for expensive clutter?

Fran rolled her eyes.

I didn't care. This was the life. A sort of payback for my struggles. I took a sip of soda and nodded to myself. Yes. I'd *earned* this time out. My eyes rested for blissful, precious seconds before I heard the commotion outside the front door.

"Son of a—" I turned to Fran and frowned. A smirk was plastered across her face. "I guess I'd better get that." I set my Coke down and went to the door.

Chapter 13

It was just annoyed mumbling at first, but Kasper quickly escalated into gruff barks. Someone was pissing him off. I set my hand on the doorknob and paused. Attempting to open the door mid-glyph could be disastrous.

I checked the peephole. Damn. Reddish ink clouded the glass. I could barely make out a blurry Norwegian waving his arms around, yelling.

I pounded. "Okay to come out?" More yelling. I banged again. "Kasper! Is it okay to open the door?"

It clicked open. Kasper wore an annoyed look. His cigar had been plunked into the water can, still smoking. Standing before him, arms crossed and wearing the most colorful blouse I'd ever seen—colorful in this case being a euphemism—was the head of my home owner's association, Carmela Flores.

"Mr. Suarez," she started, voice haughty and indignant, "I've repeatedly notified you of the interior decoration policy in the building. We can't have strange men painting up the walls. It's unbecoming."

"Strange men?" exclaimed Kasper. "I fought my heart out for this country and I won't have old bags like you telling me where I can and can't work."

Her lips jutted out unseemingly, matching her stark nose.

I massaged my temples. "Kasper, why don't you take a break inside, buddy?"

He grumbled and stormed past me. I waited for the tension to ease but Carmela was pretty wound up.

She always was. If she could somehow manage to relax, to—dare I say it—smile, she would appear much as any grandmother in her fifties. Graying hair with a disturbing amount of pink dye, stern but slight, with numerous flowers on her dress that were alien to this world. For whatever reason she marched around the building as if she was the only one in it who had any sense. It was a power trip, nothing more, nothing less, and I was getting sick of tiptoeing around it.

"No one's painting the walls," I said calmly.

"Don't lie to me, Mr. Suarez." She pointed at the door. "It's plainly evident—" She froze, eyes going wide.

I craned my head around the door to see what she was pointing at. Kasper's inks had dried and disappeared. "You were saying, Carmela?"

"But he was painting..."

I went for an understanding smile. "I can see how you would have that impression, but Kasper's not painting the walls. He's treating them for mold."

She snapped up straight. "Mold?"

"Yes." I nodded slyly. "I'm very sensitive. And Kasper's the best contractor in Miami. He needs to chemically treat all surface areas for traces of... mold. But it won't leave a mark behind."

"Well, you know I should be notified of any—"

I leaned forward conspiratorially. "Carmela, if I came to you in an official capacity, you'd have an obligation to check for mold on every floor of the building. I'm trying to take care of a problem before it *becomes* a problem. Know what I mean?" I winked.

She swallowed. "Well, yes, of course. Thank you for that. And it certainly doesn't appear that the walls are marked."

She leaned around me and poked her nose in my place. I stepped out, closed the door, and put my arm around her, gently nudging her back to the elevator.

"You do understand, Mr. Suarez, that even licensed contractors are not allowed to smoke in public spaces in this building."

I pushed the elevator call button. It opened immediately.

"The smoke is part of the test," I explained as she walked in. She gave a knowing nod. I pushed the button for the ground level and casually stepped back into the hall. "It chemically reacts with the... chemical surfactants to... hybridize the mold deposits. It's all very complicated."

She mulled it over for a second before her eyes narrowed. "Just a second, Mr. Suarez—are you bullshitting me?"

I masked the alarm on my face as the double doors shut

between us. I thought I heard Carmela release a string of profanities to the empty elevator, but she was already on her way down. I just hoped she would think better about coming back today. I returned inside.

"Can you believe it?" complained Kasper. "We've been dodging her for months, and she catches me in the final minute of work." He shook his head. "I got overeager."

"Don't sweat it, Kasper. I took care of it." I paused. "So that's it? You're completely finished?"

"It's a done deal, broham. And little Ms. No Smoking had to rain on my parade." He scratched his wild beard. "It's too bad, too. I kinda like the way she walks. Has a nice sway to her hips."

Fran giggled. The old man winked at her and sat in my massage chair. He turned it on with a long groan. I sighed in disappointment and sat on the couch.

"By the way, Kasper," I said in an icy tone, "don't worry about getting my massage chair all dirty and sweaty."

The vibration of the chair made his voice come out choppy. "Didn't even cross my mind."

I sighed again.

Fran turned sideways on the couch and kicked my shoulder with her bare foot. "Hey, grumpy pants, what was so important about today?"

Whatever slight annoyance I'd felt disintegrated at the brightness of her face. "Huh?"

"I was hoping for a lesson earlier but you weren't around."

"Oh, that."

I didn't want to tell her about the bar. The missing girl from her school would never be found. The vampires were too good for that, and whether the people they took lived or died, their mysteries had less chance of being solved if they never resurfaced.

"It was nothing," I said. "Don't worry about it." I eyed Kasper, but decided I could trust him. I stood and dimmed the lights. Then I teased the shadow with my fingers. A finger of darkness pulled away from an unlit corner. "We could get a quick lesson in."

Excitement splayed across her face, but she quickly tempered it into full concentration. She sat up straight on the couch and studied my string of shadow. Kasper peeked an eye open and watched as my construct vanished in a blink.

She laughed. "Got it! That was easy."

Unbeknownst to her parents, Fran had begun spellcraft coaching at the age of seven. Not by me—I wouldn't have crossed that line. But what was done was done. Now that she had the talent, I felt an obligation to continue her instruction. Magic without guidance was a dangerous thing. At first, I was just curious what she could do, but as we started the lessons, I was more and more fascinated by what I saw.

"Null magic," whispered Kasper with just a hint of awe. "You got someone to teach you null magic."

"Not just anyone," I said. "An egomaniacal drug kingpin."

"Connor Hatch?"

"Yes. Which is why I'm making sure she exercises proper judgment with it now." I turned back to my daughter. I wasn't familiar with her patron. I couldn't cast her spells. But magic was more instinctual than textbook. I knew what it meant to channel the Intrinsics. And I knew that she needed practice. "Let's try something a little harder."

I manifested a bundle of shadow. It took more time and effort on my part to set up, but it was in the span of seconds. I stretched it into a wall, stood behind it, and said, "See if you can get to me."

Kasper scoffed. "You call that harder? That's just a bit of darkness."

I smirked. "Try it."

"You serious, broham? You don't want to go toe to toe with me again, do you?"

I'd learned a while back that Kasper was a tank now. He had so many defensive wards tattooed on his body that he could absorb damage all day and be fine. I couldn't beat him in a boxing match, and I didn't know anybody that could.

But animists weren't built for boxing matches. There was a wide variety of spellcraft that, if not exactly harmful to Kasper, could easily defeat him.

"Bring it on, old man," I challenged.

He eagerly rose from the massage chair. "Don't say I didn't warn you." Without further pretense, he stomped straight into my shadow.

It held him back like a soft cushion over a brick wall. He grunted, stepped back, and slammed his shoulder into it. The glyphs on his body flared and he managed to penetrate the wall more than before, but it still stopped him cold.

Kasper's wards were defensive. It was his specialty, so I doubted a week of trying would net more success. I chuckled. "Now how about we allow the student to continue her lesson?"

He grumbled and pulled away. "Just trying to make you look good in front of the kid." He returned to the massage chair.

"I'm not a kid," said Fran. She walked to the wall and pressed her hands into it.

I wasn't going easy on her this time. The wall wasn't an afterthought. It was an active construct I was putting my will into. I didn't need full concentration or anything, but I was pumping power into it nonetheless. She was clearly struggling, getting about as far as Kasper had.

"It's... too solid," she said.

"Don't think about the physicality of it," I instructed. "Shadow is anything but."

"But I feel it."

"Forget about your hands. Feel it with your head. Your heart."

She scrunched her eyebrows together and leaned into the construct, breathing harder.

"Relax. Adrenaline is good. Emotion is good. Frustration isn't."

She nodded. Her breathing slowed and grew more regular. Deep breaths. Her brow eased and her eyes locked on the center of the shadow manifestation. I couldn't recall ever seeing her so serious.

Fran pushed deeper into the shadow. Kasper's eyes widened in disbelief. My daughter was halfway through it when she hit a snag. Her mouth twitched. She strained under the effort. The wall held.

"I can't," she said, giving up.

I nodded and dispersed the darkness. I could've given it to her, weakened the spellcraft so she would succeed, but she was already gifted enough with weaker constructs. I wanted to offer her something to strive for. A victory that would be meaningful when it finally came, not because it was awarded to her but because it was earned.

"Don't worry," I said, kneeling and giving her an encouraging hug. "That's a great first try. That one's not easy. It's meant to keep me alive in scary situations."

"It's just..." She chewed her lip. "For a second, it felt like I could actually do it. It was in my grasp."

"I'm sure it was. Don't rush it. That's what these lessons are for. You'll get there."

After mulling it over, she nodded. She was a bright girl, but she needed the assurance. The best thing a parent can do for their kid is believe in them. Not that I was in the best position to give advice, but I knew that much.

"You did better than I did," noted Kasper.

She smiled and gave him a high five. "Can we try that one again in the next lesson?" she asked me.

"Why not keep it up now?"

She shrugged. "I figured you had to get ready for your dinner party."

"Dinner par..." My jaw sagged.

Crap. It was nearly evening and I had dinner plans tonight. And not just any plans, but Evan and Emily's fifth wedding anniversary.

I *knew* I was forgetting something.

I swore. Briefly considered pushing the time. I had promised I wouldn't screw up their night, practically begged Evan and Emily to leave their anniversary in my hands. They'd been skeptical, maybe rightly so, which especially meant I had to pull this off without a hitch.

And really, what was stopping me? I had to eat, right? It would be a good opportunity to talk to them about the Manifesto Killer, which I was going to do anyway. I wasn't about to let a rando psycho infringe on our night.

So not only was I gonna do this, I was gonna *rock it*. And part of my responsibility tonight was...

"Hey, Kasper. I know this is last second but... can you babysit?"

Knowing Kasper, he wasn't doing anything else tonight but lounging alone at the tattoo parlor where he lived. Spending the night at my condo would be a luxurious change of pace. "Why not?" he said.

Fran was enthusiastic about my choice of sitter. "Cool! This'll be much more fun than hanging around grandpa's house with my brother. I'll text my dad."

"Just don't have too much fun," I said jokingly. Then my eyes narrowed. "And no tattoos."

The old man stood up. "Working all day left me a little sore. And a sweaty wreck." He frowned at my massage chair. "Mind if I use your shower?"

"Mind? *Mi casa es su casa*. Go for it. When you're done you can raid the fridge. I stocked it with those Cigar City brews you like."

"My man!" He disappeared into the hall.

"You're gonna be fine?" I asked Fran.

She was back on her tablet again. "I could ask you the same question, Cisco. Didn't you used to be boyfriend-girlfriend with my mom?"

"None of your business."

I pulled out my cell phone and stepped to the window for privacy. Em and I had moved on a long time ago. Evan was my best friend and was treating her right, not to mention the hell of a job he did with my daughter when I hadn't been around. There were no worries on that front. Hell, the whole reason I wanted to give them this night was to show them how good I was with the situation.

But something about dinner did make me nervous. I texted Milena: "You still on for tonight?"

Things between us had been weird ever since I came back. Sometimes on, sometimes off—after what had happened last year I'd kinda let the dust settle. And now that I'd returned and was ready to put down roots, things had never felt the same.

Honestly, it was all my jackass fault for not making a move. I was in real danger of falling into the friend zone. I'd been hoping I could change that tonight.

Kasper peeked out from the bathroom. "Cisco, your shower is next to a floor-to-ceiling window."

I chuckled, still on edge. "It's fine. No one can see in

from the outside."

He looked uncertain but shrugged. "Okay, but if I frighten any fragile ladies in the next-door building, it's on you." He returned to the bathroom.

My phone chimed. Milena had gotten back to me. "Of course I'm coming. I wouldn't miss their anni dinner!" She seemed enthused, at least. A follow-up text came in. "You're not planning on wearing your white tank top, are you?"

I looked down at my battered clothes and laughed. I guess I needed a shower too. I disappeared into my bedroom and prepared for the big night.

Chapter 14

"Wow," beamed Emily. "This is actually a really nice place, Cisco."

"Don't act so surprised."

The host sat us at a large round table with a traditional white tablecloth. I let Evan and Emily get the best view of the jazz band. I sat at the worst angle, leaving the empty seat, for Milena, with a nice view as well.

This joint was all the rage these days. Despite only being open a year, Carbon had already won several prestigious awards. It was sleek and oozed cool and the food was reportedly top-notch. The buzz assured that reservations were extremely hard to come by. My cash had greased those wheels.

I liked the place, too. Half traditional steakhouse, half modern hip fusion. The combination provided the best dry-aged beef in Miami with a jazz score that wasn't campy or stuffy. Not bad for sitting a literal block from my condo.

To properly meet the standards of the place, I'd worn a suit. The jacket hugged my shoulders as I sat so I unbuttoned it. Then I mimicked Evan's move and hung it over the back of my seat. I was hoping he'd loosen his tie so I could follow suit, but it was a no go.

"Don't look so uncomfortable," said Emily with a lilt in her voice. "You look nice. You should dress up more often."

I shrugged. I kinda felt like a Ken doll. I accepted the compliment and turned it around on her. "You look great, Em."

It wasn't lip service. An Australian bombshell with a thin frame—she was elegant fashion-model material. Pretty smile, straight blonde hair falling over her shoulders. She wore a glittery dress and long matching earrings.

I turned my eyes to Evan. "You clean up okay too, buddy."

Evan Cross was my contact in the City of Miami police. He worked for the mayor now, a special detail that looked at district-level threats. It gave him some autonomy and connections that were useful. He usually wore polos as a self-styled Matthew McConaughey, but today opted for a light-gray suit and golden shirt that matched his close-cropped hair. I like to think my black-and-purple combo made a more stunning statement. Then again, he wasn't single like me.

"As least you didn't wear your Diamondbacks tonight," I joked.

He laughed. "I hope we won't need them."

The waiter introduced himself and I ordered a bottle of red. Milena texted that she'd be ten minutes late and Emily wanted oysters, so we started off with those while we caught up.

"You got arrested?!?" Evan laughed so hard wine practically dribbled from his chin.

"It's not funny, bro. Besides, I was just questioned."

"But they took you to County?"

I nodded. "Pretty much."

He tried to keep a straight face but burst out laughing all over again.

I glowered. "I'm not even at the interesting part yet. A fed came in to talk to me. Apparently there's a serial killer in Miami they're keeping under wraps."

His mirth dried up. "What?"

"He's sending letters to the paper and everything. But get this. He's batshit. Thinks he's on a holy mission from God or something and decides to pick off occult entertainers."

Emily perked up. "Does this have something to do with the Marvelous Mordane?"

"Yes! That was the Manifesto Killer."

"Manifesto?" asked Evan.

"His anti-magic letters. He also knocked off a musician and a fortune teller just yesterday that nobody knows about yet. But here's the thing." I leaned forward and waited as guests shuffled past. "These entertainers weren't just entertainers. They were legit animists. All three of them. The last was a member of the Society of Free Thinkers."

Evan hissed. "Those are your Illuminati conspirators, right?"

"Not quite that dramatic. They're just business people.

Turns out some of them are Big Pharma. Their lawyer bailed me out. They want my help catching the guy."

They traded concerned glances. "Isn't that kind of dangerous?" asked Emily.

"No more than consulting city cases with your husband," I pointed out.

"It's not a horrible idea," said Evan. "Working with professionals should keep him out of trouble. He could even curry favor with the feds. FBI, right?"

I nodded and decided not to mention the vampires.

Emily frowned. "I'm worried about the Society. They can't be trusted."

"I'm watching my back. Besides, they're gonna help me with my *money problem*. Which Fran pointed out to me needs to be dealt with."

Evan stiffened at my castigation and stuffed an oyster in his mouth to avoid responding. Emily blinked back pleasant surprise at the news. Strengthening my income source would relieve their financial risk, after all.

"Just don't risk yourself on our account, Cisco."

"I know. But you can help me, in fact. I brought you a couple of anniversary gifts."

Evan chortled and found his tongue. "Dude, you're not supposed to get other people anniversary gifts."

"No worries. They're not fancy. Just a pair of murder weapons in freezer bags."

Their faces went hard.

"Don't look at me like that. I'm not dumb enough to bring them into the restaurant. But I was hoping you could run forensics on the knife, Evan. And, Emily, yours is something you're familiar with. A crystal ball."

Evan's face darkened. He didn't especially like the fact that his wife was an animist too. My best friend wasn't a huge fan of magic. With everything that had befallen us, he had solid justification.

Emily was a white witch. Just as I commanded darkness, she manipulated light. It was a useful talent that allowed her to refract illusions and run protection circles. She could also scry, to a limited extent.

She rested her hand on her husband's and said, "I'll do whatever I can, of course. I can finally help with police work."

He frowned. "Serial killers, jinns, voodoo gangs. Sometimes I wish I could just go back to not knowing about any of it."

I chewed my lip. This was why I didn't know how to approach him about instructing Fran. Regardless, tonight wasn't the night to open that can of worms. This night was for them, and I was already killing the buzz.

With impeccable timing to save my ass, Milena wandered into the restaurant. I raised my hand and her searching eyes found me. A smile overtook her face and she waved back excitedly. I couldn't stop a stupid grin from breaking my cool exterior.

I grabbed the bottle of red and poured Milena a glass. Emily was ahead of us so I topped off hers too. Since that killed the bottle, I spotted the passing waiter and asked for one more.

No more business. I was determined to have fun for once. I stood to greet Milena. The heat rushed through my body just looking at her. Where Emily was proper sophisticated elegance, Milena was down-and-dirty smoking hot. Short with an hourglass figure, a one-piece spandex ran from her knees to her ample cleavage. Milena's long brown hair fell down her back, and her beautiful eyes and lips smiled as she moved in for the world's sexiest hug.

We kissed cheeks. This was my babe, and I wanted to hold onto her forever.

The mood soured when a gangly waiter stood behind her awkwardly.

"We'll take her from here," I joked. I waited as Milena kissed and said hello to my friends and apologized for being late. It was the Cuban way, both the kisses and the tardiness. Then, as she sat, the waiter bumped me trying to push her chair in like a gentleman.

"Oh, I'm sorry," said Milena. "This is Gavin."

We all looked at the awkward guy.

"The waiter?" I asked.

He shuffled nervously.

Milena playfully slapped my side. "He's not a waiter, *tonto*. He's my date."

My tongue stuck in my throat. Gavin was wearing the same black-suit-white-shirt-red-tie combo as the steakhouse staff. Besides that gaffe and some nervous jitters, he was a normal-enough-looking guy, but dating *Milena*? She was a bombshell by any measure.

"Your..."

I picked up my wine glass and pulled it to my mouth. Expert stalling tactic. I killed it off, thankful it was almost empty anyway so my exasperation wasn't obvious. Hopefully.

Evan smirked and watched as Gavin held out his hand for me to shake. I made sure my grip was nice and firm.

Chapter 15

"Oh," said Milena, looking around. "We need another chair."

Everyone was sitting now except Gavin and me.

"Cisco," whispered Emily. Her eyes jerked toward the extended handshake.

"Oh," I said, releasing Gavin. He pulled his hand away, relieved.

A busboy approached with an extra chair. I frowned at the table layout and decided to scoot me and Milena down. It put my back to the jazz band. Before I could ask Milena to slide over, the busboy placed the extra chair in my old spot and Gavin sat down. Milena was already trading conspiratorial whispers beside Emily.

I ground my teeth and slid my chair further down next to Evan instead of Gavin, leaving a vacant area easily explained due to the size of the table and the position of the stage.

Evan punched my shoulder as I sat. "Sorry, dude," he mouthed.

The staff helpfully reset the table and everyone's

attention turned to the menus. We ordered steaks and duck-fat fries and roasted cauliflower and potato gratin and a host of other dishes that didn't sound nearly as appetizing now that Gavin was here. Eventually, everything was in order and the staff left us to ourselves.

"So this is exciting!" exclaimed Milena to the happy couple. "Is it five years now?"

"Yup!" Emily's response was jubilant.

"*Ay*, you have such a beautiful family."

"Thank you."

I cleared my throat. "How long has this been going on?"

Everyone looked at me except for Gavin.

Milena brushed her hair behind her ear. "What?"

"This." I pointed. "You two."

Milena and Gavin looked at each other and smiled. "Just a few weeks. You know, Cisco, we hardly talk anymore. If you picked up the phone once in a while you'd know."

"Sorry... just... busy..." I mumbled under my breath. "Vampires."

Everybody blinked.

"Anyway," said Milena, "it's no big deal. Nothing like *five years!*" She turned to Emily and they squealed at each other like hyperactive marmots.

"She gets like this with other women," muttered Evan.

We left them to their conversation and took the opportunity to talk shop. I filled him in on Special Agent Rita Bell and her suspicions. He mentioned troubling crime trends—after years of violence in Miami decreasing, it had finally spiked.

"I should powder my nose before the food comes," said Milena eventually.

She left Gavin alone at the table. He just stared at his recently filled wine glass. I wanted to see how long he could keep it up so didn't say anything, but Emily had a heart and broke the ice.

"So, Gavin, how'd the two of you meet?"

His face brightened. "Actually, it's a funny story. I was doing her taxes."

Emily nodded.

"Last year I wanted to ask her out but never did, so this year I did."

We all followed along, waiting for the punchline.

"That's about it," he said.

Evan sniggered and then immediately covered his mouth and coughed to mask his laugh. Emily chuckled encouragingly. "That is funny, Gavin."

I rolled my eyes. "Hilarious."

He relaxed a bit, missing the sarcasm. "Milena's great. How do you guys know her?" He asked the table but looked at me.

I worked my jaw. "Long story."

"You're childhood friends, right?"

Evan snorted. I glared at him to stay out of this. "Kind of, but not really. She was friends with my sister. Where's our food? I'm starving." I went for another sip of red.

Lucky for me, Emily was good at small talk. She kept the mood festive until Milena returned. Evan rode me a bit about my bad mood, but told me a couple of *actually* funny stories to get my mind off things. I realized I was being an asshole and didn't want to do that to my two favorite friends on their special night. I joined in the conversation and, if you don't mind me saying, was a bit suave myself. I could be a charmer.

The food came out picturesque. It was delicious and everybody was having a great time. Even me, I had to admit. But this wasn't just about food and drinking and "funny" stories. Not for the merry couple and not for me. So I found the right moment as dinner was winding down and the band took a break. I raised my wine.

"Everybody," I announced, "I have something to say."

I tilted my glass a bit to draw attention and everybody picked up theirs. Everyone except for Gavin. He hadn't taken a sip out of it all night, and while I was fine with people deciding not to drink, I did resent the fact that he'd taken wine from the bottle—from someone else's glass—because he was too polite to say otherwise. But putting that aside because I was in my happy place, I couldn't have the man disrespect my moment.

"Gavin," I said firmly, "this is the time when you raise your wine glass."

He looked around, unsure, but Milena nudged him and he obliged.

I nodded thanks to her, flashed a mini-scowl at my new arch-enemy, and then turned my attention on Evan and Emily.

"You could say we've all led interesting lives," I started. Evan snorted at the understatement of the year. "Seriously.

Since I first disappeared, and since I first returned, we've had a rough go of things."

Evan helpfully spoke up. "You could say trouble follows you."

I eyed him pointedly. "You could, if you wanted to ruin a perfectly good toast." He laughed, and my expression sobered. "I'm just saying that it means a lot for me to host your fifth anniversary tonight. Thanks for trusting me."

Evan clapped my shoulder and Emily smiled.

"I wanted to show you how much I love you guys. You're more than friends—you're family. And I'm really happy you found each other."

Evan grimaced at my sentimentality and spoke like he was talking to a pet. "We love you too, buddy."

Emily poked him. "He's trying to act cool but he means it, Cisco. We both love you." She looked around. "And this is an amazing restaurant you brought us to."

"You see?" I said, feeling validated. "I didn't let you down."

Milena beamed. "Wow, Cisco, I've never seen the sappy side of you before."

"I can be sappy," I said defensively. "But I'm not a sap."

She giggled. "Don't think you'll ever be accused of that."

I ran my eyes over the table. These were my people. And Gavin. But I focused on my people.

"Enough sentiment," I concluded. "I want to thank you, congratulate you on your five years, and wish you many more. *Salud.*"

We clinked glasses and drank them down. Gavin just

pretended, but that was okay. He wasn't part of this. Milena laughed and took over his wine glass after hers ran dry.

And damn if I wished I was sitting right next to her. I caught Gavin staring at her cleavage as she laughed heartily. He wasn't being rude—it was out of his control. Milena was, to put it delicately, totally stacked. And to see her in that dress with that bounce... well, let me just say I was jealous of Gavin right now.

Evan leaned over. "The look on your face."

"But you see what I'm working with here?"

"I don't blame you one bit."

The waiter appeared and handed dessert menus around.

"Oh, I don't want to do that," said Milena. "If I eat another bite after that steak I'm gonna get fat."

"Screw that," said Emily, voraciously reading over her options.

Milena shook her head. "Look at you. Happily married with two kids and thin and eating dessert. I'm envious."

"He's not perfect. You know he named our son after a character in a Bruce Willis movie."

They laughed.

Evan shrugged. "I think John McClane Cross has a nice ring to it."

Now it was my turn to console him. "A damn fine ring, bro."

As dessert arrived the band picked up again. Milena pulled Gavin to the dance floor where a few couples were sharing a laugh. I drowned my sorrow in butterscotch pudding while the married couple split a crème brûlée.

I set my spoon down. "See how he's hanging on her every move? He's infatuated with her."

Evan snickered. "You can hardly blame the guy with her wearing that dress." Emily sharpened a laser stare at him. "What, am I not allowed to see what's in front of my eyes?"

I shook my head. "And he's so polite about everything." After analyzing the situation, I nodded. "They haven't had sex yet."

"What?" exclaimed Emily.

"Can't you see it? He's putting on his first-date act."

"She said they've been dating a few weeks."

"Doesn't matter. He's still stuck at the starting line."

She arched a skeptical eyebrow. "I don't know. It doesn't look like an act."

Evan grunted while he swallowed a bite and cut in. "You're just not paying attention, honey. The poor guy's clearly afraid to let loose and spoil his chances. I'm with Cisco."

I chanced a peek at the dancing partners. It didn't look romantic to me. "What a softy. I wonder what she sees in him anyway?"

Evan laughed. "Dude, she only brought him here to make you jealous. One dinner and look how up in arms you are."

I pouted. "I'm not jealous."

Emily tagged herself back into the conversation. "Okay, Cisco, I may not be clued in to the dating games you boys pat yourselves on the back over, but I can totally tell a jealous man when I see one. And you... are... *stewing* in it."

She considered Gavin's awkward dancing. "Anyway, I think you might be right. She works in a dance club so she probably tries extra hard to be a good girl." She turned to her husband. "It's the same reason Cisco hasn't gotten any yet." Evan broke into overly boisterous laughter.

I blushed and looked around. "How do you know I haven't?"

Emily was merciless. "Please."

Evan's face slowly sobered up. "Are you kidding me, brother? You mean you haven't... Since you got back..."

"I've been kinda busy." My frustration was evident.

Emily feigned a bimbo voice. "But you're such a stud now with your new muscles."

Evan crossed his arms. "And I'm not allowed to talk about cleavage."

She laughed and kissed his cheek.

"You can only make it better by talking like that when we get home."

She rolled her eyes but I chuckled. "You brought that on yourself," I told her. "Guys like sex voices. You shouldn't have revealed the talent if you didn't intend to use it."

She pressed her lips together. "I'm not gonna do the sex voice."

"But it's my anniversary!" whined Evan.

"Besides," she said, "we're talking about Cisco's, uh, dearth of hookups." Their eyes turned to me again.

I sighed. "Don't fret over old Cisco. I've had a couple of... dalliances. I thought one of them was gonna kill me."

"You see?" said Evan to his wife. "He knows what he's

doing." He turned back to me. "But it also proves that trouble does follow you."

I was about to object when the waiter interrupted with another bottle of wine. We were all just about finished up, and I presumed we were about to check out.

"Did you...?" I asked Evan. He just shrugged and shook his head. "I'm sorry," I told the waiter, "I'm pretty sure we didn't order that."

A bus boy set five small glasses on the table and the waiter presented me with the label. "A bottle of port, sir. Compliments of the house on your special occasion." He nodded toward a table in the back corner. It was the only table in the room on a raised platform, with a good view of venue and stage but also adequate privacy, like a VIP section.

I squinted. "I, uh, who is that?"

The waiter poured all five glasses and set the bottle on the table. He leaned to my ear. "It's the owner, sir." Then he disappeared.

Emily's eyes widened. "You know the owner?"

My face scrunched as I picked up a glass. "Not me. Maybe he's a friend of the police?"

Evan shook his head. "No one I know." He tasted the strong wine. "This is pretty good."

"It tastes old," I agreed.

Emily did too and she was something of a wine connoisseur. "Cisco, I hate to spoil the magic, but how did you manage a reservation and fantastic table at one of the trendiest restaurants in Miami?"

I clinked my glasses with theirs in a standard free-booze maneuver. "No magic. I just asked really nice and then handed them a fat stack of cash."

"Look at Scarface over here," joked Evan.

"It beats expensive clutter." We sipped the port and glanced at the VIP table a few times. "So what's the procedure here? Are we supposed to go over and thank him?"

Evan frowned. "I guess we kinda have to."

"Watch out," snapped Emily, positioning her glass in front of her mouth to hide the fact she was speaking. "He's walking over right now."

We all simultaneously straightened and then relaxed so as not to appear wound up. A man stopped at our table wearing a white tuxedo jacket with a black collar, pocket highlights, bow tie, and pants. He looked rich, smug, and European right off the bat, with dark-brown hair plastered close to his head. Despite the standoffish persona, his eyes and smile were disarming.

"Good evening," he said respectfully. I detected a slight French accent but figured he'd lived stateside enough to normalize it. "And congratulations to the wonderful couple." He noted their slight alarm and said, "The waiter informed me."

"Thank you," said Emily. "The port is delicious. It's very nutty."

He took her hand and kissed it. "You have good taste. It has a wonderful color. Rather like blood."

His eyes flicked to me and I focused on Emily's hand in

his. His fingernails were black.

I rose to my feet but didn't make any sudden moves while he was so close to her. Evan noticed my alarm and went still.

"Who are you?" I demanded.

He released Emily and offered his hand. "I'm Leverett Beaumont, of the Clan Beaumont, currently pledged to the Obsidian March."

Chapter 16

Everybody was silent as I shook the restaurant owner's hand. It was a long shake, noticeably more tense than my go with Gavin, no doubt stemming from the very real possibility of ending in bloodshed.

"Cisco," tempered Emily, "is this part of your big night out?"

"Surprise?" I grimaced. "More like fallout from this morning. And afternoon." I released my grip but kept my eyes lasered on Beaumont. "He's a vampire."

Our host's eyes fluttered. "Here I am, being all debonair about it, and you go and say it out loud." He surveyed my company. "Is he always this blunt?"

Evan ground his teeth. "Blunt instruments break bones."

Milena clambered to the table out of breath. "More wine!" She grabbed a glass of port and downed it entirely too fast before noticing everyone at the table staring at Leverett. "Who's this?"

I growled at him. "You come over here and openly threaten me and my friends? That's a bad move, Lev. I have zero qualms about getting into it with you and the rest of your clan right in the middle of your restaurant."

He laughed it off. "Really, Cisco, it's not like that at all. For one, I believe it was *you* who came to *my* restaurant."

Milena rolled her eyes. "Of all the rotten luck."

"Quite," he agreed. "But there's no need for hostilities. Hence the port." He picked up Gavin's unused glass, swirled it, and took a sip. "It feels nice and viscous in your mouth, does it not?"

"Talk about blunt," muttered Emily. "What's debonair about that?"

Leverett Beaumont cleared his throat. "I admittedly get carried away sometimes." He set the glass down. "May I invite you on a tour of the kitchen?"

"Yeah, right," said Evan. "And make it more convenient for you to separate our blood from our bodies?"

Gavin strolled to his seat with a confused look. Despite everybody standing and wired for fight or flight, he absentmindedly slipped between Beaumont and me and returned to his seat. Beaumont eyed him inquisitively.

"Don't mind Gavin," I said. "He's not familiar with... your culture."

Gavin turned to us, befuddled. "Are you making another toast or something?"

"Keep it down, Gavin," said Beaumont. "I just need to talk to you, Cisco, but your friends are welcome if you like. I guarantee everyone's safety."

Milena's eyes darted to her date and she chuckled nervously. "Cisco's big on kitchen safety," she explained.

"Like your word means anything," I returned.

"If you knew me I'd be offended. Keep in mind: I'm pledged to the March, but I am not one of them."

"Safety march," whispered Milena.

I frowned. "I'll listen to what you have to say, but keep in mind the only reason I'm going is because I'm confident I can handle whatever you throw at me."

"Fine. This way, please."

I turned to tell my friends to get out of here, but Evan beat me to the punch. "Don't say it, Cisco. I'm coming."

Emily nodded. "Me too."

I almost objected, but the truth was I didn't mind them backing me up. "Okay, then." We followed Leverett.

"Watch my purse!" called Milena to Gavin. She tossed it into his lap and gave chase.

I grinned at that.

We stepped through the swinging door into a bustling kitchen. "Watch your step," cautioned Leverett, leading us over a series of rubber mats and into a back hall. As soon as we had some measure of privacy, Evan leaned down and pulled a pistol from an ankle holster.

"On our anniversary date?" chided Emily.

He shrugged. "Anniversary date *with Cisco*."

She seemed to take that as an acceptable answer.

Whether our host saw the gun or not, he continued ahead unconcerned. We walked past a stock room and turned into a wine cellar. "Get out," he ordered a sommelier. The man rushed away as if his life depended on it. Leverett Beaumont turned to us, leaned casually against a shelf, and steepled his fingers over his stomach. Something about the dim lighting made his eyes shine like a predator's.

"May I speak freely?" he cordially asked. He eyed Evan, Emily, and Milena.

"Everyone here understands the situation."

"Speak for yourself," said Evan. "What does this Obsidian March want with you?"

"It's about the bar fight in the morning. I was tracking a lost little girl. The one from Fran's school." Emily covered her mouth in surprise. "Turns out these were the guys who killed her."

Beaumont shook his head. "Not me."

"Um," chanced Milena, raising a timid hand. "If everybody's asking questions, I still don't know what that guy is." She pointed to Beaumont like he wasn't right next to us.

"He's a vampire," I said. Milena squeaked. "Can we just listen to what the man has to say?" I asked. Everyone nodded.

"Thank you," he said. "First off, you should understand my position. I am acting only as a middleman here. I harbor no hostilities toward you and I've given you no cause to do so with me. Can we agree on that much?"

"So far." I worked my jaw. "How connected are you to the Obsidian March?"

He nodded at the reasonable question. "There are many vampire clans among us, but several of the most powerful congregated into the Obsidian March. It's a hegemony, of sorts. The only way our kind can compete with the silvan circles. Even then, we're banished to the far reaches of the Nether."

"You don't look banished to me."

"Granted, the silvans play politics in the underworld while we prefer to do business topside. Can you blame us?"

"For killing kids?" snapped Emily.

He raised a calm hand. "Please. Do not conflate me with those savages. My clan doesn't regard humans as livestock. We're not leeches in this world. We strive toward full cooperation."

Milena arched an eyebrow. "You trying to tell us you're a good vampire or something?"

"Good and evil are overrated concepts."

"Not to me," I challenged. "You're an upir, aren't you? You drink blood. Kill others so that you can live."

Leverett remained cool. "In point of fact, I don't. Your people tell numerous folktales about mine. Many of them are true enough. As a species, we drink any and all blood we can get—human, silvan, or otherwise. That doesn't make us monsters. A local slaughterhouse under my ownership sources my restaurants. Not a drop of blood is wasted."

"You guys live off cow blood?"

"It's a compromise in return for an FDA-approved meal. We can tap into blood banks to complement our palates. The Obsidian March runs the American Red Cross. It's one method they use to exert control over our kind in this world."

"Damn!" snapped Milena. "I *just* gave blood to them last week!"

Leverett smiled. "How delicious."

"Wait, wait, wait," said Evan. "You're telling me that a national charity organization is run by vampires?"

"You don't really think Haiti received all that money people donated, do you? Fools parted from their wealth have no say in where it gets spent."

"Or if they're funding a vampire collective," noted Evan.

"Even the March doesn't kill as often as you might imagine," said Leverett. "Once-a-month feedings are plenty to satisfy vampires who don't exert themselves."

"Bullshit," I fired back. "Tutti told me the girl was dead. And even if they keep their victims alive, they're still prisoners. Familiars don't have a choice."

"They often do, but that's beside the point. It's not my place to dictate their methods, even if I disapprove."

"Yet you give them your pledge."

He swallowed. "The Beaumont clan is small. We're not involved with the Obsidian leadership. However, their territory is vast and... It behooves the smaller groups to make peace with those larger than them."

"So you work for them?" I asked.

"No." He said that single word with such authority that the room seemed to shiver. "As the head of my clan, I lead my people the way I see fit. I own a third of the restaurants and high-end shops in Brickell. Carbon is one such establishment. Clan Beaumont is not in the business of death. I pay good money to the March for the pleasure of running Brickell. They leave me out of their shady pursuits."

Evan grunted. "What you mean is you don't get your hands dirty. If you pay them you're funding them."

"If only we could all dictate where our taxes get spent, yes? I can only control my end, which translates to ensuring the personal safety of myself and my patrons. That includes you."

"It's not like you're a saint," I said. "You're still paying for control."

He cocked his head and flashed an easy smile. "Would you rather I cede my territory to someone more vicious? Brickell is a hop and a skip away from some rather shady neighborhoods. If I exited this stage, the Obsidian March themselves would move in. I'm doing this city a valuable service."

Evan grunted. I wondered if he bought that speech. Working in the department, he often encountered the reality of political compromise. For my part, I wasn't convinced, and Beaumont could tell.

"Consider it from another angle," he offered. "I knew you'd be dining in my restaurant tonight. I could've had you all poisoned if I so wished it."

We all blinked silently.

"I know a little about you, Cisco. Word from the santeros says you killed a jinn. That would be impressive even if it wasn't Connor Hatch. But did you think you could tear down his drug empire and someone else wouldn't fill the void?" My face darkened. "This is Miami, Cisco. We live at sea level. Whenever a dam breaks, a new flood surges in."

He stepped forward, showing something close to anger. "Except this time it was my brothers who slithered into the recesses. The Obsidian March presence in the tri-county area has tripled in the last twelve months. This is not my doing, Cisco. It's yours."

I smoldered at Beaumont's words. Something told me he wasn't too happy with the situation either. Why would he be? The group he answered to getting more powerful meant his empire was that much more tenuous. One day, they might even come for him.

And in his mind, I was the cause of his troubles.

"So you sell me out to the March. Curry favor with them and get rid of a wild card in your backyard."

Emily rested a gentle hand on my shoulder.

Leverett Beaumont appraised her with an impressed eye. He crossed his arms over his white tux jacket and waited.

"He's not issuing a challenge," suggested Emily to my dense brain. "He's offering a truce."

The restaurant owner grinned in applause. "A beauty *and* a strategist. I am quite taken with you, my dear."

Evan grumbled, but Emily simply raised an open palm and willed an orb of light into existence. Beaumont didn't hiss and recoil, but he did snap his head from the glare and raise a hand to block the light.

"That was not meant to be rude," he said through gritted teeth.

Which was interesting. Sunlight didn't kill these vamps, but it did contain them in their weaker forms and cause them discomfort.

The white witch winked out her magic and the room went dark. "Neither was that. You revealed what you were so I had an obligation to do the same. Think of it as an introduction."

His eyes flashed in rapt admiration. "The pleasure is mine."

Evan cleared his throat loudly. Beaumont turned his attention back to me.

"But it's not quite a truce I'm offering, for we aren't at war. I'm seeking a partnership."

I thought of the Society. "I've been getting that a lot lately."

"As you should," he returned. "You are Miami's most notorious necromancer, and a multi-talented shadow charmer as well. Everybody in the city knows you have a penthouse in Brickell now. But everybody in the city also knows not to bring violence to my territory. Which is the genesis of this conversation."

"The Obsidian March asked for permission to get to me."

"On the contrary: They knew I wouldn't allow it. Instead, they merely asked that I approach you. Due to recent differences, they'd like to meet and set some ground rules."

I grunted. "So, what, they're hiding in the walk-in freezer or something?"

He chuckled lightly. "It isn't wise to allow them to conduct business here. For everyone's sake." He reached into his jacket pocket. Evan brought his pistol halfway up.

Beaumont scoffed lightly and presented me with a card. "They ask to suspend all hostilities and see you tonight, in hopes of reaching a mutually beneficial arrangement."

I swiped the card into my hand. It was a business contact with a generic office number without anybody's name on it. "Lincoln Memorial Park."

Beaumont smirked. "You can't accuse vampires of not setting the mood."

Milena scrunched her brow. "What is it? What is that place?"

Evan bit down. "It's a graveyard in Hialeah."

"I know the spot," I said.

Beaumont smiled. "Of course you do."

I flipped the card over. Scraggly handwriting read, "Accord at 1 am."

I checked both sides again, making sure I wasn't missing anything. "Tonight?"

Our host frowned. "I urged them to give you twenty-four hours, but they wouldn't hear of it. They're quite upset with your tactics. If you do not present yourself and come to an accord with them tonight, they're determined to go at you with everything they have."

"Why should I care?" I muttered. "They're doing that anyway. How do I even know this meeting isn't a trap?"

"You don't," he agreed. "And my word means too much to offer any guarantees on their behalf. I'd put it at fifty-fifty that they mean to bargain in good faith."

Evan tightened his grip on the gun at his side. "And the other half?"

Leverett Beaumont calmly blinked. "Extermination."

Chapter 17

"I don't trust him," grumbled Evan as our party strolled outside. Milena lagged behind, hand in hand with Gavin.

"Who said anything about trust?" I countered.

"Oh, I don't know. Try that look on your face that says you're determined to meet the Obsidian March in a graveyard."

"Just because I'm seeing what's what doesn't mean I trust them."

"I'm talking about Beaumont, Cisco. He comped our dinner. He said all the right things. It doesn't mean he's a good guy."

I spun around. "He laid it out plain, Evan. It's not like we're besties."

Emily diplomatically shrugged her shoulders. "I don't think a partnership is that bad an idea."

"Honey!" he chided. "You don't want Cisco dealing with the Society but somehow vampires are better?"

"He's claiming to keep Brickell safe," she reasoned. "I don't know if his influence extends into the residential section, but might I remind you that's where we live? If Beaumont's word keeps vampires from our doorstep..."

Evan sighed at the thought of it. "I can't believe you started another war, Cisco."

"I'm sorry, bro. I told you I was gonna look into the missing children. I didn't discover the vampire angle until this morning. What could I do?"

He hooked his hands on his hips and turned away. He was a cop. He hated the thought of the abducted children more than I did, which was why he'd offered intel to assist my off-the-books investigation.

We frowned at each other while standing in the Brickell corridor. Cars passed, blaring Cuban music and heavy beats. Occasional well-dressed groups walked to and from celebrations, oblivious to the underbelly of the city.

Milena and Gavin stopped beside us. He was mumbling under his breath. "I was hoping we could, you know, go to my place so I could play you the new Coldplay album. You said you liked them."

"I did," she said. "But that was ten years ago when they were good."

"I have other music."

Milena sighed. "Sorry, Gavin—I really am—but something came up and I need to take a rain check."

He pouted for a moment but said, "I understand. Whatever you need."

She winked at him. "That's why you're so great." They kissed on the lips and I almost vomited. When the Uber arrived, I was all too happy to see Gavin go.

"It's cruel of you to tease the man like that," said Evan.

"It's not teasing," she said. "He's nice."

I moved in close to her. "But not exciting, right?"

She snorted. "As if."

"Please. One sniff of danger and you end the date early. You know you can't come with me, right?"

"With us," said Evan and Emily together.

I tried to vocalize the intricacies of sharp vampire teeth, but Milena forced her way between us. "The hell I can't. I've seen worse."

Which was probably true but...

I rubbed my eyes in resignation. "You guys know Beaumont was being literal when he called them vampires, right?"

Emily raised a pointed finger. "That's why you need my magic."

Evan nodded. "I'll back you up from a distance with a rifle."

We all turned to Milena.

"What?" she objected. "I can do stuff."

"Maybe you can introduce them to Gavin," I offered. "They'll die of boredom."

Evan leaned into his wife. "Cisco pretends it doesn't bother him, but it's all he thinks about."

Milena narrowed her eyes at me.

"That's not true," I grumbled. "I'm spending at least a tenth of my thought processes on the meeting with the murderous vampires." They snorted. "Seriously, Milena, what do you see in that guy?" Evan broke into laughter.

Milena didn't find it funny. "Stop being a prick, Cisco. He likes me."

Emily leaned close. "And he's reliable."

I sighed. "And so are you guys. I don't deserve you."

"Damn straight," said Evan. "Now let's go kick some vampire ass."

We had a few hours until the deadline, which was just as well. I was more or less always prepared, but Evan and Emily weren't accustomed to strolling the streets with a full arsenal. We walked back to my place where Evan's bright-yellow Corvette Stingray was parked in tandem with my silver Firebird. One new, one old—both with terrifying power on the street. They agreed to meet back at my place in an hour.

Milena and I went upstairs. Kasper was watching reality TV with a beer in hand. Fran snuggled on the couch, half paying attention on her tablet.

"No!" Kasper said to the TV. "Don't let him talk to you like that."

She giggled. "He always does. He's a major a-hole."

"I can see that." He turned to us and whistled. "Now *that* is a nice dress."

Milena curtsied.

"It's good to see you back together," he said. "Cisco's much less grumpy when you're around."

She turned to me and I just shook my head. Better not get into it. I changed the subject instead. "What're you still doing up, Fran?"

"It's only 10:30. Why are you home so early?"

"Change of plans. We're..."—I scratched the back of my head—"looking into a vampire dealy."

Kasper's eyes narrowed. Milena slapped my shoulder. "Don't tell *her*."

"What?" I said. "I don't want to lie to her about what's on the streets. What I need to deal with." I turned to Fran, whose eyes were wide with concern. "It's just a meeting. We'll talk, hash out terms, and hopefully the city will be a little safer."

Fran blinked. "Is this about Gendra?"

I frowned. Nothing got past my daughter. I wanted to be straight with her but didn't want to get her hopes up or dash them too low. I realized the corner I was in.

"It's not about Gendra. I don't know anything about Gendra. But an agreement tonight might help things in the future."

Fran studied me closely. I turned away and made a show of taking off my jacket and tie. I unbuttoned the cuffs of my lavender shirt and rolled them up, revealing the dog collar. Then I looped my pouch of spell tokens to my belt.

Kasper stood. "Should I go with you guys?"

"I can't ask you to do that, bro. You should stay here." I turned to Fran. "Where it's absolutely safe. You should go to sleep too. Your parents are coming over in a bit and they'll be upset if you're awake. You have school tomorrow. Come on."

She washed up while we prepared. When she was ready to sleep, I sat beside her in the guest room and tucked her in. She was unnaturally quiet.

"You like this room?" I asked. I'd decorated it with a few posters from music groups she liked. A pink fairy doll I'd given her a year ago sat on the night stand beside her tablet. "You can keep anything you like here. Think of it like a vacation home."

She only half smiled at the thought.

I took in a slow breath and held her hand. "You know you don't need to worry, right? I've shown you what I can do."

"I know," she intoned. "But you never know what can happen."

I ran my finger down her cheek. "Hey, I know that stuff with Connor Hatch frightened you. He was a scary guy. These vamps are nothing. They're animals. They don't use spellcraft. They can't vanish or shoot fire. They're not invincible." I pressed my lips together. "You know how to kill them? You stab them in the heart." I pressed my hand on my chest. "Right here. It's their magical core. It stores all their blood. All their life force."

"That's it?" she asked.

I nodded. "Easy peasy. Without blood they're nothing but ash."

She considered my words. "It kinda sounds like you can handle them in your sleep then."

I chuckled. "Just about. So no worries, okay? I promise I'll be back before you know it."

She nodded. I kissed her forehead. The door creaked and I noticed Milena watching with her hand over her mouth. She was one of the few people who knew Fran was my daughter.

I stood and left Fran with a long smile, and then stepped out and closed the door.

"That was a hell of a bedtime story," she noted.

"What can I say? She's been through a lot. You know that."

She nodded. "Should I stay with her?" We returned to the living room. "It might make more sense for Kasper to go with you. I'm a lover, not a fighter."

I shot her a devilish grin. "I wouldn't exactly know, would I?"

She blushed.

"Fran loves Kasper. Plus, I want someone here in case the Obsidian March tries something underhanded while we're distracted."

Kasper rubbed his fists after I said that. I'd hate to see whoever tried to hurt Fran with him around.

"What about Beaumont's protection?" asked Milena.

"I think he's being straight with us, but I can't chance Fran's life on it. You shouldn't have anything to worry about, Kasper. This is just insurance."

"The wards alone will stop anybody. The windows, doors, ceiling, floor—there's no way in."

I made sure the condo was locked up tight at all points of entry. "I wouldn't have paid you so much if I didn't have full confidence, Kasper. It's just that the wards haven't been tested yet."

"Oh ye of little faith," he muttered.

I squared up with him and rested my hand on his

shoulder. "Quite the opposite, my friend. I'm relying on you."

He nodded, suddenly solemn. We locked wrists. "I won't let you down."

Evan and Emily arrived. Like Fran, they had keys and entered without me needing to open up for them. Emily immediately checked on her daughter, and Evan thanked Kasper for staying in. Then we went over the plan. What we were up against, what might happen, and what we could do about it.

Milena burped and we turned to her. She shrugged. "Is it weird that we're vampire hunting when we're drunk?"

"We're not hunting and we're not drunk," I said. "You and Emily drink too fast."

"It's not too fast if I can handle it," returned Emily. "Milena's the tipsy one."

"Thanks," she said sarcastically.

"Besides," I added, "we only had three bottles of wine."

"Four if you count the port," said Milena.

"Who counts port?"

Stymied by my masterful argument, we finished up our strategy and filed into the elevator.

Milena sat with me in the Firebird as we followed the Corvette. Evan knew the city like the back of his hand and wanted to approach on the sly. That didn't stop us from a little friendly racing on the open road. I revved past him. He took an unexpected turn. It was a winding dance of horsepower until we rolled into the ghetto outside Miami International Airport. Some blocks were a hive of drug activity. Others had residents wandering and laughing into the night. It wasn't an ideal place to park two sports cars.

I pulled up next to Evan and told him I knew a place on the corner. He followed me down the street to a ratty concrete building. We pulled into the private lot in the back.

"Monument & Casket Depot?" Evan asked incredulously as we congregated outside the cars. The run-down storefront was jammed to the rim with headstones for sale. It reminded me of a ninety-nine-cent store for funerals.

"Don't worry," I said. "I'm a friend."

The back door jarred open. An overweight Cuban man held a gun on us, bald head dripping with sweat. His large belly peeked from under a dirty shirt. I very carefully faced him.

"Cisco Suarez," he said, lowering the weapon. "I should've known it was your flashy ass."

I smiled and approached with an alligator grin. "Hector!"

"Stop." He raised his hand and backed into the store. "You *come mierdas* look like you're up to trouble tonight. Leave me out of it." He shut the door and loudly clicked the deadbolt.

Evan cocked his head. "Friends, huh?"

My glum expression spoke for itself. "Our cars will be safe. Hector's kind of a neutral party around here. Let's get ready."

Evan lugged a tactical rifle from his trunk, dual Colt Diamondbacks already holstered on his shoulders. A blacked-out police vest hugged his dress shirt.

"You didn't lose the tie," I noted.

"Gotta look nice for the wife on the anniversary."

Emily still wore the glittery dress. I wondered if she was taking this seriously.

I disappeared to my car and returned with some gear. I handed Milena a Micro Uzi with spare magazines in a drop-leg holster. It was small enough to almost disappear when the stock was folded, and the recoil was very light.

"You keep an arsenal in your trunk?" exclaimed Evan. "Those are illegal, you know."

"Then I won't tell you what else I have. Perks of infiltrating a drug cartel."

He remained tight-lipped. Milena hiked the tight dress up her thigh and strapped on the holster.

"Damn, girl," said Emily, "you really wear that dress."

"She means you have a nice ass," I translated.

"That's not what I meant!" Emily protested.

"But you do recognize her ass, right?" asked Evan.

She straightened. "That's it. No sex voice for you tonight, mister."

"Ugh." He stomped to the lot exit and glared my way. "In case I forget to tell you later—or, you know, *die*—I wanted to make sure to thank you for a wonderful wedding anniversary."

I loaded a custom fire round into my shotgun and dropped it into shadow. "Shit, guys, I really am sorry about this. Our night out's ruined."

Emily slapped my butt and walked past. "Don't sweat it, hotshot. Evan and I celebrated our *real* anniversary last weekend on the sly."

"You what?"

"Come on, Cisco," said Evan as we walked out to the dark street. "You have a penchant for this type of thing."

"You didn't trust me to pull it off?"

"You brought us to a vampire business front and a midnight graveyard meeting that may or may not be an ambush."

"But you didn't know that last week!"

"Forget it," he said. "It's not a big deal. We had a great time tonight. I was just giving you shit."

"I'm not talking to you guys." I stomped ahead.

The businesses on our right were sparse. They were decrepit structures, many of them more likely housing transients than solvent companies. Individual houses came next, the lawns wild and overgrown. Across the street was mostly an open field before the cemetery started. Our destination was the only entrance a few blocks down.

"Hey, brujo," hissed a grungy man sitting on a stoop. "You's not welcome here."

"I'm not in the mood," I warned.

The man was a dabbler, if that, so I didn't heed him much. We continued marching through the muggy night. Whispers and strained activity followed us as I slowly realized the local voodoo community was out in force. One minute into the neighborhood and already I was made. The dabbler outright followed us. Evan, sensing trouble, hefted his rifle.

"Keep it steady," I murmured. "We're just here to talk."

Chapter 18

The man approached aggressively. He had dirty dreads and shoes that were half worn away. The sad thing was I couldn't tell if he was a vagrant or a resident. This was a rotten area of the city, but some people called it home.

"Stay back," said Evan in an authoritative voice.

The man ignored him until he reached me. Three more locals peeked from behind a house, gathering courage.

"I don't have business with you," I said.

"Dead man," accused the necromancer. "Youse bring the undead."

My eyes narrowed. "I'm not here by choice."

"No," he snapped. "Never your choice, huh? Never your fault." His friends slowly approached.

"Back away," I warned. "We're just passing through. You don't want to get involved."

"And what will you do?" asked the lone woman among them. "Bring them here and scurry away? Leave us to them?"

I scowled. They were talking about the Obsidian March.

"Do I look like I'm running?"

Her yellowed eyes shivered at the determination in mine, but the original man was not cowed. "You's..." he started, lifting a finger to pound on my chest.

Evan cracked him across the jaw with the stock of his long gun. One of the friends reached into a pocket. Evan twirled the rifle and pointed in warning. The three stragglers raised careful hands in surrender. They backed away at Evan's urging.

This wasn't going how I wanted. "Go inside your house and lock your door," I urged.

"Not wants us to see you deal against your own kind?" he spat. "Youse will not walk away from me."

Evan growled and pulled his badge. "Hey, asshole, you see this?"

The vagrant's eyes flickered in recognition—no—fear. He backed away. "Don't want no trouble."

"Then get inside."

I wondered what it said that the locals were more afraid of the police than of me. But at least the crew backed off. I scanned down the block ahead of us. White eyes dotted open windows and doorways.

"Better not rile up the locals," I whispered. We crossed the lonely street to the abandoned far side. No one followed.

The large cemetery was decrepit and unkempt. Chain link ran flush along the crumbling sidewalk. Rusted metal poles twisted into the air and gates rested at angles as the dilapidated fence struggled to remain standing. It was hardly the only sign of disrepair in the boneyard.

Row after disheveled row of stone coffins sat amongst overgrown grass and weeds. They were squeezed so close together they appeared haphazardly placed, without space to accommodate grieving family members. Many graves were inaccessible without climbing over others.

Above-ground coffins were not the norm in Miami, but this was a historic black cemetery and the tradition had been carried over from the flood-prone Bahamas. Patches of dirt marred the uneven vegetation that grew around and over the weather-stained crypts. This neighborhood and these grounds oozed the stink of neglect.

Another block took us to the pair of coral-rock pillars standing on either side of the main gates. It was the only black iron around. Above and connecting the stone pillars was an arch with the words "Lincoln Memorial Park."

Milena gulped. "Those vampires really know how to set the mood."

I pulled away the rusted metal chain and pressed the gate open. It creaked unevenly. A wide dirt path cut through the cemetery and led straight to an office building.

Evan nodded across the street. "I'm gonna set up in that tree. Should give me overwatch." He kissed his wife. "Be careful in there."

As the rest of us pushed in, the area went deadly quiet. It was as if our presence breached a centuries-old taboo. Not because the locals avoided midnight visits, I knew, but rather because we weren't locals.

"Stick close," I advised and walked ahead.

Halfway down the main path, I opened my eyes to the darkness and took it in. My enchanted eyes searched the field of coffins. A wooden cross rested on its side. A miniature flag from a country I didn't recognize was staked in the dirt. Finally, movement caught my eye at a distant bramble. I turned to Evan's position, assuming he was already scoping me, and signaled two fingers to my eyes. We'd be another fifty yards to his left. I was hoping either he could adjust his position or that he was good enough to make the shot. Regardless, the threat was more important than deadly accuracy.

We turned off the entry path and weaved between ceramic and stone. Some of the coffins were broken, with portions of their contents stolen. A goat lay decapitated, its head nowhere to be found. Emily and Milena scrunched their noses at the sights. I knew them to be common signs of necromancy. Local santeros and voodooists had a veritable playground in this unkempt lot.

It was, however, abandoned tonight. It wasn't a leap to figure why.

A man presented himself from behind a low tree. We froze as he stepped into view, hands spread.

"So," he said, "the Frenchman actually carried through. What a good little dog."

Emily shook a can of spray paint and traced around Milena. A circle of white gloss striped the dirt and weeds. "Stay inside at all costs," she reminded.

I frowned. Emily was supposed to follow her own advice, but she stepped to my side without similar protection. I didn't naysay her audible in the presence of the enemy.

The man—no, *vampire*—stepped toward us, stopping at a safe twenty feet. Well, safe was relative. His preternatural speed could cover that distance in no time. He had shaggy brown hair, a goatee, and wore a bowler hat.

"You wanted to chat," I stated evenly.

His lips curled, revealing extended canines. His black nails were still retracted. "Is that what the little dog said?" I wasn't sure why he was going out of his way to insult Beaumont in front of me. Did he know the restaurant owner would attempt to strike an alliance? "Are we here to... chat?"

I clenched my jaw, already tired of this charade. "You tell me. I can kick your ass if you prefer."

His eye twitched, equal parts shock and anger. He recovered quickly. Shadowy forms rose into view around us, each perching on a separate coffin. I turned my head to both sides, getting an idea of how many vamps we were up against. I counted seven others. Not too shabby.

"I heard you were a cocky little shit," he taunted.

His voice had a hard German twang but, like Beaumont, had been naturalized to almost non-existent. I suspected these vampires had lived several lifetimes, which could make them dangerous. I reminded myself to ask Simon about upir life expectancy.

"We should kill him, Magnus," suggested one of his underlings.

I lasered onto the girl that spoke. "Try it and you're the first one that dies."

She reared her head back, sulking.

"Enough with the second-rate intimidation tactics," I said. "You know who I am, and you know I don't scare easily."

Magnus hiked a shoulder and flashed a resigned smile. "So you don't. But I had to see for myself." His eyes darted to the women. "The Obsidian March operates in absolute secrecy. It was careless to open those doors to others. What is seen cannot be unseen."

"They can take care of themselves."

His eyes narrowed. "Wizards."

Nether creatures preferred the historical word, but I'd always thought it a bit hokey. Spellcraft wasn't about magic school and the power of love and the fight between good and evil. This was the real world, fueled by greed and lust and need and even the irrational power trip. Animists, netherlings, subhumans, primal beings—no one had a monopoly on right and wrong.

But I realized... these were fiends from the Nether, visitors to the Earthly Steppe and unwelcome by anyone's standards. Their entire existence was predicated on living in the shadows.

"You hate us," I said, "don't you?" His face was a steady mask. "It grinds your gears that animists are some of the few in our world who not only know of your kind, but can do something about it." Magnus tilted his head, not commenting either way. "I wouldn't be surprised if this animist serial killer has something to do with you."

"A wizard killer?" Magnus turned to his cohorts and laughed. "That sounds like more of a 'you' problem. We don't engage in that business."

I tried to read his face, but either he wasn't giving anything up or he was telling the truth.

"I'll be straight, then," said Magnus, approaching. "Your disrespect at my bar was reported to me."

"Your people attacked me."

"I don't doubt that. Little Tutti's a spicy peach, but she's also my favorite. A connoisseur of giving pleasure." He made an overwrought sucking motion with his lips. "I'm pissed you hurt her."

"Glad to have your attention."

His face flushed. He wasn't used to being talked to like this. "She was only trying to bring you to me!"

I shrugged and turned to make sure our audience was keeping their distance. "What can I say? No one. Brings me. Anywhere."

He watched me a long moment, craning his neck to stretch. It was clear he wanted nothing more than me dead on a platter, but he was holding back. Why? I wasn't sure. If I had to guess, Magnus was a low-level pimp with some territory. He was too conceited and too rash to have more power than that.

"I wanna talk to your boss," I announced.

His face went hard. "You're talking to me."

I shook my head. "Nope. Not how this works. I'd like to escalate this to your supervisor."

"Wha—?" He visibly shook. "You insolent prick. You'll listen to my terms or you'll die."

"Terms," I repeated, noting the subject of a higher-up

Domino Finn

was a sore point with him. "So this is a business meeting then?"

He twitched at my prodding tone but took my response as an assertion of his authority. It wasn't. I just wanted to get whatever this was over with. He took his win regardless. Magnus lifted the bowler from his head, brushed a hand through his hair, and replaced it.

"We've heard of you," he continued. "The war in Little Haiti. The confrontations with the *Agua Fuego* cartel. Your battles don't concern us. The Obsidian March prefers a more discreet line of business." He stepped closer. "To put it bluntly, the chaos in your wake helps keep prying eyes off our activities. Which means there's room for both of us in Miami."

I didn't say anything. The gang war in Little Haiti hadn't been my fault, but Magnus didn't care about that. His point was taken. The vampires worked in secrecy, otherwise I would've heard about them before now. More than anything, they wanted their business to run unimpeded.

I blinked. "That's your offer?"

Magnus snorted. "The Obsidian March doesn't make offers, especially not to rogue wizards. I'm telling it like it is. You stay out of our way, and we'll stay out of yours. The unsuspecting denizens of this city will go on living their simple lives surrounded by their simple pleasures. They, and you, will die while the March, and I, will... march on." He chuckled to himself.

The surrounding vamps hissed and cooed as I mulled over his words. There was a good chance they'd spring into action the moment I said no. However, despite Simon's impression of me, I didn't hope and dream of starting a vampire war.

At the same time, how much was I really willing to concede to these murderous pricks?

"There's something you need to know," I announced, making sure every single vamp in the graveyard heard me. "In case you didn't get the memo, Cisco Suarez is back. And Miami's under my protection."

He scoffed. "You're one man—"

I held up my hand. "I'm not done. I know about your business. You wanna keep running your scams—collecting money and blood donations? Fine. But the human trafficking is done."

He glowered at me, incredulous, as if I'd just asked him to turn off gravity. "THAT," he snarled, "is NOT going to happen. Ever."

"Then don't say I didn't warn you."

His eyes narrowed. Dark spears elongated from his fingertips. The surrounding vampires likewise brandished their claws.

"Do you think yourself invincible, shadow witch?"

I pointed my finger at him like a gun. I glanced sideways at Evan's tree, noting the clear angle to us.

"I warn you, wizard. If you invoke spellcraft against our kind, it means open war."

My finger gun locked onto his heart. "And I warn you, Magnus: you're the one with the incorrect assumption about who can and can't be killed."

Pointing at his weak spot clearly aggravated him. "So we're at an impasse."

The photograph of Gendra in the news flashed into my mind. The words came out without thought. "Not an impasse. An ultimatum. Stop stealing people or I'll end every one of you."

His eyes flared silently. And, just as silently, his vampire kin rose from their perches. A twisted, hungry smirk overtook Magnus' face. "I was hoping you'd say that."

I stretched the thumb of my pointed hand back as if cocking my imaginary gun. "Watch what you wish for, Shaggy." And then I fired with a "Bang."

It was a glorious moment, at least until nothing happened. Magnus blinked. I looked around and mimed the gunshot two more times, but Evan wasn't firing.

"Too late to reconsider?" asked Magnus with a cruel laugh. He snapped his fingers and his cohorts closed into a tight circle around us.

Chapter 19

"Stay back!" ordered Emily. As she screamed, she thrust her arms up. An orb materialized over our heads and blazed like a miniature sun.

The vamps shuddered and hissed against the sudden light. I practically did as well. My vision went white. I clenched my eyes shut and squeezed the light-sensitive spellcraft away. Black tears ran down my cheeks.

I didn't have time to let my vision readjust—at least I didn't think so. I spun and took in the blurry forms of the vampires. The three of us were in a perfect circle of death. It would've been the ideal time for Evan to fire.

Our attackers didn't immediately close in. Emily's spellcraft wasn't killing them, but it was holding them back.

Magnus darted behind the shadow of a tree. As he did, his skin blackened and solidified. His eyes glazed over with white and gleamed in the night. Emily sidestepped and the light shifted over his hand. Claws instantly reverted to human fingers, black fingernails their only vestige.

The other vampires held their ground, forced into their

human guises and utterly furious about it. They may have been declawed, but they still had plenty of juice to do damage. Milena's Uzi trembled despite the purported protection of the white circle. I stood like a statue, taking careful note of each vampire's position.

"So you brought a flashlight," snarled Magnus. He stepped from beyond the tree. As soon as the light hit his features, they reverted to human. He considered his hands. "What a bitch." Despite his flippant body language, he winced under the strain. This much light in this proximity was painful.

Magnus scratched his goatee with a thumb. "It does make you wonder, though. What kind of power does a shadow witch command in daylight?"

I gritted my teeth. Each of the vampires had a stark shadow, of course. Wherever there was light, shadow followed. But those small formations were hardly enough to dish damage, especially against the significant odds.

Magnus reached to his belt. With netherlings, you could never tell whether clothing was real or glamour. They changed guises so much it didn't make practical sense to drape themselves in physical fabric. But material palpability couldn't be completely disregarded. Magnus pulled a pistol from a holster.

The Micro Uzi zeroed in on him. He kept his weapon at his side. I fingered a plastic Easter egg of zombie poison.

Magnus chuckled confidently. "I take it this is some kind of Mexican standoff."

I liked the sound of that. Part of me wanted Milena to

open fire and let all hell break loose. The other part figured the longer we waited, the more time Evan had to get in position. Stalling wasn't the worst option at the moment.

"This is your last warning," I told them. "Back off or you die here, tonight."

Magnus arched an eyebrow. "Eight of us against the three of you?"

"Four. A sniper rifle is trained on your heart as we speak. Make one move and you're dead."

His gaze dropped to his chest. "Well, shit. I'm practically dead already then." He shrugged. "Unless, of course, I already accounted for your fourth man." My eyes narrowed, and he laughed. "Are you kidding me? Your sniper walked right up to the cemetery gates. Of *course* we saw him." He turned to his gang. "And it's a good thing we alerted the local brujos that the man they hated would be visiting tonight."

Emily and I traded a concerned glance.

Magnus stepped forward, not at all concerned about being taken down from a distance. "You'd better believe we urged them to give you trouble."

The beacon of light above us flickered. "Evan..." breathed Emily.

I scanned the distant tree across the street. I could make out movement around it, maybe, but it was too dark to see. And I couldn't use my spellcraft to enhance my vision with Emily's sun blaring above me.

Damn.

Once again I surveyed the opposing vampires. Eight of

them were a lot to take on, but I noted their positions, their stances—I had them locked down.

I turned to the women. Emily and Milena both appeared horrified at the predicament. They weren't used to this. They weren't practically bulletproof like I was. What the hell had I been thinking dragging them into this?

If it was the last thing I did, I'd get them out.

"Go, Emily," I said. I locked eyes with her. "Milena's safe in the circle. You need to go get Evan right now."

Her eyes widened. She realized what I was asking her, but I could see that she desperately wanted to save her husband.

"Now!" I barked.

In a blink, the light extinguished. Darkness took over and it was absolute, even for my eyes. I moved while still blind, knowing that a fraction of a second was the difference between success and failure. I screamed and pounded my hand to the ground.

Eight spears of shadow simultaneously spiked upwards and struck the vampires in their hearts.

Stunned cries screeched in a ring around us. My eyes went black and the night lightened as I spun low. Obsidian claws raked over my head.

I didn't have time for a hard count, but a few of the vamps had moved quickly enough to avoid my heartstrikes. Either that or I'd missed, which was a distinct possibility when dealing with so many targets.

Another vampire with a shiny black carapace dove at Emily. It had only been a second since the light winked out and she'd barely moved. I thrust my hand up to grab him with a tentacle of shadow, but I was doing too many things at once. I couldn't make it in time. The vamp barreled into her. The image of Emily flickered and bent until she was a few yards to the side, safe.

That was a good girl. She'd used her spellcraft to refract her position and slip outside the kill zone. I barely had time to see her charging away toward Evan.

All around me, the vampires I'd bull's-eyed collapsed. They weren't dead—I'd already learned my shadow wasn't able to pierce their magical hearts—but they were down for a half count.

The egg of zombie poison I'd released exploded. Dust spread in a small cloud. The two vamps most affected were already down. Magnus darted away, temporarily distracted at best.

Automatic gunfire tore through the night. I flinched as the Uzi sprayed the enemy with soft fire. Milena wisely fired away from Emily and I, but her eyes probably hadn't adjusted to the darkness yet. She was aiming over the downed vampire's heads.

The female vamp I'd initially admonished had taken a shoulder blow from my shadow spear, wounded but not stunned. She tore at Milena with murderous accuracy. Claws deflected against flashes of light that hurt my eyes.

Milena turned her weapon and fired at the new threat. The vamp darted around her in a blur, attacking all sides of the circle. My amethyst sword sprouted from my fist and straight through her back. She only had time to give a shrill scream before her chest violently erupted. Blood splattered forcefully like an overripe mutant pimple all over my face and shirt. Milena's circle of protection had spared her the same indignity.

"I told you you'd be first," I said.

Claws slashed my shoulder as the vamp who'd attacked Emily whirled on me. I rolled away in a hasty tumble, surprised to feel the warmth of my blood soaking my arm. Milena turned the Uzi and fired at his center mass. He made the mistake of going on the offensive, trying fruitlessly to get through Milena's circle. That error cost him his life. The rounds found his heart and he burst as well.

I ignored the pain and took to my feet. All the other vamps were getting up now. "Take them out while we still have a chance!" I screamed.

Milena reloaded and grunted.

The next minute was a bloodbath. Milena downed a couple of them while I held them off and killed another, but the quick reflexes of the nether fiends were costly. Milena's ammunition ran dry. The final two underlings retreated to Magnus' flank as he stepped forward, firing his pistol.

I threw up my shield. Bullets alternately ricocheted off my turquoise magic and Emily's white circle. Magnus growled and threw the empty gun to the floor. His face went black and his claws lengthened.

I squared off with him.

"Not so fast," he spat. He nodded at one of the vampires. "The girl's not a wizard. Get her out of that circle."

The blackened skin of his cohort vanished into smooth,

silky skin the color of cinnamon. A lusty woman in her twenties ran fingers up her naked side and purred, "With pleasure." The other vamp, still wearing armored skin, intercepted me.

I slashed with my sword but he wasn't engaging. I rolled again and turned the ground to sludge. He hopped through the air to change position. He was playing cat and mouse, staying out of my reach.

"Come on, dear," cooed the naked woman. "You don't really want to miss all the fun, do you?"

I turned abruptly at the sensation, foreign but familiar at the same time.

"Why don't you be a good little girl and step out of that circle?"

I felt it. That was a vampire compulsion. Netherling mind tricks didn't often succeed against animists—a working knowledge of the Intrinsics was a huge defense against such tactics—but Milena had no such immunity. Her Uzi dropped to the grass.

"Stop this right now," I said. I took a step toward them but the other vamp leapt in my path. I feinted with my energy sword. He jumped over my head.

"Come out, come out," ordered the woman.

The vamp landed behind me. I immediately lassoed him with shadow and punched my sword backward. He let out a surprised grunt when he discovered he was trapped, but he wiggled sideways enough to dodge. I maneuvered a backswing that caught him by surprise and took his leg off above the knee. The vampire crashed to the ground. My amethyst blade came down hard. It ripped through his chest and rewarded me with another kill. I spun around to assist Milena.

She was in a trance now. She lifted her foot toward the line of white paint.

"Don't do it!"

I dove into the shadow, sliding through the void at top speed. It was full night so I stretched the spellcraft to its maximum length, but at some point I had to resurface. When I did I had just about caught them. I reached my arm out.

Milena stepped on the line. The circle popped like a lightbulb. Diffuse energy washed over my face uselessly. Before I could get to her, the naked vampire wrapped her up and held a single razor claw to her throat.

"Oops!" shrieked Magnus in relief.

We all froze, wound to full tension. Vampire reflexes were legendary. A single twitch would forever end Milena's life. We'd put up a good fight—killed six of them with just two of us—but my lack of intel had been our downfall. I'd had no idea the Obsidian March were able to compel their victims. It suddenly made the human trafficking angle much more understandable.

Damn, they were able to steal people away without even an objection. No wonder the police weren't onto them.

"Now," announced Magnus, taking control of the situation, "we find ourselves in a bit of a tit-for-tat situation. On one hand, you killed six of my people." He glanced morosely as the wind picked up and swirled the ashes of dead upirs around us. He cocked his head with a grin. "On the other hand, they were assholes."

The cinnamon beauty cackled.

"So," he said, "should I kill all your friends?"

"No," pleaded the female vampire. She licked Milena's neck and sniffed at her. "This one is my type." Milena huffed at her captor, but she couldn't do anything. The compulsion wasn't on anymore, which was interesting. I wondered if the vamp was conserving her energy for the kill. She forced Milena to her haunches and stood behind. Her human breasts flattened and hardened to glossy black armor, a lone claw tickling Milena's neck. "But if you move, shadow witch, I have no choice."

I clenched my teeth. "She's the only thing keeping you alive," I warned.

Magnus paced around me. "So she is. But you know what? I'm inclined to give Alexa what she wants. She did, after all, end this. So how about this: I kill you and I let your friends live and we call it a day? Sounds fair to me." He flashed a knowing look at Alexa. "Of course, Milena might spend the rest of her life as a familiar, but why split hairs?"

I growled and took half a step. Alexa jerked Milena's head by the hair, exposing a mile of her juicy throat.

Magnus searched the ground and retrieved his gun. "You see, wizard, that's the importance of surrounding yourself with competent people." He waved his pistol. "You can't just hand them a gun and go at it. That's reckless because"—the mag slipped out of the pistol and bounced to the ground—"human weapons eventually run empty."

Magnus reached for a spare magazine to reload. A sudden burst made us both flinch. A loud bang followed, cracking through the air. We spun to a splash of vampire blood, the initial burst. Alexa was gone. Milena slumped to the ground, patting at the smooth skin of her throat, delighted to discover it whole.

Magnus stared in disbelief. I grinned as we both realized Emily had fended the brujos away and Evan had overwatch on us again. And, damn, was that an incredible shot. I brought my arm forward, dog collar twitching. Magnus clicked the magazine into place as he turned to run. The pistol barked, shot going wide. Milena was his target.

I dove and wrapped my arms over her as we fell into the shadow together. Bullets peppered the dirt around us as I hugged her tight. Milena still shivered from the previous close call. She gazed deep into my eyes, her face inches from mine, knowing she was well and truly safe in my darkness.

We waited until the gunshots stopped and then returned to the world with a lurch. I spun around with my shield out.

"Tell the rest of the March!" I yelled after him. "Tell them they've been put on notice!"

Unfortunately, protecting Milena had afforded Magnus an escape route. Emily converged on us and bathed the area in stark light. We were alone.

Chapter 20

We regrouped and headed to the cemetery entrance. I clutched Milena tight, shocked I'd almost lost her.

"That was amazing, Cisco," said Emily, eyeing me strangely.

"That's a funny way to describe a near disaster."

"No, I mean what you did with the shadow. As soon as I extinguished my light, you hit everybody at once. I thought you were limited to one manifestation at a time."

I shrugged without giving it much thought. "Ever since I returned from the Taíno underworld, I... I don't know how to explain it except that the Intrinsics flow through me faster. It's like things had been gunked up and I'd taken an entire bottle of Drano to it."

She chewed her lip as she studied me. Evan entered the gate lugging his rifle over his shoulder. "That was a close one. Would've been easier with night vision." He smiled. "I need to bring more toys when I back you up."

His attitude starkly contrasted his appearance, beaming and positive despite being sweaty and looking like he'd gone a few rounds in an illegal MMA pit fight. The arms of his gold shirt were ripped, his skin covered in cuts.

My expression sobered. "Who did this to you?"

"Two punks who got what was coming to them."

I guess I shouldn't have been impressed. Evan was a tough cop. Being ambushed by animists wasn't an easy thing. As soon as Emily evened the odds it was game over. Combat wasn't an everyday occurrence for her, but she was more talented than the local santeros by a mile.

Speaking of whom, the street outside the gate bristled with them. I popped my ketchup bottle of voodoo toxin and squeezed some over the gashes on my arm, grimacing in pain. "Just keep walking," I told my friends.

We pushed into the road. Some of the crowd parted, but the man with the dreads made his way into our path.

"You's hurt," he said.

"We don't want any more trouble," I told him, voice hard.

He shook his head. "Youse took them out, dead man. Fought for us."

"I didn't do it for you."

He leaned in and pressed a fist to his chest. "Us." Then he put a hand on my shoulder and another on Milena's. "*Us.*"

He was talking about humanity.

I grunted. The man stepped aside and let us pass. As we did, a few practitioners waved feathers and beads and chanted. Milena stiffened in my arms. "It's harmless," I explained. "They're blessing us."

"Let's just get outta here before they start breaking chicken necks," she whispered.

We made it back to the casket depot parking lot. Hector hadn't disappointed. Despite the initially hostile locals, our cars were unmolested. I'd need to thank him sometime. For now I just wanted what we all wanted: to go home.

"Maybe I should drive," offered Milena, pointing to my wounded arm.

"Keep dreaming," I said.

We hurried to my place. Evan parked behind me. They came up to make sure Fran was okay. I wasn't worried. Kasper had stayed up and reported all quiet on the home front. He took a gold paint pen to my gashes. I'd stopped the blood and ensured they wouldn't get infected, but Kasper's runes would aid the healing process.

"She's sound asleep," reported Emily, coming back from Fran's room and catching us in the middle of a postmortem.

"I can't believe it," repeated Evan. "I-95 is a major artery for trafficking. At-risk kids get taken and dragged two states away to work. We've always known that. But for the major culprit to be vampires? How are we supposed to fight back?"

We sat on stools around my private bar. Kasper was in a rare mood, probably from being close to action. He was so excited to hear our stories that he'd played bartender and mixed up some cocktails: spice rum and ginger beer.

"Dark and Stormy?" he offered Emily.

"I'll just pop open something bubbly," she said. He seemed disappointed. I pointed at the wine fridge and Emily pulled out my most expensive bottle of champagne. She had good taste, and she'd earned it.

"At least let me do the honors," said the old man. She smiled and handed him the bottle so he could open it.

"This is gonna be a new thing now," said Milena. "Isn't it?"

The adrenaline from the fight had worn off and she was no longer hanging onto me. She felt distant already; there, in the middle of the conversation, but not connected to it. To me.

"It's already a thing," replied Evan. "My unit looks for district-wide threats. Anti-trafficking initiatives are part of that—"

"You're gonna go to war with the Obsidian March?" asked Emily, concerned.

"I'm not an idiot, and the DROP team's not big enough to take down an army. These guys are too many... too strong... but they still need to operate within human parameters. They have business licenses, trucking agreements. It's gonna take a while, but we need to gather all interdepartmental evidence and see what I can put together on their enterprise."

I sipped my drink and set it down. Kasper was a natural. "How long are you talking?"

He hiked a shoulder. "A year. Maybe two. This is a sophisticated operation. But if they're growing as fast as Beaumont made out, and most of it has been within the last year, it should be easy to track. You can't hide change that drastic."

I nodded. "Sounds safe enough as long as you don't go

pissing anybody off."

"You're the renegade, Cisco. I'm part of a large force that's dedicated to protecting the city. We'll do this through the proper channels until we have enough evidence to shut them down. The Obsidian March won't even know we're looking into them."

"What if they have someone in the department?" asked Milena. It was a good question.

"Just look out for black fingernails and sensitivity to light," I instructed. "Any familiars would be too drugged up to gather effective intel. The real worry is normal people on their payroll."

Evan frowned. "That's always a concern with organized crime. I'll keep everything within the DROP team for now."

Emily leaned a tired head on her husband's shoulder. "Speaking of organized crime, what do we know about Beaumont?"

"Good question. He's not a crime figure as far as I know, just an investor in Brickell. A businessman."

"Aren't they all?" I muttered, rubbing my temples. "And he's taken an active interest in me. As if I didn't have enough on my plate."

Emily smirked. "Might this be a good time to inquire about the bloody knife you stashed in the wine cooler?"

I feigned embarrassment. "You caught me. I'm a serial killer." Which, of course, just flooded my brain with entirely separate issues I needed to address. I went to the fridge, pulled out the bloody bread knife from Marie Devereaux's house, and set it on the bar in front of Evan. "I was hoping you could run it for prints."

He arched an eyebrow. "Why was it in the cooler?"

"I don't know. Maybe in case you needed the blood." I shook my head. "It should be the kid's anyway. I just wondered if we could get a bead on the scumbag who used the knife." I stepped to the kitchen cabinet and pulled out the baggy with the crystal ball. "This one's for you, Emily. It took a salt water bath, but I was hoping you could get a trace on the last thing Marie Devereaux saw."

"I thought you said this Manifesto Killer wasn't an animist," she said.

"He's not, as far as I can tell."

She frowned. "But he's familiar with spellcraft, or at least what interferes with it, so he knows it's real enough." She hefted the ball in her hands. "It'll require a cleansing ritual before being of any use."

Their faces were solemn as I explained the crime scene to them and showed them pictures from my phone. Evan didn't like Emily using magic, but he knew what was at stake. I printed up several copies of the cipher. Evan folded one up with a promise to do what he could tomorrow.

"Letter puzzles," muttered Kasper as I handed him a copy. "You really do throw the best parties."

I grinned magnanimously in the face of his sarcasm. "I figured you were good with script..."

"This isn't really my flavor of fun." He shook his head. "Only two short lines here. 'Wivo ivo wero ev.' It isn't much to go on. But I'll give it a gander." He shoved the evidence in his pocket. "Tomorrow. I'm too drunk now."

"Mom?" squeaked Fran from the hallway. "Dad?" We turned as Emily met Fran halfway into the living room. They hugged.

"My baby," said Emily. "You should be asleep. You have school tomorrow."

"I thought I heard talking." She disengaged and went to hug Evan, who held her tight.

"It's late," he agreed. "Maybe we should all call it a night."

I pointed my drink down the hall. "You're all welcome to stay here too."

"How many bedrooms do you have in this place?"

"Five. You guys should know," I ribbed. "You cosigned on it."

Evan smiled and turned to his family with a silent exchange. "I think we'll go home anyway. Fran can come with us."

It was disappointing I wouldn't get my father-daughter sleepover after all. I turned to Fran for a hug but she gave me a high five. "That's okay, Cisco. I'll see you tomorrow," she said with a wink.

"Okay, little one."

Evan wrapped up the knife so Fran wouldn't see it and we said our goodbyes. I took a measured breath and turned to Milena, who'd been unusually quiet. I figured she was tired.

"Guess I'll turn in," chimed in Kasper with a knowing look. "Glad you kids are all right." He disappeared down the hall, leaving us alone.

I slid my stool toward Milena. She leaned on the bar, ear resting on crossed arms, empty stare filling me with doubt. I brushed a hand on her back. "You okay?"

"I almost died." She said it matter-of-factly, without emotion. That was the kind of thing usually associated with strong feelings. She was in shock.

"Sorry. I totally screwed up your night." I thought about Evan and Emily, probably too exhausted for anniversary sex and without an empty house anymore anyway. I could've spent a late night playing games with my daughter. "I bet you're wondering what it would've been like to go to Gavin's place and listen to bad music." There was no derision in my voice at the mention of her date's name. It really was a simple pleasure I'd deprived her of.

"Actually," she said, "that hadn't crossed my mind at all."

Our eyes met and we shared a longing gaze. Then she looked away with that same blank stare and sighed. "I think I'm gonna go home now."

I nodded sullenly. "Yeah... Of course." We meandered to our feet and toward the front door. "Though you should probably unstrap that Uzi first."

Chapter 21

Kasper had cleared out by the time I woke up. I would need to thank him later: the gashes on my arm were mostly healed up. I went through my morning routine with only a bit of stiffness and aching, and most of that was due to the wine. I downed a glass of water while recollecting how great it had been to get everybody together. The thought made the condo feel empty.

I was in the middle of looking for breakfast when Simon called.

"We got a letter," he relayed. "From Manifesto. The *Herald's* likely to have a similar copy so we need to move fast before the police request it."

I was still sleepy and not thinking straight. "Why would he send the letter if Marie's body was cleaned up?"

"He doesn't know that. He probably dropped it in the mail two days ago after doing the deed."

"Right."

I shifted into high speed and agreed to meet them first thing. I was good at that, rolling with the punches. Doing what needed to get done. So good it was sometimes to the detriment of other aspects of my life.

I pulled the Firebird into a strip mall and made my way to the address I'd been given. I paused on foot, double-checked the numbers of the adjoining storefronts, and finally frowned at the door of an entirely unremarkable dry cleaner. It seemed an odd place for a homicide investigation, but these were my instructions. I walked in carrying a bakery box and a Styrofoam cup. My arrival was announced by a door chime, and a cute Asian woman smiled at me from behind the counter. Not to generalize, but she was younger and prettier than I'd have expected in this line of work.

"You must be Cisco," she said with an infectious grin. Her hair curled around her face and she had a freckle in the middle of her nose.

"I sure am. And you must be..."

She giggled, hooked a finger for me to follow, and led me to the back. She was a petite thing with a playful attitude. I decided to roll with it.

"Play hard to get all you want. You're not getting a *cafecito* without giving me a name."

Her eyes flared back hungrily. I was back in my tank top and couldn't tell if she was looking at my coffee or my biceps. "I'm Diana," she said with a wink.

Progress. I was just getting into the swing of things when she greeted Shen Santos with a long kiss, extra tongue for my benefit, I was sure. He hooked his arm around her territorially. Diana tucked her head into his metallic-blue tie and smirked.

"Coffee it is, then," I grumbled.

I placed the communal Styrofoam cup on a counter with the stack of miniature plastic sipping cups and poured a round of shots for everybody, even Shen. Despite the misstep with Diana, I was determined to keep things professional today.

Simon huffed with indignation. "I asked you to come as quick as you could and you stopped for coffee and donuts?"

"No way," I contested. "I'd never do that. These are ham croquettes. You should try one."

Shen immediately opened the box and dug in. It was easy to spot the true locals.

I downed a shot of liquid energy. I'd already had one at the counter where I bought it. The second hit me like an encore. *Now* I was ready to work. Diana and Shen poured a second helping of espresso as I made my way past. "Let me see what you got."

Simon refused to partake. He sternly signaled to the letter on the table. It was handwritten in black ink on white computer paper. An original.

A NEW LETTER TO THE NEW TIMES,

THIS IS MY MANIFESTO. IGNORE IT AT YOUR OWN PERIL.

DO NOT, PLAY NOT, SEE NOT, SHOW NOT.
ANOTHER PAIR OF PERFORMERS HAS FALLEN,

THIS TIME A MOTHER WHO CORRUPTED HER OWN
SON. SHE DECEIVED HUMANITY WITH PLATITUDES
AND VISIONS. THE VILE SPIRITS COULD NOT SAVE
HER IN THE END.

HER EYES ARE FOREVER MINE BUT I HAVE
GRANTED YOU A SINGLE LASH IN HOPES YOU SEE
THE LIGHT. YOU WILL FIND HER WHERE SHE LEADS
MEN ASTRAY. SHE WAS A FORTUNE TELLER—THE
BOY HAD THE MISFORTUNE OF BEING A DEVEREAUX.

NOW THAT YOU UNDERSTAND HOW SERIOUS I
AM, YOU WILL PRINT THIS LETTER AND THE FIRST
IN FULL, INCLUDING BOTH CIPHERS. IF YOU DO NOT,
MORE BLOOD WILL BE ON YOUR HANDS. THIS IS MY
WORK. THIS IS MY MANIFESTO.

The cipher at the end of this letter was similar to the other, but slightly different.

"Any conclusions?" I asked Simon.

"Just what's obvious. This is a breaking development. We're the first to see it."

I took the note to a dark corner. Then I looked around. "Why are we in a dry cleaner anyway?"

Simon shrugged. "Shen didn't want you seeing where he lived."

The illusionist just munched on his snack silently. Diana leaned on him.

Whatever. I didn't press it. I returned my attention to the note. My eyes cracked and filled with black. I examined the ink closely.

"It's not enchanted," I said. "Nothing about the cipher is magic."

Simon's face told me he'd come to the same conclusion. I handed him the letter. "This one was more specific," he said. "It included the victim's name because there was no maid to discover the body. The police are already scouring the house."

"They won't find anything," assured Shen. "There's no proof of murder. No victim to match the eyelash to."

"That's right," said Simon. "We're counting on the FBI to keep a lid on things a while longer."

As he set the letter down, I made sure to snap a quick picture with my phone. Kasper and I weren't the sort to work out word puzzles, but I'd give him a go at it.

"I think the performer angle is interesting," I said.

Simon chewed his lip and waited for me to elaborate.

"Well, he uses that word. Performer. And besides being animists, it's a link all the victims have in common. Mordane was a card mechanic. The piper was a musician, a charmer. Marie told fortunes. So who's next?"

Shen scoffed. "It's impossible to know what two-bit performer he's gonna strike next. Or when for that matter."

I nodded to partially concede his point. "We can narrow down the timing a bit. Mordane was five weeks ago. The piper was a week ago. Marie only a couple of days."

"His timeline's accelerating," noted Simon.

"Maybe. Or the screwup with the fire forced Manifesto's hand."

Shen crossed his arms. "So we have anywhere from one week to one month. Great."

"Or only a few days," added Simon. "If he's speeding up."

Their frustration was well founded. I studied the note and recited the words aloud. "Do not, play not, see not, show not. That's the guidebook."

"How so?" asked Simon.

"Go down the list of kills. Mordane used his hands. He *did* things. The piper played."

Simon nodded. "And Marie Devereaux saw the future. Do not, play not, see not. Which means the next victim—"

"Is a show-er." I banged the table. "Show. Perform."

Diana's face brightened. "Quentin Capshaw's in town this weekend. He has a hypnotism show at the Arena. It's a pretty big deal."

Shen glared at her for encouraging me, and I couldn't say I was all that encouraged to begin with. "That hack?" I asked.

"He's not a hack," she insisted. "He's one of us. His performances are full of demonstrations of his power. Because his spellcraft is subtle, he shows everyone in broad daylight."

Simon's eyebrows went up. I clicked my teeth and repeated, "Show." It was worth a shot.

"This is your big investigative revelation?" snorted Shen. "You just wanna stake out this guy in case he gets attacked?"

I shrugged. "It's not quite Sherlock Holmes, I admit. This is about boots on the ground and knocking on doors."

Simon chimed in. "The mantra of the police detective."

"How else to catch a killer? We need to cross every 't' and dot every 'i.' I guarantee you Manifesto is meticulous. We can't afford not to be."

We stared at one another for a long moment. With nothing else on the table, it was the best lead we had.

Simon scooped up the letter. "I need to get this back to the paper. The police will want to examine it."

"Jesus, I touched that."

"We all did." Simon plucked a handkerchief from his suit, wiped the letter down on both sides, and placed it in a manila envelope. "Walk me outside, Cisco."

We left Shen and Diana whispering sweet nothings in the back room. The loud chime sounded as we stepped through the dry cleaner door and into the sun. "Good news," he said. "We've already started your bank paperwork." He led me to his Lincoln where a driver waited. The lawyer retrieved a briefcase and plopped papers on the roof and handed me a pen. "Don't forget to read the fine print."

"Don't worry. I'll read it."

And I did, because I didn't trust the Society as far as I could throw them. The papers concerned a holding company, investments in the Caribbean, and new bank accounts to link to mine. "You're gonna backdate this?"

"We don't need to. These subsidiaries exist in limbo until we need them. They're not US-based so the paperwork is dodgy."

Sketchy, maybe, but things looked legit enough to convince me. Granted, I wasn't hard to fool. I had the financial acumen of a prize fighter. But I doubted I had enough money to tempt the Society to steal anyway.

"Congratulations," said Simon. "Your stolen drug money now comes from a legitimate enterprise."

"It's that simple?"

"There's still some behind-the-scenes approvals that need to happen, but your records will be above reproach."

I handed the pen back. "Thanks," I said, surprised at the weight lifted from me.

Simon stuffed everything back in his briefcase and tossed it in the car. "What's that?" he asked, pointing to my shoulder. While mostly healed, the wound was obvious.

"I got in a scrape last night."

"Vampires?"

I nodded. "You never told me they could compel their victims."

"Don't you ever watch the movies?" He laughed, but his face quickly sobered. "Are they gonna be a problem?"

"I don't know."

"Okay. Just try not to draw attention to yourself. Remember, the FBI's looking into you."

I nodded and hesitantly shook his hand. I half expected him to zap me. Old habits and all.

I found it unnervingly odd to deal so cordially with the Society. They were doing so much for me over one serial killer. As Simon drove away I considered his Town Car and then the dry cleaner. His secret group had impressive resources throughout the eastern United States, but South Florida was a different beast. The state government in Tallahassee was light years away from this banana republic. With recent events and Connor Hatch's failed attempt to place a dirty mayor in office, the Society was desperate for any influence in the area they could find.

Their current target was me.

That's what the gifts were for. This investigation. It was a way for us to work together, to play on the same team. And that was assuming the whole thing was on the up and up.

It was tough not to be suspicious of the circles I rolled in. I told myself it was a necessary part of being back and staking a claim to the city. There was nothing to do but face the realities presented to me, realities which did not always match my ideals. I frowned and headed back inside.

Chapter 22

Shen Santos admired the silver leather from the Firebird's passenger seat. At least, that's what I imagined he was doing. I revved the engine louder than usual, but he still failed to confess what a rad car I had. Maybe he preferred to bask in glory rather than comment on it.

The silence gave me time to process recent events. The meeting with the Obsidian March could've gone better. Really, besides me dying, how could it have gone worse? Evan and the police were the ones with the right idea. Investigate crime in the background instead of introducing yourself as a target. I usually chose the latter path. It was simple and straightforward, which was nice but had drawbacks. That's the nature of Whac-A-Mole: stand up tall and risk getting beat down by a big stick. Except they don't use padded toys in the real world.

From now on I was gonna give these situations more consideration. It was just so damn hard to keep emotions out of the equation when dealing with monsters. A missing girl from Fran's school had hit too close to home.

Not this time. I was determined to handle Manifesto in textbook fashion. Today was a workday. Shen and I were two seasoned professionals. Keep it simple. No surprises. I'd do some light investigative work, knock out a training sesh with Fran, and catch up on some sorely needed Netflix. Blue-collar stuff.

I parked outside Kasper's tattoo parlor. "Wait in the car."

"Not a chance," grumbled Shen, climbing out. "We're in this together."

"This guy doesn't like strangers."

His face tightened and he slammed the car door. "Then introduce me."

"Whatever."

We approached the nondescript shop. It was by the River but in an industrial neighborhood, undesirable but exactly how Kasper liked it. I was happy to find the parlor was open, which wasn't always the case during normal business hours. We pushed into the eclectic space, not altogether distinct from a junkyard. Stray items were piled on chairs and counters and the picnic bench beside the entry. Scraps of paper covered with tribal symbols plastered the walls, interrupted only by medieval polearms and other weapons of the bashing and slashing varieties. In fact, the main feature distinguishing this from a museum was the mess. We discovered the old man inking a heart on a woman's butt cheek.

"What's with the tie?" asked Kasper without turning his head our direction. "It's the break of dawn."

Shen cleared his throat and straightened his jacket. "It's almost noon, old timer."

The buzzing of the needle paused for a second before continuing. Kasper was putting the finishing touches on the thick black outline of a red heart. I tried to read the word across the design but didn't want to stare at the woman's butt too hard... even if it was well framed by the flimsy thong.

"I drew it myself," she proclaimed proudly. "But I wouldn't trust anyone else with my ass besides Kasper." I grinned.

"You'd be surprised how many women have told me that," he remarked. He wiped the ink down with a towel and leaned back. "There you go, Melody. Why don't you walk it off and wait in the back a minute?"

"Whatever you say." She swung long legs around and stood, angling her butt to the mirror to get a better look. It was a good look.

"He means excuse us," reminded Shen loudly. Melody huffed at him and disappeared into the back. Kasper glared.

"Sorry," I said. "He's not good with people." The old man just grunted. "We got another cipher." I handed him my phone since I hadn't printed this one.

Kasper frowned and compared it to his photocopy. "This cipher has the same intro. That's good. A pattern is a clue. If we figure it out we can decode the rest of this thing."

"You think it's more than gibberish?" asked Shen.

Kasper ignored the question. He picked up a pen and copied the cipher to his paper. "I gotta be honest with you,

Cisco. This doesn't look like it has anything to do with my talents."

"Yeah," I said. "I examined the original and there wasn't a trace of spellcraft."

"Then I don't know how much I can help." He dug around the counter for a smoke and took a long drag. "I got some downtime today. I'll take a look between appointments and see what I come up with."

"Downtime. Give me a break." Shen hissed.

Kasper considered him for the first time. "Do you have a problem, kid?"

"Kid?"

"Yeah, *kid*." Kasper stepped into Shen's face. "You walk into my shop, make rude comments to my clients, and otherwise act like I'm a washed-up nobody. I know who you are. Not you, specifically, because you're less important than a pimple on my ass. But I know about your organization and you don't scare me. If it wasn't for Cisco walking you in you'd already have your arm broken in three places."

I flashed a showy grin. "I *told* you to wait in the car."

"That was good advice," grumbled Kasper. "Take it next time." He brushed his shoulder into the illusionist on his way past. "I gotta take a leak."

I managed a "Thanks, Kasper" before he hit the bathroom. We walked outside without new information.

"Too defensive, if you ask me," muttered Shen. "I never called him washed up. That's his own self-doubt chafing his ass, not anything I said. Besides, he had nothing to give us anyway."

I shook my head. "Do you wake up in the morning and decide to be an insufferable douche or do you take lessons?"

"Fuck you. You're just mad you haven't gotten anywhere yet. If we're gonna waste our day talking to a hypnotist, how about we fucking get started and talk to a hypnotist?" Shen held up his phone. Someone in the Society had texted him Quentin Capshaw's hotel information.

We loaded into the Firebird. The back end of the car swerved as I peeled out.

Despite Shen's information giving us a goalpost, he still used every minute of the drive to discredit the idea that we were doing anything other than wasting time. I had to hand it to him how well connected his organization was to locate Quentin Capshaw so fast, but the dude could be less smug about it.

It was probably that annoyance that made me sloppy, because I'd let my guard down. We were almost at the hotel when I noticed the windowless black van behind us. The compact cargo vehicle had limo tints on the front windows and even a darkened windshield. I made a few superfluous turns. Shen was navigating and complained loudly, but the maneuvers confirmed my suspicions. As we approached a yellow streetlight, I stopped short and waited for it to go red.

"What are you doing?" he grumbled. "We could've made the light."

"I didn't want to." I slipped the gear into neutral and pulled the parking brake. I waited as the line of traffic stopped behind. Shen noticed me checking the rearview mirror and turned around.

"What is it?"

"We're being followed."

"By who?" He turned back in time to see me pulling a shotgun from the shadows. "Whoa! What the hell—?"

I pushed the door open and set an alligator boot on the street.

Chapter 23

Shen grabbed my arm. "Hold it. You're crazy."

"I'm not crazy. That black van's following us. Let go of my arm."

He chuckled derisively. "Followed. Would you listen to yourself?" My eyes glared at his hand on my arm. "This isn't some old-school detective movie."

I clenched my jaw. "No, but the Obsidian March is looking to off me these days, so we'll need to call reality stranger than fiction. Let go of my arm."

His grip tightened. "I can't let you—"

I cracked the butt of the shotgun into his face and hopped from the car. My boots twisted on the asphalt and I marched along the single lane of cars. The driver of the red Ford immediately behind the Firebird laid on his horn. The stoplight was already green.

Damn. It had taken too long for the van to come to a stop because it had been following at a distance. Now I was out of time with a line of jittery drivers behind me. The man pounded his horn again but froze as soon as he saw the weapon in my hand. I stomped by him.

The motorcyclist behind him freaked out and recoiled, attempting to maneuver out of the lane but panicking and dropping his bike in my path. I tried to catch it then cursed as more cars honked. I skirted the motorcycle and picked up my pace.

The black van flipped into reverse and hit the bumper of the car behind it. I broke out into a sprint. Tires screeched as it rounded through a U-turn and made it to the opposing empty lane. I kicked the back bumper before it accelerated out of reach.

"Damn it!" I screamed as the van sped away. I considered opening fire but that would've been irresponsible. Although I had my suspicions, I couldn't be sure who or what was in the van.

I stormed back toward my car. "Sorry," I weakly offered the guy climbing back on his motorcycle. His eyes through the open helmet were angry.

"Fuck off."

Before I could explain, he veered the bike around my car and shot through the intersection.

I grumbled and returned to my seat. Shen was wiping a bloody nose. The honking had stopped but I cleared the lane, turning down several side streets to get lost in the city.

"You're a psychopath," leveled Shen.

"I'm chasing psychopaths," I fumed. "There's a difference."

"You're a menace. You can't walk around with a gun in broad daylight."

I popped a left turn and looped back toward our destination. "The van full of vampires would like that to be true."

"We weren't being followed."

"You saw them speed off."

He grunted in pain. "You were holding a gun. Of course they ran." He checked his napkin to confirm his nose had stopped bleeding. "Now you have a whole lane of civilians who called 911. And you don't even give a shit. You're gonna get arrested again."

"How about we cool it with the talk until we find the hypnotist?"

We parked and made our way into the lobby. The place was more convention center than boutique hotel, which made sense, given our person of interest. The problem was the heightened crowd demanded heightened security staff. Despite knowing Quentin's floor and room, getting to him wouldn't be trivial. A security guard was visually confirming hotel key cards before he allowed access to the elevator. I scanned for an alternate stairway.

"Keep walking," said Shen, paying attention as an elderly couple before us flashed their key. I did as he asked but didn't think we'd be able to pull off being the couple's brash sons. Aside from us being too far behind, the couple would have third-degree burns before they ever managed my level of tan. There was also the fact that Shen was Chinese.

Before the security guard could ask to see our credentials, Shen flashed a key card. The man nodded as we brushed past. We hurried into the elevator as the couple scanned their card in the reader. Shen stepped between them and the panel. "Which floor?" he asked politely whilst pushing eight, the button we needed.

"Oh," said the old lady. "Seven. Thank you, young man."

Shen nodded. He pressed seven but the button didn't light up. He waved his key card before the scanner. Nothing happened. "It's not..."

"That's okay, young man." The woman swiped her key. Shen lit up their button and waited with a smile. He charmed them from beginning to end, even holding the doors open as they filed out on the seventh floor. As soon as the doors closed, the key card in his hand flickered out.

"That's gotta come in handy," I said.

"You have no idea."

"Not a bad bit of social engineering either."

Shen pressed his lips together, unsure how to take the compliment. After a moment of deliberation, he settled on, "Thanks."

The eighth floor was quiet as we made our way to the hypnotist's door.

"So how does this work?" I asked. "Do guys like this register with the Society? You have a secret handshake or something?"

"Nothing like that. He doesn't even know who we are. So that's what we use against him."

I nodded, impressed. We stopped at the door. I signaled for him to do the honors. He knocked.

"Mr. Capshaw, we have a situation."

Chapter 24

A balding man with thick plastic glasses opened the door. He squinted at Shen pointedly. "You don't work for the hotel."

"No, we don't."

Shen pushed in. I followed and shut the door.

"Don't make me call security," he threatened. "Or worse." He ripped the glasses from his face and widened a mysterious eye at the illusionist.

"Don't bother," said Shen. He held up his palm. A seed sprouted and grew into a short vine, green and robust. The leaves curled and turned brown. Within a matter of seconds, the entire plant withered and decayed into dust.

"Oh," said Quentin flatly. "Who are you?"

"That's not important. We're like you, and we have reason to believe your life is in danger."

He eyed me as well. "Is this some kind of shakedown?"

"Not in the slightest," I assured. "A few other... talents have been murdered recently."

Shen's eyes warned me against revealing too much. "It

could be nothing, but we want to make sure your life's not in danger."

"What are you talking about? Who would want to kill me?"

"Does that matter?" Shen asked.

The hypnotist frowned.

I walked deeper into the bedroom and cleared the bathroom. "Are you staying here with anyone, Mr. Capshaw?"

"No. I tour alone. My publicist stays in the same hotel."

"Have you had any strange encounters?" asked Shen. "Any unusual threats?"

Quentin scoffed. "I get all kinds of threatening mail left for me. Angry spouses who admitted to cheating. You'd be surprised how many are women."

I arched an eyebrow. "I thought you were a hypnotist."

"I am. As a display of my impeccable power, I get people to announce their deepest secrets to each other."

"Like Jerry Springer."

He seemed only mildly offended at the comparison.

"What about someone complaining that your powers are evil?" suggested Shen. "That you consort with demons?"

"Only every other week," he answered. "Look, are you absolutely sure my life is in danger? Who do you work for? I know a thing or two about cons, and believe me, this doesn't pass the smell test."

"We don't want anything from you," I repeated.

"Of course not," he snorted, growing more suspicious by the second. "You just want to *help* me. Perhaps you can find my stolen briefcase, is that it? You can give it back. All you ask for is a nominal fee."

"What briefcase?" asked Shen.

"Get out of my room!" snapped Quentin. "You steal my belongings and try to sell them back to me? You can keep that briefcase and everything in it!"

"But—"

"Get out!"

I shoved Quentin backward onto the bed. He immediately realized his precarious position and clammed up, still bouncing slightly.

"We're not here to rip you off," I promised.

He arched one eye dramatically and locked gazes. "You *will* leave my hotel room. Now."

Strangely, I did feel a tickling in my brain.

"You *will* leave my hotel room," he repeated.

I smacked him across the face. "These aren't the droids you're looking for. Now would you quit making it difficult to save your life?"

He clenched his teeth and pouted.

"You said someone stole your briefcase. When?"

He pouted but answered. "Yesterday afternoon. I was having lunch downstairs. I set it down and went to the bathroom, and when I came back it was gone."

I turned to Shen. "He's quick. We're studying the body and he's already scoping out his next victim."

Quentin's face paled. "Body?"

"What was in the briefcase?"

"N—Nothing. My papers, my schedule. I was serious

about not needing it back. The biggest hassle was asking the maid to open my room for me."

My eyes narrowed. "Your key card was stolen?"

"Yes, but I have a duplicate." He pointed to the one on the nightstand.

"That's his way in." Shen's face tightened. He still wasn't convinced this was a practical lead, but it was hard to deny the opportunity.

"Am... Am I in danger?" asked Quentin meekly.

"Change your key card," I told him. "Change your room, even. Do you carry a weapon?"

Quentin Capshaw made his famous hypnotizing face. "I don't need a weapon."

"An actual weapon," I urged.

He gulped. "Um, I have a Swiss Army knife."

"Keep that on hand. Get a gun if you can."

"A... gun?"

Shen casually strolled to the door. "And watch your back."

"What do you mean, watch my back?"

"Someone might be trying to kill you," I reiterated.

Quentin Capshaw looked like the smallest man in the world right now. "Are you sure you don't want anything from me?" he asked meekly. "I liked this better when it was a scam."

"We can try to keep an eye on you, but there's no replacement for being cautious."

"You must have bodyguards," added Shen. "Pay them overtime." He walked out the door and waited for me to follow.

I felt bad about leaving, but we'd warned him. "Good luck, Quentin."

On the way down in the elevator, we discussed options. Shen was right that we had no idea when Manifesto would strike, but we both figured it would be before the Sunday show. That left three days, counting today. When we were downstairs, he called Darcy and caught her up. He said she'd watch the hypnotist.

It was getting late and my stomach was grumbling. Instead of going outside, I suggested we eat in. The hotel restaurant was a pseudo-hip gastropub with ample seating at high tables. We grabbed a couple of stools and ordered burgers.

After dipping a few fries in cheese sauce and chowing down, I figured we could bury the hatchet. "I can see why Simon wants you on this," I said. "You have useful talents. For a pessimistic know-it-all."

He chuckled. "You too, for an unstable hotshot."

I smiled. "I'm still not sure how much I like Darcy watching this guy. We don't know what Manifesto's capable of."

He set the remains of his burger down. "She's tougher than you think. She *wants* to do this. In all seriousness, the rogue outlaw rep you cultivate is overrated. Darcy's a pragmatist. If you're not with the Society, you're nobody."

"That's exactly the kind of peer pressure I can't get behind." I slurped the dregs of soda from between ice cubes and leaned in. "Can you honestly claim you love being their errand boy? What if you didn't need the money? Say you're a millionaire—would you still work for them?"

"I would. It's a purpose. It's a place to belong."

"Belong? You can have a life without them."

He shrugged. "I could do whatever I want. What's wrong with them?"

"I can't believe you're asking me that. My introduction to the Society was a little heavy-handed, to say the least. It's why you and I are always giving each other a hard time."

He shrugged and chomped at his burger again. I backed away from the subject. If I was honest with myself, I didn't know enough about the Society to be preachy. My distaste was more of a gut feeling.

"What about Diana? She in the club?"

"Maybe one day. She's been apprenticing with me."

"She's been doing more than that."

He laughed. "Yeah, well, what can I say?"

Despite being out of soda, I couldn't help myself with the fries. They were too good and I kept dousing them in cheese.

"I can see why you think they're bad," conceded Shen, referring back to the Society. "They're rich and they're protecting their interests. But half the time it means killing scumbags like Manifesto or..."

"Or me," I finished. "Which is the problem with personal interests. I was getting in the way of their good drug cartel money."

"It's not like that. We didn't kill you."

"Not for lack of trying."

"We just held you for Margo," he insisted.

"That's the same excuse the vampires are using on me. They wanna talk. Thing is, when talks like those go south, killing usually follows."

He shrugged. "I guess that's the way of things, sometimes."

I sighed. Shen wore rose-colored glasses when it came to his organization, but I was probably biased the opposite way. After all, the drug money and dirty politicians had been Connor's play. The Society just had to put up with him. And our past beef had more to do with me lugging a necromantic artifact of power around the city than anything else. In some ways, they had a point. I decided to take a shot. "What do you think of the idea that the Manifesto Killer is someone from the Society? Cleaning up the trash— that sort of thing?"

He killed his burger and shook his head. "You think you're smart, but you're not. You said it yourself. Manifesto's going after public figures. Performers. The fact that Marie was one of us was pure chance. The previous victims had no Society associations, and Quentin Capshaw couldn't find his ass with a mirror. I hate to break it to you, Cisco, but this is just a deluded psychopath going after low-hanging fruit."

It was a sound theory, but I didn't think it was a good idea to underestimate the killer. I didn't doubt the crazy part, but there was a reason Society leadership was taking this so seriously. I couldn't shake the feeling they knew something we didn't.

I licked my salty fingers and leaned back with a satisfied sigh. After last night's steak and this burger, I could do without meat for a week. As I enjoyed my full stomach, I spotted a security camera on the ceiling. I scanned the rafters and saw a few more.

"Hey, Quentin said his briefcase was stolen yesterday during lunch, right?" I pointed at the surveillance. "If we look up the footage, we might get a hit."

Shen looked around and slowly nodded. "You're not as dumb as you look."

I stood and tossed a few twenties on the table. "I got something to do right now. Can you take care of that?"

He paused. "Are you serious?"

"What?"

"You're ditching the investigation?"

"No. I just need to pick up my friend's kid from school."

"What happened to boots on the ground?"

"Come on, Shen. We don't both need to comb through security footage. Besides, your social hacking skills will come in handy. I would just be an 'unstable hotshot' in there."

He sniggered. "Sure, whatever. You can stick to the hard jobs, like picking up coffee and croquettes. Don't worry about me, Mr. Dedicated. I'll grab an Uber home." He stormed away from the table.

"Sorry I have a life," I called back, but it fell on deaf ears.

Jeez, buy the dude lunch and he cops an attitude. And just when I thought we were getting somewhere.

Chapter 25

I pulled the Firebird to the curb and scanned the rolling lawn of the park. Coconut Grove was a lush neighborhood of snaking roads and trees. There were nice areas and rough areas, of course, but this one was especially picturesque. Fran's magnet school was only a block away so tons of the kids congregated here when they got out. Full-on soccer games had been known to break out, but the kids mostly did whatever kind of socializing sixth graders got up to.

I didn't see Fran so I checked the car's clock against my phone's time. I was a few minutes early, likely due to Shen's incredible congeniality. I waited a minute and scanned the crowd some more, keeping an eye out for her friend Nicole as well.

With the phone in my hand I went through some of the Manifesto pictures. There wasn't a lot to go on. The ciphers were the only evidence that deserved some thought, but they were too opaque to make out. After Fran's lesson I would check with Evan and Emily to see what they had and go from there. I set the phone down and looked up at the trees through the open T-top roof of the Trans Am. The wind rustled through the leaves and I tried to relax.

A scream broke my reverie. I jerked my head around and zeroed in on it. Two boys fighting, over a textbook of all things. I took a breath and scanned the park again, growing unnaturally worried. Was this my instinct as an animist or was I just a worried father? Jeez, parenting was gonna make me go gray.

Finally, I spotted Fran at the other end of the park. She looked to be having—I wouldn't call it an argument—a disagreement with Nicole. Fran pulled her friend away from the far curb, but Nicole ignored her.

That was odd. Those two were thick as thieves. I frowned and watched as the two girls approached a parked black van.

I leapt out of the car and charged them. I couldn't be sure it was the same black van that had been following me, but it had signature Obsidian March markings. Limo tints. A windshield shade. Damn it.

"Fran!" I called as I ran. The side door swung shut. I skidded to a stop. Fran and Nicole were gone. Had they—

The van peeled out, leaving me certain the girls were inside. I realized Fran's magnet school wasn't technically in Brickell. It was outside Beaumont's protection. The vampires were coming after us.

I pulled a one-eighty and hurried back to the Firebird. I wasted no time pulling a *Dukes of Hazzard* move jumping into the open convertible, starting the car, and racing after that van.

Whoever was driving it was dead.

The residential streets were quiet, but I'd lost track of them. I swerved around a slow car with blinkers on and looked both ways down an intersection. Nothing. I cursed and floored the pedal, going from zero to sixty to zero in the span of a single block. As my tires screeched to a stop, I checked the streets. The van crossed one block over.

I growled and turned after them. They'd been zigzagging after the initial kidnapping and had almost lost me, keyword being almost. As I screamed around the corner, they merged onto a major artery ahead.

"Come on, Fran," I said to myself, adrenaline pumping fast and heavy. "Be smart. Stay alive."

I tried burning through to the street but had to veer away from a collision. Traffic was backed up in two lanes. The van swerved over double yellow lines and drove against light traffic going the opposite way.

I pulled across one lane but a Range Rover blocked my path through. I laid on my horn, but the lady either didn't notice or didn't care. Her car was stopped, and she was eyeing the mirror as she lined mascara on way too thick.

I honked, released a string of profanities, and flashed the universal gesture for "Get the fuck outta my way." She was oblivious.

I shifted into reverse and curled out of there by gunning it on the right side of the road. I flew by stopped traffic, quickly ran out of road, and drilled onto the sidewalk. It was a bumpy ride but a clear one.

The van ahead broke left down a street. By the time I

caught up I couldn't make it through. I overshot them until I could cut everyone off at a stoplight and hook around. I returned down the street and gassed it again, V8 screaming as they disappeared in the distance. Somewhere behind me, a police siren flared to life.

I didn't care about them. I wasn't the bad guy here. I wasn't even an outlaw at the moment. I had witnessed a double kidnapping and was in pursuit—no one would blame me for that. I was almost at the end of the block when the red and blues joined the chase. I skidded around the corner and hoped they hadn't seen me.

We were entering an industrial district now, with wide lanes and dead ends. It was a tactical error on the van's part, and it was only a matter of time before I cornered them. The Trans Am roared through a final turn and my eyes widened. The van was parked in the middle of the road, doors open. I hit the brakes and slammed to a halt.

"Fran!"

I leapt from the car with my shotgun ready. The smell of burnt rubber wafted over the hot asphalt. I flanked the van. A man in the driver seat hissed at me from the open door. Before he could move, I blasted him, center mass. A cone of fire tore him apart and blood gushed from his magical heart.

I furrowed my brow. I couldn't tell why the van had stopped. The police siren closed in. I ran to the far side of the van. The sliding door was open. The vehicle was empty. My heart fluttered.

I spun to the nearby warehouse. An access ramp beside the building sloped down into a subterranean parking lot. I charged that way.

"Fran!" I bellowed.

I turned the corner in the darkness and saw them. Nicole, huddled on the ground, hugging her knees. Fran stood between her and a fully transformed upir in a menacing stance, salivating wildly.

Except... he wasn't moving.

The vampire hissed, eyes white and wide, tongue blood-red. It trembled with rage. I rounded on them as Fran, eyes narrowed, held a single hand forward. She was shaking too, but her words came with practiced calm.

"Leave... us... alone."

She hissed. Something in the vampire snapped. He choked out some kind of embarrassing squeak that surprised even him. Then his heart exploded from his chest.

The blackened husk toppled to the cement and crumbled to ash.

"What the hell?" I said. I scanned the room for more vamps. We were alone. Fran was okay. Nicole was crying, but unhurt. I ran to Fran and hugged her. "What did you do?"

She blinked several times, having trouble focusing on me, or on anything for that matter. But she came back to me. "Null magic," she said, putting her hand on my chest over my heart. "You said it was their magical core."

I just stared at her in shock: that she had done what she did, that she was still alive. I had no idea null magic could disenchant the very body of a vampire.

"Police! Don't move!"

Footsteps stomped down the ramp. I dropped my shotty into the shadows where it vanished. I lifted my arms as two men surrounded us.

"Don't shoot," I said. "They're kids. They were kidnapped."

"Get down!"

The man threw me to the floor. My chest crunched ash that split apart and drifted away.

"It wasn't him!" snapped Fran. "Leave him alone!"

"They went that way," I said, pointing deeper into the warehouse. "I scared them off."

The cop grabbed my arm and pulled it behind my back as he cuffed me. The other cop lifted his pistol to the darkness and cracked a flashlight. "How many?"

"Two," said Fran. "Scary men wearing masks." She went to console Nicole, who was whimpering quietly. Fran sat beside her and latched on. "We scared them away," she said softly.

Chapter 26

"Thank God you're okay," cried Evan. He and Emily were simultaneously smothering their daughter from both sides. It seemed more dangerous than the vampires.

I sat in the hallway of the police station in handcuffs. I smiled and waited for them to get the worry out of their system. Who was I kidding? They were parents. After something like this, they would worry the rest of their lives. But I let them have their moment.

"You see?" I grumbled to the nearest officer. "Everything's fine."

These were City of Miami Police, thankfully. It hadn't made things easier on me per se, but they'd kept me on the holding bench while they notified Evan of what had occurred. I could only guess that he'd been too mortified to clear my name and that was why I was still in cuffs.

I cleared my throat loud enough to get Evan's attention. He peeled his face from his daughter's shoulder and spotted me. Evan Cross ground his teeth and came over.

"This guy says he's your friend, Lieutenant," said the

officer.

"Never seen him before in my life," he joked. "Looks like a kidnapper to me."

The other officer grabbed me roughly by the shoulders before Evan burst out laughing.

"Very funny," I grumbled. "You know I hate these things." I wiggled the iron bracelets around my waist to put them on display.

Evan nodded to the officer. "Is he booked?"

"Not yet. He broke some traffic laws but if he says what happened happened, he's a goddamn hero."

Evan smiled. "Don't say that. It'll go to his head. I'll take him from here."

The officer unlocked the handcuffs and walked away.

Evan sat on the bench beside me. "What the hell happened out there?"

"Well, it's not the statement I gave for the official police report, I'll tell you that much."

His eyes darkened. "The Obsidian March."

I nodded grimly. "Same way they nabbed that Gendra kid. Her school's not in Brickell."

Evan worked his jaw. "We'll need to move her."

"No, Dad. I like it there." Fran and Emily approached in a huddle. Emily wouldn't let go.

He shook his head. "You don't understand, honey."

"About the vampires? I know about them."

Evan hurriedly checked the hallway. We were alone.

"Cisco told me," she said.

His eyes narrowed. "He shouldn't bother you with that

stuff. And it's not safe at that school if they're after you."

"They were after Nicole, Dad. Not me. I got in the van to save her."

We all blinked dumbly, the thought having not occurred to any of us.

"You what?" he said. "That was a very dangerous thing to do, Francesca."

"Not really," she returned. My eyes shot to her in warning.

I successfully hid the gesture from Evan, but Emily caught me. "What is it?" she asked.

"It's nothing."

"Cisco," she warned in a low tone.

Evan swiveled his head between us. "What is it? Did you have something to do with this, Cisco?"

"No," I said truthfully. "I'm as surprised as you are. These guys don't know about Fran. In fact, she mentioned some creeps were bugging Nicole at the park yesterday afternoon, before our meeting with the vamps." I looked up at them with relief. "This was completely random."

Evan was still processing that, but Emily wasn't satisfied. "But..." she prodded.

"We have to tell them, Cisco," said Fran.

"Tell us what?"

I jutted my lip out. "Let's go somewhere more private first." I stood to go.

Evan nodded authoritatively. "Let's do that."

We marched down the hall just as Special Agent Rita Bell turned in and approached.

"Aw, hell," I said.

"What is this man doing out of custody?" she demanded to the general vicinity. "I asked for him to be held until I arrived." The officers in the distance spun around and pretended to be mid conversation. She rolled her eyes.

The tall woman stopped before me with hands on her hips, reminding me entirely too much of Evan. "Cisco Suarez. How is it you find yourself arrested twice in two days?"

"He's not under arrest," stated Evan. "He was a witness to a crime."

She stared at me pointedly.

"And what are you doing?" I fired back. "A police department goodwill tour?"

"I'm working a case. And I'm curious to know how you're involved."

"This is a completely separate matter," assured Evan.

Her indignant expression only heightened at his presence. "Where were you two days ago?"

I grumbled. "I didn't kill the fortune teller."

Her eyes suddenly lit up. She drew her gun in a flash, stepped backward to create distance, and kept it pointed at the low ready.

"What are you doing?" demanded Evan.

"Marie Devereaux's murder hasn't been announced to the public," she said hotly. "How do you know about that?"

She had me. She was digging into my alibi. Rita hadn't known about Devereaux yesterday—the letter had only come out this morning, after the scene was all cleaned up—

so now she wanted to question me about it. Only I wasn't supposed to know about it at all.

Evan stepped between Rita and Fran. "*Alleged* murder," he corrected. "Holster your weapon, Agent Bell. This is my family."

She lowered the firearm further. "He's my suspect and he has information he shouldn't have."

"About the Manifesto Killer," said Evan. "I told him about Marie Devereaux. City searched her home first. We handed over one of the letters to you. Of course we know about it."

A crowd of officers gathered close. Rita was suitably admonished and quickly holstered her sidearm. But then her lashes flared. "Have you told the locals what we talked about?" she asked me.

I shrugged. "He asked, I answered. I couldn't interfere with an active police investigation."

"I could bring charges against you."

"Cool down," ordered Evan. "We're supposed to be cooperating on this, aren't we?"

"This is a federal case. And since Devereaux hasn't been found yet, the only confirmed murder happened in Fort Lauderdale. Outside your jurisdiction."

"Wrong," he said. "Victim number two, one Javier Gomez, was recovered over a week ago in Homestead."

Both Rita and I simultaneously said, "Who?"

Evan turned to me and shook his head slightly. "The piper."

"Oh." I'd never actually gotten his name.

"What are you talking about?" demanded Rita. "There was no victim a week ago."

Fran broke from my grip and headed into the room where Nicole sat. Her parents hadn't arrived yet. Emily brushed her hair on the way past and made sure she was okay before returning.

The group of cops grew and closed in as Evan explained. "Sure there was. Manifesto killed a performance magician but accidentally burned his house down. We believe the mistake precluded a note."

She frowned. "You're required to forward us all related information, officer."

"Lieutenant. And it was just a normal homicide case until we linked it."

"To *my* case."

"Even though the first homicide was outside city limits, subsequent actions have proved the killer is operating in Miami. We're investigating this case alongside you, like it or not."

That actually shut her up for a second. The officer peanut gallery chuckled, enraging her even more. "Who's your supervisor, Lieutenant? In fact, belay that. I can put a call directly to your police chief if you like."

Evan smiled. "That's all right. I'm on special assignment running the DROP team for his boss, the mayor."

The officers couldn't contain their bellows. Rita bit her lip and ignored them. One cop behind her pulled out his ASP and put it up to his mouth. He made a sucking motion to the delight of everyone else. As Rita was staring right at me, I pretended not to notice the show behind her back. It was hard.

Rita remained rigid. "I want everything you have."

"Of course," replied Evan. "If you follow in kind."

She sneered. The officer behind her held the ASP to the side of his face but stood in profile. It achieved the masterful effect of appearing to deep throat the baton. I tried to keep a straight face, but when he tickled imaginary balls I lost it. Rita spun around. An officer clapped the offending cop on the back and he swung the ASP low and starting coughing.

"What is going on back there?" she demanded.

The cop coughed some more to sell it. "Sorry," he groaned. "I swallowed something."

An older cop with a gray mustache bellowed, "You sure did!" The entire crew exploded into guffaws.

Agent Bell shook her head. "It's a frat house in here. You all should be ashamed." She withdrew her card and slapped it on Evan's chest. "I expect to hear from you later today."

"I look forward to working with you. And look me up if you don't believe me."

"Oh, I will." She stormed down the hall. The officers parted and did their best to stifle their mirth, but it was a lost cause.

"Officer," snapped Evan. "That behavior is not appropriate in the workplace."

The room immediately sobered up. "Sorry, Lieutenant."

Emily shook her head and sighed. "Thank you, dear." She stormed off into the room with Fran.

Evan whispered, "Good technique, though."

We choked out laughs but immediately hushed as Emily peeked her head around the doorway.

Chapter 27

"Agent Bell's not wrong," I commented as we left the station. "I can't believe our taxes pay to arm those frat boys. For a second I was afraid it was gonna turn into a rap battle in there."

"To protect and serve sick burns," chuckled Evan. "And the kids do dance-offs these days."

Fran laughed. "No we don't, Dad."

We filed into Evan's unmarked car so he could drop me back off at mine. Luckily, Fran's protests had kept my car from being immediately impounded, despite the precaution to take me into custody and sort things out.

We arrived back at the warehouse and the Firebird was parked on the side of the street. The van was already towed. A stray police car lingered. The uniform reported to Evan that there was nothing odd about the building. It turned out the vamps had randomly stopped there—either to shake me or because of Fran's meddling with their life force.

I still didn't know how to tell Evan and Emily, but it was clear they needed to know. Em would take it better, I knew.

Even though she'd once sworn off spellcraft after almost ruining her life, she was an animist at heart. She understood the calling. Evan had no such fancies. He stopped his car beside mine.

"I still get to go to Cisco's house, right?" asked Fran.

Emily was sitting in the back seat next to her. "I don't think so, honey."

"Come on." Our lessons were important to her.

"No," said Evan. "I'm canceling my plans tonight. We're gonna stick together as a family and talk things over."

"Cisco."

My little girl appealed to me with her eyes, but I softly shook my head. "You should listen to them, Fran. What you went through was a big deal, even if you feel fine right now. Just relax and take things easy."

She pouted but didn't object. She was a strong girl, much stronger than any of us had realized, maybe. Things weren't as I'd feared. The events today didn't paint Fran the victim, they made her the hero. She'd willingly jumped into a van of vampires to save her friend, and although I helped with the driver, she'd practically taken care of the situation all by herself. It was an understatement to say I was both proud and terrified.

"Should I swing by?" I chanced. "See what we can get on that crystal ball?"

"Can we just get a night without magic?" Evan snapped. He stared hard at the dashboard.

Emily shook her head. "You'd better not, Cisco. We just... need a family night."

Evan's eyes locked on her as she said the words. She hadn't meant to exclude me in that way, but there it was. I bit down and nodded, trying not to show emotion.

"I'll call in the morning then."

She nodded with a silent apology in her eyes.

I shut the door and watched as they pulled out. Evan had the presence of mind to wait until my car started after them. Maybe he wanted to make sure the cop didn't hassle me as I left. Then we were both on the same road going to separate destinations.

I made sure we weren't followed again. My confirmation wasn't especially comforting. Not only was the Obsidian March trolling for humans, but they had a hard-on for me as well. For all I knew, the feds were keeping tabs on me too. And all the while my new home was nestled in the territory of a Brickell restaurant mogul-cum-crime boss.

The sun was still out so it was early enough to be productive. I was reminded of that as I noticed a missed call from Shen sans voice mail. I considered hooking up with him again, putting some hours in. It might mend fences with the chain of command. Then again, I needed some time to decompress. I swiped away the notification and called Milena.

"Hiya!" she chirped. Her positive attitude was a far cry from the last time I'd seen her. It had the effect of immediately lifting my spirits.

"You sound better."

"I am! I was just in a funk last night. Probably from being mind-assaulted by a vampire. Sorry about that."

"Don't apologize."

"Other than that part the night was actually pretty fun, Cisco. I forgot how exciting it was to hang out with you."

I laughed. "Adrenaline junkie. You see? You like me."

She snorted. "You think chemistry is all about excitement, don't you?"

"Isn't it? Chemical reactions are based on heat."

"Oh, so that's all it takes?"

"Nah," I admitted. Then I decided to go for it. "Chemistry's also about physical contact. Which is why you should come over."

The silence was deafening.

"Or I can swing by Midtown. It's been awhile since I've been to your place."

"That sounds really fun, Cisco." Score. Then Milena cleared her throat. "But Gavin's on his way over as we speak."

"Oh." Cars crashing. Dive bombers plummeting to the ocean. "Two dates in two days. You must really like this guy. What makes him the one?"

"Please. I never said he was the one. He's a nice guy who has his life in order."

"You mean he doesn't have issues."

"I didn't say that."

"Bet he doesn't battle ghosts and vampires," I teased.

"Some would say that's a good thing. But don't take it the wrong way. He's gentle. He's kind. He's a nice guy, and I feel bad about the way I ditched him last night."

"How many dates is that?" I asked suddenly.

"What?"

"How many dates?"

She took a long breath. "Tonight makes eight or nine or ten. I don't know. Who counts those things?"

"Ten dates and you still haven't had sex?!?"

"What? Cisco, I'm not having this conversation with you."

"Fine, but you know I'm right. I'm wearing you down. In fact, if you wanna ditch him mid date again and give me a call, I'll be around."

She laughed. "In your dreams."

She didn't know the half of it. We both laughed for a minute, but what started out genuine became forced. I didn't want to overstay my welcome. "I guess I'll leave you to it," I said.

"Okay, Cisco. I'm glad you called."

"Yeah. Nice talking." And then, "Hey! Why don't we do something tomorrow night then? I guarantee it'll be more fun than whatever Gavin has planned."

She sighed. "Don't make this a competition, Cisco. But that sounds fun. If you promise not to turn it into a dating situation, you have a deal."

"No date here. Just a couple of chill platonic bros hanging out," I said sarcastically.

She laughed. "You sure you still want to hang if you're not gonna get in my pants?"

"What kind of thing to say is that, Milena? Of course I wanna hang. Let's do it."

"Okay, then. Look, I gotta go."

"Yeah. Cool. Talk to you later."

I hung up before I said something else stupid. Maybe I'd finally get some time with Milena, but it didn't feel like a win. Not when Gavin was seeing her tonight. I made the rest of the drive in a detached stupor. When I finally parked the car in the underground lot of my condo, I decided I felt worse than before.

The elevator ride up was a lonely one because I knew my place was empty. When I unlocked the front door, I ripped off a notice from the HOA and took it inside to read. Apparently my last payment had been declined by the credit card company. I immediately called them up, knowing Carmela Flores would begin eviction proceedings in a second given the slightest provocation.

Apparently, Fraud Protection had canceled the card because they believed I was dead. I was already braced for the issue because this was the third time it had happened.

"I don't care if you have a copy of my death certificate," I fumed. "I can assure you I'm very much alive and can send you the documents to prove it."

Ugh, modern necromancy was a nightmare. It must've been so easy in the Middle Ages to resurrect from the dead without needing to wade through a bureaucratic mess of paperwork.

I popped a beer and chugged down, phone at my ear. It was gonna be a crappy night.

Chapter 28

Milena never called back, and my adolescent mind couldn't stop wondering how far Gavin was getting on date number ten. Between that and the Manifesto case, I was up half the night.

Thankfully the morning proceeded as planned. I cooked up some *café con leche*, touched base with Emily, and headed over right away. I was eager to start another day on the right foot and hopefully not have it hijacked by a kidnapping. And I wanted to have something new before the next time Simon called.

"Fran holding up?" I asked Evan as he led me upstairs. She was playing with her younger brother in the den.

"She's fine. Nerves of steel, that one."

"Takes after you."

"I was gonna say the same about you."

I bit my lip and smiled. With the lessons I'd been giving her, he didn't know how right he was.

Emily was upstairs in her bedroom. "Wow, you guys," I said. "I feel like I visit your bedroom much more than is healthy with platonic friends."

"Shut up," she muttered, unamused.

"I'm just saying. Maybe you should invest in a war room or something."

"Let's just get the spellcraft over with," said Evan.

"Look at you using the proper terminology. You're all growed up."

"After meeting Agent Bell in person, I'd do anything to beat her to the punch. You'd just better hope we have something here because the knife was a bust. The blood was from a young-adult male and there were no prints or aberrant DNA."

"Damn."

Emily decided to kick me while I was down. "The salt water did a number on the crystal as well. It soaked almost a day. I buried it with purifying stones to try to undo the damage, but it was too late." She revealed the crystal ball on a piece of soft leather in the middle of the bed. There was a slight crack in it.

"It's destroyed," I said, downtrodden.

"Not completely. I attempted a scry this morning and the Intrinsics were too hostile. It's a good thing we gave it extra time to cool down, otherwise we would've lost it all."

"Did you see anything?"

"I didn't get that far, and I was afraid to try again after it cracked. Remember when I had trouble finding Fran with my crystal?"

I nodded. "I helped dim the light with my shadows."

"I was hoping you could do that again."

I scratched my head. "Wouldn't that be even more unstable?"

"Possibly, but the energy is too erratic now. It needs something to soothe it, bring it down to make it readable. Can you do that?"

"I'll try."

If she said this would work, I believed her. We'd done this once before to great effect. It was funny how sometimes opposites working together were stronger than either alone.

Emily massaged the air around the crystal and intoned under her breath. She was a skilled white witch even if scrying wasn't her specialty. When it came to seeing the future she was no Marie Devereaux, but she brought the goods.

"I think..." started Emily, peering into the ball, "I think I see a reflection."

I squinted and drew closer, using the shadows to tone down the light's intensity. It made for a dim scene, but a picture came into focus. We all leaned in to see it.

The image was skewed. Marie Devereaux's face was rounded, with squished eyes and an enlarged nose. Her mammoth-sized hands hovered over our view.

"This is a reflection of her final session," whispered Emily. She concentrated and the scene exploded outward, nearly filling the room.

"You come to me a troubled man," said Marie in a dramatic whisper.

"Yes," answered a hoarse voice.

I spun around to see a man in a gray Dolphins hoodie

and sensible working jeans. He was a bit overweight, but mostly normal-sized with a nondescript face.

That's Manifesto? I'd figured him for a scarier persona. I mean, he wasn't even wearing the skin of his victims or anything.

Marie rolled her head as if in a trance. "You seek something to ease the burden."

"Yes," the man said, but the fortune teller didn't respond. She was intent on the performance. Marie continued teasing the crystal, and while we could see their faces we couldn't see what she saw with her spellcraft.

"You hurt," she whispered. "Tell me what it is you desire."

The man grunted. "Aren't you supposed to tell me?"

"The truth will come in time. Have no worries. I'd like you to tell me what it is you *think* you want first."

He frowned. "Fair enough. I want it to end. Can you tell me when it will end?"

"Your life?" she asked with an arched eyebrow.

"No. My tribulation."

She took a patient breath and rubbed the crystal. "All life is a test, sir."

"Life is easy," he scraped out. "Death is the true test."

Marie Devereaux chewed her lip, unsure what to do with his query. I realized that simply seeing glimpses of the future wasn't enough to get a full understanding. If she was to truly guide people to better paths, she had to understand them. Get a feel for them. We were watching spellcraft and dime-store psychology all at once.

"Hold my hands," she commanded. Their arms wrapped around us in the real world as they placed locked hands on either side of the crystal ball. "You seek an end to your trials, but you must first remove yourself from them if you are ever to find the way out."

He accepted the apparent truth with anticipation. "Yes."

Marie pumped her forehead back and forth, rhythmically, feeling out the aura extruded from the stranger. "You think yourself trapped."

The man's eyes flickered.

"It is not so," she assured. "Desperation slicks from your being like oil, but there is no need to drown."

Between scrying, Marie stole glances at his reactions. It was obvious to me that, while insightful, most of what we'd seen so far was a show.

She was a performer. A deceiver.

The corner of the stranger's mouth crooked up.

"I *am* trapped," he said, "but I don't seek escape. I was promised life eternal."

Marie's brow furrowed ever so slightly. Who didn't want to escape a trap? "The fish in the bowl bumps against walls. It sees more. Imagines more. Yet it could never comprehend the ocean."

Manifesto's face twisted. "No. This isn't what I want." His grip tightened and he rocked with agitation. "Tell me what you see."

She was losing him, and it was obvious. She flashed a hurried nod and pulled a hand away. The man reluctantly gave it up. Finally, the fortune teller traced a finger around the curvature of the crystal.

"Well then," she said, bringing her chin up. "You are... afflicted."

He leaned close, face in darkness. "Yes. Tell me my future. How many more?"

Marie's eyes quivered as she peered through dimensionality. "You're forced to do horrible things..."

"Not forced. It is my holy charge. How many more?"

Marie tried to pull her other arm away but the man held tight, white knuckles trembling. She attempted to continue without distress. "How many?" she asked, slightly out of sorts. She shook it off and stared deeper into his future. Into hers. Marie's eyes snapped open.

Manifesto grabbed her free hand and pinned it to the table. He leaned forward and growled, "How many more must I kill?"

Marie's entire body trembled, horrified gaze fixed on Manifesto's face. Plain, nondescript, but his eyes were perfectly round, like dinner plates, and lidless, with large fixed pupils. Black tears rolled down his cheeks. She recoiled, but his strength was too much.

"You and the flower maker are just charlatans, aren't you?"

"Please..."

Manifesto groaned in pain and frustration, body racked by anguish, but perfect open eyes not so much as quivering. "See not," he growled. "Show not."

He flipped the table into her and the entire room jarred loose. Evan, Emily, and I were so focused on this reality that we nearly lost our balance in the bedroom. A shambled image jerked all around us. I struggled to maintain concentration, but Marie Devereaux's piercing scream penetrated my mind like a lobotomy pick. The shadow snapped free. The light crackled. And Marie's yellowed crystal ball shattered into a thousand pieces.

Chapter 29

I grabbed ahold of Evan and Emily and tore them into the shadow as a crystalline grenade went off. Jagged projectiles peppered the walls and ceiling. The overhead light cracked into pieces. A large slug embedded itself into the couple's espresso-colored dresser.

It was all so fast and disorienting that they jerked free as soon as we rematerialized.

"What the fuck was that?" asked Evan, checking his wife's face for glass.

"She's fine, Evan."

They hugged each other as they recollected their bearings.

"Did you see his eyes?" asked Emily.

"Yeah, they weren't human eyes. They weren't mammalian."

"Snake eyes?"

I shook my head. "Maybe."

She breathed heavily. "But I thought Manifesto detested spellcraft."

Evan ground his teeth. "He's a Nether fiend, like the vampires."

"No," I said. "I don't think so. I think he's human."

"But you just said—"

"There's something wrong with him. You heard Marie Devereaux. He's forced to kill."

"So he doesn't die himself."

"No," I said. "It's just the opposite. He wants to die." They looked at me uncertainly, but for the first time everything was clicking into place. "Agent Bell thought Manifesto was claiming to be invincible, to be a dead man like me, because he initially wrote that he would never die. Except he wasn't talking about this life, he was talking about the next."

Evan gritted his teeth. "You're saying he wants to be caught. To be killed."

"Whenever his trials are over, anyway. He said death was the true test. Manifesto hopes to be rewarded for his actions. He's continuing this string of killings as long as necessary. Until it kills him. This is his final death march."

Emily nodded. "The afterlife fits with the trappings of a holy mission. All his talk of angels and being chosen."

Evan traded glances with us. "Do I need to point out the obvious? This guy's obviously *not* on a holy mission."

"I know. I know." I put my hand up, trying not to get distracted from the vision we'd witnessed. Manifesto's eyes were seared into my brain. I now understood why Marie's son had run from the terrifying sight. But there was more. Black tears. The anguish. "I think he's cursed."

Emily pressed her lips together. "He was certainly suffering. His voice was strained. Maybe he's been dealing with this for a while and killing is the only way to alleviate his agony."

We didn't really know what to say to that. But it did track in a twisted sort of way.

"He mentioned a flower maker..." I massaged my eyes. "See not. Show not. Those were the last two clues. Marie was the fortune teller; she saw things. I was pretty sure Quentin Capshaw was the one who *showed* things but..."

I marched to the door. Fran sprinted past me into the room to find out what the commotion was about.

"Shen's an illusionist," I realized. "Spellcraft that *shows*. Yesterday he spawned a flower in his hand to display his power. If Manifesto knew about Marie, he knows about him. These murders aren't random."

I stomped down the stairs and picked my phone from my pocket. Interestingly, I had another missed call from Shen. I dialed him and went straight to voice mail. "Damn it, Shen, call me back," I barked.

Evan followed me outside. "What's the plan?"

"I'm touching base with the Society. You can't come. They don't want people to know about them, especially the authorities."

"You think they're in danger?"

I opened my car door and sat. "I don't know, but if anybody can handle it, it's them."

Evan clapped my shoulder through the open T-top. "Watch your back."

"You too."

On the way, I called Shen again. When he didn't pick up I tried Simon, who actually answered.

"The wonder boy checks in," he said magnanimously.

"Are you absolutely, positively sure Manifesto can't be someone in the Society?"

"You're still on this? It wouldn't make sense, Cisco. And Shen doesn't have anything to gain."

"Not him. Has he pissed anyone off? Did Marie?"

"I mean, Marie was outspoken. Shen can be a braggart but he's too low on the food chain to seriously piss anybody off." Simon cleared his throat. "So let me get this straight. First you think Shen's a suspect, now you think he's a target?"

"I'm not sure what to think. Where's Shen now?"

"I talked to him earlier. I figured you guys were meeting at the laundromat."

"Good. I'm already on the way."

"I'll call Darcy," he added. "Round up the troops, and all that. I'm a little ways out but I'll be there."

"Make sure you are." I ended the call.

I was starting to have doubts. I wasn't sure it was smart to pull Darcy off Quentin. At the same time, getting the whole band together was just what the doctor ordered. If we were organized and had a plan, Manifesto wouldn't be able to come at us. Better yet, I was starting to formulate a plan to dangle a little chub for the killer. If he wanted Shen so badly, maybe we could give him the perfect opportunity.

I pulled into the parking lot of the strip mall and spotted

the illusionist getting out of his black Mercedes. Luck was on our side. I honked several times to get his attention. He'd recognize the Firebird anywhere. I parked diagonally over two spots in front of the laundromat and hopped out to intercept him.

"That's a dick move," said Shen. "They're both fifteen-minute parking spots."

"We don't want anybody dropping off their Sunday dresses. Why didn't you pick up your phone?"

"Why didn't you?"

I hissed at his juvenile antics. "You might be a target."

"Yeah, I just got off the phone with Simon. He said you thought I was in danger."

"Could be. I saw Manifesto in the crystal ball. He was a normal-looking guy wearing a Dolphins hoodie. He all but said he was going after a flower maker next."

He paused thoughtfully. "He said that?"

"It makes sense after Devereaux. See not, show not. You're an illusionist. It makes sense."

"It doesn't make any sense. Devereaux was a performer. Quentin's a performer. Manifesto is going after animists in the limelight."

I threw my hands up. "Maybe that's how it started. I don't know. He knew about and killed Marie's kid just the same. He wasn't a performer. I just don't think his choice of victim is entirely random."

"You're overthinking this, Cisco. I admit I was wrong about you, but you're overthinking it." He flashed a CD case in his hand.

"What's that?"

"Security footage from the burger joint. You remember boots on the ground and knocking on doors, don't you? The theft of Quentin's briefcase was captured on camera. The hypnotist went to the bathroom and a middle-aged man slipped by and snatched it as if planned. He was wearing a gray Dolphins hoodie."

My words caught in my throat. That was him.

"You want me to say it?" asked Shen. "Fine. Your hunch was right, and I was wrong. You have a good eye for this stuff. Come inside. I'll show you the video."

I was... stunned. Not that I'd been right with my previous leap of faith. It was a gamble but a sensible one. It was just that I'd felt so sure about things a few seconds ago. Manifesto's circular eyes flashed through my brain. I tried to shake them away. Had seeing the vision screwed with my judgment?

The lone chime introduced us as we entered the dry cleaner. Half the overhead lights were off. It was quiet.

"That's strange," noted Shen. "Someone should be at the counter by now." He moved towards the back. I gripped his shoulder to stop him.

"I'm telling you, Shen. We need to be careful."

He swallowed and scanned the lifeless room. It was a snapshot of how it appeared every day, except it now lacked the vitality that made a room warm. The cleaner seemed closed for business, but the open sign was still on display and the door wasn't locked.

Shen turned to me and dipped his head in

acknowledgment. His entire body flickered. I released him and stepped back. He was still there, unchanged. That was strange. He set the CD case on the counter and crept toward the back room. I drew my shotgun and followed, blinking unsteadily.

"Diana?" he called. "Baby?

No answer.

Shen took a breath and entered the back room. A flurry of motion exploded faster than I could react.

Chapter 30

Shen spun to the side, alert to a threat. Someone barreled into him, pinning him to the wall with what could only be called a sword. They struggled in a disorienting fashion. Both attacker and defender seemed confused. They twisted around each other awkwardly. I pointed my shotgun but they were too entwined to risk it.

I charged through the narrow doorway. The man's attention snapped to me, off guard. It was him. Manifesto. He slashed in a defensive arc and retreated deeper into the room.

I burst through but suddenly tripped for no apparent reason. The weapon lurched from my hands. I tumbled to the floor. For a second I thought I'd run into Shen, but he was drooping against the wall where he'd been impaled. A line of thick blood traced down to his slumped form on the floor.

Manifesto, still holding the sword, went for my shotgun. Shadow lashed out and knocked it away. The gun slid to the back wall. I hopped to my feet and he stuttered in place, hesitating just long enough for me to square off with him.

And when we did, I have to admit I was a little disappointed. The Manifesto Killer was just a normal guy. A little past his prime, a little extra cushioning around the belly, and slightly balding. Even his gray football hoodie was so unimpressively... regular.

Of course, his inhuman eyes ruined any sense of normality. Large round pupils dominated his visage. They were fixed in place, forcing Manifesto to snap his head around like a bird to appraise me.

"You're one of them," he said knowingly.

I risked a glance at Shen. He wasn't breathing anymore. Diana lay in a pool of blood, half obscured by the counter. Manifesto had laid his trap and I hadn't stopped him in time. I was damn sure gonna stop him now.

"That's right," I fumed. "I'm one of them."

"Then it's my holy duty to remit you from this world."

I chortled. "Sorry to disappoint you, but I think you're punching a little out of your weight class."

I thrust my hand forward. A javelin of shadow exploded from the wall. Manifesto's head twitched to the side in surprise. He was many things, but he wasn't a physically gifted opponent. The slow man had no hope of dodging the strike.

Instead, the spear simply passed through him without effect.

"What the?"

His laugh was full of scorn. "I've been tasked with hunting magicians. Spellcraft doesn't work against me. I'm fearless in the face of your power."

My eyes widened as he came in with a downward sword swipe. I raised my armored forearm to meet the blow. It struck with a flash of turquoise. Manifesto recoiled, nearly losing his grip on the weapon.

"What's this?" he spat.

My tattoo pulsed strangely, my arm stung, but the armor had held. Maybe it was because the rune was defensive, or maybe it was due to being grounded in physical place by ink. Either way, Manifesto had failed to counter it. By his quivering face, it might've been the first time he'd seen such resilience.

He pulled a pistol from the small of his back. I slipped into the darkness as he unloaded on me. The first few shots were wild. After two more, he realized the bullets were unable to find me. Instead of panicking, he let off a few controlled shots and walked to the door. His pistol turned to Shen's head and blew a hole in the side of it. He fired at me again to keep me pinned. Then he ran from the room.

I sprinted to the doorway. The second I poked my head out, Manifesto fired. I pulled back and stood there, staring at Shen's dead body. I turned to get a better angle on Diana and confirmed she wasn't moving. The chime at the front door went off and I seethed.

"What am I doing? I can take a bullet or two."

My skin had been enchanted with zombification toxins that made me somewhat bulletproof, at least to small civilian rounds. I was never totally confident in its ability, since the physics and dynamics of such things were a total crapshoot in real situations, now being a prime example. But I was angry enough that my apprehensions didn't matter. I was willing to get hurt if it meant putting this animal down.

I burst into the front room and chased the killer outside. A motorcycle roared to life and sped down the lot. He wasn't wearing a helmet or jacket now, but it was the same blue motorcycle I'd seen in traffic behind us. The rider who'd freaked out when I walked right by him holding a shotgun. The motherfucker had been following us the whole time.

I charged. He was too fast. He sped off and skipped into the street. I spun to the Firebird and deflated as I reached the driver's door. Manifesto's sword was impaled in the front tire.

"Shit!" I screamed, kicking the wheel.

Strangely, I heard the motorcycle return. I ran toward it before noticing it was red. Darcy. I flagged her down and we converged.

"That was Manifesto! On the bike!"

She was stunned for a moment as she processed my words.

"He got Shen," I said.

Her face tightened. Darcy revved her bike and gazed down the street. I wondered if it was already too late to catch up, but she was determined.

"All right," I said, approaching the bike to mount up behind her.

She accelerated into a spin and kicked me out of the way before bursting out of the lot on her own.

"Dolphins hoodie," I yelled. The sports affiliation wasn't a big help in Miami, but the hoodie wouldn't be a popular choice in the heat. I ran to the street and watched her, mad that I hadn't warned her about his magic resistance.

"Damn bratty punk," I muttered. "Thinks she can take on the whole world by herself." It took a full three seconds to realize people often accused me of the same thing. Hi, Cisco, my name's Karma, and I'm a raging cunt.

After idling there another minute, I felt about as useless as I could. I wasn't sprinting anywhere in cowboy boots and my car was out of commission. My eyes trailed to Shen's Mercedes. I could get his keys from inside, but there was no way I'd be able to track Manifesto by then.

Fuck. The visceral back-room scene crammed into my head and wouldn't get out. I'd thought Shen had a chance there before that final bullet to his brain. At least I'd saved him the dignity of having Manifesto take a piece of him as a souvenir.

To make matters worse, the logistical hot mess of the situation started to dawn on me. Call me an asshole but there was a giant crime scene to consider. I figured it wasn't my problem and I would stay out of it, but my shotgun was still in there and boy wouldn't Special Agent Bell just love to find it at a Manifesto murder.

I hissed, scoped down the street one last time in case the killer was dumb enough to circle back, and made my way inside the dry cleaner. As the adrenaline started to wear off, my worry for Darcy inversely increased. Then I wondered if there was a tiny chance Diana was still alive. I stepped to the back room and grimaced at the pathetic sight of Shen crumpled against the wall. My eyes dragged over to Diana's body. She was half sitting up.

"What the hell?" I said, jumping like a kid at a horror movie.

Suddenly, Shen's body at my feet flickered and faded away. The blood too. It just disappeared.

The illusionist reappeared, propping up Diana's body. She wasn't sitting up—he was holding her.

Anger flooded me. "You played dead?"

He sat there sobbing, Diana in his arms. "Did you get him?"

I recalled seeing the awkward melee as the killer struggled with Shen's illusion. Tripping over something—some*one*—that wasn't there. "Did *I* get him? What about you?"

"He surprised me. I let him think he got the drop on me, all right? My priority was to get to Diana."

I stomped toward him. "You could've given me a bit of help! He was distracted by me!" I passed him and scooped up my shotgun. "You could've picked this up and shot him in the back instead of leaving me on an island!" My rage was boiling over at his display of cowardice.

In the face of my anger, Shen attempted to pull himself together. He went to wipe his face but regarded the blood on his hands. He set Diana down and wiped with his shoulder instead. That was when I noticed Manifesto had tagged him. Shen's button-up was slashed across his side. His entrance into the back room under the guise of an illusion was clever, but there hadn't been ample space to hide in. Manifesto had gotten lucky with a wild swing.

Then I realized I was screaming at a wounded man with a dead girlfriend. He'd ignored the battle and turtled, but maybe it had broken him.

"I need to wash this off," he said, rising and heading to the bathroom.

I shook my head. This was a mess. At least Shen was alive. I dropped my shotgun into the safety of the shadows and called Simon. I reported the news in detached precision and hung up before he could gather a response. I didn't want to hear it.

Chapter 31

I studied Diana's body. She might've been dead for an hour, with Manifesto lying in wait for Shen. Then again, her body hadn't been stripped or butchered past the stab wounds. I considered invoking spellcraft to see Diana's last moments of life or speak with her. In the end I didn't think it would help, and I didn't want to do that to Shen. I'd already seen Manifesto face to face.

Shen returned from the bathroom, shirtless but still wearing a tie. His chest and stomach were well-muscled. I would've made a Chippendale's joke but even I knew it was poor taste. Shen held his bloody shirt to the wound at his side.

"I got something for that," I offered, digging into my belt pouch.

"I don't want that toxic crap," he said. "It's not too bad."

I shrugged. He seemed to be pulling himself together pretty well. Night and day, actually. "I've got a spare shirt in my car."

"Yeah."

We emerged into a day so bright it made our moods all the more stark, like shadows. For some reason I thought of that scene from *Reservoir Dogs* when Mr. Blonde, after spending so much time in a dingy safe house, casually strolls outside to his car to get a can of gasoline. We were outside in broad daylight in clear view of maybe a hundred people, and not a soul was privy to what had happened indoors. To what was thirty feet away. I couldn't shake it.

I opened the trunk and grabbed one of a few spare tank tops. Ruined clothes were a job hazard and I had a look to maintain. Under present circumstances, I didn't mind letting Shen borrow that look. I tossed him the shirt and he gingerly stretched it over his head and his makeshift bandage.

I shut the trunk and looked through the rear windshield right to the dash. It hit me, right there.

"The dash cam," I said, rounding my car and wondering if I had a day's worth of data.

Shen came around and eyed the sword in my tire.

"Manifesto escaped on a motorcycle. He was the same rider behind us when I caught the vamps tailing us."

He scrunched his face as he considered the ramifications. "So?"

"So I must've freaked him out. He thinks he's just a normal guy following me and I get out of the car with a shotgun. He practically craps his pants and drops his bike. Then he sees I was scoping somebody else, but still wants nothing to do with me. He's still hiding, right? He tells me off and speeds away, right past my car." I tapped the video recorder. "Right past my dash cam. We could get his license. His address."

Shen was dumbfounded. At a total loss for words.

The hum of Darcy's sports bike announced her arrival. I stepped out of the car as she pulled up beside us.

"You're okay," she said to Shen.

I pointed to her scraped up motorcycle. "Your bike's not."

She clenched her jaw. "I had him. He was right there. I pulled out my Hecate fetish and tried to nail him to the street. Nothing happened."

"He's running some kind of magic resistance. I couldn't hurt him either."

"It's worse than that. He uses spellcraft. Since I was holding my statue, I was riding one-handed and couldn't maintain the best control. Something black came out of nowhere and hit my bike. I crashed."

"That can't be. Maybe he has allies. A vampire?"

"Way too small and in broad daylight."

I moved to study her bike. Shen remained distant, understandably distracted. I picked at a melted scrape on the engine block.

"What is that?" she asked.

"I don't know. It's like acid. And you dropped your bike on the other side. What could have melted this?"

"Spellcraft."

I gritted my teeth. It didn't fit.

Shen shook his head. "We can't kill this guy."

"Sure we can."

"Our spellcraft doesn't hurt him."

"Your illusion tricked him. My defenses held up too."

"He's some kind of monster."

"He's just a normal man. Maybe normal is relative, but I've faced worse."

"I fucking haven't." Shen grimaced and paced a few yards away.

Some onlookers nosed around for evidence of wrongdoing—they'd probably heard the gunshots. Their inspection passed over us as we were acting normal enough.

I pulled Manifesto's sword from my tire. "We should get inside." Darcy parked her bike and came in. Shen reluctantly followed.

Careful not to get prints on the sword, I hurried ahead and set it by Diana's body. I rushed back to stop Darcy from entering the back room. "You don't wanna go in there," I said, blocking her path.

"I wanna see," she said. She brushed past me and I didn't stop her. I moved to the front room where Shen was idly staring out the window.

"The Society's out of town," he mused. "They left us to deal with this fuck. Maybe we should get out of here too."

"You wanna run?"

He turned to me. "Shouldn't we? It's the smart play."

"What about Diana?"

"She's dead. I can't help her. Besides, it's not like she was the love of my life or anything."

I flushed. "What the hell kind of thing to say is that?"

He palmed his forehead. "Fuck. I don't know. She was a

good girl. She didn't deserve this. But it's the truth. Diana and I had another three or six months tops before we went our separate ways. I'm still alive. I wanna keep it that way."

I turned and saw Darcy leaning in the doorway, watching us with the same forlorn expression she'd worn after seeing the body of Marie's son. Shen was only slightly embarrassed she'd overheard.

"This guy's smarter than us," he reasoned. "You were right, Cisco. The murders aren't random. Maybe they were at first, but this guy's directly targeting the Society now."

I growled. "What the fuck good is a secret society if you can't catch a serial killer?"

"That's just it. Secrecy is more important than catching killers. That's how we stay hidden. Manifesto is threatening to expose us."

Darcy stomped forward. "That's exactly why we need someone to stop him."

He snorted. "Well, we should send professionals then."

Darcy hooked her arms across her chest. "He saw you?" she asked me.

I nodded.

"He knows you now, then. Me too. You gonna run?"

I set my jaw. "I've never run from anything in my life. Except zombie pit bulls. And giant Aether squid whales." I cleared my throat. "Actually, running is often a tactically superior strategy. But I'm not letting Manifesto chase me out of my own town."

She took a moment to mumble and nod to herself. I'd seen this before. She was gathering her courage. "I don't

Domino Finn

want to run either." She turned to Shen, but the illusionist remained quiet. "What can we do?"

"I think I have the asshole on camera. He was following us the other day and sped past my car. I'll put on a spare tire and check the video on my computer at home."

"Sounds like a plan. Let's go." She pressed outside.

"Hold up," I said as we followed her out. "I let Simon know what happened. I imagine he's sending the cleaners to... the cleaner. Shouldn't you wait for him?"

"Screw that," she said. "I'm done sitting on the sidelines. I'm following you."

"I'll wait here," Shen called back. He stood propping the front door open. "I want to say goodbye."

I chewed my lip and nodded.

"We'll call you with news," said Darcy.

"Don't bother. I'm... I'm not pursuing this anymore. I'm heading upstate. Manifesto was waiting for me in here. He thinks he killed me. I'm gonna let him keep believing that."

I almost said something but Darcy squeezed my arm, her features hard. I often wondered what kind of friendship they had, now more than ever. It never seemed very strong, but maybe she was giving him what he needed.

Me? I was disappointed Shen couldn't find the will to man up. It's not like he was a complete stranger to action, even if his skills were on the more visual spectrum. Manifesto had killed his girl. The least he could do was reward him with a slow death.

Maybe that was easy to say coming from a tough-guy ex-zombie hit man.

236

"Fine," I said, relenting. I turned to the Firebird and dug out the jack.

Chapter 32

Darcy followed me back, and I made sure she was the only one. No Dolphins hoodies or windowless minivans in sight. By the time we rolled into Brickell, I suspected we would be left alone completely. By the Obsidian March, anyway. I was still trying to figure how the serial killer fit in. That black form that had attacked Darcy still had me worried.

The parking elevator let us out in the lobby. We made our way through the decadent space to the main building elevator. I hurried but Carmela Flores was like a viper lying in wait. She struck right as the doors were about to close and joined us inside for the ride up.

"The payment cleared, Carmela. I confirmed it with the credit company last night."

She sucked in her cheeks. "I expect nothing less, Mr. Suarez, and must warn you that being late in the future may carry severe penalties."

"Can't you give a guy a break? You know about my tragic past. Every now and then I get flagged as a dead person again. It's out of my control."

"I can sympathize," she said in the most unsympathetic voice ever, "but rules are rules. Without them we'd be outlaws. And we certainly wouldn't be voted most coveted condominium in Brickell, would we?"

I rolled my eyes. "That would be tragic." Darcy glared at my HOA director and chewed gum loudly. I was hoping she didn't go for one of those eighties-movies bubble blows. That would've crossed the line.

Carmela was unruffled. "Also, about the strange men and women you keep company with..."

"Strange?" complained Darcy. Carmela eyed the carved statuette of the god Hecate in her grip. The teenager moved it behind her back.

"Yes," continued Carmela. "Some residents have concerns that you're running an illegal business from your home. That's expressly forbidden in the bylaws—"

"What business?" I snapped. "Which residents? This is harassment."

"It is my duty to act for the community."

"Duty," I snorted. "You make it sound like a noble calling."

"It *is* noble. This is a prestigious community, Mr. Suarez. Residents rely on each other to keep our property value maximized."

The elevator thankfully dinged. We hurried out with the nosy old lady in tow. "Go home, Carmela. I'm not running a business."

She cleared her throat with a shrill cough. "I'll need visual confirmation that you aren't engaged in illegal activities."

"Not gonna happen."

Darcy popped a bubble in Carmela's face. I opened the door and pulled her inside before barring Carmela's path.

"Mr. Suarez, your housing agreement states that you must give me access to verify resident concerns, otherwise I can place a lien against your unit."

"It's my unit! I own it!"

"You don't technically own it until it's fully paid off. Until then, I am free to place a lien for any minor infraction in the bylaws. You signed the agreement. You should have read the fine print."

I grumbled and held the door open for her. "Be my guest then." Ugh, what was I thinking buying into an HOA?

I pushed inside and headed straight to my office computer. Yes, I still have a desktop. Call me old-fashioned. In my defense, I was kinda dead throughout the smart phone boom so I'm a little behind the curve. Sue me. I plugged in the thumb drive, copied the buffered video data to the computer, and went to work locating the moment.

Darcy wandered by. "You didn't tell me you were rich."

"What can I say? Caribbean drug money is good." I turned and found Carmela's eyes fixed on me. "Joking." I wasn't sure she believed me.

"This is so cool," said Darcy. "Can I go swimming in your balcony pool sometime?"

"Yes. Ask your parents." I pulled away from the computer. "How old are you? Do you have parents?"

"I'm eighteen. And not really."

I scratched my head. "Oh, well, then knock yourself out." I wanted to ask for further details but she wasn't the type to open up. I could see her as a runaway, maybe, or an orphan. It would be pointless asking with Carmela snooping around anyway.

I scrolled forward through the video until I found our little outing. Since the dash cam was forward facing only, I didn't have any evidence of the tail or the encounter. I searched for the moment the car was stopped at the light that turned green. I played it through. Manifesto's bike raced through the intersection and made the first turn.

"Found it," I called out.

Darcy hurried over and I replayed it. This time I paused and copied down the plate number. Some letters were hard to make out. I scrolled forward and back a bit until all the digits were confirmed.

"We've got him." I called Evan, gave him a quick update, and relayed the plate number.

"This guy sounds wild," he said.

"How fast can you run the plate?"

"Assuming it's real, I'll call you right back."

I smiled as he hung up. Darcy said, "That asshole's going down." Carmela peeked into the room and blinked dumbly.

"I consult for the police," I explained. "It's not a business run from the penthouse."

"Yes, well, it appears everything is in order here."

"Great. You can close the door on your way out." That's what I said out loud, anyway. My tone clearly implied a more colorful ejection. She took the hint and excused herself.

I paced back and forth along the window overlooking the Miami skyline. Evan was taking a while to call back. If the plate was fake, I wasn't sure the image of Manifesto was enough to catch him. I was getting worried when my phone rang.

"We found him," he said. "It's an apartment in Flagami registered to Nathan Bartlett Jones. No record. Single, lives alone. He fits the standard profile. I'm putting together a team."

"Wait a minute, I need to be in on this. We're still not sure what he's capable of."

"You said he was resistant to magic, right? My guys will pound in there equipped with full BDUs and automatic weapons. What more could you want?"

Actually... my friend kinda had a point. He gave me the address and told me to burn rubber. My poor Firebird was wounded, but I did what I could on the undersized donut.

Chapter 33

The DROP team unloaded from an unmarked delivery van. It was Evan and four guys in SWAT gear. Their faces were covered and they wore tactical webbing with plentiful equipment. White letters across their backs spelled out DROP.

Evan sharply appraised the teenager with gummy bracelets.

"I've seen her stop bullets like in *The Matrix*," I said. "Don't worry about her."

He grunted. "Okay, then." He handed us both ear plugs. "We go in first. You follow."

I nodded and stuffed the protective plugs in my ear. These guys weren't playing around. I hurried after them through the main entrance. Once in the hallway, I pulled my shotgun from the ether. To minimize collateral damage, I loaded it with standard buckshot instead of anything with magical components. From what I'd seen of Manifesto, the standard stuff would take him down just fine.

We crept down the hallway and up a staircase in a line.

The DROP team moved with lethal efficiency. They were the right people for the job. Full helmets and lowered weapons. Hand signals and contact for communication. The point man held a body shield. Kinda made me feel like a scrub.

The breezeway overlooked a central courtyard. We rounded to the back of the building where the DROP team confirmed the apartment number. Evan nodded to initiate the door breach. An officer from the rear came up and pegged the deadbolt with a battering ram.

"Miami PD! Get on the ground!" The door crashed open and they flooded in. "Left clear." "Right clear." They tapped the shoulder of the man ahead and advanced with full coordination. Darcy and I entered, ready for just about anything.

The main space was empty. There were no finger necklaces strewn about or severed heads on the dining table. The apartment appeared well lived in. A remote on the sofa and a box of frozen pizza on the kitchen counter. Once again, I was stunned by how innocuous everything was.

"Pot!" called out a masked officer. "Possible explosive device."

One of the cops rushed to switch off the gas stove.

"Back away!" ordered Evan. "Are we clear?"

The officer in the kitchen retreated. Pistol shots echoed loudly in the small apartment. It was hard to tell where they were coming from, but small holes punched through the closed bedroom door.

"Taking fire!"

The DROP team recoiled from the door and behind cover. The lead officer with the shield immediately opened fire, shredding the bedroom door with three controlled bursts. Everybody paused, weapons ready. Another pistol round burst through the door.

Before the officers could return fire, the pot on the stove whistled sharply. "Down!" cried Evan, but he was interrupted by the explosion of the makeshift bomb. Darcy swung her statue at it and did the impossible: she froze half the explosive force directed our way. A blinding burst of light preceded the concussive tremble that shook the entire floor. Darcy jerked to the carpet. A second explosion was released, reflected away from us. The apartment filled with smoke that tasted of gunpowder.

The DROP team locked eyes and assessed each other. The two closest to the bedroom door pelted it with return fire. It wasn't chaos, exactly. Despite the unexpected blast and the low visibility due to smoke, the trained officers executed their roles perfectly. They covered the door in tight bursts to suppress incoming fire.

My problem was it was a little too controlled. A little too safe. Manifesto wasn't engaging the police force. That wasn't his style.

"Stop!" I yelled. "Stop!"

Evan ordered the cease-fire and they pulled away, dropped their spent magazines to the ground, and reloaded. Darcy was still on her hands and knees, distraught after her effort. I charged the door, bashing my boot through the splintered remains.

The bedroom was empty. Smoke roiled from the closet, filling the room and escaping out of the open second-floor window. I huddled back around the wall. "Another explosive!"

Everyone ducked. Darcy tried to crawl forward to contain it but only succeeded in collapsing. She was hurting. I chanced a peek. Saw the smoke thickening. Orange light reflected from the closet interior.

"It's not a bomb," I called. "It's a fire."

I re-entered the room and cleared the closet. The flames raging within obscured my vision. I cautiously approached the window next, slicing the pie with one eye to minimize my exposure.

Manifesto was already on his bike, revving down the alley.

"It's him!" I yelled.

I was glad I'd gone with standard buckshot for the raid. My specialty rounds were low powder. They weren't meant for this range. I pointed the shotgun out the window and fired. The rear wheel of the bike kicked at the impact. Manifesto almost dropped the bike, but set his foot underneath and revved in the opposite direction, regaining his balance.

Evan converged behind me. I leapt through the window and landed on the dumpster cover below. I pulled a shell from the sidesaddle attached to the shotgun and fed it into the breach. As Manifesto sped down the alley I took careful aim and pulled the trigger.

He pitched sideways off the bike. He skidded on the

asphalt into the cross street. The motorcycle continued across the street without a rider and crashed into a wall. I reached for the last shell in the saddle to go again.

Manifesto was in obvious pain as he rolled to his feet. His pistol was already loaded so he was faster. More shots rang out. I ducked and threw up my energy shield. In his state and at this distance, his shots were wide. Their impacts echoed throughout the nearby alley.

Above me, Evan's burst fire suppressed the killer. Manifesto cursed and retreated around the corner. Evan ordered his team to the front door, but jumped onto the dumpster himself. I was already sprinting after the wounded killer. Gunshots rang out in the street before I rounded the corner. A car swerved and rear-ended another. I regained visual with Manifesto just as he emptied his weapon into a stalled Toyota's windshield. I aimed the shotgun but a bystander ran across my firing line.

I opted instead to close the distance. He limped to the door and shoved the dead driver aside. I lashed out with a twine of shadow. It failed to grab him. I cursed and skidded to a stop as he took control of the wheel. One steady breath and I pulled the trigger.

The driver's window shattered as Manifesto slammed sideways out of view. I rushed forward amid honking horns and the sounds of panic. I was almost at the car when he sat upright in the seat, head fixed on me with those preternatural eyes.

Rifle fire pelted the rear of the vehicle. The DROP team had made it back to the street and was flanking him.

Manifesto gassed the stolen car and peeled out. I lunged and grabbed the window frame as it jerked into motion. The officers ceased their fire.

And then we were racing down a street in the afternoon with me gripping broken glass. My jeans scraped asphalt. I tried to kick my boots up and over the rear end, desperate for a steadier perch. One hand slipped and caught the metal handle. My other hand reached through the broken window and clawed at Manifesto's face.

His pistol peeked over the door and barked. I jerked my head out of the way and grabbed his wrist. He struggled momentarily, but I banged the gun into the door frame until it plummeted to the street. We were still locked together when the car swerved into the oncoming lane.

Looking ahead, I saw the Metrobus he was maneuvering to sideswipe. It came at us too fast, and I had very few options. I released my grip and fell to the street, immediately sinking into the shadow beneath the car. As soon as it passed over, the sun flooded me and I came tumbling out onto the street. Horns blared as the bus narrowly avoided my flailing, rolling body.

I scraped to a stop and hurried to the curb on hands and knees, wincing at the road rash I'd just incurred. I could do nothing but watch as Manifesto once again eluded capture.

Chapter 34

I passed an officer examining the fallen motorcycle. "You okay, bro?" he asked in awe.

I shrugged. "Nothing a hot tub won't cure."

He watched silently as I trudged toward the apartment building.

It must've been wild for non-practitioners to see stuff like this, but Evan's DROP team had already been introduced to the fire. They didn't have special training against spellcraft or any targeted education regarding the preternatural, but they knew it existed. That was usually enough to stand a fighting chance.

I passed more officers in the breezeway. Some nodded my way, others establishing a perimeter. A fire extinguisher cabinet on the wall was empty. I walked through the open door into the foggy apartment, equal parts bomb dust and fire smoke and propellant agent from the extinguisher. Evan was on the phone while Darcy chilled on the couch.

I collapsed beside her. "You holding up?"

"Yeah. I just... There was so much kinetic force in there. Kinda left me in a daze."

My eyebrows climbed my forehead. "I've never seen anything like that before. I'm impressed."

"And I need to thank you again," said Evan, slipping his phone in his pocket and approaching. "That was a small improvised device, but you very likely saved lives." Evan eyed my shredded clothing and smiled. "You look like you've been through a cheese grater."

"I got spare clothes in the car."

"You have spare skin in there too?"

I checked wherever I hurt. I was scraped up pretty bad, but I didn't see any blood.

"Officers pegged the car he jacked. We put a BOLO out."

"He's not stupid enough to keep it for long."

Evan nodded in agreement. "Either we catch him in the next few minutes or he's in the wind."

I pulled the pistol and slapped it on a side table. "I recovered this from the street if it helps."

"It might. Might be registered to an accomplice or linked to another crime. We'll check it out."

I really didn't want to get up, but I was determined to make something out of this mess. I strained to my feet. Just as I made it, a tall black woman with big hair stomped into the apartment. "What happened here?" She paused when she saw us. I collapsed back on the couch.

Evan winced and spoke under his breath. "I advised the feds right before we stormed in. I had no choice."

The look on Special Agent Bell's face was priceless. "What is *he* doing here, Lieutenant Cross?"

"Material witness."

I'd already worked on covering my ass and picked up the slack. "I caught someone following me on the road yesterday. The same guy ambushed me in the street earlier today. It was the Manifesto Killer." I kept mention of the dry cleaner out of it.

Rita's eyes went wide.

"I'm fine," I said, "but I realized it was the same guy and I had his plate number on video. I reported it to the police and..." I shrugged to the interior of the apartment. I was pretty proud of the story. It simultaneously explained why I looked beat up while also keeping me out of the police raid.

The FBI agent frowned. "And who's she?"

"No one. I'm babysitting."

Darcy slapped my chest. "No way. I'm"—she turned to Agent Bell with a straight face—"his girlfriend."

I jumped up so fast pain shot through my back. "No," I said firmly. "No, you're not. It's not smart to lie to FBI agents."

Darcy smoldered, but she curled her lips and spoke in a throaty voice. "That's not what you said last night, sweety." She smacked my ass and I jumped again.

Jeez, maybe she was eighteen and all, but she was kind of a kid to me. Watching her pouty lips was more than enough to arouse a guy, but I didn't think of Darcy that way.

Rita Bell clicked her tongue. "Whatever, lovebirds. I don't care about Cisco's choice in women. What happened here?"

Evan gladly took the ball. "Everything he said is true. We identified Nathan Bartlett Jones, found the address, and notified you."

Darcy was still making kissy-faces. At first she was fighting to be a respected adult, but now she was definitely screwing with me.

"You didn't wait for me to enter," noted Agent Bell.

"We felt, with Manifesto's increased activity and erratic behavior, that the circumstances were exigent. We breached the door, contained an improvised explosive, and exchanged gunfire through a locked bedroom door before Jones escaped."

She brushed past him and into the bedroom. Shreds of wood and drywall salted the floor. She stopped at the window. "You didn't have officers outside the rear exit?"

The lieutenant's face flushed. "We had no way of knowing where the apartment was located in relation to the street before we found the door. At that moment I made a judgment—"

"You could've had the building surrounded."

He ground his teeth. "I didn't have enough men."

"*That's* why you should have waited." A few suits entered the apartment. "We'll take over from here, Lieutenant Cross."

"We have a right to share this crime scene," he pressed. "You're not kicking us out that easily."

I saw the writing on the wall and pushed past her into the bedroom. A discarded fire extinguisher lay on the floor beside the blackened walk-in closet. Everything inside was toast. From the metal trays and the chemical smell, I figured it was where Manifesto manually developed his photographs the old-fashioned way. I could only wonder how much evidence was destroyed.

"What do you think you're doing, Cisco?" asked Agent Bell with a self-indulgent smirk.

I turned to leave the otherwise nondescript bedroom when a string of pictures along the entry wall caught my attention. Color prints of people taken from a distance. Some I didn't recognize. Others I—holy crap.

"You know them?" asked Rita.

I stifled a cough and tore my eyes from the pictures. These could expose everything the Society was trying to cover up.

"Good God!" cried one of the older feds. We peeked out. The older man was covering his nose with the fridge open. "We have multiple mason jars with human remains in here. Eyeballs. Hands. What are those... Lips? Jesus Christ."

While everyone huddled around with morbid curiosity, I melted back into the bedroom and returned to the photographs. I studied the shot of Shen outside Marie Devereaux's house.

I grimaced as I stringed the narrative together. The first two performers were murdered. Random targets, probably. Marie Devereaux was assigned to investigate. Manifesto followed her and took her out. Then it was Shen's turn to take the case, and Manifesto was on to him too. The killer had been scoping out his own crime scenes. He'd killed animists and waited to see who'd take notice. That was how he knew to target Shen. That was why he was following me.

The two photos of Quentin Capshaw confirmed this was a list of potential victims. The hypnotist had also been watched from a distance.

I checked the door again. Evan was arguing with Rita over jurisdiction. He was buying me time. I continued piecing together the photos. Shen outside Marie's house, but no proof of Simon or myself there. That was lucky. Evidence of me at that location would prompt a lot of questions from the feds. It must have been after we'd left, when Shen was cleaning down the house.

Manifesto followed Shen home. Diana was there. He tailed them the next day. I stopped cold at the picture of the dry cleaner, right in plain sight. A picture of me standing beside the Firebird. Fucking hell. The next few shots transferred Manifesto's focus to me. Once again I was lucky. No proof of me interacting with Shen, who'd been pictured at Marie's house. Diana was the only link. Not much of a loose end because she was dead, and we could always propose that Manifesto followed her and randomly targeted me for getting a shirt pressed. After all, it's not like the feds knew about animists in any real sense.

Running out of time, I hurried to the end of the string. Manifesto had followed me that day, I knew. I'd all but caught him in traffic before scaring him off.

Only I wasn't so lucky that time.

Manifesto had snapped a photo of me leaving Capshaw's hotel. I didn't know how he'd done it. Maybe after losing us he decided to surveil Capshaw again and caught a lucky break. He'd found me again. Alone again. But not for long.

The next photo was me waiting in my car outside Fran's park.

My heart stopped. The last photograph in the sequence was a group shot. Me, Emily, Evan, and Fran outside the police station after the vampire confrontation. Manifesto had tailed me through it all. Depending how much he saw and who he followed next, he may have even guessed Emily and Fran were animists. I yanked the photo off the string and crumpled it in my fist.

"See anything interesting?" inquired Agent Bell as she returned to the room.

I held the crumpled picture tightly in my fist. "He has pictures of me," I said, motioning to the wall. "This is proof that what I said is true. Proof that I'm not the Manifesto Killer."

Her attention immediately turned to the display, eyes lighting up at the influx of information. I backed away and twisted my arm around my back.

"Did you know you were being photographed?"

She turned to me and I froze. I shook my head. Agent Bell curled her lips. Her eyes shot to my hands, behind my back.

"What do you have there?"

I backed up, my entire body tensing as I weakly shook my head again.

Darcy strolled into the bedroom. "What's going on?"

Rita turned for the briefest of seconds. I tossed the

balled-up photo out the window. I hooked my thumbs in my back pockets and spun around casually, showing my hands without being obvious about it. Rita narrowed her eyes.

"Hey," exclaimed Darcy, "I know that guy." She drew the FBI agent's attention by rapping her finger on a photo. "That's Quentin Capshaw, the famous hypnotist. He has a show in town this weekend."

"Another target," Rita surmised. She pulled out her phone and made a call. When her back was turned, I gave Darcy a thumbs up. She came back with kissy lips again. My thumb went down and my middle finger cranked up in its place.

Relieved, we retreated to the main room and dragged Evan to the breezeway. "He had a picture of us together," I said under my breath. "You, me, Emily, Fran."

His eyes went hard.

"Don't go too far, boys," called Rita from inside, still on the phone but apparently on hold. "I'm gonna need your statements." Darcy followed further down the hall.

"You need to go get them," I told Evan. "Right now."

"Why would—"

"Don't ask questions, Evan. Just trust me. You have a spare key. Get your family and take them to my place. The wards will let you in and keep you safe."

We all stomped down the stairs in unison.

"I'm coming with," said Darcy.

"You sure are. Everybody." I put my hand to my head, trying to cover loose ends. Milena was safe. She wasn't an animist and Manifesto hadn't been on to me that night. The next day it was Shen, Quentin, and...

I dug out my phone and dialed Kasper. He didn't pick up. I called again. "Come on, buddy. Come on." No luck. "This isn't good," I muttered as we went outside. "Manifesto could've seen us question Kasper about the cipher. That old man's covered in runes. Anyone in the know could practically see the magic dripping off him."

"You think he's a target."

"I didn't see any pictures, but a bunch of them were burned. It's possible. You get your family. I'll pick him up and meet you at the condo."

He nodded and we split up.

I passed through the back alley and recovered the crumpled photograph, which I hoped was the only evidence of my kid's attachment to any of this.

Chapter 35

The evening was in full force. I weaved between the lit towers that form the Miami skyline. My experience at the dry cleaner had turned my worry-dial to eleven, but I could only go so fast on the spare tire. The little donut was partially flat itself and made a disheartening *whump whump* that echoed off nearby buildings and cars. I took comfort in the fact that Darcy's follow motorcycle drowned out the embarrassing noise.

As if we didn't have enough to deal with, a windowless black minivan pulled behind. I scowled. My first thought was to take them on right then and there, but I didn't think Manifesto would wait on my vampire crusade. If we continued right into Brickell maybe they'd call off the tail entirely. I decided to drive by the tattoo parlor without stopping, just to get eyeballs on the situation. The old man would kill me if I led the Obsidian March to his doorstep.

I traversed the construction-filled neighborhood, in transition but tightly clutching to its previous industrial identity. Rough and dirty—that was how Kasper liked it. As the Firebird rumbled by the small tattoo parlor that would soon be out of place in the area, my grip squeezed the steering wheel.

Another black minivan was parked out front. The vampires were already here.

And why not? Manifesto hadn't been the only one following me yesterday. I'd chased the black van away after visiting Kasper's shop. I'd already put him in danger.

I waited at the stop sign an extended beat, playing through possible scenarios. I drew my shotgun and loaded fire rounds into the breech and the two-shot sidesaddle. Darcy revved the bike impatiently before pulling to my left and stopping by the window.

"What gives?"

"Vampires. Tailing us and in Kasper's shop."

Her eyes discreetly scanned the area.

"We're gonna go get him," I said.

I peeled the car around and swerved to a stop in front of his parlor. I leapt from the car and aimed at the parked van's windshield. No one was inside.

The tail van realized the jig was up. They accelerated directly at us. Darcy jumped off her bike and brandished the Hecate statue.

While she could make the van swerve if she wanted to, the effort would knock her out of commission. I couldn't babysit and save Kasper at the same time, so I charged between her and the van and fired. A cone of fire smashed into the hood and windshield. The van veered to the side and hit a telephone pole. I pulled Darcy into the shop.

Kasper often kept the lights off so it was dark. The red-and-gold flashes going off like strobe lights weren't normal. A vampire sailed past us and crashed into the wall. Kasper's fist glowed with residual energy. "Good timing, broham."

Another upir leapt on his back. The runes flared and fended off vicious teeth. Several more surrounded him. I knew from personal experience what a handful that could be, and with everybody moving so fast it would be impossible to stun them all.

I phased through the darkness, appeared next to a surprised black carapace, and shoved the sawed-off into his chest. The resulting boom sprayed the wall with blood and fire. Darcy swung her fetish and a vamp went flying. The grotesque creature's neck snapped on impact and he fell in a heap. Only a second later he regained his feet and snapped his head back into place.

Kasper reached for the wall and tore down a double-sided ax on display. He swung and swiped, putting real power behind his blows, failing to do lethal damage against the quick vamps but forcing them back.

Which was all a way to say that we were doing all right until the second van of vampires flooded around us and opened fire.

At least five pistols barked. A cacophony of lead rained over us. I dissolved into shadow as nearby cabinets shredded apart. Kasper buried his face in his arm and huddled over. Blue runes sparked across his body. Darcy just stood there holding her statue out like the chosen one. Wood witch-god eyes stared deaden at the barrage of bullets suspended in the air. There is no spoon.

The firearms were spent fast. Vampires hissed and licked their lips. To their utter disbelief, the three of us squared off without so much as a scratch.

"This is gonna hurt," said Darcy.

She flicked her statue sideways. The bullets hovering before her rocketed into the vamps like a frag grenade. They flinched and jerked and rolled away in agony, empty black holes popping their skin or bouncing off completely. Those upir carapaces weren't just for snazzy looks.

I dropped my shotgun into the shadow and spawned my darksword. "They're not invincible," I assured my friends. I lunged and sliced a recovering vampire from the shoulder to the chest. The wound was dry and black until I struck the pumping organ that sourced his unholy power. Blood rushed like a geyser. The vampire exploded and turned to ash. "If you hit them in the heart, they're big softies."

Kasper grinned. "So that's what I was doing wrong." He charged two vampires with reckless abandon.

Darcy arched an eyebrow, considered the various medieval implements adorning the walls, and said, "This is gonna be fun."

A spiked mace on the wall wiggled. Pairs of monstrously white eyes faced the new threat. The heavy weapon careened into an armored carapace and sent it flying.

The paused combatants sprang into frenzied action. They were fast but, when everything was a weapon, they were surrounded. Spears and swords whizzed through the air with deadly accuracy. Kasper rent limbs and heads askew.

While not usually fatal, the damage he caused neutered the incoming attackers. All the while I danced among them, slipping into and out of shadow, making sure obsidian claws never reached their marks. Blood and ash rained in that room.

Somewhere in the chaos, I spotted a third group sneaking from the back room into the hall. They wore black tactical gear, all helmeted except for one, and I'd recognize her twin pigtails anywhere. Tutti's second arm had regrown and was in a sling. "Let's get out of here," she ordered. Her small team exited the back door.

My friends were doing fine. Kasper was mostly indestructible against tooth and claw and Darcy had a knack for keeping bodies away. I charged after Tutti's group and glanced in Kasper's office slash bedroom on the way past. Boots scraped the floor as I skidded to a halt. As much as I wanted to teach Tutti a more permanent lesson in manners, I had to confirm what I'd just seen: a slab of C4 attached to a timer, with only seconds left.

"Everybody out!" I yelled. "Now!" I rushed through the tattoo parlor and dragged Kasper and Darcy after me. "Let's go!"

Darcy sprinted outside but Kasper gave some resistance. "I'm not running!" he answered. "This is my shop!"

The two vamps left inside swiped at him. The old man spun and deflected the claws away with his ax.

"It's too late, Kasper!" I tugged his shoulder but he rebuffed me.

I ground my teeth and summoned a tentacle of shadow. I

hooked it around the old man's waist and burst out the front door, yanking him with me. At the same time, the entire storefront erupted. Lightning cracked. Glass exploded. An assortment of tattoo needles and furniture and body parts ejected outward.

Darcy hit the floor and attempted to shield us from errant projectiles, but the whole thing was too sudden. Kasper took a polearm in his back. I held up my armored forearm and deflected a vintage tattoo chair away, but the heavy cast-iron swung around and knocked against my temple. The concussive force of the blast finished the job and sprawled us across the street.

I could make out the tail lights of a van speeding away. I couldn't hear it. I couldn't hear anything, for that matter. Beside me, the smoking top half of a vampire pulled at the ground, struggling to prop itself up. Its red tongue lolled from its mouth as it searched for blood.

I blinked. Kasper was sitting up. Darcy dragged me away, which was an easy thing with assistance from her spellcraft. The first hearing I recovered was the sound of glass on the street scraping under my jeans. I think the sound was traveling through my body rather than into my ears.

Kasper's eyes shimmered as he considered the remains of his parlor. Some of the walls had held up okay due to the wards, but they hadn't been intended to protect from the inside. Darcy screamed. My ears were ringing, and I figured that was something, at least. We watched the old man lumber toward the last living vampire. The burnt husk without legs. Kasper flipped him to his back, growled, and dug bare fingers into his chest. Yellow fire rushed up his arm as he ripped the creature's heart out and held it overhead in a mighty Viking roar. Blood popped and rained down on us.

I rubbed my ears. I heard that, but it was distant, like a dream.

Darcy said, "We have to go."

I pushed to my feet and wobbled. Kasper caught me.

"You hurt?"

I shook my head and stumbled to my car. "Get in." It sounded like someone else speaking. I made my way to the driver's seat. Kasper didn't move.

"Come on," urged Darcy. "Your shop's gone."

He stared at the burning war zone and set his jaw. "So it is." The old man settled into the Firebird and we took off.

Chapter 36

I parked behind Evan's car in the tandem parking space, glad to find them safe. Darcy squeezed her motorcycle behind and we wordlessly took the elevator to the lobby. Our faces broadcast stern conviction so well that even Carmela Flores gave us a wide berth. It wasn't a good time to fuck with us.

Pushing into my place, I was relieved to lock hands with Evan. We were all here. Emily, Fran, and even her four-year-old brother John. The little guy was playing with my tablet and had already figured out the wireless Sonos system. Apparently he was fond of Nine Inch Nails. Kasper made a beeline for my favorite recliner—after a pit stop for beer—and Darcy hovered idly at the edge of the living space. Emily watched everyone from the balcony before turning back to the Miami skyline. It wasn't just us with a lot on our mind.

"My team pulled out," reported Evan. "The FBI took over my scene. Bell's pretty pissed we skipped out but it's equitable payback. We'll need to straighten things out with the feds later."

"Can't be helped," I agreed.

"So what are we doing here? What are the chances we're in real danger?" Fran perked up.

"It's worse than I thought. Manifesto is a wildcard with an ax to grind, but the Obsidian March are doing their darndest to make my life hell. They just blew up Kasper's shop."

Evan's eyes widened. "Metaphorically?" He raised a hand to stifle my answer. "Never mind, Cisco. I should know by now that explosions are always literal with you."

My daughter wandered over to Darcy and offered her hand. "Hi. I'm Fran."

Darcy feigned a polite-but-grim smile. "Darcy. I work with Cisco."

"You're an animist."

The teenager bit her lip.

"Can I see your fetish?"

Evan watched with a critical eye as Darcy turned to me. I just nodded. The witch offered the statue of Hecate, her patron, to the preteen. Fran ogled it before handing it back. "It's cool. Don't let my brother touch it or he'll break her head off."

Darcy chuckled. "Got it."

I continued as Emily returned indoors. "Any one of us could be a target, including a couple of Society guys who won't be joining us."

"How safe is it here?" asked Emily.

"You see the walls, don't you? The glass?"

Emily waved a palm over the ceiling-to-floor windows. Prismatic colors reflected from microscopic etching and filaments, lighting up glorious runework plastered over every exterior window and wall. She blinked. "This is beautiful."

"*Gracias*," said Kasper in horrifying Spanish. "Took me months."

"You." I briefly wondered if Emily remembered Kasper at all, not that he was forgettable.

Evan put his arm around his wife. "Should I point out that your store is nothing but rubble now?"

He sighed. "It was a public business. The walls were fortified some, but my doors were always unlocked. No point protecting heavily when trouble could walk right in. The wards didn't protect from a bomb on the inside."

"So what stopped that from happening the entire time you've been in business?"

He shook his head and flicked on the massage chair.

"Kasper's neutral," I answered for him. "He's Switzerland. No animist wants to screw with him because they might need his scripting or medical talents at any point. It's why he never entered the business of offensive runes. As long as he was a protector, a medic of sorts, no one ever took the fight to him." I canted my head. "Aside from the random clueless biker who'd take a bat to his window."

That drew a smile from the old man. "Happened a few times. My response always staved off that behavior for years after. Another reason I didn't bother with the windows."

"So if you're Sweden," interjected Darcy, "why come after you now?"

Once again, Kasper decided to leave the question unanswered. He closed his eyes and relaxed. John switched to a Nirvana song.

"I didn't know you like classic rock!" said Fran excitedly.

Evan and I muttered to ourselves under our breath.

She traded glances between us. "What?"

"Way to make us feel old, honey," he said.

I scoffed. "We're not old. Only a millennial would call Nirvana classic rock."

"I'm not a millennial," returned Fran. "The youngest millennial is drinking age by now."

I slapped my face. "Okay, mind blown. We *are* old." I decided to address Darcy's question to change the subject. "I don't know why they attacked Kasper. The Obsidian March must've known who he was and what he did. They knew he wasn't a threat."

"They're not animists," pointed out Emily. "They're a criminal enterprise that doesn't make use of his services."

"A growing criminal enterprise," added Evan. "Leverett Beaumont said the void created by defeating the *Agua Fuego* cartel had given rise to a new Obsidian March. One whose footprint in Miami has tripled in size over the last year."

I nodded. "So they're taking out any and all potential threats to their empire. It's all-out war."

Everyone in the room let that sink in for a second. No one said a word except for Kurt Cobain. It was Fran who finally spoke up.

"If it's a fight they want, let's kick their ass."

"Honey!" hushed Emily.

"What?"

"She's right," I said. "We need to make a statement. We need to make them back off. Otherwise they'll take potshots at us any time we step out of Brickell."

"Which generously assumes Beaumont can keep order for more than a few days against the larger hegemony," pointed out Emily.

"Another reason to take them on now."

"You make that sound easy," said Evan.

"The Obsidian March isn't unbeatable. It was three against ten at the tattoo parlor and we kicked their ass. Vampires go down if you hit them hard enough."

"The problem is there's a metric shitload of them."

"Metric, imperial, what's the difference? Your task force is sixteen strong, right?"

"Cisco, I can't just mobilize them any time you want to pick a fight. If there's a crime in progress and we have probable cause, I can go in."

"They're criminals."

"And a case against them will be built from the ground up over the course of a year. Even if I rushed it past the point of irresponsibility and reckless disregard for the law, we're talking a few months at the very least."

"Well, *that's* not going to work." I huffed and continued pacing. There had to be an angle here. A way to make the vamps back off, capture Manifesto, and put a pretty bow on the whole thing for the feds. Staying alive would be a desirable side effect. "Okay. For now the important thing is that we're all here. While holed up in the condo, we're safe. While we're together, we're safe. No one's gonna take us all on at the same time."

"That would be suicide," chirped Kasper.

Emily put a gentle hand on my shoulder to halt my nervous pacing. "Cisco, dear, everybody can't just camp out in your living room until this is solved."

"That depends how quickly we solve this."

"I've got nowhere else to go," said Kasper, seeming to realize it as soon as the words left his mouth.

"I have bedrooms. You and Evan take one," I told Emily. "Kasper has his, and the kids can share."

"What about me?" asked Darcy pointedly.

"Sorry. You're not a kid. I know."

"I can sleep in your room," she said slyly.

"I don't like this new bit you're doing," I said. "There's a futon in my office. If this goes long term I can move the desk to my room."

She crossed her arms, only partially satisfied.

"It's not a plan," said Emily, "but it makes the most sense for tonight. But I do wonder why Fran and John need to be here. The Obsidian March didn't go after Fran—it was Nicole they wanted. And our house is presumably protected from them in Brickell. I think we should take our kids home. Away from all of this."

"It's not just the vampires." I pulled the crumpled photo from my back pocket and unfolded it. "Manifesto keeps tabs on possible victims." John was pleasantly distracted, having moved on to Alice in Chains, but Fran was avidly hanging on my every word. I decided not to sugarcoat it. "You've caught his attention."

Emily took the photo from me. Her eyes flared as the scope of this lockdown dawned on her. Her voice came out strained. "Manifesto doesn't care about the Brickell protection."

"That's right. Your house might be safe from the March, and that's a big if, but the Manifesto Killer doesn't check in with criminal organizations before striking."

She breathed in and out, trembling at the thought of our daughter in his sights. "But Fran and John should be okay. They're not animists." She looked at me. "Evan can take them home. Manifesto only wants practitioners."

My jaw tightened. "He's killed at least one civilian before," I reminded. While there was a good chance the random killings he'd claimed were bullshit, I'd personally witnessed him murder a woman during a carjacking not a few hours earlier.

"No," said Emily, denial overtaking her. "My babies won't be hurt. They're not animists."

I worked my jaw. I had wanted this conversation to go a different way, to be under different circumstances, but there was no avoiding it anymore. Fran's talents were a material concern now, and Evan and Emily deserved to know.

"Yeah," I squeezed out with a wince, "about that..."

Chapter 37

"She WHAT?!?" fumed Evan, taking an angry step toward me.

"Cool it, buddy. We're all grown-ups here."

"You just told me my daughter is a... a..."

"An animist," I repeated in the soothing voice of a therapist, hoping the manner of what I was saying distracted from the actual content of my words. All eyes in the room turned to my daughter. To her credit, she took the attention with a half-baked shrug. "I know it's a lot to take in..."

Evan did a poor job tempering his anger. "This wasn't your decision to make." Even his neck flexed.

"Buddy, hear me out. This wasn't me. This was Connor Hatch."

At the mention of the drug kingpin's name, Emily went white as a sheet.

I summoned Dr. Phil and explained. "Dirty politics, the DROP team, the Miami Covey—you guys have always been in his sights. What you didn't know is he'd secretly been giving Fran spellcraft lessons for two years."

"WHAT?!?" Evan had gone full circle. His runtime was broken.

"It's like Emily said before. That's how Connor operated. He got his hooks into family members, enticed them while they were young."

Emily's wet eyes quivered as she considered her baby.

I raised calming palms to the air. "But it's okay, because we got her back. Fran's fine."

Evan swallowed and nodded. That had been the night we all realized we were on the same team. The night all the internal bullshit between us was nothing compared to the evil in the world. We'd banded together and taken it head on, and although complete success arrived at a later date, we knew we could trust each other after that. From then on, old friends were true friends. Only there had been a price.

One was my reputation in the Miami necromancer community. I'd effectively sold a lot of them out and was still trying to make amends for that. Another side effect was Fran, bearing a new talent but left stranded, without the wisdom to channel it.

"I..." I swallowed and started again, hoping my best friend wouldn't see this as a betrayal. "It was a while before I looked into it. Maybe I ignored it and hoped it would go away. Maybe I had problems of my own. But when I got back to town to lay roots..."

Fran helpfully chimed in. "Cisco's been training me once a week for the last three months."

Evan's face went stone cold. "You're training... MY daughter... how to use magic?"

"She's good at it."

"Cisco! You know how I feel about magic."

"And she'd begun instruction before I ever came back from the dead." Again, the state of affairs pointed squarely at Emily's past affairs with the drug cartel. She was grief-stricken. She dropped to her knees beside her daughter and embraced her. Fran latched on tightly while her mother wept.

"It's not gonna go away, Evan," I insisted. "She needs someone who'll teach her to be responsible with it. Teach her right. You know... you know why that person should be me."

He lowered his head, unable to shoot me down. He couldn't deny my love for my daughter. He knew I would literally walk to the ends of the steppe and into the others to save her. Still, the mood in the room was all wrong.

I took a breath and changed tack. "You need to understand what a gift it is."

He turned away abruptly. "I don't want to hear it." For a second I thought he might cry like his wife. A year ago he hadn't known about Emily either. Now his house was harboring two animists.

"It's purely defensive. You'll like it. It's null magic. By itself, it doesn't do anything at all, but it voids the spellcraft of others."

Emily pulled her head away and considered her daughter intently. Null magic wasn't very common, and it took an animist to understand how truly formidable it could be. Kasper went for the fridge—this was old news to him—but

Darcy watched from the corner with interest.

"It's true, Mom, Dad," affirmed Fran. "Cisco saved my life yesterday."

They turned to me. I cleared my throat. "We've been doing drills. Getting her to concentrate under pressure. Dispelling my constructs. Simple stuff. Nothing dangerous. And when the Obsidian March had her in that van, she disrupted their hearts. Their magical cores." I shook my head. "She exploded one of the fiends all by herself."

That news was bittersweet for them. No one wants their baby to become a stone-cold killer. In my book, black-armored monstrosities with daggers for fingers didn't count for human, but nobody would discount putting them down as a kill.

"It's a great defense," I assured them. "For moments like right now, when we're under assault by the things that go bump in the night, it could mean the difference between life and death. *Her life*. That's what matters, isn't it?"

Emily was already wiping her tears. She still wouldn't let go of her daughter, but I saw the turn in her. She was an animist, after all. Her daughter following in her footsteps must have come with a certain amount of pride.

Evan, well, he was a practical guy. I was sure he would come around. Just not right now.

He shook his head. "I'm happy to hear that, honey. But what if your power was what put you in that position in the first place? Would you have jumped in that van if you didn't have null magic?"

"To save Nicole?" she asked incredulously. "Yes!"

"You're in sixth grade!"

"And she's *not* a crime fighter," I stressed, to parent and child both. "And she absolutely *won't* take part in our offensives."

Fran's face soured. "But—"

"NO EXCEPTIONS!" said the three of us at once.

We looked at each other and almost chuckled, but we weren't quite there yet.

"I was gonna tell you," I said, mostly to Evan but giving a nod to Emily as well. "I was just wrapping my head around it. Waiting for the right time."

He pressed out his lips and looked at everything in the room besides me and Fran. He nodded slightly. His gaze lingered on Kasper, relaxing with a bottle of ale. "I know," he said begrudgingly. "I need a beer." He stomped to the kitchen. You see? Practical.

I took a relieved breath. Months of stress and the worst of it was done. Fran beamed at me. I crooked only the corner of my mouth. I didn't want to gloat.

Her mother doted on her some more as Evan dug through my kitchen. I scratched my head and retreated to the balcony, unsure what to do with myself but glad to be done with the conversation. Longer ones would follow, I knew. Ground rules would need to be set. Everything was changing so fast—I just wanted to stop and breathe.

Leaning on the railing, feeling the cool breeze high over the streets, was therapeutic. I took in the city lights, the current of the river. Seagulls dove and dipped. An owl passed over the moon. People scurried in the distance.

Miami was alive with energy tonight.

Having everyone here was a boost to my mood as well. I turned and rested my back on the railing, watching my people through the window with a stupid grin on my face. The moment was almost perfect.

A hard knock on my door invaded the fantasy.

Evan set his beer down and drew a Colt Diamondback. I rushed past him. "Easy. We're safe in here." Despite my reassurance, everyone took appropriate precautions. Emily pulled Fran and John into the rear hall and Kasper peeled himself out of the massage chair.

The knock came again, heavier. I slipped my eye to the peephole and exhaled. I waved everybody off. "Don't worry. It's cool." I swung open the door and smiled at Milena.

"You never gave me the gate code so I had to park on the street—" She paused in the doorway as she noticed the congregated audience. "This looks like a party. I thought we were gonna have a 'chill platonic bros' night."

Evan snickered. Well, that was embarrassing.

"Show's over," I snapped, waving them away. I shut the door and led Milena toward the balcony.

"Hello, hello," she mumbled, passing everyone with a wave. Milena gave Fran a kiss on the cheek. "You're getting so big, girl." Her eyes lit up at little John McClane. "*Ay, que* cute!"

Great. As soon as she started playing with the toddler, I knew it was over. There zero chance to get Milena alone for a minute now. I secured the balcony door and sat at the bar with Evan, eyes on Milena lighting up the room.

She was probably the friendliest person I knew, and it was infectious. As promised, she was dressed for a casual night in. Jeans, a tight red shirt that showed a respectable amount of cleavage without advertising. Her long hair was wavier than usual. Milena flashed me a wink between playing with the kids, smile from ear to ear, unable to help being beautiful. She went over and gave Kasper a kiss on the cheek before settling beside Emily on the sofa.

"The Avengers are assembled," said Evan.

I admired the room. "They are, aren't they?"

He chugged deep and sighed. "Somehow I thought it would feel different."

"We'll get there." I held up my bottle. He clinked his against it with a nod. I had time to finish half the beer before Evan got a couple of urgent texts preceding a phone call.

"Now?" he asked gruffly. "Where?" He stood and paced to the others. "Turn on the TV."

I grabbed the remote and flipped to the news. Two news anchors were discussing a new development. A photo overlaid the background with the caption "Manifesto Killer."

Chapter 38

The talking heads consulted with a legal expert. I switched stations until I found one showing the action. An evening scene on the street with the word "Live" in a border graphic at the bottom.

"Once again," said a male voice-over, "this is the horrific scene just twenty-five minutes ago when a man interrupted a live broadcast with a gun. Here it is in full and without interruption."

The recording showed a female field anchor interviewing an elderly woman on the sidewalk for the evening news. Storefronts and light foot traffic created the backdrop.

"That's Miracle Mile," noted Evan.

Off camera, a car swerved and skidded, drawing the attention of the news staff.

"Watch your equipment," said the anchor with practiced efficiency, pointing behind the cameraman. The camera sidestepped but didn't swing the focus off the interview. A moment of puzzlement gave way to fear. The news anchor let out a hurried yelp as Manifesto appeared onscreen and forced a pistol to her head.

"Is this live?"

"Please," she begged.

"Is this live?" he snarled.

She nodded. Both women were paralyzed with fear. Manifesto yanked the anchor by the shoulder and held the gun to her head. "You keep rolling or I blow her head off, is that understood?"

"Y—Yes," came the muffled voice of the offscreen cameraman.

Manifesto still wore the gray Dolphins hoodie. He looked straight at the camera, regular eyes but stressed features. Just a normal guy with a gun.

"I can't force the truth on you," he said, voice harried. "It's something you can only accept after searching your soul. But I damn well will scream to get your attention if I need to." He shook the trembling news anchor by her hair. "I'm murdering Miami's best and brightest magicians and your authorities are hiding the truth from you."

Evan dropped his phone to his side and traded a glance with me. Everyone leaned toward the seventy-two-inch screen.

Manifesto scouted the street for a moment before again facing the camera. "The police know about me. The newspapers refuse to print my letters. The FBI has already named me the Manifesto Killer. Yet why haven't they told you?" He stepped closer and the cameraman's hard breathing became audible. "All you need to do is open your eyes. See what I see. Accept your salvation." There was a dead moment while Manifesto switched his gun hand and dug into his jacket pocket.

Milena grumbled. "Why do I get the feeling everybody's not here for a super awesome adult slumber party?"

I snorted. "Never a dull moment."

"I should have known." I could've sworn she smiled.

Manifesto withdrew papers into view. "My ciphers," he said, unfolding one. "Unlike the authorities, I kill out of necessity. And I bring you proof." He held both edges of the paper so it was unrolled. The first cipher. "You have that?" he asked.

Barring the jerky movement of the nervous cameraman, the focus and zoom adjusted to capture the cipher perfectly, a handwritten strip of paper that looked well worn.

"Next one," said the killer, cycling to another. "And the last." He flashed a third cipher, which to my knowledge hadn't been released yet. It was also worn, which meant he'd planned these long ago. Manifesto stacked the papers and shoved them into the news anchor's chest. "Take these," he demanded. "Refuse to shut your eyes against the cold light. Take these, know the truth, and *live*."

She nodded frantically. Manifesto looked around again. People scrambled in the distance. The killer reached toward the camera and jerked it. "You—you're coming with me." The view swung to the sidewalk.

"No... Please!" said the man.

"Come. With. Me!" The video flashed to black.

As the program returned to the studio, the two anchors took a heavy breath and turned to each other with practiced concern. "It's... it's uncanny," said the female host.

"That it is," said the man who'd introduced the segment. "And the latest word from police is that this Manifesto Killer is still at large with the kidnapped cameraman as a potential hostage."

"Our hearts go out to his family."

"Yeah," said Evan, phone back to his ear, "I've seen it. Did your perimeter go up in time?"

I lowered the TV volume as Evan spoke. It sounded like he was going through the police grapevine more than official channels, but his info was likely to be better than whatever the media reported. Besides, the talking heads were just speculating now. They returned to live coverage of the scene. Several police cars lined the block, red and blues flashing. The camera zoomed in on Special Agent Rita Bell asking the locals questions. This was turning into a shitshow, and the FBI's immediate presence all but confirmed Manifesto's claims. The media was gonna have a field day with this one.

I rewound the TV to catch the ciphers again. I paused on the first. It was grainy.

"That's the one we already have," said Fran, pulling out a folded paper.

"Where'd you get that?" asked Emily.

"You were all looking at a stack of them the other night," she said. "I've been trying to solve it for the last two days."

"Fran!"

I printed the second cipher from the image on my phone. I handed the paper to her. "Kasper says the more ciphers, the better." Emily didn't look happy. I paused the TV on the second and confirmed the match—Manifesto was showing these in order. The chronology was important. I played to the next one and paused several times, failing to get a good image.

"Don't bother," said Evan, rejoining the group. He was browsing on his phone. "The three ciphers are all over the internet. There's already a 4chan group trying to crack it. This was a bold move that got a lot of attention, which is exactly what Manifesto wanted. With this kind of mystique and the group computing power of the internet, it's only a matter of time before the ciphers are solved."

I gritted my teeth.

"He's right," said Fran. "Look, the third one's right here." She held up her phone too.

"Are they gonna catch him?" I asked Evan.

He worked his jaw. "Ten square blocks are closed off. The problem is it's a busy area with lots of pedestrians. It won't be easy to find anyone in there."

"What about us?" asked Darcy, suddenly motivated by the development. "We can go find him."

He scoffed. "Nobody's going in right now. This is a citywide emergency."

"He's right," I said. "Let the police find him."

"But—"

"We know he's not going down without a fight," I explained. "It's kill or be killed for him now."

Evan shook his head. "With the amount of heat out there, he doesn't have a chance."

"I think our focus should be the ciphers. We need to solve them before anybody else."

"Fat chance," said Kasper. He reclined the massage chair just as someone knocked on the door again.

"Ooh, more party peeps," said Milena. "I'll get it."

"Wait." I furrowed my brow, going over everyone here. Who else could it be?

Milena cocked her head and glared. "You didn't invite a date to a 'chill platonic bros' night, did you?"

"Would serve you right for that Gavin stunt," I quipped.

"Ha, ha."

I approached the door just in time to hear a rustle. I checked the peephole. It was blocked. "Who is it?" No one answered. I peered through again. While I couldn't see the hall, I could make out light straining through some kind of covering. A paper was stuck to the door. "I swear, Carmela, if I get one more HOA warning..."

I flung open the door. The landing was empty as she rounded into the elevator. On second thought, I'd never seen Carmela wear solid black before. I arched an eyebrow at the paper taped to the door exterior. The scrawl wasn't on the usual HOA stationary.

"What the... Carmela?"

I stepped into the hallway and approached the elevator. As the doors closed, I locked eyes with the lone passenger. Wide eyes, like dinner plates.

Chapter 39

I lunged at the double metal doors, but they shut on me.

"It's him!" I warned.

I tickled the shadow. Two hooks grabbed the doors and forced them open. The elevator car had its own set of doors and rapidly descended. I reached at it with another hook but it dropped below the floor.

My friends spilled into the hallway. "Who?" cried Evan, pistol in hand.

"Manifesto."

"Here?"

"Yes!" I pounded the call button and watched the floor indicators to see where he stopped. The elevator plummeted toward the ground floor. The second elevator was also descending but stopping at every floor on the way down. "He must've pushed all the buttons and sent an empty car down before calling the other. We're stuck here."

"You're sure it was him."

"Yes. Except he had a black jacket on. No more hoodie."

Evan was immediately on his phone and reporting the

development.

Milena huddled at my door, afraid to come out. "We just saw him on TV. How could he be here so fast?"

"That was half an hour ago," pointed out Darcy. "He fled the police raid, freaked out, and did the first thing he could think of to get attention."

I nodded. "I agree that he's desperate—he wouldn't come here if he wasn't—but this isn't panic. He had forty minutes to gather his resources. He had that third cipher ready. This is part of something."

"Got it," said Evan, hanging up the phone and uselessly pressing the elevator call button. "Help is on the way. I'm gonna go down and coordinate as they arrive."

"Not without me," I said.

"Suit yourself."

Everybody stood in the small landing and awkwardly watched the elevator light. Manifesto's elevator was already on the way back up. It finally arrived and Evan and I entered, telling the others to keep safe. On the way down, annoyed residents piled in, having likewise been blocked from elevator access the last few minutes. We smiled pleasantly but impatiently until everybody spilled out at the bottom.

The lobby transitioned from hip lounge couture to bustling command center very quickly. Police all over the city were alerted to the new threat and they made the spacious lobby look more crammed than the elevator had been. It was a madhouse, much to the dismay of the residents.

We approached another Lieutenant. Evan shook his hand. "How you doing, Lucky?"

"Not so lucky, actually. I was in the middle of taking a shit. They say you saw this guy?"

"I did," I said. "Right before the elevator closed."

Evan chimed in. "He's in a black jacket now. No hood."

"We got that," said Lucky. "It belonged to the cameraman. He's probably dead in the trunk of a car somewhere. What did our guy do up there?"

I shrugged and hurried for a cover. "He was trying to get in, I think. He made some noise and left. That was it." I realized I'd left the letter taped to the front door.

"Did anyone see him on the way out?" asked Evan.

"Not so far. We're checking security footage."

"The elevator stopped on the ground floor and the garage floors too," I added. "He was smart and covered his exit point."

"We'll check them all," he said with a nod.

"It also stopped on the tenth floor," noted Evan.

"You think he's still in the building?"

"It's possible, but it's more likely it was a random resident stop. It might be smart to track them down."

Lucky nodded. They continued discussing police procedure. I kind of tuned out at some point because I noticed Simon Feigelstock in the frenetic lobby. I stepped aside and made my way over. He waited for me in a quiet alcove beside locked glass doors leading to the street-front coffee shop. It was closed this late at night and gave us a nice spot to chat out of traffic.

"There you are," he said, frowning at me. "Look at this gong show."

"What can I do? The man practically knocked on my front door."

Simon hissed and watched officers march past. "The last thing we need is spectacle. You shouldn't have called the cops here. This is getting out of hand."

"I hope you're not blaming me," I warned. "You brought me into this investigation unaware you were being surveilled. You pulled me into Manifesto's crosshairs. One investigator's dead. One ran. That leaves me and mine as targets. My picture was in his apartment. Manifesto was already in the news. The police presence here won't change anything."

The Society enforcer almost apologized after considering that. I never got the pleasure because Carmela Flores ambushed us.

"Mr. Suarez, did you bring this mess to us?"

I sighed. "I didn't bring anything. The police are looking for a criminal."

"Is it you?" she snapped.

"Ugh," I said out loud.

"I wouldn't be surprised if it's one of those strange people you keep bringing around. I've warned you about them. I could start eviction proceedings."

"You know, Carmela, that blond officer over there"—I pointed to Evan—"was asking to talk to someone in charge. He said he had really important questions for really important people with really important fake jobs. Like the head of a condo homeowner's association, for instance."

I'd already lost her attention by the time I got to the last part. She straightened and eyed my friend from a distance. "Oh, yes. I'd like to give him a piece of my mind about how to conduct oneself in a community lobby."

"He'd be really interested in that," I said, but she was already loping his way. I was so frustrated with her I almost sobbed in relief.

Simon snickered. "She giving you a hard time, huh? This kind of stuff is why you need to align with people like us."

"Not to mention perks like being hunted by a serial killer."

He pressed his lips together. "Have to admit, didn't see that one coming. Do the police have evidence of the organization?"

"No, but the dry cleaner is blown. Pics of Shen and Diana there and at a house. He caught me there too, but there's no proof of association. Right now I'm floating the theory that Manifesto turned on me while I was getting a shirt pressed. That should fly as long as nothing else gets revealed."

"Fat chance with Manifesto taking to the limelight." He scowled. "It gets worse. This is high profile now. Margo canceled the agent she was gonna send. She's ordering all Society members out of town, including me."

"You're leaving?"

He angled his head. "Order from the board. She believes the damage is done. It's about containment at the federal level now."

I couldn't believe the ease with which he was abandoning the case. It's what Shen had said: secrecy was more important than solution. Did it really surprise me?

Simon's expression softened. "You should come with me. Get out of town a while. Let the police do their jobs. It's only a matter of time. Manifesto's a ticking bomb."

My face darkened. "Don't worry about him. He came to my door with my friends inside. It's personal now."

I considered mentioning the new letter but held back. It wasn't that I didn't agree with the Society's interests—nobody wanted Manifesto stringing up animists and spreading mass panic—but Simon was already cashing his chips. He had one foot out the door. He wasn't involved anymore.

"Have you heard from Darcy?" he asked. "She's not picking up her phone."

"Huh," I offered noncommittally. Evan and Lucky were heading to the elevator, no doubt to take a look-see upstairs.

He hissed. "That kid is always a little hard to reach. If you see her, let her know about the order."

I barely nodded, distracted by the police. Manifesto's letter was on my front door. If it was a personal message to me, I didn't want Lieutenant Lucky getting his grubby hands on it. Details about me and my friends could be in there.

"Keep your phone close," I called to Simon as I sprinted away.

Evan and Lucky entered the elevator. For once, Carmela saved me. She slowed the closing of the door by following them in. I weaved through personnel as they reactivated, slipping my hand through the doors just in time to stop them. Lucky grumbled.

"Sorry," I said. "I gotta use the bathroom, and I really prefer my own toilet."

Evan rolled his eyes as the doors slid shut. I shrugged meekly.

"And that's another thing," complained Carmela as we ascended. "People live here, and they'd appreciate it if your officers didn't block off the entire lobby."

Lucky grumbled even louder. "Ma'am, I'm gonna ask you to stop talking."

The elevator stopped on the tenth floor. I arched an eye as Lucky brushed past me.

"Step back, please." For a second I thought I'd gotten lucky and Lucky was gonna get off, but no such luck. The lieutenant held the door while he scanned up and down the hall then returned to the elevator. "I'll do a full check on the way down, but it looks clear. Ma'am, I'm gonna need the names of the residents on that floor."

As we approached my penthouse, I tried positioning myself so I would get off first. Lucky angled in my way.

"Sir, I'm gonna have to ask you to wait a moment. I want to make sure the hallway's clear."

"But Manifesto's not there anymore," I said.

"It's just a precaution."

I pressed to the door. "I really need to go to the—"

The door opened and Lucky set his arm across my chest. He barged into the hallway first. I shoved past him as he turned toward my door, which was hard to miss because the penthouse took up the whole floor. I lunged but couldn't beat him to it. Not only did I trip face first to the carpet, but Lucky's eyes fixed on the only door in the landing.

The letter was gone.

Chapter 40

"Aha ha," I chuckled nervously, picking myself up. Everyone stared. "Sorry. Just had an almost-pissed-out-of-my-ass situation there. I'm okay now."

Carmela pointed an offended nose in the air. Lucky's hard glare softened. "I know the feeling," said the grizzled lieutenant. "I got half my remaining business knocking on the door myself." He surveyed the landing. "Looks like there's nothing to see here. No point getting prints if we've already identified the suspect." He nodded to the door. "Go ahead and take care of it."

"Thanks."

"And, sir," he called as the door was half open, "I'd strongly suggest using your peephole next time a stranger knocks. It's there for a reason."

"Yeah. Thanks again."

Evan asked about widening the perimeter as I shut the door. I didn't have high hopes this time. Manifesto was no stranger to avoiding detection. Given his close calls, he almost had it down to an art.

An entire living room switched their gazes from me to the letter in Fran's hands.

"You took it down," I realized, joining the pile. "You shouldn't have done that." I snatched the letter and ruffled her hair. "Good girl."

The single page of copy paper had handwritten blue ink hastily scrawled across it. No special symbols or ciphers, just an all-too-straightforward message.

TO MY NEMESIS,

WE ARE MEANT FOR EACH OTHER. I SEE THAT NOW. I FINALLY UNDERSTAND THE TASK BEFORE ME.

MY WORK HAS RESULTED IN THE EXTERMENATION OF SEVERAL DEMONS, BUT THEY'VE ALL BEEN INCONSEQUENTIAL AND UNDESERVING OF MY FOCUS. YOU WILL BE MY GRAND FINALE.

OUR DESTINIES ARE ENTERTWINED. WE EACH REPRESENT BANNERS OF THE WAR TO COME. HUMANS WITH EYES OPEN FACING OFF AGAINST FURTIVE MAGICIANS. NO LONGER CAN THE CURTAIN HIDE YOU. LET OUR CONFRONTATION BE A RALLYING CRY TO THE WORLD. LEAVE MY NUMBERS TO THE SHEEP. FOR YOU, I WILL

> ADDRESS A SPECIAL INVITATION. KEEP A FIXED EYE OUT FOR IT.
>
> AND IF YOU DON'T, I'LL PICK OFF YOUR MAGICIAN FRIENDS AND CONSORTS, ONE BY ONE. THIS IS MY MANIFESTO.

I nearly crumpled the paper in anger. Instead I handed it to Emily so she could have a look. "He's not a very good speller, is he?" she noted.

"He'll get the electric chair for sure."

Evan entered while fending off Carmela. He eventually closed the door with her on the outside. He huddled with his wife and went over the message.

Milena punched my shoulder. "This guy really wants to kill you, huh? What'd you do?"

"Probably my stunning good looks. Anyway, don't be jealous. He wants to kill you too."

"That's reassuring."

Darcy didn't appreciate the casual banter. "How are we gonna find him?" she demanded.

"I'm not quite sure. Manifesto has a method to his madness. This letter is proof that he's setting something up."

"So we hit him before he's ready."

"That's a nice idea if we know where he is."

Evan handed the letter back to Emily and said, "I'll be notified if anybody spots him. That doesn't mean the DROP team's free to act. This is too high profile for us to get involved off the books."

"Screw that," said Darcy.

"I'm serious," he returned. "Half the police force is on the streets as we speak. I'm gonna need to mobilize for any SWAT eventualities. There is way too much heat on this thing."

"I don't see a way around it," I agreed.

Darcy crossed her arms and dug in. "Come on, Cisco. They need us."

"I don't disagree, but you have to keep in mind that the feds are out there too, and Rita may have her suspicions about spellcraft. Manifesto's actions have only shed more light on this." I paused before I revealed the next point. Part of me didn't want to tell her, but she had a right to know. "Margo recalled the Society. Simon's leaving town."

Her eyes widened. "What?"

"He said he called you."

She snorted. "I lost my phone when I took a spill on the bike."

"I can call him back to come get you—"

"Fuck that. They're cowards. I'm not scared of this guy."

I watched her for a second to determine whether she was pushing out false bravado or actual feelings. "Can you do that? Go against the union?"

She set her chin out. "I'm my own person."

A smile I didn't know I wanted stretched across my face. "Good. So we wait for Manifesto."

"Wait for him to do what? He wants to kill you," pointed out Emily.

"He can get in line."

She chewed her lip. She wasn't usually the nervous type. Then again she didn't usually have crosshairs on her back. "I don't like this at all. He didn't give us any leads. He told us what he wants but not what he intends. His only instruction is to keep a look out. He doesn't even say for how long."

"His time frame has moved up," said Evan. "It took a month between homicides one and two. Another week for Marie Devereaux. Then just two days before attacking you. Given his reckless public statement, I wouldn't be surprised if he makes a move tonight or tomorrow."

"But no leads," repeated Emily.

"Actually," contested Fran, studying her papers and holding a hand up as she would in math class, "I think I can solve this cipher."

Everybody turned to her. Even Kasper peeled his eyes open and sat up.

Evan shook his head. "Fran, I don't want you investigating something so dark."

"It's not dark. It's just a number puzzle." She smiled confidently. "He said 'numbers,' remember?"

I blinked. "What?"

"In the letter. Manifesto said, 'Leave my numbers to the sheep.' You get it? He *did* give us a clue, only he didn't mean to. Look here."

We huddled over her shoulder.

"Look at the cipher fragment: wivo ivo wero ev. It's gibberish, but there's not a lot of variance. It doesn't use the whole alphabet and there are repeated letter pairs. I thought it was curious while studying it. Then looking at the second line. And the other two ciphers, the pattern is undeniable."

"But those are letters," noted Evan, "not numbers."

"And that's the key." Her face lit up. "Look here. There are no 'A's or 'U's. You know what words don't have 'A's and hardly any 'U's in them? Numbers."

Kasper mouthed them out loud while he ticked his fingers. "One, two, three, four—that's a U. Five, six, seven, eight, nine, ten—"

"Skip ten," she said. "Add zero. Those are the ten numerals you need to build a number."

"So what's 'wivo ivo' then?" I asked.

"Well, the W stands out. The only number with a W is two." She grabbed a pen and wrote it above the top line of the cipher.

"Okay," I granted, not quite sold yet. "What's the I?"

Kasper grunted. "Five, six, eight, nine."

Fran nodded. "Right. The 'I's not unique, but the V is, except for seven which doesn't have an I. So what if the letter pairing IV represents five?" She scribbled that next in the sequence. "You see what's going on here now, right?"

I scratched the back of my head, glad I wasn't the only one holding back.

She sighed. "These are numbers, but starting with the second letter. No 'T's—two, three—and no 'F's—four, five. So the next O is four, not two or zero. Second letter, right? 'Wivo' is 254. The next 'ivo' is another 54."

Kasper nodded. "I get it. And the reason some numbers, like five, are two letters instead of one is because the single letter's not unique to their second position."

"Exactly!" she said, huddling closer to the tattoo artist. "The rest of the line is 'wero ev' which is two... ER is zero... four, seven. And last is this strange spiral symbol. I'm not sure what that is."

We studied the string of numbers as Fran worked on the second line: 254542047.

"Twenty-five," muttered Evan, bringing up something on his phone. He peeked at the beginning of the next sequence as Fran filled it out. "Eighty. These are GPS coordinates."

I turned between them. I couldn't believe this was working.

"Twenty-five degrees by eighty degrees is a location in Miami. The first line would be 25° 45' 42.047, assuming three decimal places. The spiral is probably just the end of the number. Or where GPS users would put the cardinal direction. In Miami's case, that would be north. If we assume the second spiral signifies west, because it wouldn't be anywhere near us if it was east, then we have a very specific location in the city."

Fran smiled. "It's a geocache! Dad and I did some a few years ago."

Everybody was thoroughly impressed. I swatted Evan's back. "You done raised her right," I joked. He was beaming. Fran's first police work. I waited as she copied down letters and translated them into numbers. "So what you're saying is we have a physical location to look for Manifesto?"

"Three," she said. "Three ciphers, three locations."

Emily shook her head. "But we won't find Manifesto at any of them. He said these numbers were for the sheep. This puzzle is meant for the general public."

"And if these are true geocaches," explained Fran, "then there should be an item or stash at each one." She finished with all three and spaced them out correctly so they could be easily read. All nearby locations.

"There's one problem," returned Emily. "The whole world has these ciphers now. We might not be able to get to them first."

"No one else had the clue," said Fran. "No one's thinking only numbers. And the fact that some numbers are a single digit and some are double will throw people off."

"That's for sure," I said. "The FBI's had the first cipher for over a month and they think it's gibberish."

Evan shook his head. "I dunno. Never underestimate the power of 4chan."

"You're right. Let's split into three teams and grab these caches. Emily and Evan—"

She shook her head. "No way. I'm staying here with John and Fran."

"Mom," whined Fran.

"I'm sorry, honey. You did a great job with the evil ciphers, but you're not leaving this house while that man's out there. He had a picture of you."

Her darkened face turned to me. I ignored her appeal. Her mother was right on.

"Don't worry about me," said Evan. "I need to step out and mobilize my team. We'll take the first location." He grabbed an extra copy of the cipher and jotted down his coordinates.

"Okay, then." I noted how eager Darcy was to get moving. She was already copying the second location down. She was a formidable witch by herself, but I didn't like the thought of anyone being alone. "How about you stick with Kasper, Darcy?"

She flashed him a sidelong glance and nodded. "Sure."

Milena hopped up to me like an excited puppy. "That leaves you and me!" She accepted the master list from Fran and pulled out her phone. I almost objected but realized I had no idea what to do with those coordinates. And, well, I could finally get my Milena alone time.

We said bye to Emily and the kids and headed down together. Police still patrolled the lobby but their presence was less dense. We easily transferred to the parking lot.

"I would ask if you know how to sit on a bike, old man," said Darcy to Kasper, "but you look like a crazy biker yourself. Hold on."

They straddled the motorcycle and took off like a missile.

I popped the trunk and handed Milena the same Uzi from two nights ago. "You should probably just keep this." She had jeans now so couldn't hide the drop-leg holster under a skirt. She ducked into the car with it.

"I hope we don't need this."

"Better safe than sorry." I gave Evan a nod before I pulled out next. He followed me out but quickly split off on his own mission.

Chapter 41

"Can't this piece of junk go any faster?" teased Milena.

"It can, but I don't want to blow out the spare tire."

I pulled onto Red Road and slowed as we neared the location. A park the size of a small block. No lights or infrastructure, just grass and trees. The area was well covered and abandoned; the park was closed from dusk to dawn.

"At least the Obsidian March isn't following us," I said.

I pulled onto the swale. The entire park was sunken into the ground, a gentle slope from all perimeter streets to what was a hilly picnic paradise during the day. At night the stillness was eerie, only broken by passing headlights that didn't reach the bottom of the basin.

"I didn't know you could dig that deep in Miami without hitting water," said Milena. It wasn't much—fifteen or twenty feet—but her point was taken. She double-checked the coordinates. "It's definitely in there."

I shut off the Firebird and scanned the park with my night vision. My spellcraft couldn't detect infrared heat signatures or anything like that, but it pierced the darkness well enough. "It looks empty."

My phone buzzed. Evan had set up a group in a messaging app. Me, Milena, Kasper, him, and Emily. Darcy no longer had her phone. "Recovered 1st cache in Allapattah," he texted. "Diary pages. Grisly photos of Mordane, postmortem. Rant about magic."

I frowned and texted back. "You named this group Team Evan? Not gonna fly."

"My group. My name."

Milena shook her head. "Focus, Cisco."

"Right."

I texted, "Magic rant?"

He took a minute to come back. "Handwritten account of Mordane's magic."

"Proof?"

"Questionable. Need to finish with my team. Unless anyone needs assist?"

Kasper interrupted the textathon. "Would you clowns quit hogging the airwaves? We don't need help. Public park. Have it soon."

I chuckled. "Evan, hold off on handing that over until we're all clear. Then you can take credit for solving the cipher."

"I'll tell Agent Bell in person," he replied.

I smiled. Then I changed the name of the group to Team Cisco and put my phone away.

"Real mature," said Milena after getting the last update.

We exited the car and I pointed. "Lead the way,

navigator."

"Aye aye."

We carefully descended the rocky grass to the bottom and headed toward the center of the park. I surveyed a wide swath around us to make sure there were no surprises. We weaved between a few trees, over a small hill, avoided a wayward boulder, then approached an oak. Milena moved to pass it on the left but looped around back to her starting position.

"I think this is it."

Milena's phone flashlight blinked on and momentarily blinded me. I squeezed the shadow from my eyes as she searched the tree. She bent over and her shirt rode up her back. I took special notice of the black frilly thong she wore.

"You wore that to our 'chill platonic bros' night?"

She spun around and reached her arm behind her back. The effect enhanced her bust. The frilly edges of her black bra squeezed against supple flesh. At this angle, the modest cleavage wasn't so modest. She caught me looking, and I didn't care.

"It's just a shirt and jeans," she said.

"I'm talking about the sexy underwear."

She pursed her lips, shrugged, and turned back to the base of the tree.

"I see what's going on. You're teasing me."

"No," she returned, not bothering to turn back to me. "But I do like the way you look at me."

I groaned in pure torture. My phone buzzed, and things were already tingly down there.

"Watch it," texted Evan. "Had some hooligans approach the geocache. Having officers lock area down."

I scanned the trees. I didn't see anybody, but my eyesight was still recovering from Milena's flashlight. I held off on the spellcraft. "The cipher's already solved," I told Milena. "People were scoping out Evan's site."

"What? How could the internet do in minutes what the FBI couldn't in a month?"

I shook my head. "Having three ciphers at once must've made the pattern obvious. I don't know these kinds of things."

A car passed in the distance. Headlights swept over the branches above our heads. I caught the gleam of a metal box. I chuckled.

"What?" asked Milena, on all fours and peering between the tree's exposed roots. Her tight jeans waved in my face.

I crossed my arms. "Is this a pole-dancing technique or what?"

My phone buzzed again. Kasper messaged, but it wasn't him. "Darcy here. Found more notes. Has pics of piper marie and nick. Inside stuff that proves he murdered them. Rando pic of Shen too. Gonna sanitize it."

Evan texted. "That's evidence!"

"Sorry, it's what they pay me for," she replied. "I'll leave pics of them being scouted, but not of their bodies. They deserve more dignity than to be highlights in a Manifesto documentary. Plus, they're technically missing, not dead. I'm removing Shen too. He's been through enough."

Shen was already in the photos at the apartment, but

maybe this would lessen the emphasis on him. "She's right, Evan. This is the job."

He answered quickly. "Fine. Leave rest at location. Sending my sergeant to recover before other civilians arrive."

All she said was, "Word."

I pocketed the phone and laughed when I saw Milena digging through the dirt with her hands. She was almost up to her elbows in it. "What are you doing?"

"It has to be here," she grumbled. "I think the dirt's loose."

My voice went deadpan. "Oh, look. Up in the tree. There's a box."

She spun the flashlight upward until she found it. I scratched the back of my head nonchalantly. I was confident of the act until Milena got up, pulled on my belt buckle, and dropped a handful of dirt down my pants. "Maybe *that* will settle you down," she hissed.

"You're sexy when you're dirty."

"Good." She dusted her hands off on my jeans, which would've felt better if my crotch wasn't all grainy. When she was done I shook the soil down my legs. The process involved removing my boots and upending them as I hopped awkwardly on one leg. She watched me fussing with my clothes for a minute until she asked, "What are you waiting for? Do your thing." She motioned up to the metal box.

I considered explaining the intricacies of grains of dirt near my junk but decided to keep what dignity I had left. I nudged the geocache with a shadow and smoothly caught it. How's that for sexy?

I set the box down and opened it. It was just a brown leather journal in a plastic bag. Folding open the pages revealed stacks of photos sleeved between. Shen, Diana, Simon, Darcy, Quentin Capshaw, me, Kasper, Evan, Emily, and Fran. The only dead body pictured was Diana, and it was a single uninspired shot. I quickly realized what this was.

"Manifesto watched his victims before taking them on. He keyed in on signs of spellcraft and documented them. He was methodical. Look at this." Covering up the photo of the murder, I showed Milena a scene through the window of Shen's house. He stood before Diana, holding a glowing rose in his palm. An illusion, like he'd spawned at Quentin's hotel. The flower maker. And Diana was mirroring the same spell.

"Beautiful magic," whispered Milena.

"He was tutoring her, just like I do with Fran. Manifesto caught them, and she died because of it." I ground my teeth together so hard it hurt.

While Milena caught up with the group chat, I flipped through the journal. I wasn't sure what the other geocaches contained, but what I had was a goldmine. Page after page of crazed serial killer ramblings. Several pages had been torn that likely coincided with the notes in the other boxes—maybe even the ciphers. The book I held was more than that. This was Manifesto's master journal.

"Whoa."

The pictures too. Much had evidently been destroyed in his apartment fire, and some had remained on display, but the stacks in this book were his active cases. His leftover murder targets. Flushing him out of his apartment had escalated his timetable. Manifesto had dropped whatever notes he had left in hopes of revealing the truth to the people of the world.

I wondered if I had a right to take that away from them.

But this was surely not the way. Killing innocent animists trying to make a buck. Besides, this was the job, right? Sanitize the Society's involvement. I didn't kid myself that they were the good guys, but they weren't going around murdering entertainers.

I drew a single photo from the collection, careful not to get prints on it, and slipped it into the plastic bag. I wiped it down, closed the box, and repeated the precaution. Then I dropped the box in the hole Milena had dug and kicked some dirt over it for good measure.

With Manifesto's journal tucked under my arm, I texted the group. "Found box. Sanitized."

Evan responded with, "..." and then, "On my way."

Good. The fewer questions, the better. I steadied Milena's hand as we climbed out of the park and returned to the car. We'd done it. Manifesto's master plan had been derailed. Plenty of people would whisper in macabre awe at his killings and motivations, but no proof against us would surface.

As for Manifesto's last box? A ruse to throw the authorities off my scent. A single photo of a single person:

what would have presumably been Manifesto's final target. The hypnotist, Quentin Capshaw.

I knew he was safe, but Special Agent Rita Bell didn't. The police would deem him in immediate grave danger and pick him up. Call it an inconvenience for saving his life—I wouldn't feel guilty over it. The crafty hypnotist would no doubt spin his near-death experience into a TV special or two.

The crux of the ruse was a common magician's deception. Watch the hand that's moving, not the one hiding the real trick. The police would be all over Quentin tonight, leaving me room to do what needed to be done. Finding and ending Manifesto.

Chapter 42

We were both unusually quiet on the drive back. I didn't know why, exactly. The quick success had gone off without a hitch. The entire team played their parts. Sometimes it felt like, together, we could do anything.

But what was left unsaid intruded on the ride. I glanced at Milena as the lights of the city washed over us. She idly hummed beneath her breath, probably imagining a multitude of ways tonight could have been normal. Still, she was completely content. That was part of why I liked her. Both our lives were fucked up in so many ways. It was a shit connection, maybe, but it was an undeniable one. Besides, with her, nothing felt fucked at all.

I should put that on a valentine. Cisco Suarez, a regular Romeo.

She turned and caught me staring. We locked eyes for a moment. She straightened and bit her lip. The only thing I could imagine was kissing them. I tried to clear my head. Well, I didn't try *that* hard.

I flicked my gaze to the street and swung into a turn.

"What's next in the plan?" she suddenly asked. It broke the silence. Broke the moment.

But that had already happened. I sped forward and through an intersection as the light switched to yellow. Behind us, a windowless black minivan accelerated.

I cursed. Being followed was getting real old real fast. Admittedly, a silver T-top straight out of the eighties with a giant black phoenix on the hood didn't exactly blend in. A man still deserved his privacy.

So I ran through the calculations. Four or five in the van, probably. I wasn't scared of that, but I had Milena with me, and busy city streets to boot. I was trying to shift the attention *away* from me, not attract it.

As I crossed into Brickell and approached the main drag, the follow van pulled away.

Which simplified matters. It also gave me an idea.

I drove under the skyline of condos and past the Friday celebrations. It was just about ten at night, which meant I had an hour or so to hit up one particular restaurant. But why wait?

As a double-waxed Aston Martin pulled away from the curb, I veered into a strip reserved for valet and parked right in front of Carbon. I wasn't a dick about it—they had four spaces and I was only taking one. Besides, I was trying to make a statement.

"You don't need to take the keys out," instructed the valet, assisting Milena out of the vehicle. She thanked him while hiding a bundle under her shirt. He rounded the car and held out a hand for them. I stuffed them in my pocket as

I passed. "Sir, you can't—"

"Take it up with the owner," I replied.

"But—"

"I'll be quick."

I pushed into the door with Milena's arm hooked under mine.

"Reservation?" asked the hostess. She wore a backless evening gown and was a model in her own right. Her eyes flitted with horror over our ensembles. Scratched-up tank top, both wearing jeans, and mine weren't even the fancy kind. For her part, Milena was pretty but looked like she'd been digging holes in the backyard all evening. Black dirt stained her forearms and knees.

Present company excluded, the chic restaurant was filled to the brim with well-dressed well-to-dos. A hip jazz fusion group lined the stage in baby blue duds. The bustling wait staff slalomed through the hive of activity with practiced ease.

My eyes landed on Beaumont, white tuxedo jacket and all. Given current events, I figured he'd be stationed at his corner table in the back. "He's my reservation," I told the hostess while brushing past.

The vampire's eyes fixed on me almost instantly. He nodded along as a pair of business associates in the booth chatted him up. The men were white collar, lawyers or financial advisers or something. I didn't clock them as vampires. Then again, I knew next to nothing about Clan Beaumont.

"Where are they?" I demanded as I strode up to his

table.

His cheeks twitched. "Mr. Suarez. This is ill-advised."

Milena's sharp intake of breath alerted me to the converging security. A heavy hand plopped on my shoulder. I shoved him away without looking, stepped up onto the platform of the VIP booth, and slammed my fist onto the white-clothed table, rattling their cocktail glasses.

"WHERE ARE THEY?"

This time the men behind us ripped Milena off my arm. A large man grabbed me in a bear hug. I snapped my head backward and broke his nose. While he stumbled, I spun and hit him in the belly, just a touch of shadow lacing my fist. He doubled over hard. I feinted at the one escorting Milena away. He flinched, never noticing the shadow wrapped around his ankle. He fell unceremoniously on his ass. I stepped toward them and barred my arm over Milena protectively.

"Stop," said Beaumont, and his voice was so commanding that everybody immediately complied, including me. For a second I wondered if I'd been hit with a compulsion. I dismissed the thought and chalked it up to being pragmatic. I came to get answers, not to fight, and Beaumont's goons had backed down.

I glared at the restaurateur. "I want them," I growled.

Leverett Beaumont held a hand up and faced his associates. "Excuse me, gentlemen. We'll resume this tomorrow. Same time, same place?"

They nodded emphatically and showed themselves out. Beaumont wiped his lips with the napkin on his lap and motioned for the kitchen. "Shall we?" I backed away as he stepped down. The security staff grumbled. "That will be all," he told them. Cars honked outside and he noticed the flabbergasted valet appealing to the hostess. "And make sure my guest doesn't get towed. He'll be leaving in a minute." That last statement was made with a huff of annoyance and was directed at me as much as to his employees.

The real estate broker headed into the kitchen without checking whether we followed. In a minute we were again in his impressive wine cellar.

Leverett Beaumont casually wiped his hand over his hair, making sure it was still plastered to his head. "It's unwise to treat our arrangement so publicly," he said tersely.

"What arrangement? You delivered a message from your vampire bosses. That's your job as a lackey."

His eyes snapped into vicious slits. "I am under no one's heel, vampire or human."

"Tell it to your employees or your groupies or whoever you're trying to impress. I don't give a shit about your disdain for the Obsidian March. So what? We both have the same enemy. What does it count for if we don't help each other?"

He sighed patiently at Milena. "Is he always this obstreperous?"

"Obstrepe-what-did-you-call-him?" she snarled. She pulled the small Uzi from under her shirt.

He sighed again. "Unruly. Difficult."

"Oh." She relaxed. "That's actually pretty accurate."

"I had a feeling." Beaumont ignored the firearm, crossed

his arms over his tuxedo jacket, and appraised me. "What is it you want?"

"This is about what *you* want. A partnership, right?"

He nodded.

"It's pretty obvious you need an enforcer in Wynwood. Someone to wreak havoc with vampire operations. It's pretty obvious you're maneuvering me into that unwitting position."

That had him pause a moment, hesitant to cop to the charge. He finally gave a level nod.

"Well, I hate to break it to you, but that's never going to happen. You don't work for anyone; I don't work for anyone. Understood?"

His jaw flexed. "But... ?"

"But I am going after the March, for my own reasons, and if you want some semblance of a partnership, I need something in return."

Leverett leaned against a nearby shelf. "You do have something in return. The protection of you and your friends while in Brickell."

I snorted. "We have that anyway. This is an upscale district. You don't want violent crime scaring away the locals. It'd be bad for business. And that's especially true if someone came after me, because I have a habit of breaking things. Look what happened at Kasper's place."

"The tattoo artist." He swallowed in clear distaste. "I didn't know about that before the fact. They don't inform me of their idiotic offensives. Already they're positioning that as the Manifesto Killer's doing."

"So they *do* know about him?"

He shrugged. "There's little they don't know about. The Obsidian March has informants within police and government offices. Usually their actions are very shortsighted."

"And this isn't?"

"That attack most definitely was. The cover-up, not so much. Using the Manifesto Killer for shade is not the Magnus I know. It's far too clever for him."

"It won't be clever when I smash his face in."

The vampire calmly pursed his lips. "It's an ugly business —the violence—which is why you have my protection, freely given, as you point out. Your vendetta against my brethren is also freely given. That is a fair trade to my eyes."

I shook my head. "It's not enough. A few days ago I didn't even know vampires infested this city. I've... been away a while. I've been distracted with *Agua Fuego*. And I'm sick of being tailed by the Obsidian March. I need more info on them. Safe houses, waypoints—how to get to that dickhead Magnus."

The vampire shook his head. "Out of the question."

"It gets you what you want."

"Regardless, I can't give you anything you couldn't get on your own."

My tone soured. "If I could get it on my own, I wouldn't need your partnership."

"Yet that is where we find ourselves," he explained. "If you act on inside information, the March will be quick to figure where it came from, especially after your little show this evening. They would eviscerate me."

I growled and turned away. "What are you worth then? This isn't an alliance." I nudged Milena's back. "Let's get out of here. I was wrong about this guy."

She gazed back and forth between us before tucking the subgun away and heading up the narrow staircase.

"Hold it," relented the vampire.

I turned slowly, expectantly.

Beaumont sighed. "I can't give you Magnus. He's too careful about security. You missed your chance at him," he added with a tinge of disappointment. "But I can give you something. A stepping stone."

I closed in on him. "Who?"

"I understand you've already met her. Magnus' favorite companion, Tutti."

The corners of my mouth slid into a devilish grin.

Chapter 43

We stopped back at the condo to rendezvous with the others. Darcy handed me the contents she'd sanitized from her geocache. Evan wasn't around—still managing his team —but he only had specifics of the first murder, which was well known by the police. Nothing there needed censoring.

I slipped into my bedroom and shut the door. Usually I would've been content to just drop Manifesto's journal onto my nightstand, but Fran was around and she'd already displayed a penchant for curiosity. The last thing I wanted was her perusing the ramblings of a psychopath. Call it dad instinct. I moved into my closet and shut it behind me.

To call it a walk-in closet was criminally unimaginative. I'd seen smaller kitchens, and few shared the same luxury accents. Manufactured hardwood flooring with a weathered gray finish, espresso shelves and glass-door cabinets against the walls, an island with a marble top in the center, and a leather chair beside a double-wide mirror for soaking it all in. Every drawer and shelf was equipped with accent lighting.

The funny thing was, besides two suits and a few going-out duds, the shelves were just lined with stacks of jeans and white tank tops. I kept telling myself I needed a makeover, but there were always more pressing concerns.

I set both hands down on the island, closed my eyes, and concentrated. When I looked again, I was in the same place, only I wasn't. Every single shelf and floor detail was the same, except the door was gone. The lights, too, existed but didn't. They were only faint glows to mark their presence without illuminating much. It would've been too dark to see without my enhanced eyes. Instead of clothes and accessories on the shelves, rows of antiquities I'd reclaimed from Connor Hatch were on display.

This was my shadow room. Similar to the hidden shadow box I lugged my shotgun around in, but woven into the Intrinsics that surrounded my closet. This room was grounded here, inaccessible from anywhere else and, more importantly, *by* anyone else.

It was also a bit of a mystery. I'd never been able to manage anything this scale before. My shadow box was simple and, as such, could only afford to hide simply. My shotgun had been imbued with spellcraft to allow it access—I could stuff nothing else in the box, at least not without dedicating significant time to it.

The shadow room had taken two months and I was still working on fortifying it from prying eyes. It was a recent hobby. Some guys worked on cars, some built train sets—I studied and experimented and tinkered with making this the most secure room possible in hopes that even the Society wouldn't be able to breach it.

For now, at least, I was confident it would keep Fran out.

I strolled past my cache of items. A Taíno zemi, an amulet, a cracked mask. These were holy objects and spell tokens collected over the ages by a long-lived jinn with more power than Scarface. As far as I knew, they each fell short of being categorized as true artifacts. I wasn't sitting on a cache of super weapons or anything like that. These were still items I wasn't keen on allowing into the wrong hands. But first came security. Only after that would I properly catalog them.

I had mundane items as well, like the MP7 and other *Agua Fuego* weapons I'd "liberated." I set Manifesto's journal on an empty shelf, vowing to peruse it later, then blinked back to my actual closet. When I rejoined the others outside I stated my intentions.

"I'm going after the vampires who blew up your tattoo parlor."

Kasper was already ready and standing, having sensed something in the air. "I wouldn't mind running into them again," he said.

"What about Manifesto?" asked Emily.

"What about him?" I returned with a shrug. "He's out there. The police are looking for him. He's setting up his grand finale."

"Shouldn't we try to get a lead on him with the stuff you recovered?"

"It's just a record of his past moves. It won't help us."

The truth wasn't so black and white. It was very possible

Manifesto's journal contained clues about his enlightenment and empowerment. I would dig into those when the time came. At the same time, I didn't want the girls poring through pictures of mutilated bodies. It wasn't sexist. Nobody should see those things. Evan was a high-ranking police officer and Kasper had been a medic in Vietnam. They were already well familiar with the horrifying brutalities men could inflict upon each other.

"Besides," I said, changing the subject, "I just got a hot tip on the Obsidian March. One thing at a time."

I tried handing Kasper the Micro Uzi but he waved it off and tested the weight of the ax in his hand. It was the only thing he'd brought from his shop.

"What's the big idea?" asked Milena, tugging the Uzi back.

"We're raiding a vampire brothel. You shouldn't come. You're a liability."

She lowered her head. I stepped close and lifted her chin. "It's not because you can't take care of yourself. It's their compulsions. I can drill you on defending your mind another time, but for now you need to sit this one out."

Emily flashed Milena an affirmative before turning to me. "I'm still staying with my kids."

"I know," I said, embracing her. "You're a wonderful mother. The best." I gazed deeply into her eyes, silently thanking her for the years she'd raised our daughter without me. I gave little John McClane a high five and said, "Yippee-ki-yay, mother—"

"Cisco!" snapped Emily.

"My bad."

I moved to Fran, already accepting her fate of staying in. I mussed her hair. She jumped and hugged me tight.

"I guess I got nothing better to do," piped up Darcy. Kasper and I turned to her, standing by the front door holding her Hecate fetish. She shrugged. "What? Killing vampires sounds like fun."

I nodded. "It is, actually. Autobots, transform and roll out!" I was talking to a Baby Boomer and a Gen Z kid, so both their responses were lackluster.

Kasper took the passenger seat while Darcy followed on her bike. The first course of action was a pit stop all the way across the city. After confirming we had no tails we drove west, leaving the city lights behind. The edge of the Everglades was the creeping wilderness ever present throughout South Florida. Muggy wetlands rampant with chirping insects and small wildlife. I turned off Tamiami Trail onto the pitch-black dirt road.

We parked and trudged alongside a swamp in darkness. The path was dated and only used for occasional water access. The abandoned boathouse and the overgrown jungle were my old digs.

I shuddered as I remembered my time spent sleeping on the concrete foundation, wet and alone. Nowadays I was a new man, and this place was relegated to my cookhouse. People in my line of work can't boil blood and bone dust in swanky condos. While necromancy wasn't strictly itemized in the HOA bylaws, the toxic stink would turn heads real fast.

I pressed open the rusted back door and entered. The place was exactly as I left it, crumpled Taco Bell wrappers and all.

"What is this place?" asked Darcy.

"I used to live here, believe it or not." The dirty bedroll in the corner proved the truth of that statement.

"It's in the middle of nowhere. No wonder nobody could find you." She took in the damp shelter, half in awe and half in disgust. "What are we doing here?"

"Preparing for war."

I stopped at a bent metal shelving unit and eyed the knickknacks left behind. Powders and poisons and other tributes. Also a set of metal asanbosam teeth. I chuckled, remembering the plight with the Nether fiend that had started my story. Asanbosam were West African vampires, much worse than upirs on an individual basis. It was a good thing they were nomadic loners.

I had other souvenirs. A ruby red mermaid scale. A piece of igneous rock from an elemental. Even a shimmering short sword dropped by a dragon. I decided to take them to my cache later. For now I had more practical concerns.

I retrieved a reserve of spark powder. It was low and I didn't have time to cook more so I funneled what I could into red-jacketed shotgun shells. The process involved removing the wad and replacing some of the powder as well as the buckshot. It made for a big boom at short range. I emptied the road flares from my belt pouch. They were large, and I used the extra space to top off with components of black magic I was likely to use.

While I worked, Darcy browsed the curiosities. Kasper pulled a rusty machete from a wood block. Beside a cast-iron camping pot was a cloth breathing mask for filtering away toxins while cooking. It was also useful to mask my identity. I tied it so it hung loosely around my neck. Finally, we gathered outside and locked up.

"How cute!" said Darcy with uncharacteristic excitement. "A bunny." Sure enough, a rabbit hopped up the path toward us. "She's not afraid of us." The teenager crouched to give it a pat.

I dropped the silver whistle from my mouth. "He," I corrected.

She furrowed her brow. "He's your pet?" As soon as her hand brushed his fur, she recoiled. The small marsh rabbit didn't react at all. He just sat there, still, like a drone.

"Of sorts," I chuckled.

"It's a zombie," said Kasper gruffly.

Darcy's face twisted. "That's gross."

"Give him a break. He's a couple of months old and neglected. He's a little rotten."

My explanation didn't comfort her.

"Come on, Thumper," I called, leaning down and scooping the little guy up.

Darcy shook her head and hissed. "You have problems, dude."

They continued along the dark path to the street while I gave Thumper a chin scratch. These little guys weren't practical in a scrap, but they had many other uses.

Before I started after them, a strange red glow caught my

attention. Two dots, like eyes, fixed on me from across the swamp. I checked my companions. They were oblivious to the presence. When I turned back to the wraith, he was gone. I swallowed hard and made my way to the Firebird.

Chapter 44

The three of us crept down a Wynwood alley as casually as we could. It was past midnight now; while the streets were mostly empty, the area was a burgeoning hipster hot spot. Pockets of sweaty dudes sipped overpriced beer and chilled on makeshift patios because the rundown establishments couldn't afford AC.

"Remember," I said, "our number-one priority is minimizing collateral damage. We're vampire hunters, not criminals."

They nodded. "As long as the vamps are fair game," muttered Darcy.

"All except for Tutti. Beaumont wants her alive."

Kasper gritted his teeth. "Bitch blew up my parlor."

"You gotta leave it alone for now. She might know where Magnus is hiding."

I set Thumper down and picked up an empty beer bottle against the wall. The marsh rabbit hopped ahead under my silent command. I closed my eyes as he stopped at the edge of the next building.

Yellow light. A man with black fingernails sits against the wall. No cameras.

I blinked away the animal's view and signaled to the others. This was good. A quiet back entrance to a drug house. "Got one at the door. I'll distract him."

I stumbled around the corner, pulling the beer bottle from my mouth. I wouldn't win an Oscar but my inebriated condition was apparent enough. The vampire bouncer watched me like a hawk. A muted drumbeat pounded inside the door at his back.

"Cool!" I slurred, approaching him. "You guys open?"

The vampire stood, ready to take action and perhaps alert his friends inside if needed. Instead of spooking him by pressing close, I passed by with a healthy berth and headed to the wall ten feet down. He checked the alley before snapping his eyes back to me. I faced the wall and unzipped my pants.

"What are you doing?" he demanded, equal parts angered and repulsed.

"*Ay dios mío*," I drawled, only partially feigning supreme relief.

"You can't do that here. Get away." He walked toward me.

I whistled as soon as his back was to the others. They charged in with bandannas over their faces. Before the bouncer could reach me, Darcy's spellcraft dragged him backward through the air. He was impaled square on Kasper's machete, right through the heart. His eyes widened at the rusty blade protruding from his chest before he exploded.

"One down," muttered the old man. They approached the door and waited. Darcy clicked her teeth loudly.

I halfway turned away from then. "What? I had a lot to drink." I finished as quickly as I could, being careful to shake stray grains of dirt from my underwear. Darcy gave me kissy lips again. "Fine, back to business."

I approached the back door and tried it. Locked.

"I'm a decent hand at metallurgy," I boasted.

I eyed the lock and cracked my knuckles, dreading using my weakest spellcraft in front of the others. Darcy pulled me away and waved her statue. The door wrenched off its hinges and bounced across the asphalt. Loud trance music filled the alley.

"Or we could do that," I said. I raised the cloth mask over my nose and charged in.

Two vamps spun to us, in human form but elongated claws already drawn. I blasted one with a fireshot, center mass. The other sped toward me but froze at the teenage witch's behest. The machete finished him off.

A scream pierced the blare of techno and surprised me in the middle of sliding a fresh cartridge into the shotgun's breach. I snapped the sawed-off closed and raised it to my attacker, a thin redhead that reminded me of Tutti. At the last second, I pulled my aim to the floor and let the woman bowl into me. We tumbled. It was only a second until Darcy telekinetically dragged her off me.

As Kasper's blade came down, I jumped through shadow and appeared over her. The machete rang loudly against the forearm tattoo Kasper had inked. A flash of blue filled the hall.

"No!" I said sharply, grabbing the woman's hand and holding it up. "No black fingernails."

The half-crazed woman wiggled and spat against the clutches of spellcraft. Darcy could secure a human in place but not every joint in the body. She clawed at me with the human fingers I held on display.

Darcy twisted the small knife from her other hand. It clattered to the floor. "She tried to kill you."

My eyes ran to the slashed hole in my shirt. I hadn't even felt that. My hardened skin had deflected the weak blow. "She's a familiar, not a vampire."

"They're bad guys too," she insisted.

"It's not that simple." I still held the woman's wrist. Track marks ran the length of her malnourished arm. Vampire bites. Her mouth foamed and her eyes were dull. "They're like drug addicts, out of their minds, waiting on their next vampire fix. It's not their fault."

I dug into my belt pouch and retrieved a capsule of white powder. I separated the two halves and poured it down her nostrils. The frantic woman's heavy breaths immediately sucked it in. Her eyes relaxed and she settled into a stupor. When Darcy released her, she lay still on the floor, eyes open.

"No killing familiars," I repeated.

They nodded.

We peeked down the dim hall. Recessed yellow lights set the mood. Several doorways on either side, some open. The loud music had thankfully covered the commotion of our entrance. I jerked my head and Thumper hopped down the hallway. I pulled his vision into mine.

I switched the shotty to my offhand and an amethyst longsword melted from my palm. I waved Kasper and Darcy to the next set of doors, both closed, and folded into the open room.

"Yes!" moaned a skinny little thing.

She bounced up and down, straddling a man. They were both naked, and while I appreciated the jiggle of the girl's thick ass, I could've gone the rest of my life without seeing jostling vampire balls.

"Oh, yes! Give me more. More!"

I approached, techno masking the creaks under my boots. I stood right behind the girl, surprised I hadn't been noticed yet. She was leaning forward, butt springing up and down wildly, hair masking her face. The vampire's head was turned toward the wall while he chewed on her wrist. Blood dribbled down his cheek.

"Yes! Yes! Yes!"

Her free hand brushed back her long hair, and I finally saw the human fingernails. I wrapped the shotgun around her neck, pulled her up straight, and plunged the energy sword into the vamp's chest. Both of them stiffened and screamed for entirely different reasons. The guy blackened and exploded. The exhausted woman shivered and collapsed in the ashes.

"You'll thank me later," I said.

She spun in confusion, dazed from the sudden halt of the

vampire's pleasure. I pinched zombie toxin into her mouth and she drifted off to sleep on the mattress, ashy and wet, nipples still perked in the air.

I exited the room to find the next set of doors open. Vampires flew between rooms and broke their necks on the walls. A man flung himself at me. He was a familiar, so I spun around him and knocked his head into the wall. He spat on the floor, in a daze. I shoved my boot into his ass to herd him toward the back door.

It turned out the next set of rooms were larger than the one I'd cleared, with several beds in each. In the span of seconds, what was once a perfectly reasonable vampire orgy flipped into a fight club. With the droning electronica, the next minute was a scene from a violent music video.

Kasper used a super-powered punch to launch unsuspected vamps away. He tossed the machete and buried it with the kind of expert precision only a jungle fighter could have. Then he spun and started lopping off limbs with his ax.

Darcy played interference, sweeping fiends this way and that. She took Kasper's alley-oop and suddenly the machete danced through the air searching for targets.

I all-too-willingly sailed into the ruckus. Days of investigation and harassment had led us here, and we were done being whipping boys. And girls. Non-gender-specific whipping people. We were done. My darksword sailed through the nether fiends and the cheap walls of the drug house; if they were butter then I was at an all-you-can-eat brunch.

The vamps couldn't touch us. Ash exploded everywhere. It filled the air and the walls slicked with blood. Five dead vamps. Then ten. Fifteen came at us all together but they never had a chance against the ambush. Most of them had been literally caught with their pants down.

I tried pacifying what familiars I could, but they weren't all as easy to handle as I'd hoped. This wasn't a black-and-white proposition. It was very likely that many had chosen to be here. Kasper had to break a big guy's arm. Darcy turned to playing warden, holding humans out of the fight, but she could only focus on one at a time. Several others fled down the hallway and into the alley, joggling boobs and dongs alike. It was... kinda hilarious.

I stopped laughing when what must've been a twelve-year-old boy sped past. My stomach turned. I thought of Gendra, and Fran and Nicole in the black van.

Stray claws came at me while distracted. I dipped into the blackness, becoming ethereal. Instead of going for the easy kill, I grabbed the vampire by his wavy hair and smashed his head into the wall. Over and over and over, until the crater formed by his head was filled with brain matter. He slumped to the floor without turning to ash. I marveled at the resilience of these foul things.

All threats neutralized, Kasper bashed the next door open. He paused, eyes wide in shock. Darcy entered the room and walked out several bound women in the barely twenty-one category. They were frightened, leaning on each other for support, and—thankfully—mostly clothed. I just hoped they were lucky enough to have been untouched by their captors. My heart stopped when I saw the pair of middle schoolers.

"Gendra!"

The young girl was dazed, curly black hair hiding her eyes. I dropped to my knees and grabbed her in a mighty hug. Then I checked her face, neck, and arms for signs of abuse. I didn't find any physical damage, but it was obvious her head had been messed with.

As a few more people shuffled from the holding cell, Darcy returned. Her grim expression as she saw the two kids broke my heart. Not because she was shocked, but because she wasn't. Darcy was only eighteen and had already seen so much of the world that the lucky ones managed to avoid. I could only imagine what Gendra and the others were going through.

Darcy took the two middle schooler's hands and filed them out the back door with the last of them. I swallowed hard as Kasper approached the last door at the end of the hall.

Suddenly, the music stopped. Although it was probably just someone hitting pause on an iPhone, it had the dramatic effect of a record scratch. We froze and looked around. The only sound was the last of the victims shuffling to safety.

A concussive bang ripped a basketball-sized hole in the door. Kasper recoiled as blue runes all over his body flared. I charged past him and fired the shotgun, creating my own hole in the door and igniting it for good measure. Kasper and I swung sideways into opposite rooms for cover. I dispersed my sword and cracked my shotgun in half to reload.

Another blast powered through the door. Darcy was near the back door holding her statue to cover those retreating from errant projectiles. I pulled a couple of green eggs into my palm—sickening agents. After the next blast I spun into the hall and tossed them through what remained of the door. Shuffling movement was followed by retching and coughs. I emptied a container of snake dust into a palm and stomped up the hallway. I released a shell of fireshot to clear the way and dropped the shotgun into my shadow box. I kicked down the door and clapped my hands together, throwing a cloud of chalky bone dust into the room.

A vampire darted for me. I blended into the shadow and sidestepped as she flew past. I solidified and tossed the moccasin fangs deep into the room. The mask I wore filtered the toxins from my breath. Shadows swirled as I retreated.

Kasper swiped at the vampire who darted into the hall. She rolled under the ax and raked his stomach. The blow barely pushed him back. The old man kneed her in the face. Her head banged against the wall. He swung the ax and she attempted to spin away. It would've been easy with her heightened reflexes had Darcy not been pinning her down. Her skull split in two. Kasper yanked the blade out and reversed the blow to bury it in her heart.

Meanwhile, phantom snakes slithered through the smoke-filled room. They snapped and struck the defenders with ghostly fervor. Several vampires spilled into the sweet release of the hallway. I kicked a Mossberg out of my face and shoved them past, waiting for Tutti to clear the room. Each successive escapee increased my disappointment. With the others squaring off in the hallway, I dove back into the poisoned room.

Shadow filled my eyes, but there was enough smoke to keep my vision clouded. Strangely, the sounds of combat were muffled. I stepped forward, pleased to find a cage locked over the front door. Nobody had exited this way.

I took another step and ducked as black fingers nearly decapitated me. I dashed behind my attacker and pulled the darkness to my fist, but the black beast leapt out of the way. She came back with an almost full-grown arm. Despite her blackened carapace, I knew this was Tutti. I batted it away with my forearmor and slugged her in the jaw. Her shiny head snapped toward me and I slugged her again. She fell to her side, head down. An animalistic canine tooth bounced on the tile.

Enchanted slithers surrounded her. Tutti hollered and uselessly swiped the air. Gagging, she clawed the floor and crawled away from the poison. The vampire emerged into the back hall just in time for her last ally to burst all over her face. She hissed.

I put my boot on her back and shoved Tutti to the floor. Her black carapace melted away and she looked human again. She turned puppy dog eyes to Kasper. "Please! Please help me. He's hurting me." Kasper swallowed hard as energy tickled the air. "Please, mister! I'll do anything you want." I held a glowing purple darksword over the vampire boss as Kasper approached.

"Honey, even if I wanted the dirtiest, stankiest sex I could imagine, I'd only touch you to kill you." He curb-stomped her face into the floor. "That's for blowing up my house."

I defused my magic and leaned down, worried he'd killed her. She was out cold, but she wasn't dead. Tougher than human.

"I'll take her from here," said Darcy. Tutti's unconscious body unceremoniously slid along the floor.

The three of us lumbered outside, victorious. Even Thumper had a jubilant hop in his step. Our actions, however, had attracted an audience. Most bystanders attended the victims, but a few others noticed the three figures exiting the smoking back doorway wearing masks. Gendra stood beside a middle-aged couple with a stroller. The husband was doubtless on the phone with the cops. A few punks with bleached hair had no problem manning up to our presence. I pointed my empty shotgun to stall their approach before lifting Tutti over my shoulder and hauling ass down the block.

Chapter 45

I dumped Tutti in the back seat of the Firebird. She was already stirring. Darcy stood outside the car to hold her in place while I pinched some sleep toxin over her face. After inhaling some she nearly took a bite out of me. She was still lucid. I tried another dose but she wasn't having it. The vampire had displayed incredible resilience against my powders back in the brothel too.

"It's no good. You're gonna have to hold her in place, Darcy."

"One of you is gonna need to take my bike, then." We traded keys. I felt slightly self-conscious about the David Hasselhoff key chain. She ignored it and eyed the Firebird instead. "I've been wondering what it's like to drive this thing."

"Whoa," I cut in. "What are you doing?"

"What?"

"You need to concentrate on the vampire."

"I can do both." Her expression was indignant.

"Yeah, 'cause a distracted teenager driving a fast car has

never ended tragically. Besides, I can drive and Kasper can take the bike."

The old man raised a finger. "Actually, broham, choppers are more my speed, and it's been a looong time since I've gotten behind the wheel of a Trans Am." He held out his palm expectantly. Darcy tossed him my keys.

"Fine, old man, but only 'cause I like you."

I straddled the bright-red race bike and waited for them to pull out. It had been a while since I'd sat on one of these as well, but my body hugged it like a second skin. More muscle memory from my days as a thrall. Kasper redlined the V8 and peeled down the street with an enthusiastic hoot. The smell of exhaust and burning rubber followed.

"I should've let the teenager drive."

I set Thumper in my lap and revved the bike a few times, getting a feel for the throttle. The tire gripped the road and pent-up torque shot me off the line. Once on the road I settled into a reasonable cruising speed. As the spotter, it was my responsibility to keep an eye out for trouble. No black minivans. No vamps. Not even any speed traps. I relaxed as we rolled through Downtown Miami and entered Brickell.

It was a nice night with the wind in my face. Somewhere in that zone between cold and hot where the breeze wasn't necessary but still a welcome bonus. It made me briefly consider getting a bike of my own. I abandoned the thought as I rolled to a stop behind my own car. In neutral, Kasper gassed the Firebird and she answered with a throaty rumble. What a beauty. Race bikes were nice, but it was hard to beat an American classic.

The light turned green and Kasper gunned it. About to pursue, I halted the flick of my wrist when I saw it: a pitch-black owl with large orange eyes landed on a nearby ledge. Now, I'm no NatGeo expert but I do know a thing or two about the local wildlife due to my stint in the Glades, and black owls are pretty much not a thing. Not only that, but my background and body of experience clued me in to the supernatural significance of owls. As if to confirm my unnerving suspicions, the bird of prey seemed to bore into my soul.

The eyes sent a shiver down my spine. It took a second to hit me. I'd seen those eyes before. Malformed, cursed orbs. Of course, the man didn't possess eyes as starkly orange, but the large irises and wide pupils were identical. It brought Darcy's collision with a mysterious black form into perspective.

"Manifesto."

I pulled the motorcycle to the curb, cursing as Kasper sped away, showboating. I reached for my phone but the owl took flight down the cross street. I couldn't let it get away. With a hiss, I roared after it.

The owl landed at two other spots on the way. When I neared it took off again. It not only knew I was following—it was leading me by the nose. Just a few short blocks from where I'd first spotted it, the bird flew into a gated construction site, out of sight. I parked the bike and waited, but it was gone.

Large, half-built skyscrapers towered over my head. Two

heavy-duty cranes stretched even higher, their crossbeams slicing the night sky. This lot was the second phase of the new Brickell City Centre, one of those mixed-use residence/shopping spaces that was all the rage these days. It was a huge multi-block square that would one day be full of life and energy. For now it was an empty blight in the Downtown landscape.

I hit the kickstand and sucked my teeth. It was one in the morning. Bars and lounges were open just a few blocks away. What was going on here? The deserted construction site had all the trappings of the climax to an eighties movie.

I recited the serial killer's last message aloud. "Keep a fixed eye for it." This was Manifesto's invitation. It was a final showdown all right.

I brought out my phone to text the group but paused. I was sometimes unsure where to draw the line with the information I gave Evan. He had an obligation to uphold the law. Telling him the truth often put him in compromising situations. I backed out of the group-chat app and texted Kasper directly.

"Taking detour. Make sure Beaumont gets Tutti."

I cradled the rabbit in my arm and dismounted. The street was dark, with only sparse spots of lighting. A high fence with a cloth wrapping skirted the property, but there were rips and tears in it. I dove through the shadow and the chain link and appeared on the other side with Thumper.

Leveled terrain, huge concrete foundations, parked construction vehicles. The skeleton of an enormous building towered above. It was about what I expected.

I set the marsh rabbit down to scout ahead. A nagging feeling tugged at me. I was alone, playing into Manifesto's hands. I twiddled the phone in my palm and wondered if I was making a mistake. I grappled with the decision as my pet bounded ahead.

Screw it. They're my bros. Either I trusted them or I didn't. I opened the group chat and typed, "I think Manifesto's at the City Centre construction lot. Checking it out."

A sudden squawk scraped my ears. Claws raked my hand. The black owl's wings didn't flap until it was in my face, harassing me. I ducked into the shadow and recoiled, but the damn thing had swiped the phone from my hands.

I solidified a few feet away, phone tumbling in the air. The owl screeched and caught it in deft talons before flapping away. I lunged but the hunter made the sky in a blink.

"Damn it!" I hadn't sent the message yet. I'd typed it up but hadn't sent it. My friends didn't know where I was.

I clutched the top of my hand. A gash was open across the surface. I balled my fist tight as the wound seemed to steam for a moment. Manifesto was determined to keep this an intimate affair. I was willing to comply.

The first thing I did was sprint to the safety of the building structure. The first-floor ceiling was high, making it possible but difficult for the bird of prey to dive-bomb me. I imagined this space the center of a lobby not unlike the welcoming center of my own condo. Either that or a Chipotle. I crouched against a support pillar and squeezed a tube of gel on my wound. The toxin burned at my blood and I bit down. The pain was worth it. It guaranteed nothing else would be infecting my bloodstream.

I closed my eyes to scout ahead. Nothing came to me. I scrunched my brow and brought the silver whistle around my neck to my lips. A gentle blow that only the undead could hear. Thumper didn't answer. Not only was he dead, but he'd been dispelled without me noticing. That had never happened before.

I chided myself. I was distracted or wound up or something. Not an ideal way to start a showdown. I tugged my shotgun from the shadow and loaded it with a fire round. I slipped two plastic red shells in the sidesaddle on the stock. Even though I planned on facing Manifesto, I wasn't taking any chances.

Glancing back and forth, I considered my next move. It was dark enough out here that I was relying on my ensorcelled eyes to see at any distance. I wouldn't have a problem with access to my shotgun wherever there was shadow. At the same time I wasn't sure what spellcraft, if any, would be effective against Manifesto. The spark powder was magic, but it was also a chemical reaction that resulted in fire. More to the point, there was enough buckshot left in the cartridge to perforate anything I could get a bead on. I gripped the shotty in my right hand, held my left ready, and advanced through the steel and concrete husk.

My boots scraped grit and grime. They were lonely sounds. It was impossible to stifle my presence completely without going shoeless, and I wasn't about to do that with scraps of metal and glass lying about. My opponent most likely had a pistol on him. I just needed to gamble that he wouldn't get a good enough drop on me to do damage. At least not before I could return fire.

I passed a wall that opened up on the far side of the building. A small form was ripping at the ground ahead. I aimed and pulled the trigger in a blink. A cone of fire engulfed the nearby room and tracers barreled into the night, narrowly missing the owl. With the decreased powder and reduced buckshot, it was no surprise I missed at this range. The bird flapped away in a mad scramble and was gone, off to one of the many floors above me. Instead of reloading from the emergency saddle, I pulled another fire round from my belt pouch and slipped it into the breach.

I approached the edge of the building cautiously. As soon as I stepped out I'd be opening myself up to attack from above. Then again, the bird would be easily shredded by my twenty-gauge. If the thing had any rational thought whatsoever—and my experience thus far hinted that it did— it would sit back while I held the weapon. These shotties were practically engineered for popping birds from the air. Even though I didn't have a proper shell of birdshot, I was good enough to make up for the deficit if it made the mistake of closing in.

At the building's edge, a breeze of open air greeted me. At my feet, where the owl had been feasting, lay the remains of Thumper. The zombification process had stalled the putrefaction, but nothing could change the fact that he'd been dead for months. Either the black owl was ravenous or it wasn't a normal owl at all.

I pulled the silver whistle to my mouth and attempted to reach out to the bird. If it was an undead thrall, I should be able to feel a remote connection to its master. I didn't get anything at all. I could only conclude the thing was alive.

I lifted the mask over my nose again to take advantage of what little protection it offered. It sounds silly until you have a bird clawing at your face. I wished I had protective glasses as well, but it couldn't be helped. I leapt from my shelter to the outskirts of the building, sawed-off braced against my shoulder and pointing up in case the owl came swooping in.

Just as I'd expected, it was sitting this one out.

"Wizard," called Manifesto.

My weapon swung to the courtyard. My concrete structure was only one of several lining the block. They framed a wide center expanse. Like the park Milena and I had visited, this courtyard sloped down. A concrete platform rested a story below, no doubt waiting to be filled in with a raised park, fountains and trolleys, and whatever else executives figured increased foot traffic.

Unlike at the park, however, a set of flood lights circled and pointed into the depression. The high-powered beacons at multiple angles killed almost all the shadow in the courtyard.

Manifesto stood in the center of the pit beside a dump truck with a tire as tall as him. I raised my weapon to cover him and he slipped behind it.

"I thought we should talk, you and I," he proclaimed.

Chapter 46

My eyes scanned the courtyard perimeter and the surrounding buildings. Level upon level of unglassed stories surrounded us. Good perches for snipers, if Manifesto was a tactical man. I didn't think he was up to it, personally. This was his calling. He worked alone. Barring the owl, of course, but I was beginning to wonder about the damn thing.

I transferred my grip to the sawed-off barrel and used my other hand to steady my descent. Slow and stable, I watched Manifesto from a distance. He waited without movement. I had no idea what gave him such supreme confidence.

My boot caught a loose bunch of gravel. The slope gave way and I slipped. As my hand skewed to the air for balance, the owl swooped in and tore my weapon free. I tumbled to the bottom and turned just in time to see it flying away, shotgun in its claws like a helpless field mouse. Maybe I should've kept it in the shadow box after all.

I growled in frustration. That meant Manifesto wasn't the owl. Another possible theory shot down. When dealing with the unknown, guesswork was part of the business. I had other guesses too. The problem was, I was running out of them.

As I tracked the surprisingly silent flight of the predator, my field of view crossed over a floodlight. Now that I was in the lowered courtyard, the massive downward beams shone directly on me. I squeezed the shadow from my eyes before it blinded me. I wouldn't need the hyperawareness here.

I faced the dump truck. Manifesto stood beside it patiently, hands clasped behind his back. I rotated in a circle, taking in the whole courtyard depression, feeling like a speck under the looming towers and cranes. With the overhead lights dimming anything outside our makeshift arena, the structures seemed to stretch into infinity.

If I'd prepped and positioned a few undead sentries at strategic points in the rafters, I'd have eyes on the whole battlefield. The black owl wouldn't be able to surprise me like that.

As unnerving as it was, I had to focus on the larger threat. This was the serial killer's playground. He'd had hours to set his trap. And here I was, good and caught all right. I had done this all wrong. I could just kick myself, but I was definitely gonna kick him first.

I approached Manifesto guardedly. Same normal-looking guy, no more hoodie.

"Not a Fins fan anymore?" I asked.

One hand came around and unzipped the top of the black jacket. Like Superman, he brandished the Dolphins logo below. It was impressive to wear so many layers in Miami, even at night. My only thought was he wanted to die in his favorite hoodie.

"You realize you won't live to see them win a Superbowl," I said grimly.

He casually returned his hand to his back. "Who will, really?"

I didn't have a comeback. He kinda had a point.

I checked for the owl every twenty seconds or so, not that I could get a good view of the buildings. It kept me on my toes, and I was guessing Manifesto wanted that. For his part he just stood and waited, not afraid of me at all. That confidence was grossly misplaced.

"So I'm here," I said. "What is this about?"

Manifesto didn't answer.

"Why are you killing animists?"

He waited and watched.

My cheek twitched in anger. I checked for the owl again. "Where's the reporter? You kill him too?"

"I do not take the lives of the innocent," he proclaimed loudly. "I was bluffing about the shotgun murders. They were just a side effect of the filth in this city."

"You killed that woman you jacked the car from."

He bit down. "That was beyond my control. She gave her life to save humanity."

I scoffed and stepped closer. His hands were still behind his back so I was wary of getting too close while unarmed. I stopped at twenty feet. "You killed to save humanity. Tell me how that works."

"The people of this world are blind. I used to be as well." He raised a hand to the heavens. "But I shall illuminate the truth."

"You could've done that without murdering people."

"I had a hard enough time getting everyone's attention even after I did. Besides," he spat, "those who engage in devilry aren't to be saved. It's my mandate."

I clenched my jaw. I'd had the fortune (or misfortune) of meeting a real-life angel before. At least a self-styled one. I'd never heard of a Celestial mandate to take out animists. This guy was straight-up crazy.

But he was dangerous. I had to keep in mind that he'd taken out at least one competent animist.

"I hate to break it to you, Nathan Bartlett Jones, but you're not special. You're just an everyday person let down by a complicated life. A menial job, a sports team that never gets deep in the playoffs. I'm sure a lack of respect plays in there somewhere. It doesn't matter what triggered this killing spree of yours—it doesn't make you special. You've offed a few people. So what? You'll be a footnote in Miami history."

He sneered. His eyes dilated and grew to twice their size. His owl eyes resurfaced. Large fixed things that forced him to cock his head in jerky motions like a bird.

"You ignore my gift."

"It's a curse."

"No!" he snapped. He winced and fought off a moment of pain before regaining control.

I stepped closer. "I can help you," I gently offered. "Spellcraft can alleviate your hurt. I saw you ask Marie Devereaux for help. I know you want it. We can lift your curse if you would just tell me what happened to you."

His body twitched in indecision. I cut the distance between us to ten feet.

"Who did this to you?" I asked. "They're your real enemy."

His dominant hand swung around gripping a pistol. I froze. "Proof!" he announced loudly. "You would decry the holy angels themselves!"

I raised my hands slowly and shook my head. It appeared I was surrendering but I wanted my palm up to ready my shield. There was shadow beneath the dump truck but I was standing in a wash of light. The shield was my only defense.

"They're not angels," I calmly asserted. I glanced around for the owl and turned back to him. "You have the gun. You have control. You need to tell me what happened to you."

"I was given sight," he answered. "I was chosen. For this." Manifesto cocked his head. His entire body tightened and his arm wavered for a split second. Everything told me he was about to fire.

The Intrinsics sprouted through my palm tattoo as he pulled the trigger. A burst of turquoise energy flared before me and caught the round of lead. I was surprised by how measured his barrage came at me. Fire. Pause. Fire. Pause. It was mechanical. He wasn't even attempting to aim below my relatively small shield.

I continued deflecting bullets and closed the distance. Finally Manifesto showed an ounce of humanity. Panic. He backed away and lowered the gun to my legs. I dove sideways, under the massive dump truck. The construction vehicle had high clearance but the floodlights were angled enough that substantial shadow enveloped me. I slid from one flank of the truck to the other in a blink. I appeared behind Manifesto. He spun around in surprise but he was slow. I charged the last few feet of bright light to him and batted the pistol from his grip. He reached for my neck and I decked him. Manifesto dropped to the ground.

I stomped toward him. He pulled a small knife from his ankle, sharp eyes zeroing in on me. He scooted away defensively, further from the shadow of the dump truck.

"You think I need spellcraft to kill you?" I snarled.

He jumped at me with a sloppy blow. I barred the weapon with my arm. Protective magic battered the knife from his hand. I caught his neck with one hand and pounded him in the face, again and again. He collapsed, blood spouting from his nose and mouth. He hacked and clawed at the concrete.

I once again checked for the black owl, but we were alone. "Tell me who did this to you," I demanded.

Manifesto laughed.

I glowered, paced away, and scooped up his pistol. I slid the mag down. It still had a round, with one in the chamber. I snapped it back and pointed at his head. "TELL ME WHO SENT YOU!"

"Idiot!" he spat. "You're under the delusion that I can die." He fixed on a point past the floodlights. "My life will be eternal."

I followed his gaze but there was nothing to see under the glare. Manifesto shuffled. He reached to his other ankle.

His other knife. I rapped his head with the butt of the pistol and laid him out on his back. He coughed viciously and laughed some more.

The short blade in his grip had blood on it. His opposite arm relaxed beside him, wrist awash with blood. Manifesto had hacked his arteries open. I pounced to stem the flow of blood, but his knife swung again. I shielded my face and recoiled. The knife wasn't meant for me. Manifesto plunged it into his neck.

I lowered the gun and watched as the man's life left his body. He gurgled in wanton pleasure until he had no more breath. He released a long, final sigh; his eyes returned to normal. Manifesto was finally at peace.

I swallowed restlessly, knowing I'd defeated him while at the same time doing exactly what he'd wanted.

Chapter 47

I paced around the killer's body. He was dead. I didn't know owls, I didn't know curses, but I *knew* death. Manifesto had come here to execute his final mandate, willing to pay the full price because of his belief in the reward of a lofty afterlife.

I searched his body. He'd been a bit of a knife nut. A strap on each ankle and a sheath for his lost sword still on his belt. A wallet with a credit card, an ID, and a few bucks cash. That was it. He didn't even have spare ammunition left. I was betting the sum of his possessions had been dropped in that final geocache: a journal and some photos.

I stomped my heel on the floor. Manifesto hadn't meant to kill me. Not at first, anyway. His initial shot grouping had been directly at my shield. So what had he accomplished here? I checked the sky again. I couldn't see anything past the damn floodlights.

I aimed his pistol with both arms and fired toward the sky. The bang echoed through the courtyard. I suddenly wondered if the rest of Miami could hear me. I didn't care. I took careful aim and hit the target on my second try. A single floodlight shattered and went dark.

I still had plenty of light on me, but I could now see in the direction I'd come from. The direction Manifesto had looked up to right before he slit his wrist.

I was being watched.

As much as I hated leaving his body, I sprinted toward the sloped edge of the courtyard and tossed the empty pistol. I used my hands to claw at the gravel and climb up. Once outside the glare of the construction lighting, I pulled the shadow into my eyes and zeroed in on movement on the third floor. Someone quickly pulled out of sight.

I set my heels and charged into the towering husk, scanning for a stairwell. A building this size must've had several. There was no way I could cover the whole thing at once so I opted instead for closing speed. I made a beeline for the nearest stairwell, rushed up two flights of stairs, and shambled toward the window position.

As soon as I cleared the hallway and barged into the room, the black owl swooped in and scraped at me. I executed a low roll and slid through the darkness. It flapped wildly as I appeared behind it. I snatched it through a shower of feathers. It was huge up close, and vicious. Razor claws gashed my chest and ripped my mask away. I held on despite the pain. Wings thrashed, but they were useless in my grip. My right hand punched a stream of amethyst energy right through the thing. Its screech cut out suddenly as it died, probably not even aware of what had hit it.

Blood splashed my face and dribbled down my arms. I

dropped the bird as my skin hissed. I was burning. I rubbed my hands on my jeans and my shirt on my face. The cloth sizzled too. I slipped into shadow. Extraneous clumps of blood glopped to the floor, but much of it made the trip with me. It continued searing my skin, in or out of the darkness. I stifled a scream as it gelled into a substance not unlike napalm.

I shuffled through my belt pouch, desperate for something to cut the burn. My powders were all toxic and the gel wasn't meant for skin application. I opened a small jar of graveyard dirt and rubbed it on my face. While not enchanted, it was still a useful voodoo tribute. In this case I just wanted the soil to scrape away the acid.

That small amount done, I bit the bullet and squeezed the toxic gel on my arm. It burned as I rubbed it in. I emptied it over my exposed flesh and dropped the bottle to rub it in. After a stinging flare, the pain slowly faded.

I panted heavily as I regained my composure. I swallowed bitterly and crawled close to the owl. It had melted into a puddle of goopy tar surrounded by stray black feathers. Whatever it was, good riddance.

"That was for Thumper," I strained out.

Satisfied that I'd mitigated the acidic blood, I carefully grabbed a large feather for later study. Then I remembered what I'd come up here for and looked around.

The large space was mostly empty. A chair rested on its back by the ledge. I trudged over and flipped it to its feet. Bindings on the front chair legs had been untied. Someone had been here. I turned to the well-lit courtyard below.

Someone who'd had a front row seat to our little showdown.

Whoever it was had been afforded ample time to get away. Between needing to navigate up here and the distraction of the burning blood, our surprise guest could be a mile away. The black owl had seen to that.

I turned back to Manifesto, a lone figure sprawled out in a pool of red. Even in the end, the spotlights were on him. Maybe I should do something about that.

As I gazed at the ground, shadowy figures darted between the buildings. Humanoids, pitch black from head to toe except for milky-white eyes and ravenous teeth.

I stepped away from the vantage point. Vampires.

This wasn't right. How did they know I was here? I scanned the room for any other clues before my eyes landed on my sawed-off. The owl had been kind enough to drop it up here for me. I stomped over and recovered it. The stock felt reassuring in my grip. It was still loaded.

"Cisco!" yelled Magnus from somewhere out of sight. "We know you're here. We can smell it."

I hurried back to the window and crouched. More and more vamps flooded the construction site. I stopped estimating their numbers at forty. I was an eternal optimist and didn't want to see that change.

"This is unfortunate," I admitted.

Pops echoed off the surrounding buildings. Something whizzed past my face and struck the ceiling with a bang. I was taking fire. I lowered my head and weapon and pulled the trigger. I caught a bloodsucker taking aim. He caught fire but at this range the buckshot didn't destroy his heart.

Suddenly a host of weapons turned my way. I ducked as semi-automatic fire riddled my perch.

Time to dig deep into the well. I emptied the plastic Easter eggs from my belt pouch and bombed the gunners below. Green for sickening agents, white for sleep powder, blue for hallucinatory poison that utterly confused enemies. Eggs burst and clouded the grounds. I rained down my entire arsenal into their ranks. None of it would do any real damage, but the lot of them scattered. Toxins swirled across the front of my building. Hopefully they would delay any kind of united offensive.

Besides a few shotgun shells, my only remaining spell tokens were things like a mirror and some birthday candles. Necromancy stuff that didn't do me much good under present circumstances. I had sidewalk chalk to make a protective circle, but I wasn't versed in Emily's white magic. I could secure a perimeter against spirits, but physical Nether fiends would laugh off the barrier.

Sounds echoed from the stairway. I loaded a round from the belt pouch and converged on it. They burst through the door before I got there. The first one took a load right into the heart and exploded. I cracked the breach and reloaded from the sidesaddle in a smooth motion. The second vampire lunged. Still going full speed, I slid to my haunches as the black carapace shot over me. While it passed, my sawed-off emptied into its chest. Blood rained like a sprinkler.

I skidded to the doorway as a third emerged before I could reload. A freight train of shadow collided with it, large and impenetrable. The vampire bowled over her friends, stuttering their advance. By the time they got around her, I blasted another cone of magical fire down the narrow stairway. They sizzled and screamed.

My sidesaddle was empty, so I reached for my belt one after another. Crack, chamber, crack, BOOM. Crack, chamber, crack, BOOM. The spark powder did much more than burn unnaturally—it filled the entire stairwell with smoke and flames. The concentrated heat wafted through the doorway over me. It was so hot I had to step away. The effect inside the confined space was easily multiplied.

The vampires bellowed. Reinforcements charged up the steps only to find themselves trapped in a kill box. Superheated buckshot tore into hearts at point-blank range. Where the pellets missed, the magical flames finished the job. It was utterly glorious, but it couldn't last forever.

I slotted the last shell into the chamber, cursing when I saw it was nonlethal. I aimed at the next bunch of attackers and fired. Glue expanded outward and plastered the bottom of the steps. It quickly hardened and gummed up a pack of bloodsuckers. I dropped the shotgun into the shadow and dove into the smoke.

As I flew past surprised vampires, the darksword sprouted from my fist. Dramatic purple light slashed through two vamps on the way past. I skewered a third against the wall that stopped me. It was a ballsy move they hadn't expected, but they were carnivores through and through. They brandished daggerlike claws and came at me.

In close quarters, with this many of them, they were

faster than I thought. It had been one thing in the drug house when three of us had surprised them, but these vamps were a tactical kill squad. They came fast and heavy. My sword dismantled incoming black claws, but I only had one of them. Others raked at my arms and sides. My toughened skin only barely kept the wounds from being lethal.

I muddied the entire room with shadow and slipped into it, darting here and there. Rather than it holding me back, I thrived in the claustrophobic space. I only became physical when it was time to strike. I lunged from my protection, spawned my darksword mid swing, and retreated. It was maddening for them, especially since they kept slipping in the bloody ashes of their fallen. Amid the chaos, I spawned several tentacles to grasp at anything nearby.

Hearts burst faster than I could count. The air was thick with blood. So many down, but ten more filled their ranks. Then ten more followed. The bottlenecked quarters were to my advantage, but the vampires grew wiser. They crawled along the walls and the sloped ceiling to come at me in larger numbers. Their attacks came faster. Slowly, they backed me up the steps. They were overtaking my position.

I yelped as a claw caught the side of my head and nearly tore my ear off. I lunged through the shadow and dove through the doorway at the top of the staircase where I had started. An arm of spellcraft slammed the metal door tight and jammed it in place. Powerful fists dented the door. It deformed and bent away from the frame. Even with my spellcraft propping it up, the barrier would only hold for seconds.

Footsteps skittered around me. A vampire scaled from the exterior of the building and mounted onto the floor. They already had me surrounded.

I lived in the shadows. I was formidable in enclosed spaces, but there were too many of them. As the stairwell door burst open, I charged the lone vampire approaching from the window. Two others surged into the room, but they couldn't catch me. I used the black to dash ahead. It surprised the upir meeting my charge. My shoulder barreled into him and took us both clear out of the third-story window.

Chapter 48

Midair and falling fast, the vampire clutched me. Amethyst energy exploded through his heart. I ducked into the shadow as we hit the ground, ashes bursting outward. The landing still hurt, but I slid with the force and mitigated the impact.

I spun to find Magnus beside my dead rabbit. He held a submachine gun against my sword. "Cisco. You're somehow still alive."

"I'm stubborn like that."

Vampires filled the ranks behind him. Over my head, others leapt to the ground behind me. Magnus was the only one in human form. He put a palm in the air to hold everyone off. I was surprised he was being so sporting.

After all the damage I'd caused, after all the chaos and death and resistance, at least twenty upirs formed a circle around me. They kept their distance, and many of them had guns.

Magnus smiled. "I can see it in your eyes. How did I know you were here?"

I scowled. "Beaumont."

The vampire boss laughed. "That upstart? The Frenchman likes to play puppet master, doesn't he? Since you mention it, I did just speak with him on the phone a few minutes ago. He reports he has Tutti, safe and secure and wrapped with a bow."

My face darkened. If Beaumont was gonna sell me out, why would he give me Tutti's location in the first place? Why would he wait till now?

"Oh, I knew about your little deal," taunted Magnus with triumphant flair. "You think they'd make an idiot the boss of Wynwood? You wanted to become Beaumont's little mercenary in exchange for protection."

I frowned. That wasn't exactly right.

"Well, Cisco, I got news for you. This right here is Brickell. Beaumont has delusions of grandeur, but he knew he had to stand down or it was his ass. Your offer of protection was a dream."

My eyes flicked from one threat to the next. I spun in a slow circle, growling, daring the first one to make a move. None of this made sense. Beaumont hadn't led me here. He was a businessman. He wasn't supporting Magnus, just hedging his bets. That had to be what was going on.

Not that the facts helped me a whole lot where I was standing. The property was saturating with vampires in both human and Nether forms. Thirty. Forty. There was no way out of this.

I worked my jaw and faced the vampire boss. I would at least kill him. No matter what happened to me, one way or another, Magnus would go down.

I pointed the darksword. "You and me, Magnus. Let's end this."

He turned to his people and laughed. "That sounds like a waste of a good crew. Who wants to do the honors?" he asked them.

A towering bald man stepped through the ranks, mostly human except for lengthened black-armored arms and claws. I snagged his ankle with shadow. He sneered and tugged at it. Another vamp in full creature-feature mode tried next, but I bound him too. A petite redhead raised a pistol. The shadow disarmed her with a slap to the wrist. I lassoed several others in turn, straining against managing so many manifestations at once. It wasn't just the number, either; vampires were hella strong.

A few more raised firearms. Magnus ducked low. "Watch the crossfire," he snapped. The idiots had formed a circle around me. If they opened up, they'd be more likely to hit each other than me.

I grinned and pulled one more manifestation from the night. A twine caught Magnus by the neck and squeezed tight. "Call them off," I demanded.

He fired his sub gun before lifting it to me. I vanished into the ground as automatic fire kicked up dirt. I wasn't sure if upirs needed to breathe but it looked painful enough. The choking boss panicked and squeezed the trigger with abandon. Besides popping a round or two into an ally, he emptied his mag all too quickly.

The big guy who'd first volunteered to take me out

barged ahead, stretching his shadow tether with brute force. His claws waggled in anticipation. I was channeling too much spellcraft to do anything about it. I was too thin. I turned my sword from Magnus to him. He chortled, deep and mighty, bare pectoral muscles flexing like a giant Russian strongman.

"Little man," he boomed. "I will snap bones like twig."

He took a lumbering step toward me. My tether snapped. He was free. His eyes lit up.

And then a hole three inches wide hollowed out his chest cavity.

The massive vampire stood in stunned silence, blinking. A rifle report echoed off the surrounding buildings a split-second later, and the big man dropped to his knees.

Sniper fire. Evan Cross was here.

I rammed my eyes shut, forcing black tears down my cheeks as I squeezed every drop of the enchantment away. In the next second, an orb of light sprang to life above my head. Everybody recoiled from its unyielding brilliance, including me. Luckily, I'd seen the play coming and had averted temporary blindness.

The Obsidian March had an altogether different problem. See, the construction floodlights might've been as bright as the sun, but their luminance was artificial. The orb above us was Emily's magic, blazing and fierce and as elemental as the sun. It terrified the vampires.

In a blink the battlefield was transformed. Every single vampire shuddered into their weaker human forms. That got rid of my claw problem. On the other hand, the amethyst darksword winked out. That and every other shadow manifestation I'd spawned. There was no more of that, either.

Despite my being neutered, my enemies were flanked and caught in an ambush. Magnus dropped to the ground, clutching his sore neck and inhaling hard. I ducked, suddenly aware that I couldn't avoid all the impending gunfire. The petite redhead was the first to take a go at it. A round pummeled my shoulder before I got the shield up. Her next shot was deflected away. As she adjusted her aim low, she suddenly rocketed a hundred feet into the air. Darcy must've decided to tag gravity back into the ring because somewhere up there the redhead went idle and fell. She screamed the whole way down and landed with a sickening splosh-crack. That must've done a number on morale.

I lunged at Magnus, but the crazy vamps opened fire. Surprised, blinded, and poorly disciplined, their firing lanes intersected and cut friendlies down. My boots skidded backward as the ground between me and Magnus was torn to shreds. I raised the shield over my face and stayed low, crawling toward a soft spot in the circle.

Now declawed, the vampires without firearms drew blades. Daggers, machetes, tactical knives—it was a regular Hialeah flea market over here. I wasn't sure how I'd be able to get out until an old man covered in tattoos bowled through a line of them from behind. Kasper decapitated a vamp with his double-bladed ax and stood tall before me. Bullets flared and bounced off his armored body. One ricocheted into my hip. It stung but bounced away harmlessly.

Kasper grabbed my arm and yanked me through the crowd. As we passed the still-standing headless vamp, I scooped the AutoMag from his hand and turned it on our foes, only taking shots when I had clear heartstrikes lined up.

Darcy entered the battlefield and sent more vamps flying. She neutralized the ones with the biggest guns first. Evan picked off whatever targets were easiest at range. Emily was back there, too, mostly keeping up her portable sun, but every once in a while she flung a spear of light into an unsuspecting vampire heart. I hadn't even known she could do that. It seemed to tire her.

There were still plenty of vampires, but the ambush had wreaked havoc. Half the crew was mowed down before they could properly get their bearings and counterattack. When the AutoMag ran dry, I picked up a Kimber and chased Magnus into the cover of the building. As soon as I was out of the light, I switched the pistol to my offhand and spawned the darksword.

"Come out, come out, wherever you are," I mocked.

My boots pattered against the foundation. I raced to the other side of the building, spotting a bowler hat on the floor. Gunfire came from an entirely unexpected location: above. I slipped and ducked behind a steel pillar. A breath later I peeked out. Magnus was in his true form, attached to the ceiling. When he opened up on me again I swung to the opposite side of the pillar and returned fire.

Bullets rang against his carapace. I couldn't tell if they did any damage, but the vampire fled. Still maneuvering like a spider on the ceiling, he vaulted around the edge of the building to the second floor. I followed and stopped in the small area between the building and the road. A line of rebar spiked the ground, likely the frame of a future wall. Past that the only barrier to the street was the tarp-covered chain-link fence. Red and blue police lights blinked chaotically on the other side. Evan had secured the perimeter, which quite possibly royally screwed me. I figured I'd deal with that part after Magnus.

I sprinted back into the building and charged up the main staircase. These steps were wider and thankfully not slathered with Nether juice. The gunfire in the central yard began to subside. With numbers no longer on their side, the Obsidian March wouldn't fare well against a team of animists and a sniper. They'd likely fallen into defensive positions or were straight-up hiding. Just like Magnus. This was a clean-up job now.

I turned the corner. The cool glow of my darksword did nothing to illuminate the surroundings. As pretty as it looked, it wasn't light so much as a beautiful void. I scanned the surroundings with my spellcraft, using the pistol to brush back sheets of plastic hanging from the ceiling. He was in here somewhere.

A rustle of gravel spun me around. Magnus pressed through a sheet of plastic. It tore away and clung to him as he attacked. I brought the Kimber up and fired. *Pop, pop, pop.* The rounds didn't even slow his charge. I lowered the weapon and swung my magical blade as he converged on me.

The darksword slashed clean through the plastic. It wasn't until the end of my swing that I realized I hadn't caught any vampire in it. Magnus had halted his charge just before coming into range while flinging the sheet forward. It split into halves, one crashing into my face. I pushed through and tried a backhand swing, but the vampire's claws caught my wrist. The dog collar tore off my arm, and as I pulled in and punched out again, the purple energy sputtered and died. My fist banged hard into his armored chest, cracking my knuckles. My sword was gone.

Magnus quickly snatched my wrist anyway. "Oops," he jeered.

I brought the Kimber to his face and fired. The bullet pulped his eye. Either the round never entered his skull or he was powerful enough to shrug it off. Sharp claws raked my other hand and I dropped the pistol. I grabbed him to prevent another swipe. While we clutched each other, it was all I could do to hold off his snapping incisors.

Magnus was large and powerful in his full upir glory. I kneed his stomach, attempting to fortify the blow with shadow magic. As powerful as I was, even I relied on my fetish for physical manifestations. I came up empty. The impact hurt me more than him. I stared horrified as his ruined eye massed together and healed.

We struggled, locked, each with an arm holding the other. He punched at me. I did my best to fend off the blow, but unnatural speed and strength outmatched mine. He pounded my head well and good a couple of times. I lost hold of him and he wound up and struck me harder.

Dazed now, I went on the defensive. I backed away and fell into the shadow. I could manage that much without the collar. Since we were grappling, however, the vampire came with me. We slid across the floor, materializing on the ledge of the building. Magnus slammed me to my back and put a knee in my chest. Still pinning one arm, possibly to prevent a sword he didn't know I could no longer spawn, he tightened his grip around my neck.

I craned my head, now suspended over the edge of the building. Police muttered somewhere below. The fence was tall enough to conceal us. Just when I could've used some support fire. Then I remembered the scene on the ground below.

"I win, Cisco," boasted Magnus. "And I don't care if Manifesto's dead or not. I'll hide his body and continue his work. It's open season on wizards. You're all going to die."

I groaned and pushed away. He was too strong. I could only slide an inch further over the edge. "You first," I said.

I screamed. Not on the outside, but within me. I blared with the full content of my raging being and willed the Intrinsics to well up inside me. Darkness flooded my soul and I held it there, forming it into something scary and real. I released it in the form of a wrecking ball.

A huge mass of shadow collided into Magnus from behind and swept him overhead, just barely clearing me. I spun and watched as the vampire boss plummeted and hit the ground.

It wasn't a long fall, especially for a supernatural being, but he impaled himself facedown on the rebar. I recovered my breath and rubbed my wrist, amazed that I'd been able to form a shadow construct without employing my fetish. It had physically taxed me, and I was sure my capability was limited without it, but I had done it.

I stuttered to my feet and swayed, finding a wall pillar for support. I stumbled to my dog collar and snatched it up, gradually feeling stronger. I made my way to the edge of the building and hopped down. I landed in an unceremonious tumble. I pushed myself back up and made my way to the still-living vampire.

Magnus gagged and coughed. With a stake of steel piercing his chest, I was surprised his lungs weren't full of blood. These vamps really were cold, dry husks. Despite him once again wearing his earthly form, he wasn't human in the slightest. I didn't know if he was lucky or not that the rebar had just missed his heart.

"That looks like it hurts," I said, crouching in exhaustion beside him.

He glowered. "You... You cannot stop the endless March."

"Figured there were a bunch more where you came from," I snickered. "And maybe you're right. But I can stop *you*."

Black fingernails clawing the ground, Magnus summoned insatiable will and pressed up to his hands and knees. The rebar scraped drily against crusty ash in his chest cavity. I couldn't believe it, but he lifted a foot higher and freed himself. "You..."

"Yeah, me." I stood with a scowl. "Remember that. For the rest of your miserable life."

I placed an alligator boot on his back and forced him down. With my weight on him, the rebar punched through his chest again, only this time I'd nailed his magical core. Magnus opened his mouth to scream but willpower only went so far. Blood and ashes were his only reply.

Chapter 49

Rather than face the cops, I trudged back to the central yard. My friends had finished off the last of the kill crew.

"You should've told us you were doing this," chided Evan.

I shrugged and shook his hand. "An owl stole my phone." They watched me dubiously.

"Is that him?" Darcy asked. "Manifesto?"

She stood at the edge of the courtyard where the killer's body was bathed in high-powered lights. I nodded. "It's over. You guys were pretty badass. Thanks."

The vampires had been utterly routed. We'd exterminated the better part of eighty Obsidian March members over the course of days. It wasn't anywhere near the entire hegemony. It wasn't even the majority of their Miami footprint. With the March's recent expansion, they were an infestation that wouldn't be easily eradicated.

We sure as heck stomped on a sizable fraction, though.

"It's not over yet, cowboy," returned Evan. "I can't keep the department out of this any longer. We need to get out of here." He started toward the entrance he'd come from.

"Wait. We didn't uncover Manifesto's plan." I started down into the lowered platform.

"Cisco, we don't have time for this. He's dead. It's too late."

"Never tell a necromancer it's too late."

Evan got a radio message and replied. "I can't hold them out. I'm not even their field commander. Miami PD's on their way in. The DROP team is posted this way. Let's go. NOW."

I grimaced as the group turned to go. "Just need to wipe the gun down," I called back. I did that but also made a pit stop at the body and reached for my belt pouch. Darcy was the only one that waited behind and watched me.

I hurried from the pit and we caught up to Evan. His team manned a tactical van on the outskirts of the property. They remained stoic as we loaded up. The back shut. An officer pounded on the door twice. We pulled away from the team and cleared the police perimeter another block down. It was all very efficient.

"I don't know how the hell we're going to spin this," said Evan. "We got Manifesto, but the entire city of Miami heard that shootout. There are too many weapons and spent shell casings without a single vampire body to match."

"Can the feds help?"

"A better question is would they." The van stopped on the street in front of my condo. Evan swung open the back door. "I need to stay with the team and smooth things out. I'll catch you later, Cisco."

We exited to the sidewalk. Fire Rescue vehicles with droning sirens sped past. Instead of going inside, I pulled the team along for one last detour. Beaumont's restaurant was only a block away. Unfortunately, at this time of night the place was locked down. Not a soul stirred inside, human or otherwise. With the heavy presence of first responders in the area, maybe the restaurateur had the right idea.

I hated not having a resolution with Tutti but relented and retreated indoors. The police no longer patronized the lobby. We returned upstairs without seeing a soul. Milena and Fran were happy to have us. I was ecstatic. I didn't even give Fran hell for being awake so late.

"We did it," said Darcy. "It was easier than I thought, too."

"You call that easy?" I was still slashed up and sore, with bumps on my head and burns on my face. I was scraped, beaten, aching, and bloody. I couldn't stop smiling.

Emily hugged me gently. "I'm glad you're safe again. All of us. Thanks for taking care of us."

I scoffed. "Thanks for saving my ass back there." I turned to the team. "All of you."

Milena pouted. "I missed out on all the fun."

"Me too," said Fran.

I wanted to tell her the fun was right here, but Emily beat me to it. "Honey, get your stuff. I'm gonna get John so we can go home."

"You don't want to stay the night?" I pressed.

"No offense, Cisco, but I'm exhausted and want nothing more than to relax in my own house, with my kids safe and sound."

Kasper had been eyeing the fridge for a beer. He suddenly abandoned the idea. "Yeah, I'm tired too. Seeing as how I don't got a home anymore, I'm gonna turn in here, if that's all right with you."

"Of course, brother. Always here for you."

"I'm out too," said Darcy. "We all know the cops will be swinging by tomorrow asking questions." She rapped me on the shoulder as she headed to the door. "I don't want any part of that."

I looked around, aghast. "*Really?* Nobody wants to stay?"

Milena returned from the kitchen holding two beers. She handed me one. "I'm not going anywhere. I wanna hear all about what happened." She sat on the couch expectantly.

I gulped the suds and started the story. At first, everybody listened in rapt attention. They all wanted the deets on my encounter with Manifesto: the man, the myth, the legend, but especially the enigma. Unfortunately, his end was as esoteric as his beginning. It was hard to decrypt the ravings of a sociopathic killer, and I wasn't so sure it was worth trying.

As soon as I got to the part where everybody introduced themselves, they headed out, one by one. That story was old news to them. By the time I finished the whole shebang, Milena and I sat alone on the couch.

"Look at you," she said. "Becoming quite the leader."

I scoffed. "I'm not a leader. I'm just a guy who doesn't like being pushed around."

She gave me a peck on the cheek. "Same difference."

I mused thoughtfully over everything that had happened as Milena scoured my tablet for the latest news. "Downtown shootout." "Major gun battle echoed through Brickell today." "Police fired upon and killed the Manifesto Killer." Information was sparse but coming in quick. Only half of it was factual.

I started to wear down after the long night. Here I was, spending quality time with Milena, and I was too exhausted to make a move. I watched her beautiful brown eyes as they reflected the light of the tablet.

"*Mierda*," she cursed. "I think you need to see this, Cisco."

She played a high-definition video of the scene at the construction site.

"Breaking news: Our very own cameraman, kidnapped by the Manifesto Killer, has returned with shocking and exclusive footage of his final confrontation."

The video was angled above Manifesto, facing into the brightly lit courtyard from the third story of the building where I'd found the chair and bindings.

"In order to respect the privacy of an ongoing investigation, we're not releasing the name of the cameraman, but we can report that he is safe. Nathan Bartlett Jones captured and forced him to record a bewildering spectacle."

A figure stepped into frame and my jaw dropped. Cisco Suarez calmly approached the Manifesto Killer, except billowing shadow encircled me. Just as with the security footage Rita had shown me, *and* despite standing in sharp lighting this go around, *and* not remembering having done it, the shadow obscured my identity. I appeared humanoid, for sure, but overall on video I didn't look very... human.

"I don't know what we're witnessing here," said the commentator. "A Shadow Man, of some sort. Some kind of strange liquid or energy coating is pulsing off him."

The full color of my turquoise shield was followed by my ghostly dash under the dump truck. I was shocked. It was plain as day in full HD. My on-camera speech was muted as I mostly faced away, but Manifesto called out in crisp syllables, every word perfectly enunciated for an audience.

After the very brief struggle, Manifesto sat on his haunches and directly faced the camera. "My life will be eternal," he proclaimed.

I had turned to follow his gaze after that. For a split second the camera recorded the best view of my face. I could almost see a masked man if I knew what to look for, but it was a stretch. I hoped a positive ID was impossible.

The video cut out when Manifesto spiked a knife into his wrist. The commentator explained the scene in lurid detail without broadcasting it. I stopped listening. Complete stupor overtook me.

This had been Manifesto's endgame all along. He'd resolved to out spellcraft. We had stopped the killings, solved his puzzles, and cleaned up his tracks—and at the last second he played a gambit which made none of it matter. It was a masterful stroke.

"He wanted to be a sacrifice," I growled. "He wanted to show the world what he was willing to do for attention."

My face sank into my hands. An overwhelming victory had flipped into near disaster. The public now knew the police didn't kill Manifesto. They knew *someone* was out there. Spellcraft would dominate the national media and focus on the Shadow Man, on me. I was a spectator sport all over again.

The shadows tickled me. As Milena scrolled through posted stills of the event, I couldn't get over the cloak that had hidden me the whole way through. One image in particular drew my attention. Right before I'd ducked under the dump truck, the shadow had spread to either side of me, almost like...

"The Wings of Night," I muttered.

"The whats of who?"

I shook my head. "Something changed after I visited the underworld. The flow of shadow is more direct through my body, like an artery. I can do things that weren't possible before." I frowned at the dark envelope that smothered my video persona. "Apparently I can even do things without actively trying."

She pressed her lips together, unsure what to say but resting a hand on my lap.

"Put it away," I said.

She set the tablet aside and leaned on me.

"I don't think today could get any worse."

Milena rubbed my back sympathetically. "That's a good thing when you think about it. It's only up from here."

I worked my jaw as Milena tried to comfort me, dreading the impending visit from Special Agent Rita Bell.

"Did you hear what I said?" asked Milena.

I jerked, realizing I'd zoned out. "Huh?"

"I broke up with Gavin last night."

I blinked in confusion.

"Last night," she explained. "It's why I wanted to meet him so fast after our date. I figured... he's a really good guy but I wanted to do what felt natural rather than push things. Life's too short, you know?"

My mouth froze open as I took it in. Milena had her arm around me. Our faces were close. She cared about what I was going through. She was here for me. "You didn't roofie my beer, did you?"

She laughed and pretended to take offense. She sat up straight, arching her back and puffing her chest out. "I'd like to think I don't need to—"

I tackled her onto the couch before she could finish. Our lips locked and we kissed hard, pent-up worry and rage and adrenaline and even exhaustion giving way to one forceful expression. Milena moaned as I pushed my body into hers. She angled her leg around and locked ankles behind my back. I could feel her heat. She wanted me. Her nipples perked through her bra.

I paused and backed away for one aching moment. Milena watched me expectantly, eyes blinking slowly, breath baited.

"Sorry in advance," I said with a smile, "but I always wanted to do this."

"Do wha—?"

I grabbed her red shirt by the collar and tore it off. She

yelped as it ripped away, exposing the black lacy bra she'd definitely meant to show off. She hurried to unhook it before I tore that off too. Her full breasts quivered in glorious freedom. I caressed them. She was everything I wanted in my life, heaving breathless beneath me. I leaned in for a gentle kiss, snaking my lips from her nipple and up her neck. Then we smiled at each other, face to face, lips barely touching.

Milena kissed me and said, "*This* feels natural."

I picked her off the couch, carried her not-so-gently to the bedroom, and slammed the door.

Chapter 50

The night was heaven. We went so fierce and hard that I reopened a few wounds. I should've looked to them better, but nothing was more important to me than living in that moment. After we lay spent and panting on the bed, we chatted a while. We laughed about our lives and everything we'd been through. We kissed, barely able to get enough of each other, and then we made love again. Gently this time. Measured and easy, savoring every moment.

I was so damned exhausted I didn't remember falling asleep. I woke in the morning with Milena at my side, not a worry on my mind. I beamed as she slept. Sleeping in late and hitting up a fancy brunch was fine by me.

It was a nice fantasy until someone pounded on my door. I shoved on underwear and a pair of jeans and answered.

"You don't pick up your phone anymore?" snapped Simon Feigelstock. His wingtips and pinstripes and briefcase at this early hour were hard to shake.

"I thought you left town."

He shrugged and wagged a finger. "Something you

should know about me. I don't always do as I'm told. I had faith in you. Hey, you mind putting a shirt and shoes on? We have business downstairs. It'll be quick. I promise."

Half of me wanted to slam the door on his face, but the other half was intrigued by the offer of a speedy resolution. I was willing to skip sleeping in if it meant I could still enjoy pancakes. I returned to the bedroom. Milena was still knocked out well and good. I'd need to tease her about that later. I dressed without waking her and slipped down the elevator with Simon.

"That was a cool trick," he remarked, "hiding your identity like that."

I canted my head. I couldn't unravel the mystery myself and didn't try explaining. We exited into the lobby. The morning light hit the walls and furniture at a different angle. The chaos the night before seemed a week old. Once again we headed to the doors of the adjacent coffee house, only this time they were wide open. He ordered two lattes and we sat at a high table.

"I like this place," he said. "Best coffee in the city."

"Eh, it's not bad. They could use a colada though."

He laughed. "Maybe you should do something about that." I watched him strangely as his head snapped away.

"That was fast," he announced.

I turned and realized this was an ambush. Special Agent Rita Bell joined us at the table. She was freshly showered and changed, but a new coat of makeup couldn't hide the long night she'd had.

"You should order some coffee," offered the high-priced

lawyer. "It's the best—"

"Cut the shit," she snapped before zeroing in on me. "You have a lot of explaining to do."

I sipped my drink. It needed more sugar. "I don't know what you're talking about."

Annoyance flashed across Simon's face. He raised a hand and said, "I'll be the one doing the speaking, if you don't mind. It's why I'm here." He turned to Rita. "This is a courtesy sit-down, Agent. On behalf of my client, I'd like to say how relieved he is that the threat to his person has been eliminated. The Manifesto Killer is a big win for you."

"Don't give me that," she said. "We all saw the video in question. What was on it?"

"Special effects," he assured. "I don't know who rendered that but they did a hell of a job. I'm sure Shadow Man will be Miami's next big urban legend."

"We both know who the Shadow Man is. It's the second video I have of Cisco."

Simon frowned. "I don't understand. My client was under police supervision the entire night. I have numerous witnesses who can attest to that."

"Yeah? I want their names."

He didn't hesitate to flick open his briefcase and present a slip of paper with said names. I had no idea who was on it. This was Simon's play. This was what he was good at. "I also have Cisco's typed statement detailing Manifesto's attack and the *single* encounter that followed when the killer knocked on his door."

"What about the shootout?"

"My client couldn't hear the reports through the triple-glazed windows of his penthouse. I believe the police are attributing the gunfire to gang activity. You'd need to confirm that with them."

Rita forced thin lips together. She was a dog with a bone; she refused to bury it, but it was obvious she wasn't ready to chew it up. I suspected Simon had already warned her about harassment and my rights as a victim. There was definitive proof I'd been in Manifesto's crosshairs. With the backing of the local police, the FBI didn't have a lot of room to free-ball this, especially given the unexplainable phenomena.

She frowned and swiped her buzzing phone. "I'll be watching you, Cisco. This isn't done. I'll have more questions later."

"You have my number," Simon reminded. "We're happy to cooperate."

She huffed and stormed off.

"Wow," I said after another hit of coffee. "That's it?"

"It hardly ever is, but it will be taken care of. You did what you were asked, Cisco. Darcy checked in. Updated me on your work sanitizing the evidence. It was a job well done, and the Society keeps its promises."

Carmela Flores had obviously been spying on our exchange because she entered the coffee shop as soon as Agent Bell cleared the building. She dove straight in like a hawk, sharp nose and all. "Mr. Suarez, that strange character you've been employing spent the night at your house. Don't deny it. I saw him leaving this morning."

"It's a free country last I checked."

"I've seen the traffic through your home lately. I certainly hope you're not subletting rooms to vagrants. It's against HOA bylaws, you know."

I ground my teeth. "Could you just leave me alone for a single day, you dried-up c—"

Simon clapped a hand on my shoulder. "It's okay, Cisco. I invited her."

Carmela visibly trembled. Her jaw hung idly.

I blinked. "—Coffee? You tried the coffee?"

Simon withdrew official documents from his briefcase. "Mrs. Flores, it's my understanding that you've been threatening my client with eviction."

She swallowed. "As the head of the HOA, it is my—"

"I've been handling my client's financials," he continued, "and I wish to inform you that Mr. Suarez's full balance on his home loan has been paid off." My eyes widened as he slid over a stack of paper. "He's a full owner now, which grants him additional protections as per his lease agreement. You're no longer able to execute a lien against his home."

She stiffened uncomfortably as she browsed the documents. Either that or the stick up her ass had shifted. The papers were legit. A full title wasn't included under such short notice, but he'd greased the wheels with letters from the bank.

"Well," she replied haughtily, "since you're a legal expert you should be aware that Mr. Suarez still needs to abide by the housing regulations. Failure to do so can still result in a lien."

"Only if you bring it to a vote with the board," he

countered.

She nodded hesitantly. "I sit on the board and my opinion is well respected. Mr. Machado always sides with me. I can call on a vote if I need to."

"Great!" he chimed. "I'll be there."

"Well, I—what?"

He planted more paper before her. "Cisco will be, actually, but as his lawyer I can vote in his stead." She started to object but he steamrolled her. "I know what you're going to say. Residents don't automatically qualify for the HOA board. You should know that my client purchased this coffee shop this morning. As a business owner in the building, he's granted full status on the board. That also means Mr. Machado, our former coffee shop entrepreneur, is no longer on the board to give you an automatic vote."

Carmela jerked at the sudden news. She opened her mouth a few times and tried to fashion a suitable response. Nothing came. For the first time in my life I saw her speechless. The defeated HOA director finally decided on a terse nod before turning on her heels and clacking away.

I was still in shock. "I... *own*... the coffeehouse?"

He slid the papers to me for signatures. "Hope that's okay. Sorry about the short notice. Your accounts need to be tied to a business venture, and I opted for growing cocoa beans in South America. That's officially how you made your fortune. When I saw that bitch pile onto you last night next to the coffee shop, well, I suppose it was serendipity."

"You're telling me." I sipped the latte and snickered at

his earlier statement. "Maybe I should do something about the colada." He smiled. "I don't know what to say, Simon. You really came through on the financials."

"You scratch my back..." he said with a full set of teeth.

"Right."

I picked at the disposable cup and looked around. I could deal with a joint like this. It was exquisitely normal. A place I could take my daughter. Maybe Kasper could sling ink in the back.

A legit business. *Outlaw Coffee*. I liked the sound of that.

"Great work, Simon," I reiterated. "Also, you're fired." His smug smile vanished. "Don't take it personally. I'm glad everything worked out, but I don't want you or the Society in control of my finances."

He chuckled. "I can't blame you." He slid over a paper terminating his power of attorney and handed me a pen. By now I had a brick of papers to go through with him. He warned that while my money issues were cleared up, aspects of the Manifesto case would still be a headache. Maybe I did need a lawyer a while longer. "Besides," he added, "you're not up for membership in the Society."

I admitted to being surprised by that.

"It's not you, Cisco, it's me. But really, it's you. The Society strives for secrecy, and you're too hot right now. You're so hot you're nuclear. When and if you can find a way to keep off the ten o'clock news, we'll lift the hiring freeze."

I rolled my eyes. These guys really didn't get the message.

"Until then, my last piece of advice is to slow down. I understand what happened with Connor Hatch. That was personal business. But this vampire stuff, being the local tough guy—in a city this big it's bound to get you torn to scraps and eaten for breakfast. Physically as well as metaphorically. My services will get you through the fallout of Manifesto and establish you as a legal entity, but that's where the charity ends. If the police or feds pick you up for something unrelated, call that guy who advertises on bus benches and rides a Harley. I hear he's used to hard cases."

After he was gone and my coffee was long empty, I sat pondering the abrupt transition in my life. Cisco Suarez, the upstanding member of society. Very rarely was a fork in one's road so obvious. One promised happiness and a full life, the other a bumpy ride and a possible dead end. It was a lot to think about. Right now, I wanted nothing more than to head upstairs and return to Milena's side.

Unfortunately, some roads were under construction and riddled with detours. Tutti strolled outside the storefront's window. She was dressed more respectably. Her arm was fully grown back. She still had the pigtails but wore less paint on her face. The vampire in human guise posed outside and winked at me. I tossed the paper cup in the recycle bin and followed her out.

Unsurprisingly, she led me to Carbon. The steakhouse wasn't open mornings but the front door was unlocked. We passed several employees on the way to Beaumont's VIP table in the back. I didn't sit.

"Leave us," he said to her while appraising me.

She nodded her head, patted my chest seductively, and disappeared somewhere into the back.

"You played me," I said.

His eyes flared. "I did nothing of the sort."

"Did you tell Magnus where I was?"

He chuckled and shook his head ponderously. "I thought you were smarter than this, Cisco. I didn't tell Magnus—he already knew."

"How?" I demanded. "I wasn't followed. I'm sure of it."

Leverett Beaumont motioned for me to sit. When I didn't, he gave a lackluster shrug. "The Obsidian March was working with the Manifesto Killer." He noted my shock. "I knew Magnus hadn't figured on taking out that tattoo parlor by himself."

"Manifesto and Magnus were in communication?"

"It would appear so. When your people brought Tutti to me, I quickly broke her. She isn't very high in the Obsidian March ranks, but as Magnus' personal pet she overheard a few things. She knew Manifesto was setting a trap for you at the construction site. Magnus was giving him room but planned on moving in afterward if necessary."

"Why would the combined vampire clans wait on one human to make his mark?"

"Unfortunately, we can't ask them because they're both dead."

I hooked hands on my hips. "You were the one that told my friends where I was. You saved my life."

He nodded without fanfare.

"And Tutti's in your pocket, *safe and secure and wrapped*

in a bow."

His eyebrow arched at my emphasis.

"That's what Magnus said. You had her safe and secure and wrapped in a bow. You told him about just enough of our arrangement that you'd look clean in case he succeeded in taking me out. You were playing both sides."

His lips curled into a devilish grin. "The best lies are truthful actions with false intent. *Of course* I told Magnus about your visit. It made him feel in charge."

"And covered your ass if I failed."

"That too. Would you expect anything else? Is investing against annihilation such a poor strategy that it would sour our partnership?" My demeanor said yes. "Don't overthink it. It worked, didn't it?"

"Sure, but my secret's out. There's not enough physical evidence for now, but the heat will only amp up from here."

"An unfortunate turn of events for an ally."

I grumbled the word. "Ally."

"You held up your end wonderfully. The press coverage will be a hindrance, but it will only add to your rising infamy. I'll leverage my influence to sway the Obsidian March from war. After their casualties and near exposure, whoever fill the shoes Magnus left will be more conservative."

"And Tutti, she's your agent now? A mole?"

He licked his lips. "Girls like that are attracted to strength. I just proved to be the bigger dog. She'll do what I say from here on out."

I frowned. The Frenchman had it all figured out. "Can

you trust her?"

He swigged the last of his drink. "I don't trust anybody."

"Right."

Chapter 51

Milena and I ended up having that brunch, only it wasn't so fancy. Pancakes, bacon, and the best hash browns in the city. Milena got zucchini shreds, claiming they were healthier. They tasted just as fried to me.

We picked things up right where we left off the night before, without any hesitation or regrets. It was fun to think about the future for once. I think she was even more excited about the coffee shop than I was.

While we enjoyed a relaxing weekend, the public dove headfirst into the Manifesto craze. As incriminating as the video was, it kind of worked in our favor. The spectacle stole focus away from the gun battle. The grotesque allure of a deranged killer combined with mystical sights—it was a sensation. Most accepted that a street gang had slipped away before the police arrived. Sure, that fudged the timeline a bit, but who was keeping track? With zero fatalities resulting from the shootout, those details were buried in the frenzy.

The Firebird got her tire replaced. Somehow there

wasn't a scratch on her. I happily drove around Miami without serial killers or mysterious black vans in tow.

We didn't let that fact lull us into complacency, though.

A few days later, when everyone else was scurrying around the city dealing with rush-hour traffic, a few of us worked in my cookhouse on the edge of the Everglades. It was hot and humid as the sun began to fall, but that's why they call it hard work.

"Again," I instructed.

Darcy and Fran squared off in the dilapidated boathouse. They were ten feet from each other. My daughter took a few steps toward the telekinetic before encountering resistance. Fran twisted in place, looking like her arm was caught in an invisible fence. She took a measured breath, set her jaw, and pulled free.

Fran was growing cooler under pressure. Emily wore a proud smile as she watched from the background.

Darcy flicked the statuette of Hecate in alarm as Fran nonchalantly strolled up to her and tagged her arm.

"Gotcha."

I stifled easy laughter. "Just remember that this isn't a playground game in the real world." I set my boot to start forward before realizing I was stuck in place.

"What are *you* laughing at?" needled Darcy.

I tugged at her spellcraft. My torso was fixed in position, causing me to moonwalk in place. "Now, now, Darcy. There's no reason to take it personal."

"It's not fair," she said. "Magic just doesn't work on her."

"That's her thing."

Hecate taunted me in her grip. "That doesn't give you a right to laugh. It's not like *you* can do anything about it."

I watched her plainly a moment, considering my expression and patience fair warning. The chip on Darcy's shoulder had grown over the weekend. Whether it was about me getting with Milena or her difficulties against Fran, she was in a more grumbly mood than usual. After she refused to release me, I shrugged and tweaked the shadow.

A tentacle lashed out and struck her hand. Hecate flew from her fingers and toward the corrugated ceiling. The spellcraft ensnaring me evaporated.

"My fetish!"

I stepped forward and casually caught the wood statue. I considered the teenager with a smug grin. "Don't suppose you can do a whole lot without this, can you?"

Darcy blinked and looked away. Fran and Emily quietly watched us.

"You're strong for your age," I continued, "but your youth is still a crutch. You lack depth of experience. It makes you rigid, unable to compensate for unpredictable outcomes. Half of what I do is dealing with bad breaks." I handed the statue back to her. "A missing fetish, for example."

Darcy snatched it away in a huff. "Always a teaching moment with you."

"That too. That attitude. You're so used to full control that when it wavers you lose confidence. It gets you off your game and your powers falter. That's why Fran's getting to you so easily. Even though you have the experience edge, you're panicking. If you wanna have a long career in this city, you need to work on your focus."

She swallowed, trained mollified eyes on me, and nodded.

The metal door creaked open and Evan Cross walked in. I was surprised to see him at the cookhouse, much less holding bags of hot dogs and buns. He kissed his wife and set the food down beside the grill. "This is the one you don't cook animal bones on, right?"

I chuckled and grabbed the bag of charcoal. "Only pork chops and ribs. How's news?"

"Eh, the mayor's all over my ass about Shadow Man. I was expecting a suspension for failing to contain the shootout with the resources that were out there, but so far the shoe hasn't dropped." He nodded to Fran and Darcy chatting. "How's this going?"

I scratched my neck and gambled. "I could show you, if you want."

He flexed his jaw. "Sure. After we get this fire started." He noted my bewilderment and shrugged. "This supernatural stuff isn't going away, is it?"

I shook my head.

"And the Obsidian March and worse things are still out there, right?"

This time I nodded.

"Then I figure the only thing to do is take it head on. I want my family to be able to defend themselves. And not just them, but the DROP team as well. My guys have repeatedly seen what's really out there. It's about time they had the tools to do something about it."

"Well, all right." We pounded fists. I hadn't even thought of arming the police for this fight. The idea opened up countless possibilities.

We laughed and talked smack around the grill. Practiced some more. I wished Milena could've been there but she was at work. Kasper was taking time off, crashing at my place. He was in his sixties so he deserved it. The old man was clearly torn up about the shop. He didn't blather on about it or make me feel guilty, though. He was good like that.

I appraised the crew with a good feeling about things for the first time in a long while. Charred hot dogs, mustard stains on paper napkins, and the collected implements of our spellcraft. I just hoped we knew what we were doing.

By the evening, everybody had taken off and I was alone tidying up the place. I packed the mementos from my shelf to transfer to the cache back home and locked up. On the hike back to my car on the gloomy Everglades path, the hairs on the back of my neck stood on end.

"Brujo," came the voice of the Spaniard.

I turned to see the wraith hovering beside me. His white skull glistened in contrast to his scratched and dull conquistador armor. Black rips of cloth swayed around his desiccated body. He watched me intently with glowing red eyes.

Face to face while he was no longer bound to the Horn, it almost made me tremble. His visage was ghastly, his might palpable.

"I was waiting for you to show your face," I said. "In a

manner of speaking—no offense."

The skeletal features remained emotionless. The wraith was a formidable necromancer, much more powerful than I, but he was also a distant relative. I handed him a single black feather.

"Netherlings," he spat in a heavy Spanish accent. "Vile beasts."

"This came from an owl of some sort."

He cocked his head with a penetrating stare. "Owls are symbols of death in many cultures."

I snorted. "Look who's talking. You know what it is?"

"Does it matter?"

I took the feather back and trudged to the Firebird. "I suppose not." I unloaded the items in the trunk before recovering a single metallic birthday balloon. It was so underinflated I'd been able to ball it up and stuff it into my empty belt pouch the night I handled Manifesto's corpse. "I'm gonna need your help with this." The Spaniard eyed me with distaste before I undid the lock and headed back inside.

He made his way in, as I knew he would. The wraith had wandered Miami idly over the course of the year. There was no telling what he'd been up to. After five hundred years being bound to an artifact, a person can only go so long being alone. Maybe this was his fork in the road.

I set the scene by drawing a chalk star on the cement. It was fortified with lit candles at each point. In the center was a sixth candle, melted wax fixing it upright on a small mirror. I pricked my finger with my ceremonial bronze

Domino Finn

voodoo knife. As my blood dripped onto the reflective surface, I brought the balloon over the circle and stabbed it open.

A wave of crimson washed over the cookhouse. In the eerie bath of bloody light, we were no longer alone. A formless wisp of gray curled within the pentacle. I had been too late. Gotten too little of what I needed.

The wraith pointed rotting fingers and whispered to the darkness. The hapless ghost within solidified in answer. Manifesto loomed before us, neck and wrist still pumping out his life force.

"Am I saved?" he asked precariously, gaze desperately darting from wall to wall. He was no longer burdened with cursed eyes. "Is this Heaven?"

"Far from it," I spat. "You haven't even left yet. And I got bad news for you: You were right about life being eternal, but you probably won't like where you're going."

His brow furrowed. His eyes squinted as if having trouble focusing on me. "Who is that? My nemesis? This isn't possible."

"Oh, it's possible all right. You and I didn't finish our last conversation. You want out of here? You wanna see what awaits you in the beyond? All you have to do is tell me who cursed you."

The Spaniard's skeletal face hardened at my threat. Hundreds of years had taught him the evils of subjugation. I'd had my share as well. I wouldn't carry through with an act so merciless, not even for Manifesto, but he didn't know that."

"Please," he protested. "This isn't right."

"How long were you working with the vampires?"

Confusion painted his face. The man whimpered as he set eyes upon my companion. "Are you an angel or a demon?"

The wraith's glowing orbs flickered uncertainly.

"I did as I was tasked. Your black sisters stole me away in the night. They stripped my clothes, washed away my sins with blood, and delighted me with pleasures of the flesh until I was reborn. Their songs opened my eyes. I did everything they wanted."

"Who were they?" I pressured. "Where are they?"

Manifesto regarded me, and an almost-exalted patience overtook him. "They are supreme beauty, heathen. Angels well beyond your understanding or reach."

I gritted my teeth. "Try me."

The spirit chuckled lightly. "You will not find them, but they will find you. This I promise. All men must face judgment." His laugh grew more boisterous. I sneered as a cold breeze blew over the ritual. The candles flickered. A few went out. Manifesto choked on his mirth and spun in panic. "What? Who?"

I backed away as the remaining candles circling the star went out. Only the central fire remained. The wraith's red eyes flared indignantly at the intrusion.

"No!" pleaded Manifesto, jerking in pain. "I was promised salvation."

I channeled more energy into the blood rite. The circle didn't respond.

Manifesto flailed and thrashed in greater agony than he'd ever experienced. With one last appeal, he cried, "I am the chosen one!"

In a deathly scream, his ghost withered into nothing. A final buffet of wind hit us like a hurricane. The last candle snuffed out, releasing him. The crimson aura winked away and we were left in smoking darkness.

I stared at the spot Manifesto had occupied. He was long gone now. So was whatever had interfered with my ritual. I turned to the Spaniard. His red eyes smoldered.

"That was no vampire magic," he spat.

I shook my head in agreement. "The owl is the key. We need to track down its origin. Find out who or what got its hooks into this guy."

"The Nether will be the death of this world," muttered the Spaniard in disgust.

I ground my teeth into a snarl. "Not if I can help it."

-Finn

If you're reading this, it means you demand more from your urban fantasy. Bullets and fireballs are a riot, but they're nothing without a layered cast of characters or realistic plot drivers. *Black Magic Outlaw* is my stab at a cut above the rest: non-stop action, true friends banding against impossible odds, and themes that hopefully make you put the book down and ponder, even if for only a minute.

My writing process demands quality control at every step of development. I hope you agree that *Black Magic Outlaw* is the premium product I strive to make it. Unfortunately, doubling down on originality and quality in an on-demand world has drawbacks. It's simply impossible for me to get you a brand-new novel every month or two. The process takes time.

That's where you come in. If you want to be a part of building a better book, consider one or all of the following shows of support. The best part? They don't cost you a penny.

- Join our private Facebook group.
  (www.facebook.com/groups/dominofinnfans/)

- Leave an all-too-important review on Amazon.
  Each one helps more than you can imagine.

- Recommend this book to your friends. Link it
  on social media.

- Join my reader group newsletter, get a free
  gift, and only hear from me when I have new
  releases or important news.
  (dominofinn.com/newsletter/)

Simple, right? Five minutes of your time makes a world of difference to me. Thank you for your heartfelt support. I'll keep writing as long as you keep reading.

-Domino Finn

Also by Domino Finn

BLACK MAGIC OUTLAW
Dead Man
Shadow Play
Heart Strings
Powder Trade
Fire Water
Death March

AFTERLIFE ONLINE
Reboot
Black Hat
Deadline

SHADE CITY

SYCAMORE MOON
The Seventh Sons
The Blood of Brothers
The Green Children

About the Author

Domino Finn is an award-winning game industry veteran, a media rebel, and a grizzled author of urban fantasy and litRPG. His stories are equal parts spit, beer, and blood, and are notable for treating weighty issues with a supernatural veneer. If Domino has one rallying cry for the world, it's that fantasy is serious business.

Take a stand at DominoFinn.com

28231666R00242

Printed in Poland
by Amazon Fulfillment
Poland Sp. z o.o., Wrocław